PORTSMOUTH
POLICE

0333

BLACK MAGICK™

Created by Greg Rucka and Nicola Scott

VOLUME 1: "AWAKENING"

Writer: **GREG RUCKA**

Artist: **NICOLA SCOTT**

Color Assists: CHIARA ARENA

Letterer: JODI WYNNE

Cover: **NICOLA SCOTT**
(with ERIC TRAUTMANN)

Follow Greg on Twitter: @ruckawriter • Follow Nicola on Twitter: @NicolaScottArt
Follow Jeanine on Twitter: @j9schaefer • Follow Eric on Twitter: @mercuryeric

IMAGE COMICS, INC.
Robert Kirkman – Chief Operating Officer
Erik Larsen – Chief Financial Officer
Todd McFarlane – President
Marc Silvestri – Chief Executive Officer
Jim Valentino – Vice-President

Eric Stephenson – Publisher
Corey Murphy – Director of Sales
Jeff Boison – Director of Publishing Planning & Book Trade Sales
Jeremy Sullivan – Director of Digital Sales
Kat Salazar – Director of PR & Marketing
Emily Miller – Director of Operations
Branwyn Bigglestone – Senior Accounts Manager
Sarah Mello – Accounts Manager
Drew Gill – Art Director
Jonathan Chan – Production Manager
Meredith Wallace – Print Manager
Briah Skelly – Publicity Assistant
Sasha Head – Sales & Marketing Production Designer
Randy Okamura – Digital Production Designer
David Brothers – Branding Manager
Ally Power – Content Manager
Addison Duke – Production Artist
Vincent Kukua – Production Artist
Tricia Ramos – Production Artist
Jeff Stang – Direct Market Sales Representative
Emilio Bautista – Digital Sales Associate
Chloe Ramos-Peterson – Administrative Assistant
IMAGECOMICS.COM

Editor: JEANINE SCHAEFER

Book and Logo Designer: ERIC TRAUTMANN

Special thanks to **Juliette Capra and the Valkyries**; **Sebastian Girner**; **Casey Gilly**

http://blackmagickcomic.tumblr.com

BLACK MAGICK VOLUME 1: AWAKENING.
First printing. April 2016. Copyright © 2016 Greg Rucka & Nicola Scott. All rights reserved.

Contains material previously published as BLACK MAGICK #1–5.

Published by Image Comics, Inc. Office of publication:
2001 Center Street, Sixth Floor, Berkeley, CA 94704

Printed in the U.S.A.

For information regarding the CPSIA on this printer material call: 203-595-3636 and provide reference # RICH -675126

For international rights contact: foreignlicensing@imagecomics.com

ISBN: 978-1-63215-675-4

ISBN Newbury Exclusive: 978-1-63215-829-1

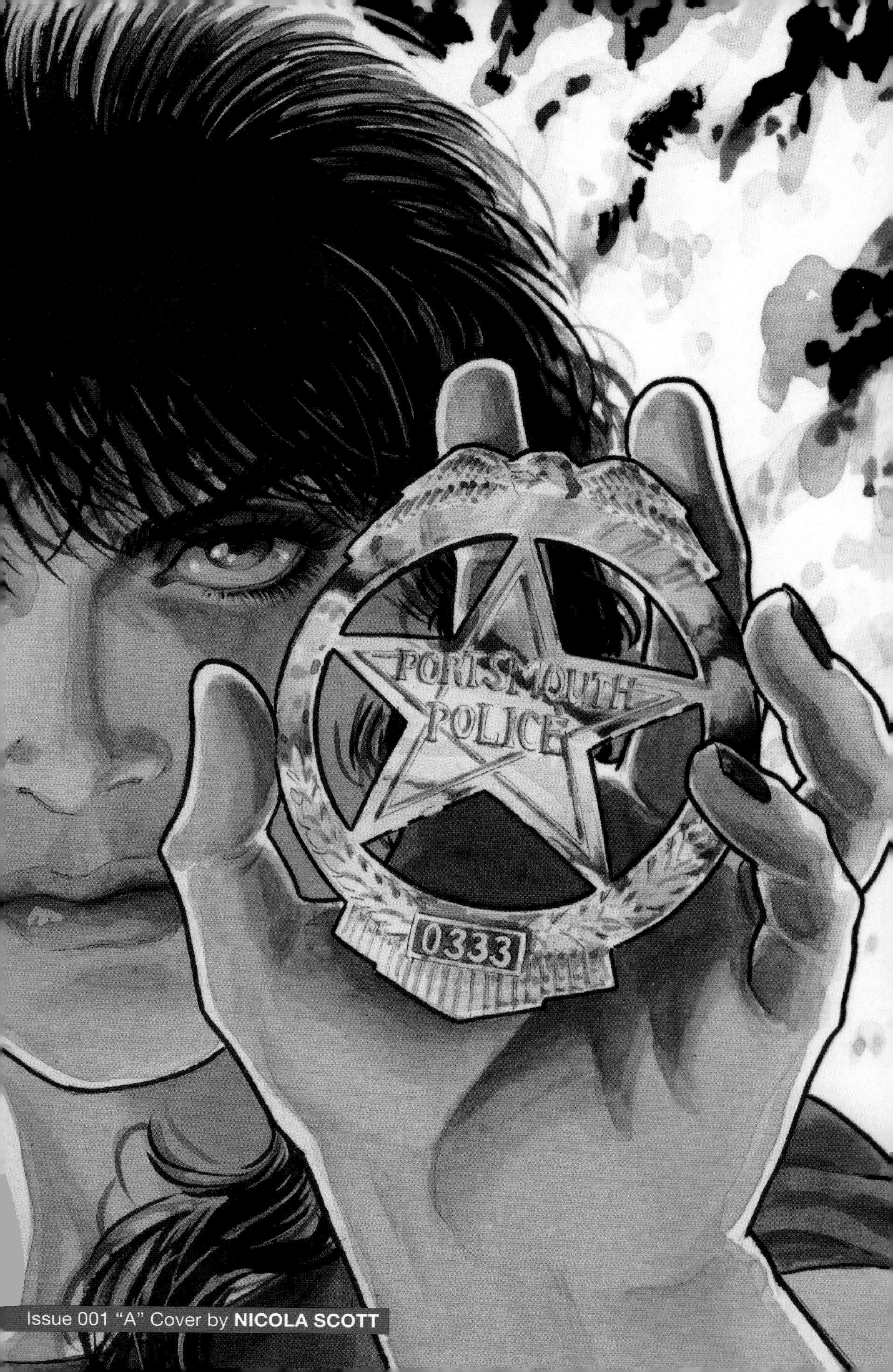
PORTSMOUTH
POLICE
0333
Issue 001 "A" Cover by **NICOLA SCOTT**

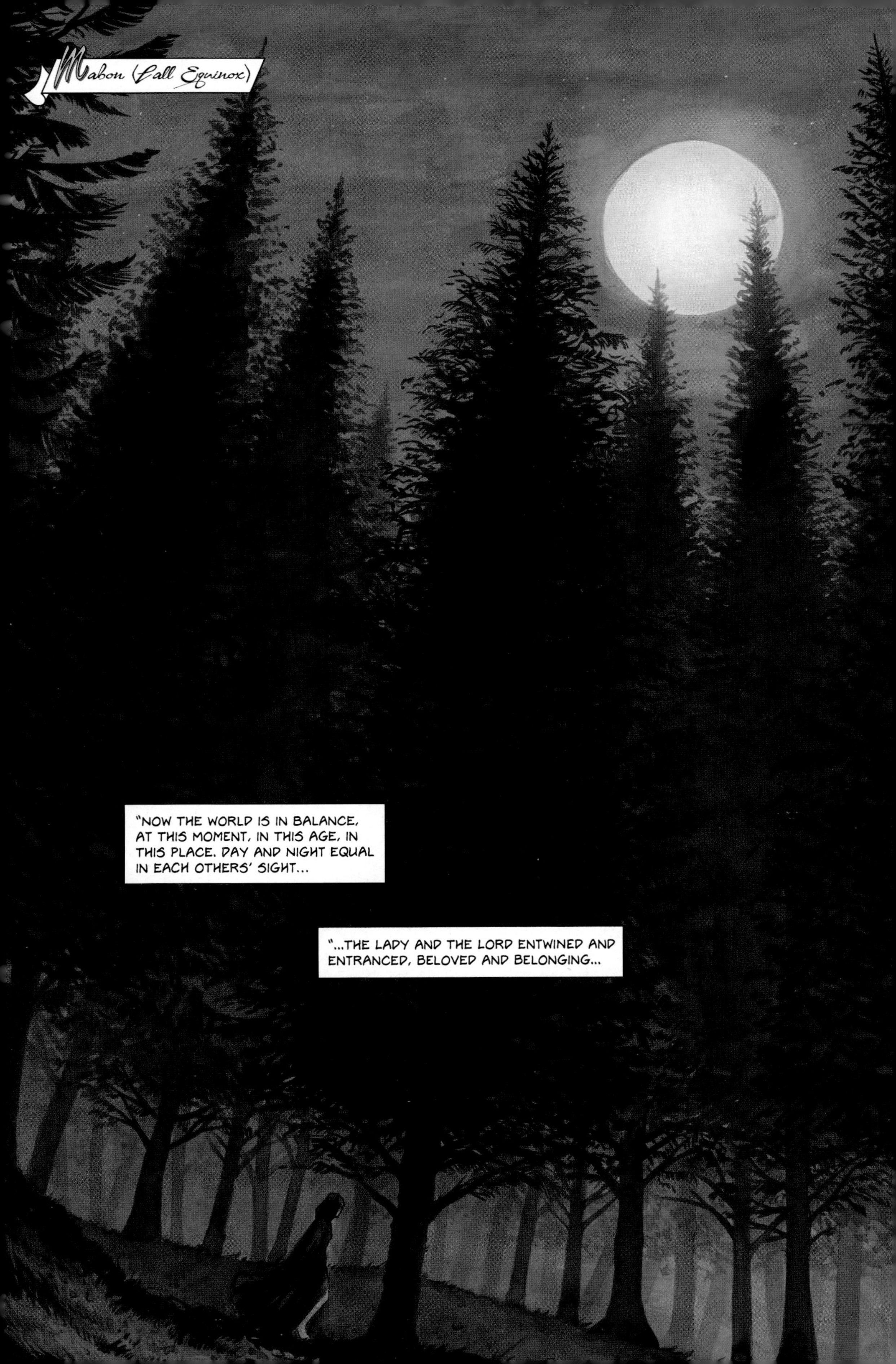
Mabon (Fall Equinox)
"NOW THE WORLD IS IN BALANCE, AT THIS MOMENT, IN THIS AGE, IN THIS PLACE. DAY AND NIGHT EQUAL IN EACH OTHERS' SIGHT...
"...THE LADY AND THE LORD ENTWINED AND ENTRANCED, BELOVED AND BELONGING...

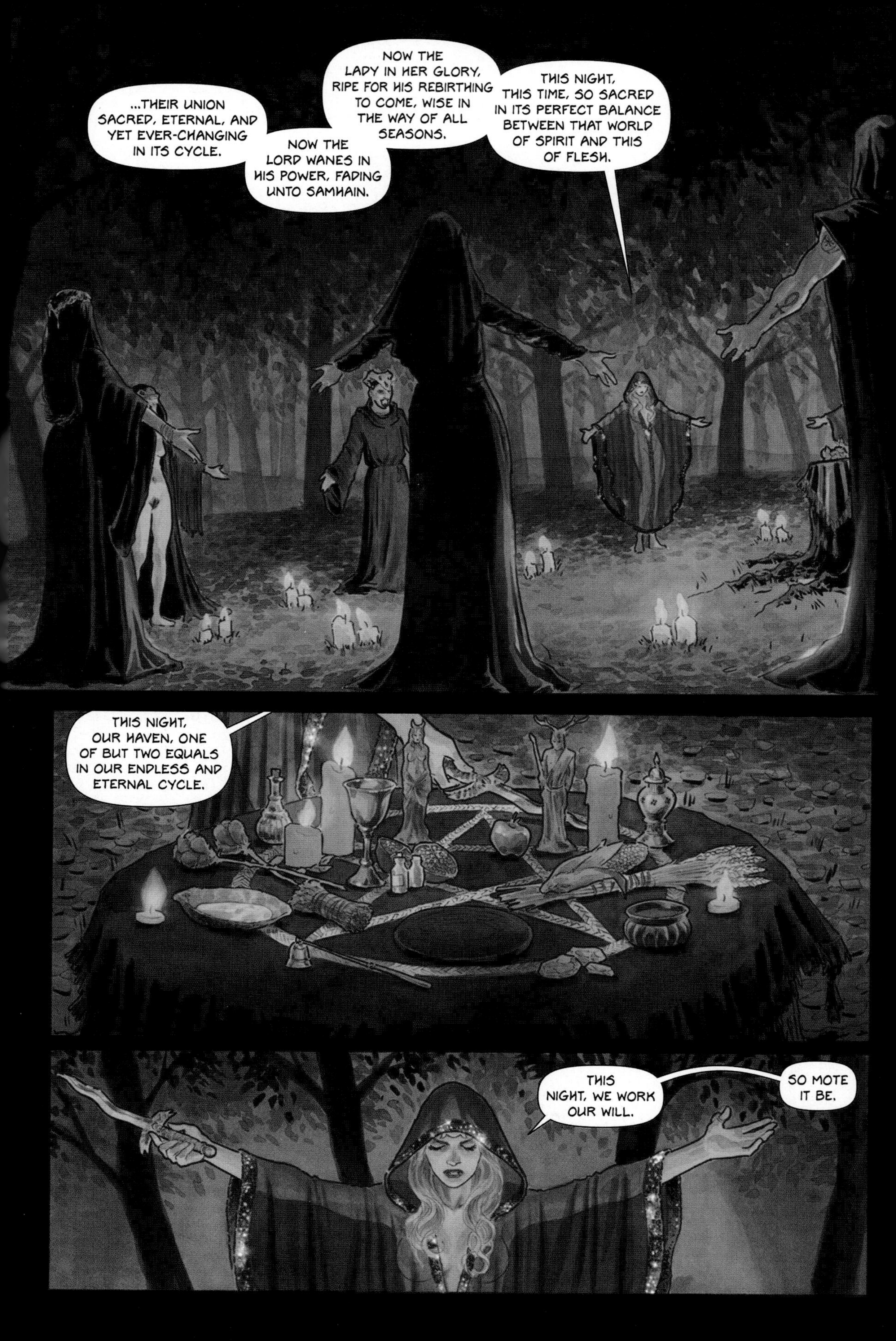
...THEIR UNION SACRED, ETERNAL, AND YET EVER-CHANGING IN ITS CYCLE.
NOW THE LORD WANES IN HIS POWER, FADING UNTO SAMHAIN.
NOW THE LADY IN HER GLORY, RIPE FOR HIS REBIRTHING TO COME, WISE IN THE WAY OF ALL SEASONS.
THIS NIGHT, THIS TIME, SO SACRED IN ITS PERFECT BALANCE BETWEEN THAT WORLD OF SPIRIT AND THIS OF FLESH.
THIS NIGHT, OUR HAVEN, ONE OF BUT TWO EQUALS IN OUR ENDLESS AND ETERNAL CYCLE.
THIS NIGHT, WE WORK OUR WILL.
SO MOTE IT BE.

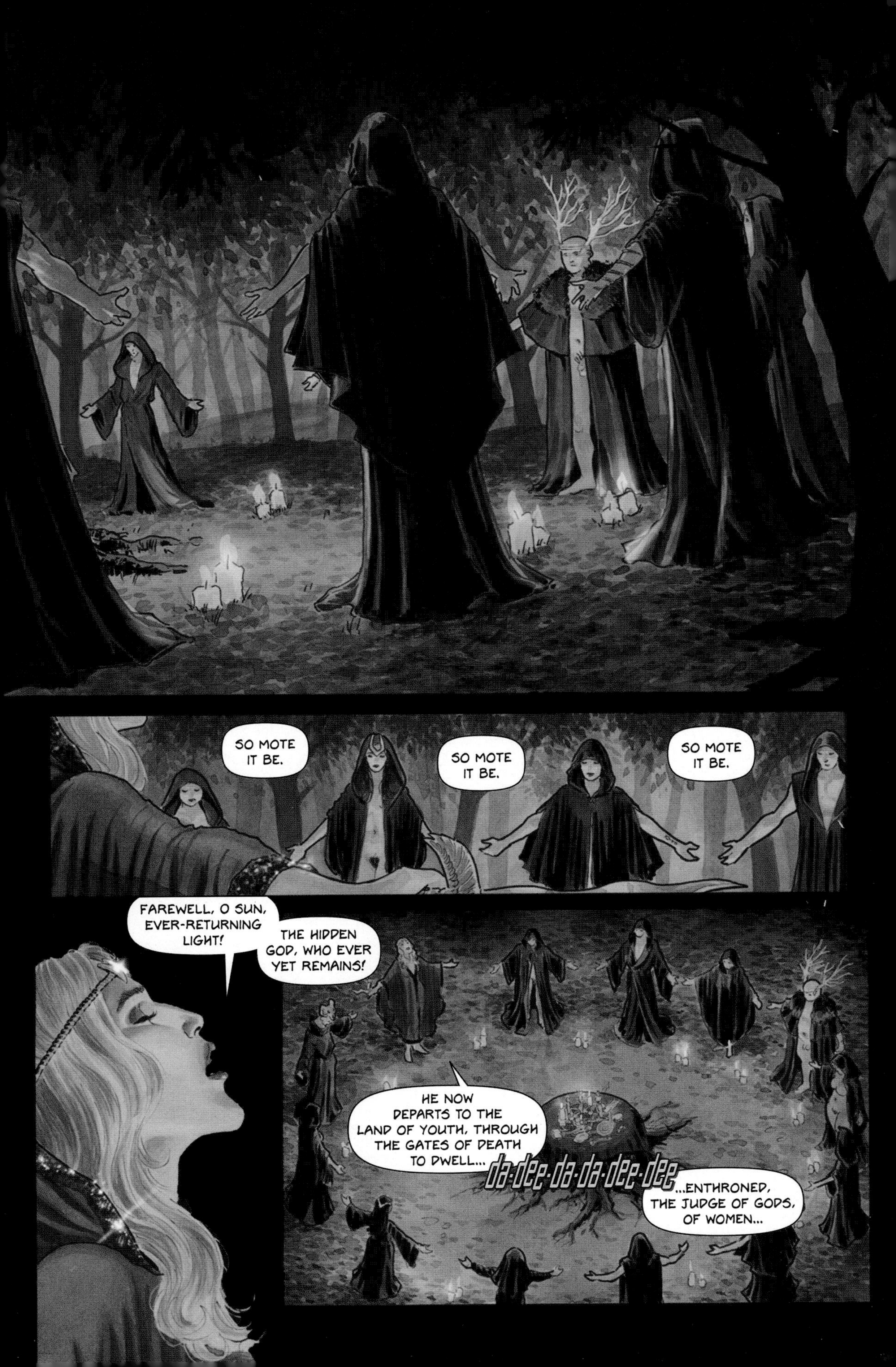
SO MOTE IT BE.
SO MOTE IT BE.
SO MOTE IT BE.
FAREWELL, O SUN, EVER-RETURNING LIGHT!
THE HIDDEN GOD, WHO EVER YET REMAINS!
HE NOW DEPARTS TO THE LAND OF YOUTH, THROUGH THE GATES OF DEATH TO DWELL...
DA-DEE-DA-DA-DEE-DEE
...ENTHRONED, THE JUDGE OF GODS, OF WOMEN...

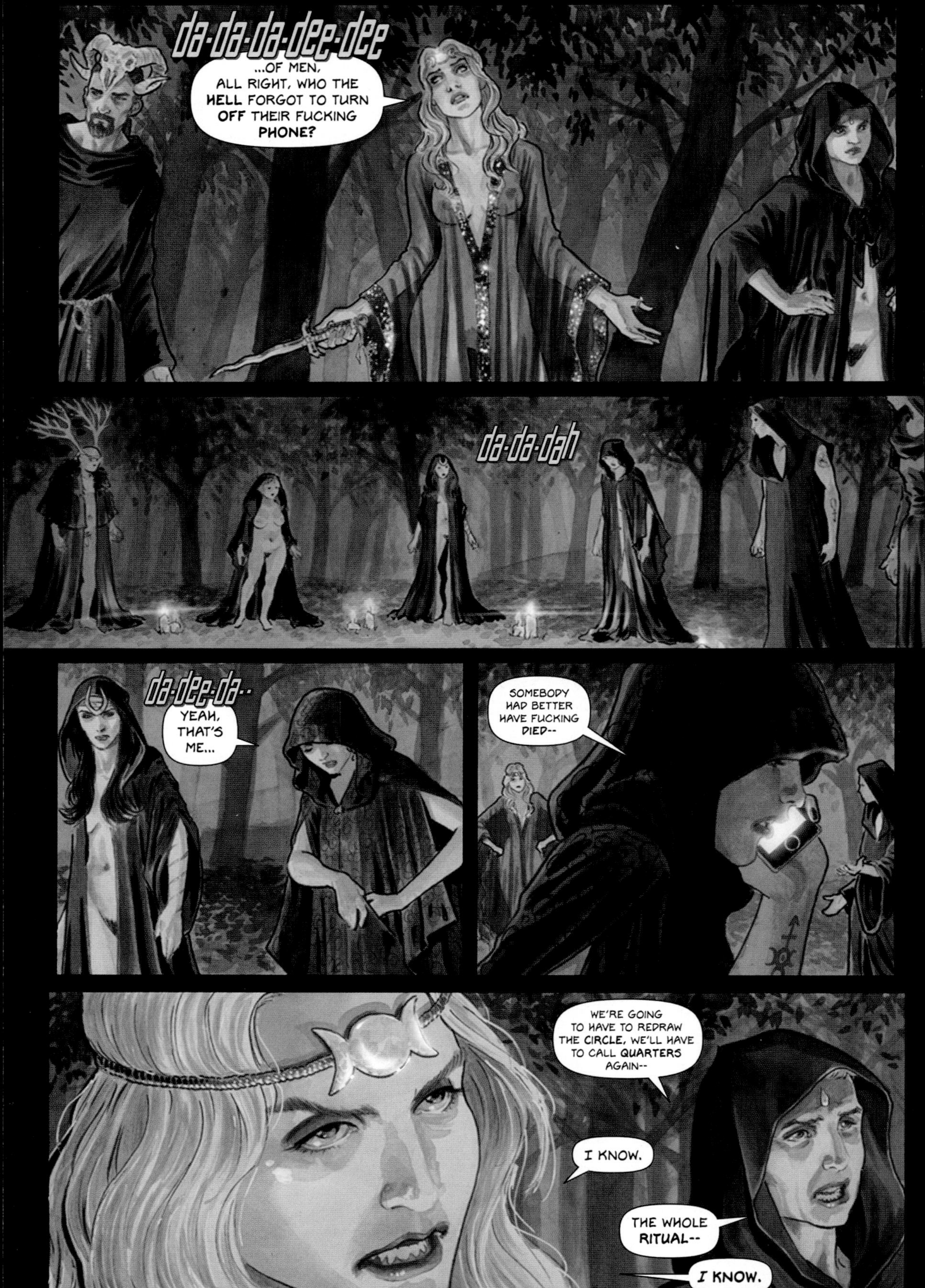
da-da-da-dee-dee
...OF MEN, ALL RIGHT, WHO THE HELL FORGOT TO TURN OFF THEIR FUCKING PHONE?
da-da-dah
da-dee-da--
YEAH, THAT'S ME...
SOMEBODY HAD BETTER HAVE FUCKING DIED--
WE'RE GOING TO HAVE TO REDRAW THE CIRCLE, WE'LL HAVE TO CALL QUARTERS AGAIN--
I KNOW.
THE WHOLE RITUAL--
I KNOW.

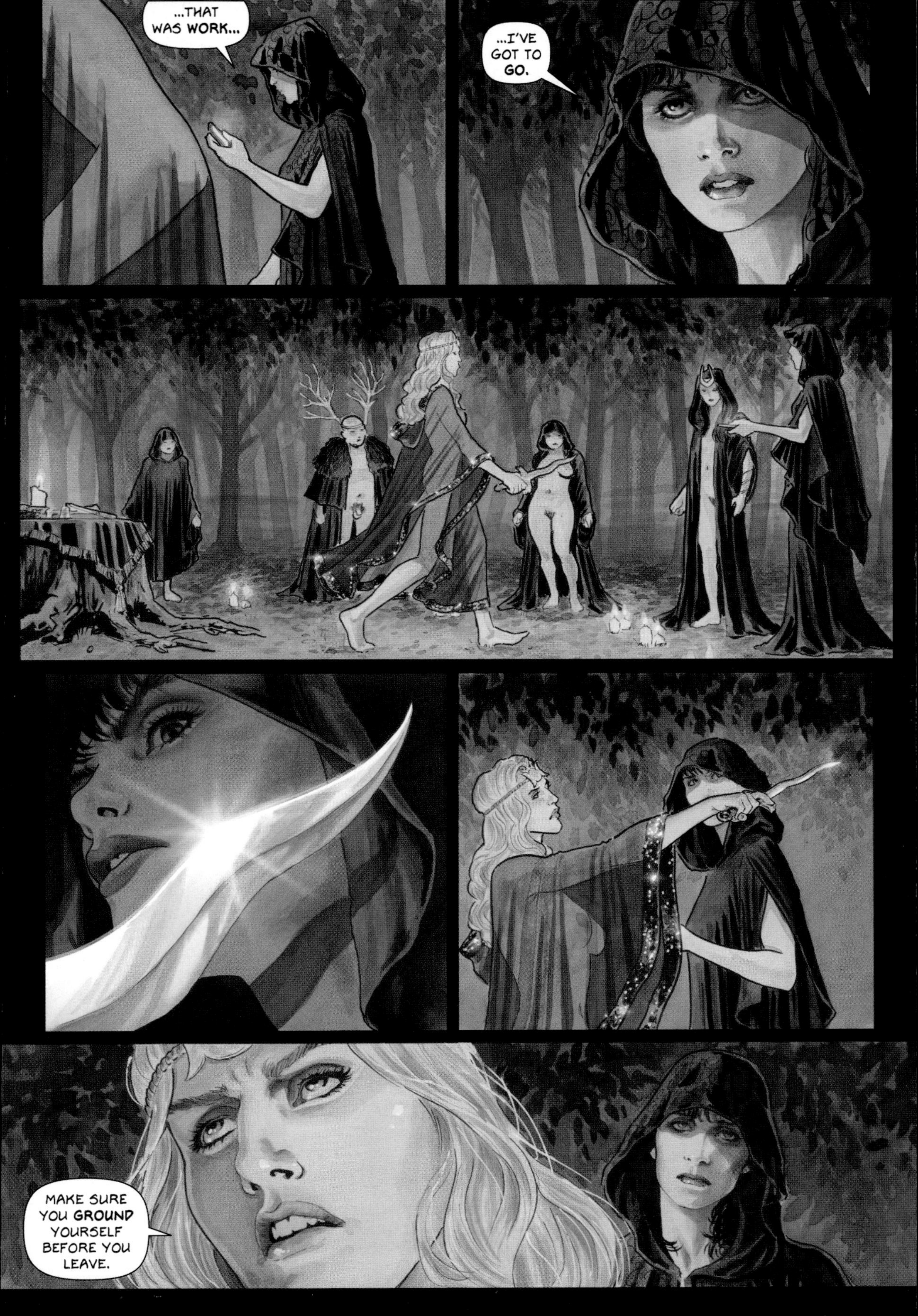
...THAT WAS WORK...
...I'VE GOT TO GO.
MAKE SURE YOU GROUND YOURSELF BEFORE YOU LEAVE.

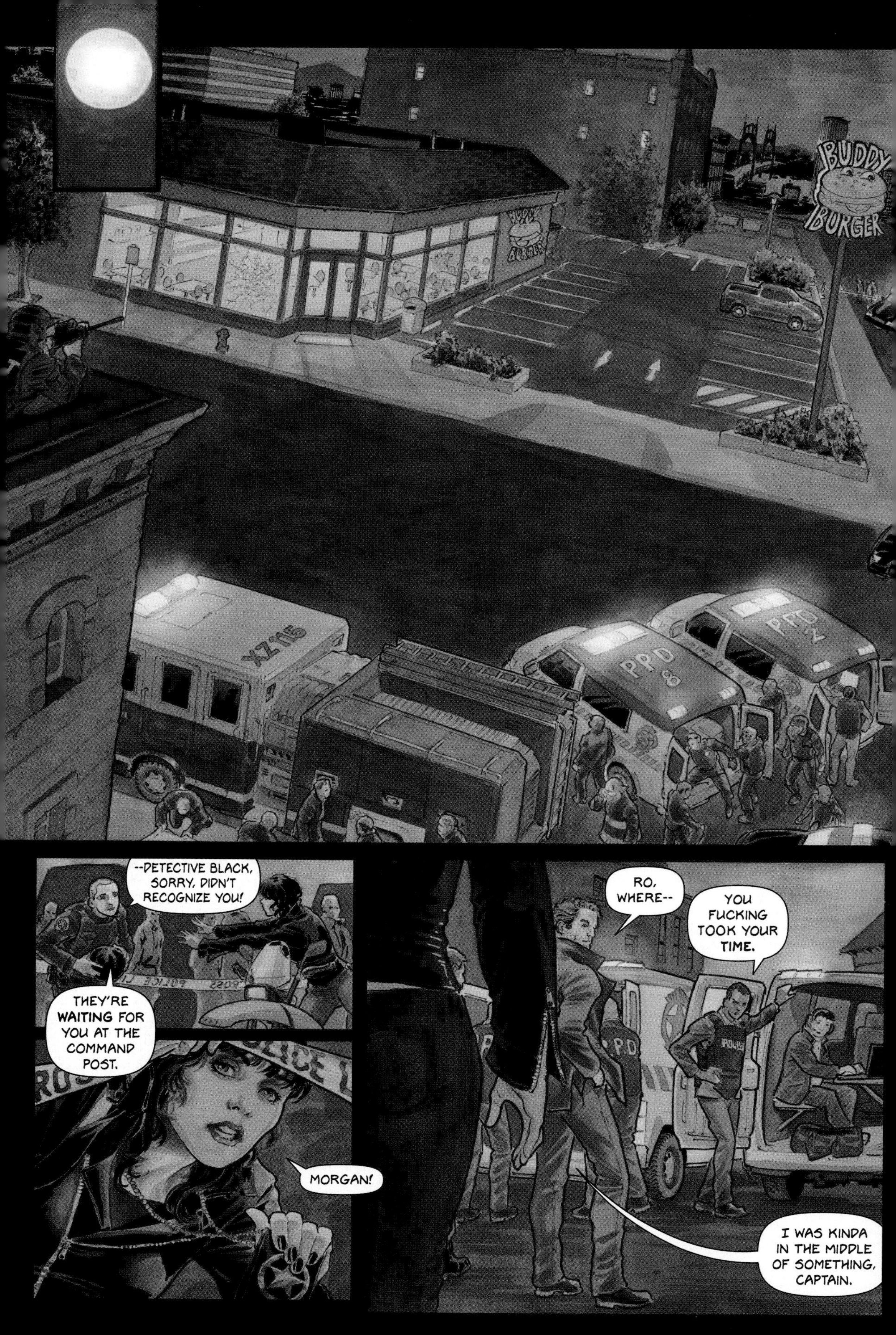
BUDDY BURGER
--DETECTIVE BLACK, SORRY, DIDN'T RECOGNIZE YOU!
THEY'RE WAITING FOR YOU AT THE COMMAND POST.
MORGAN!
RO, WHERE--
YOU FUCKING TOOK YOUR TIME.
I WAS KINDA IN THE MIDDLE OF SOMETHING, CAPTAIN.

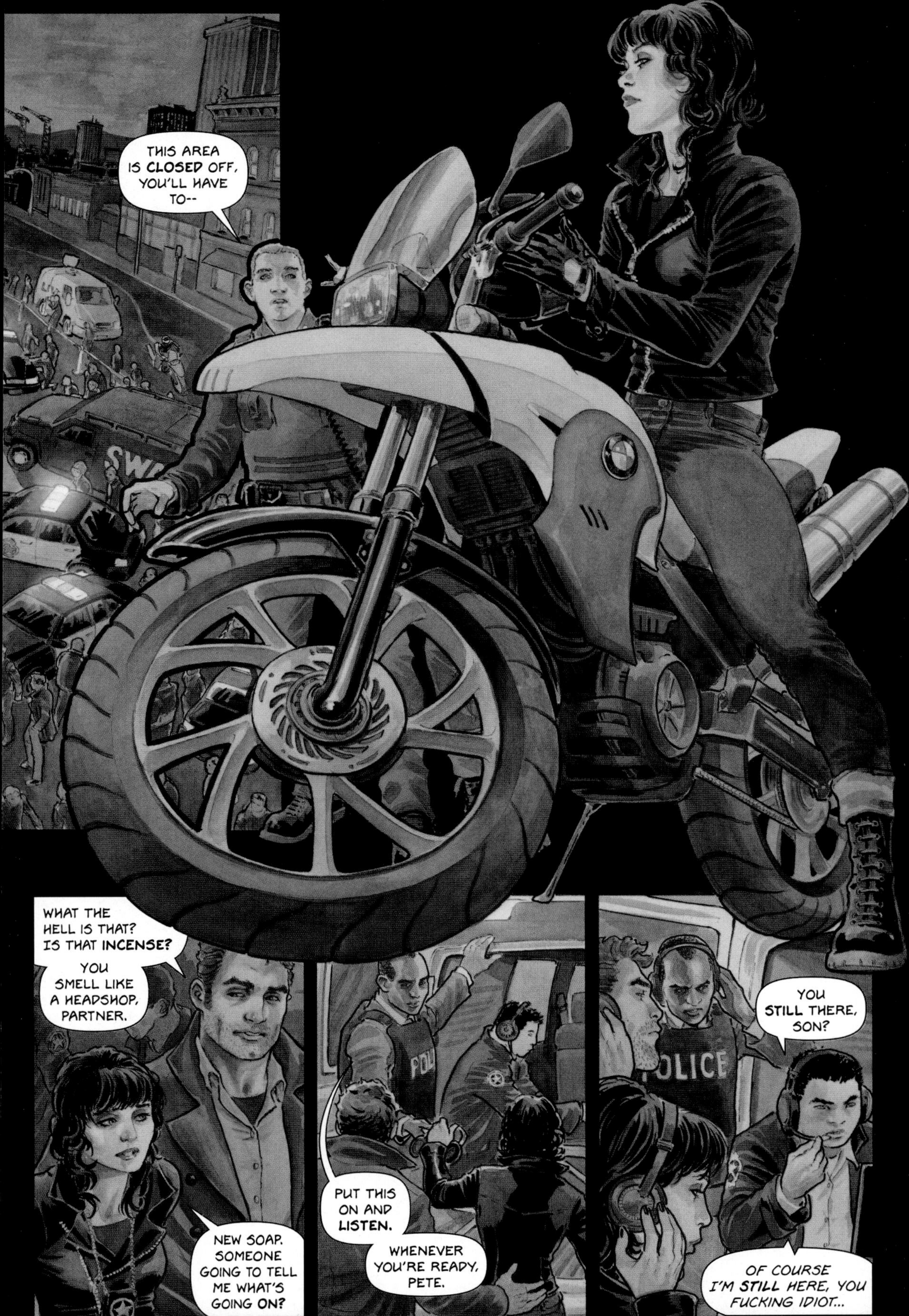

THIS AREA IS **CLOSED** OFF, YOU'LL HAVE TO--
WHAT THE HELL IS THAT? IS THAT **INCENSE?**
YOU SMELL LIKE A HEADSHOP, PARTNER.
NEW SOAP. SOMEONE GOING TO TELL ME WHAT'S GOING **ON?**
PUT THIS ON AND **LISTEN.**
WHENEVER YOU'RE READY, PETE.
YOU **STILL** THERE, SON?
*OF COURSE I'M **STILL** HERE, YOU FUCKING IDIOT...*

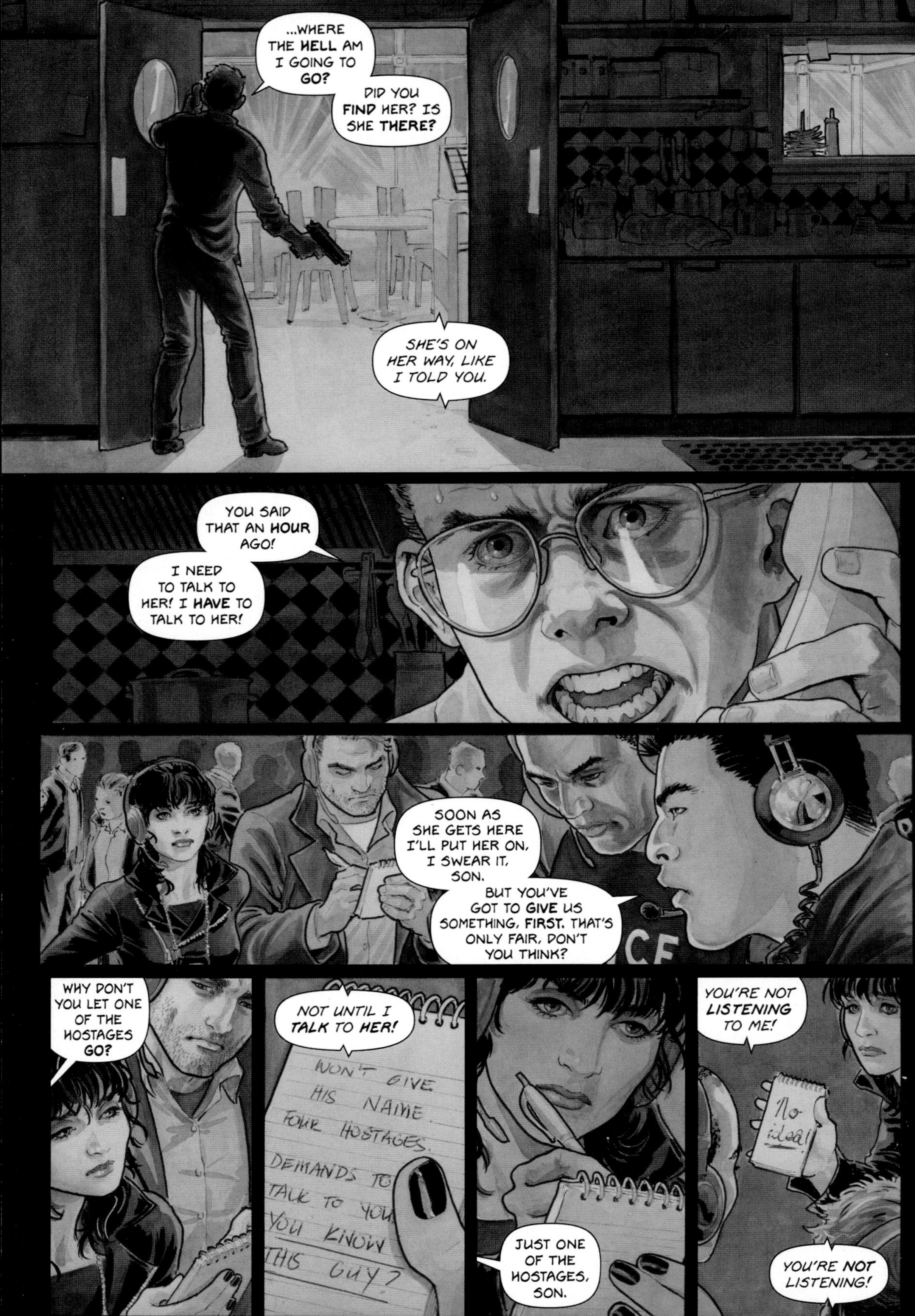
...WHERE THE HELL AM I GOING TO GO?
DID YOU FIND HER? IS SHE THERE?
SHE'S ON HER WAY, LIKE I TOLD YOU.
YOU SAID THAT AN HOUR AGO!
I NEED TO TALK TO HER! I HAVE TO TALK TO HER!
SOON AS SHE GETS HERE I'LL PUT HER ON, I SWEAR IT, SON.
BUT YOU'VE GOT TO GIVE US SOMETHING, FIRST. THAT'S ONLY FAIR, DON'T YOU THINK?
WHY DON'T YOU LET ONE OF THE HOSTAGES GO?
NOT UNTIL I TALK TO HER!
WON'T GIVE HIS NAME.
FOUR HOSTAGES.
DEMANDS TO TALK TO YOU
YOU KNOW THIS GUY?
JUST ONE OF THE HOSTAGES, SON.
No idea!
YOU'RE NOT LISTENING TO ME!
YOU'RE NOT LISTENING!

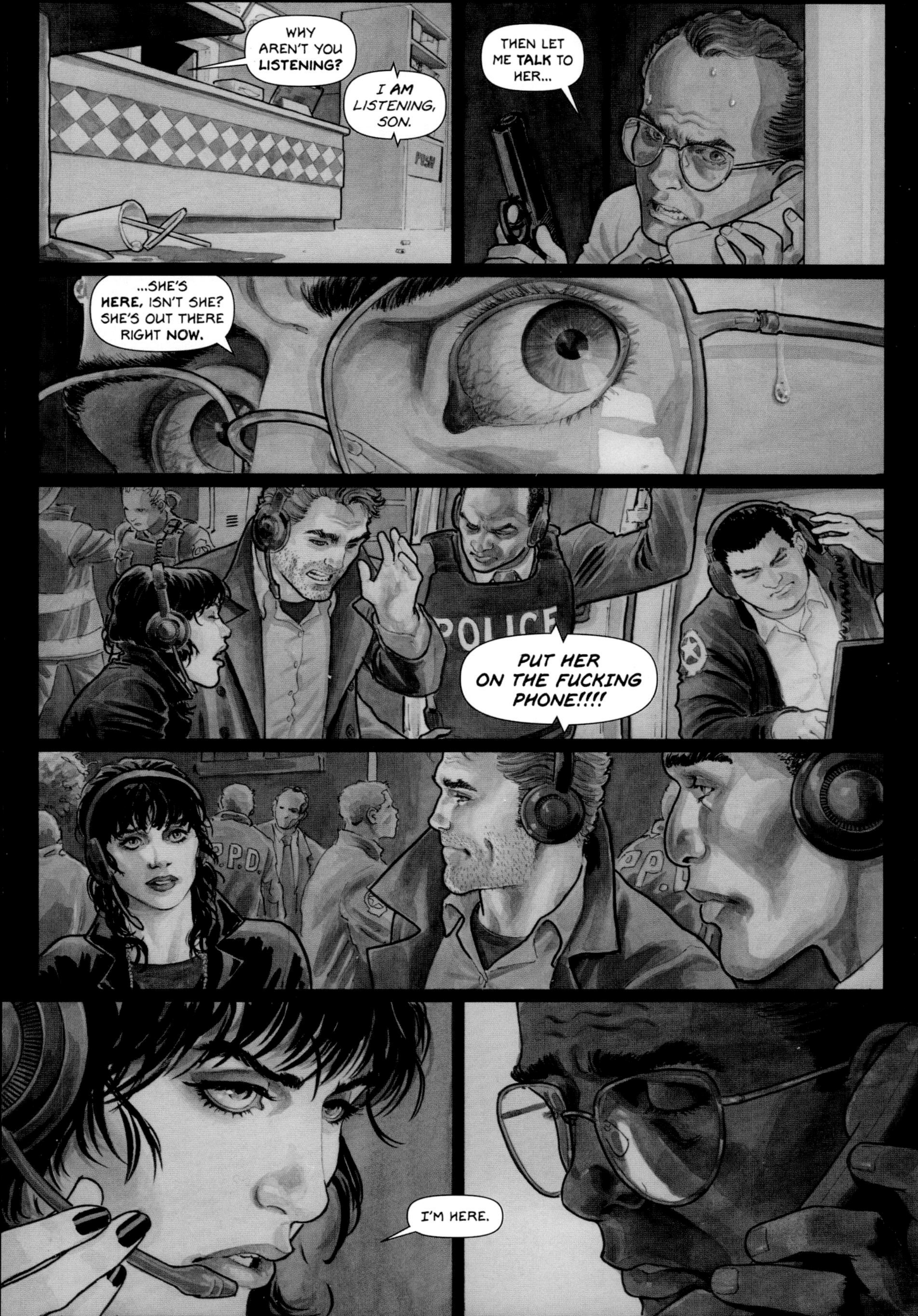
WHY AREN'T YOU LISTENING?
I AM LISTENING, SON.
PUSH
THEN LET ME TALK TO HER...
...SHE'S HERE, ISN'T SHE? SHE'S OUT THERE RIGHT NOW.
POLICE
PUT HER ON THE FUCKING PHONE!!!!
P.P.D.
I'M HERE.

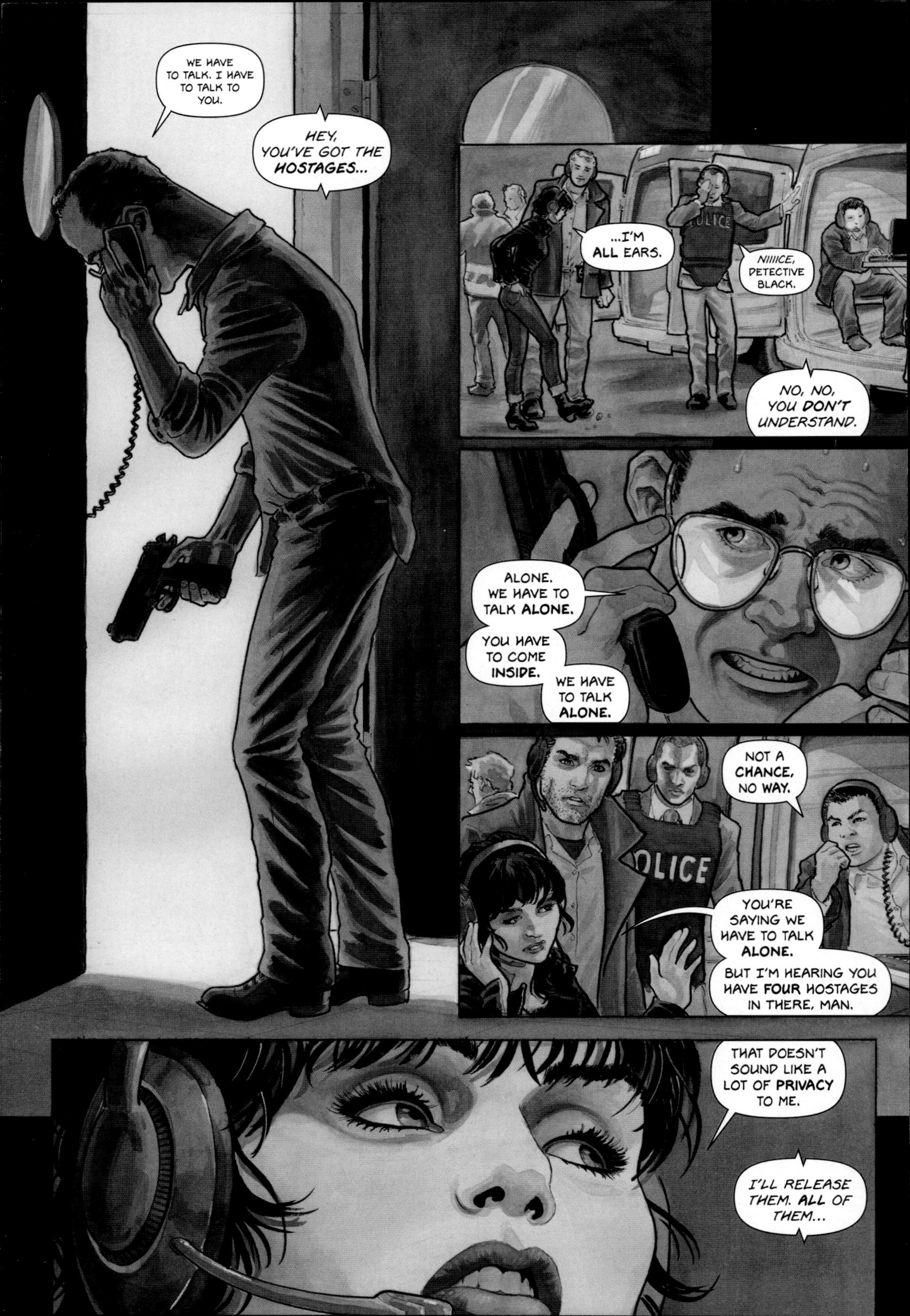
WE HAVE TO TALK. I HAVE TO TALK TO YOU.
HEY, YOU'VE GOT THE HOSTAGES...
...I'M ALL EARS.
NIIIICE, DETECTIVE BLACK.
NO, NO, YOU DON'T UNDERSTAND.
ALONE. WE HAVE TO TALK ALONE.
YOU HAVE TO COME INSIDE.
WE HAVE TO TALK ALONE.
NOT A CHANCE, NO WAY.
YOU'RE SAYING WE HAVE TO TALK ALONE.
BUT I'M HEARING YOU HAVE FOUR HOSTAGES IN THERE, MAN.
THAT DOESN'T SOUND LIKE A LOT OF PRIVACY TO ME.
I'LL RELEASE THEM. ALL OF THEM...

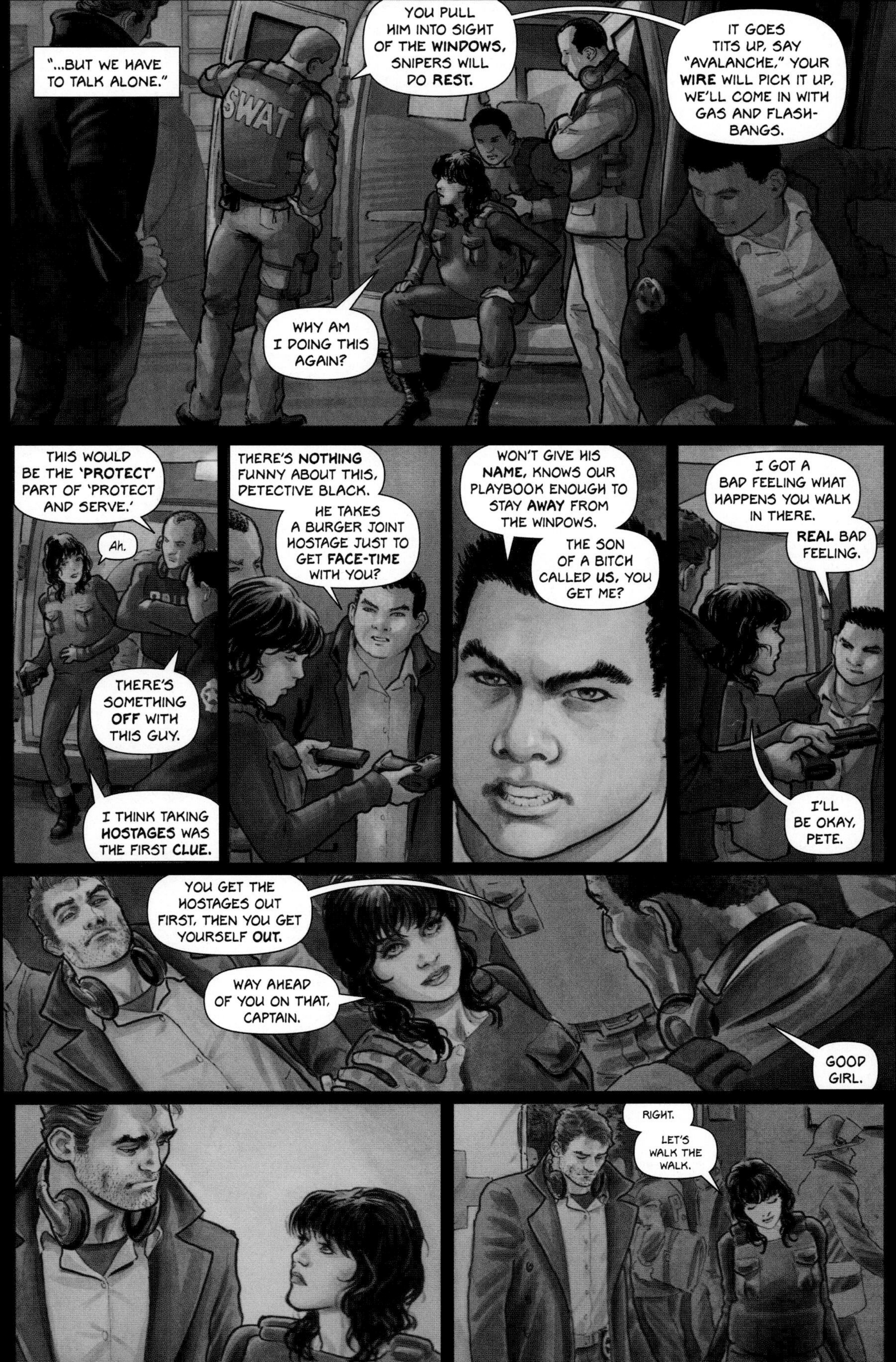
"...BUT WE HAVE TO TALK ALONE."
YOU PULL HIM INTO SIGHT OF THE **WINDOWS**, SNIPERS WILL DO **REST**.
IT GOES TITS UP, SAY "AVALANCHE," YOUR **WIRE** WILL PICK IT UP, WE'LL COME IN WITH GAS AND FLASH-BANGS.
SWAT
WHY AM I DOING THIS AGAIN?
THIS WOULD BE THE **'PROTECT'** PART OF 'PROTECT AND SERVE.'
Ah.
THERE'S SOMETHING **OFF** WITH THIS GUY.
I THINK TAKING **HOSTAGES** WAS THE FIRST **CLUE**.
THERE'S **NOTHING** FUNNY ABOUT THIS, DETECTIVE BLACK.
HE TAKES A BURGER JOINT HOSTAGE JUST TO GET **FACE-TIME** WITH YOU?
WON'T GIVE HIS **NAME**, KNOWS OUR PLAYBOOK ENOUGH TO STAY **AWAY** FROM THE WINDOWS.
THE SON OF A BITCH CALLED **US**, YOU GET ME?
I GOT A BAD FEELING WHAT HAPPENS YOU WALK IN THERE.
REAL BAD FEELING.
I'LL BE OKAY, PETE.
YOU GET THE HOSTAGES OUT FIRST, THEN YOU GET YOURSELF **OUT**.
WAY AHEAD OF YOU ON THAT, CAPTAIN.
GOOD GIRL.
RIGHT.
LET'S WALK THE WALK.

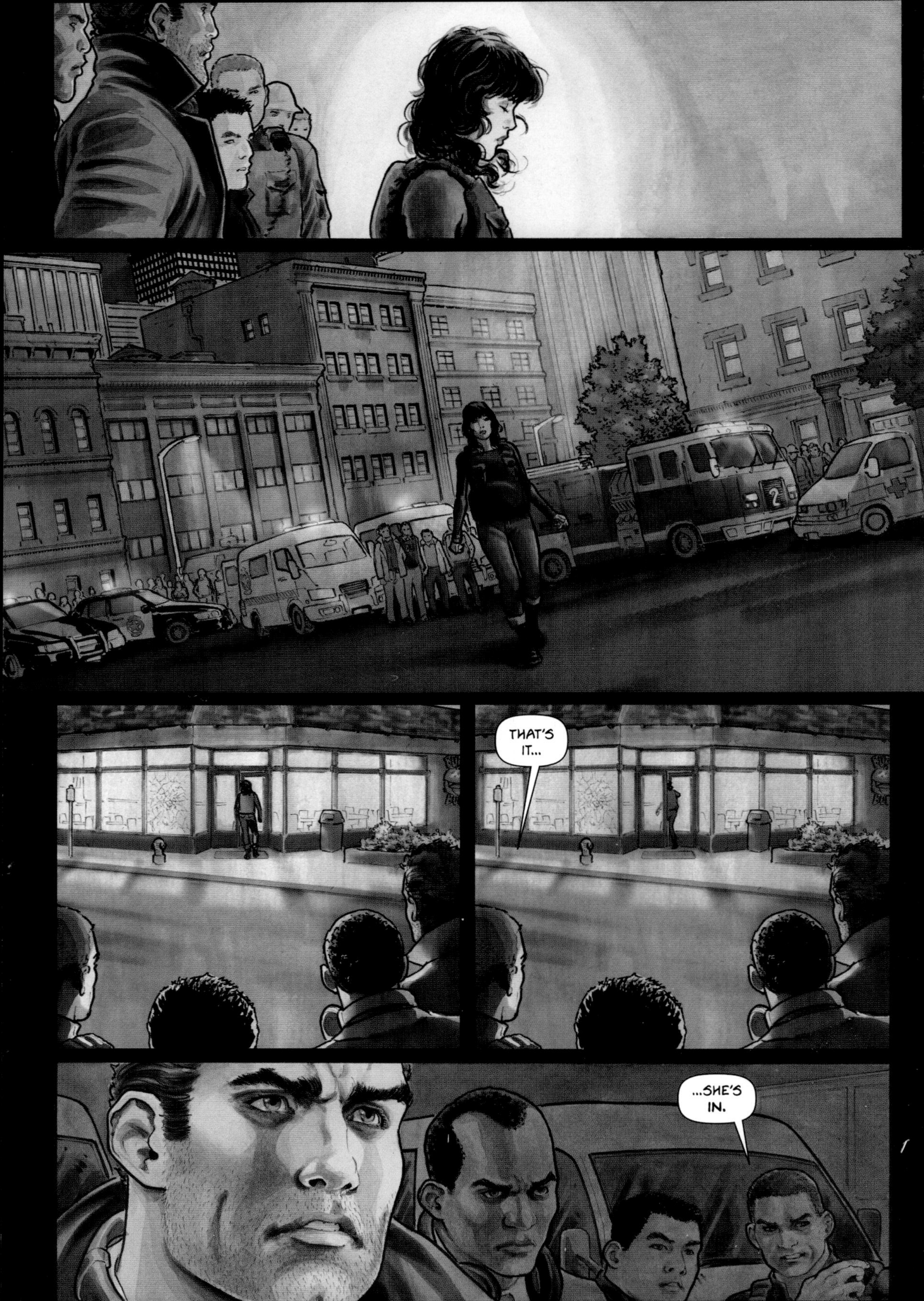
THAT'S IT...
...SHE'S IN.

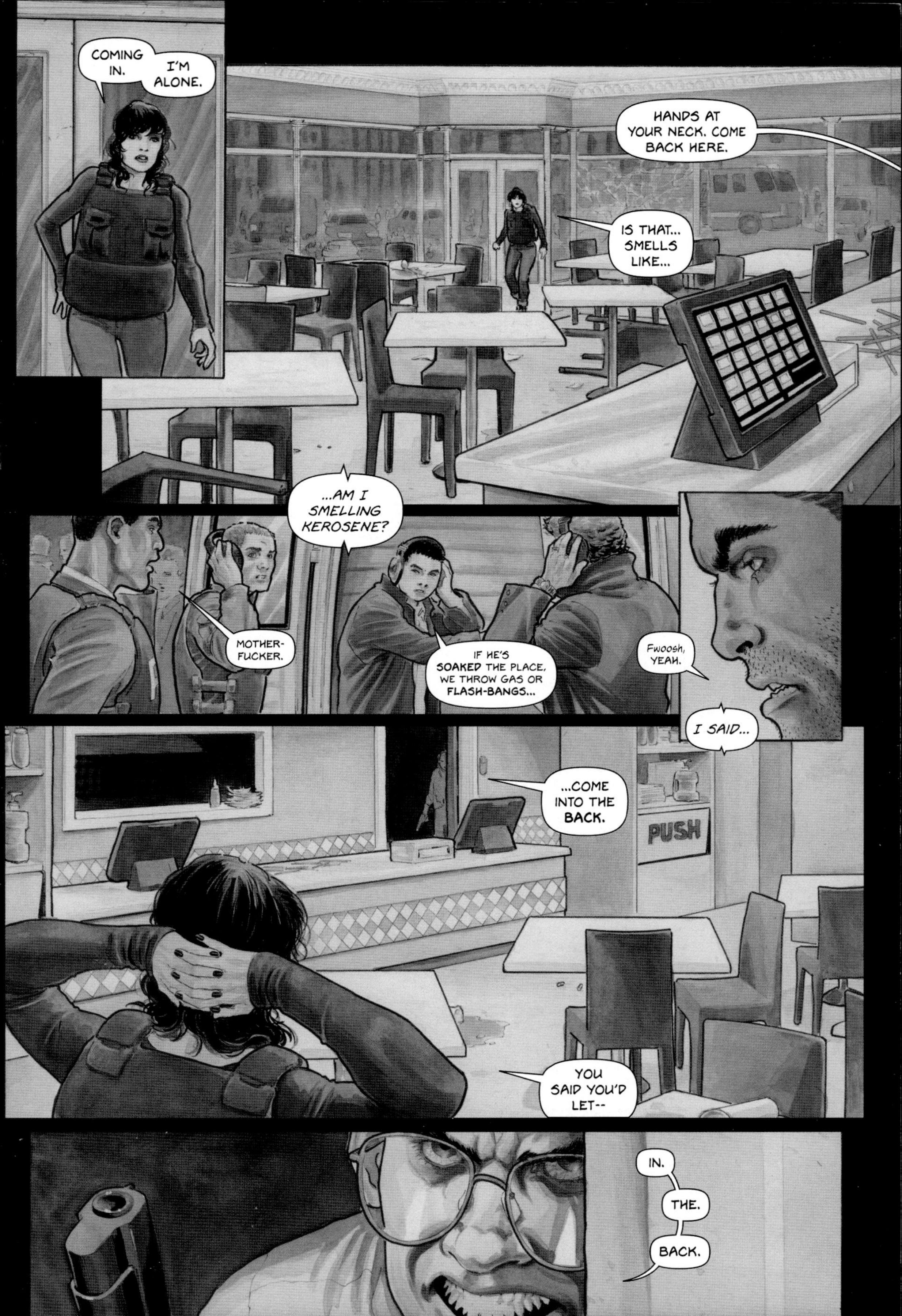

COMING IN.
I'M ALONE.
HANDS AT YOUR NECK. COME BACK HERE.
IS THAT... SMELLS LIKE...
...AM I SMELLING KEROSENE?
MOTHER-FUCKER.
IF HE'S SOAKED THE PLACE, WE THROW GAS OR FLASH-BANGS...
Fwoosh, YEAH.
I SAID...
...COME INTO THE BACK.
PUSH
YOU SAID YOU'D LET--
IN.
THE.
BACK.

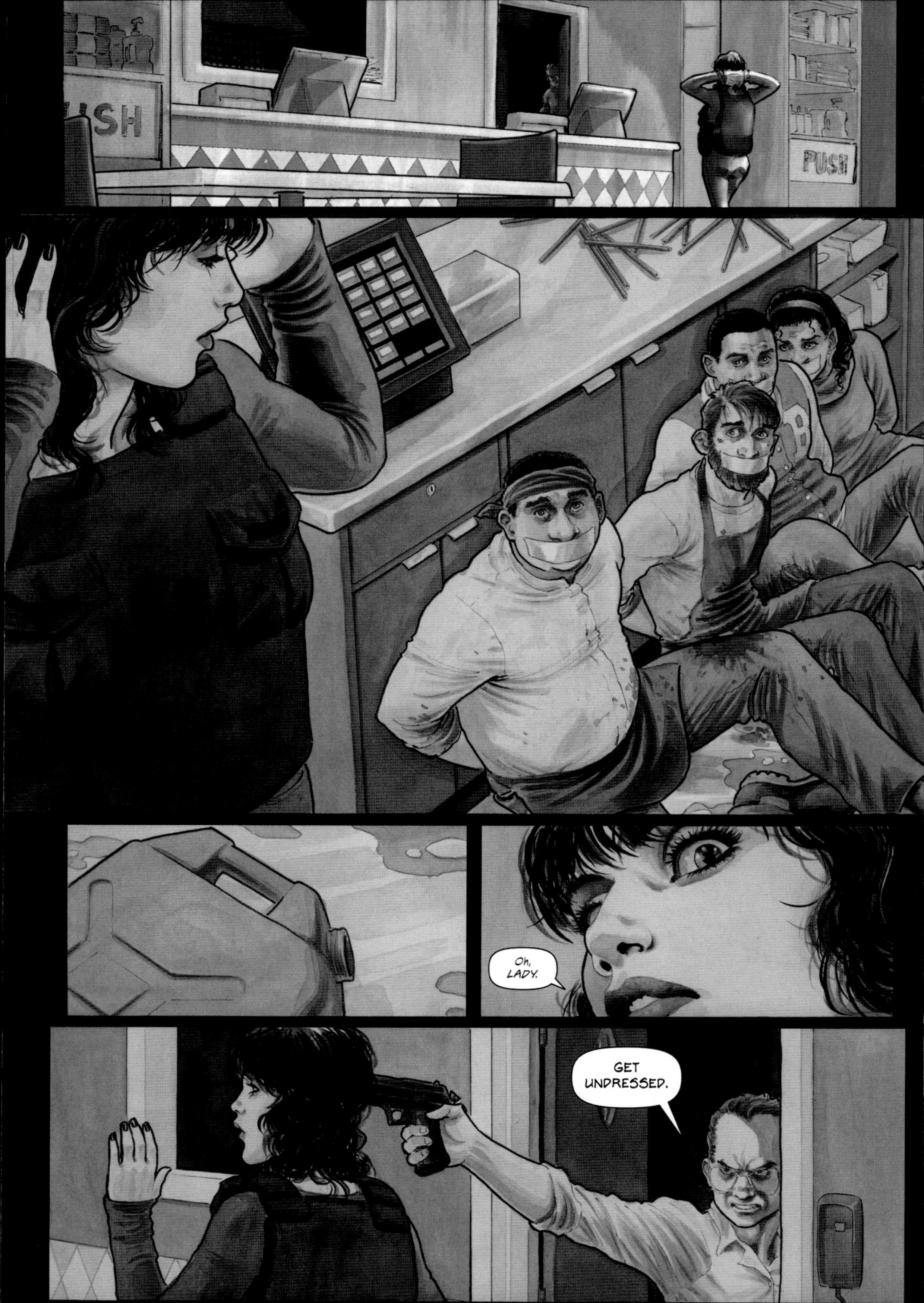
PUSH
PUSH
Oh, LADY.
GET UNDRESSED.

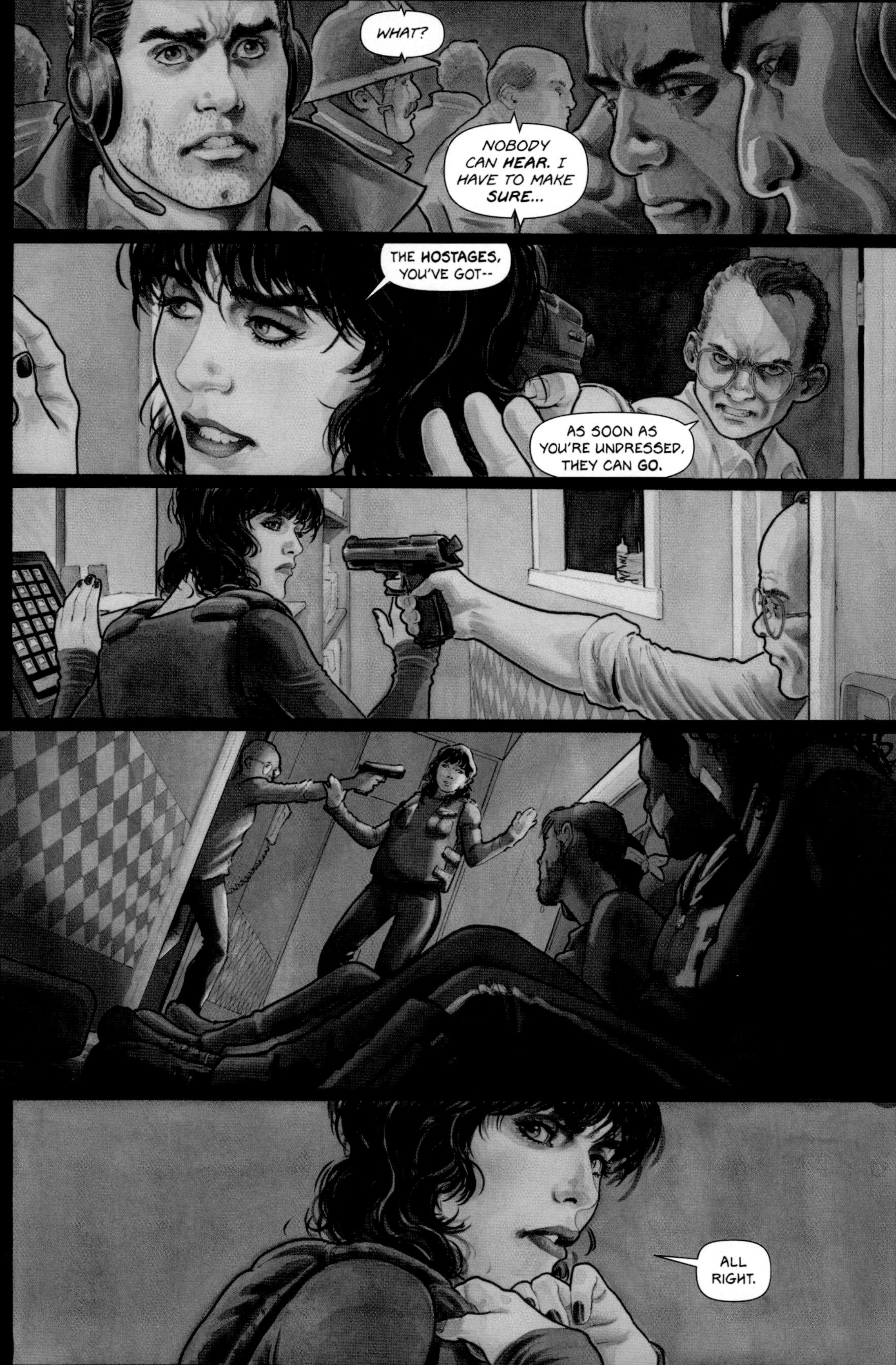
WHAT?
NOBODY CAN HEAR. I HAVE TO MAKE SURE...
THE HOSTAGES, YOU'VE GOT--
AS SOON AS YOU'RE UNDRESSED, THEY CAN GO.
ALL RIGHT.

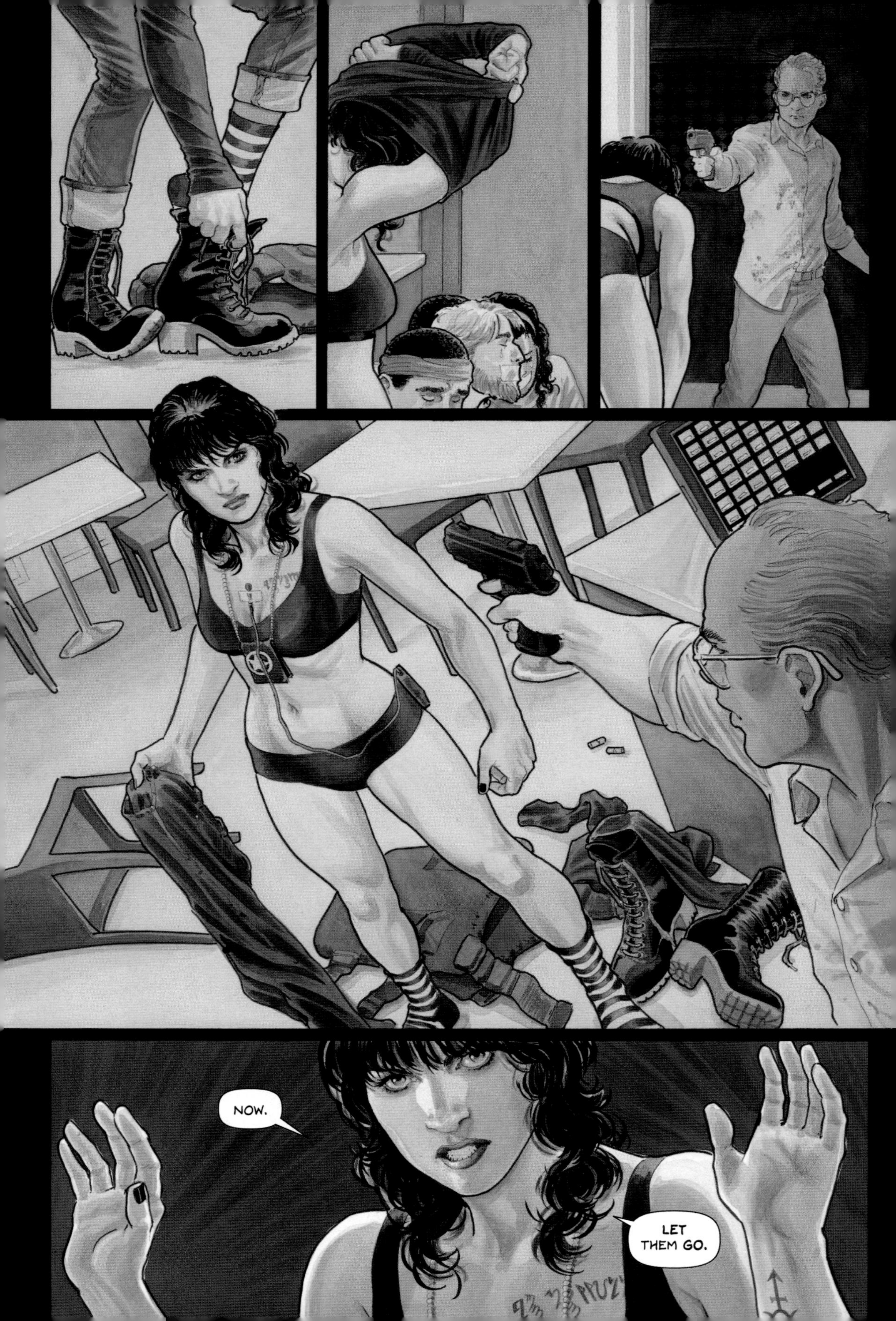
NOW.
LET THEM GO.

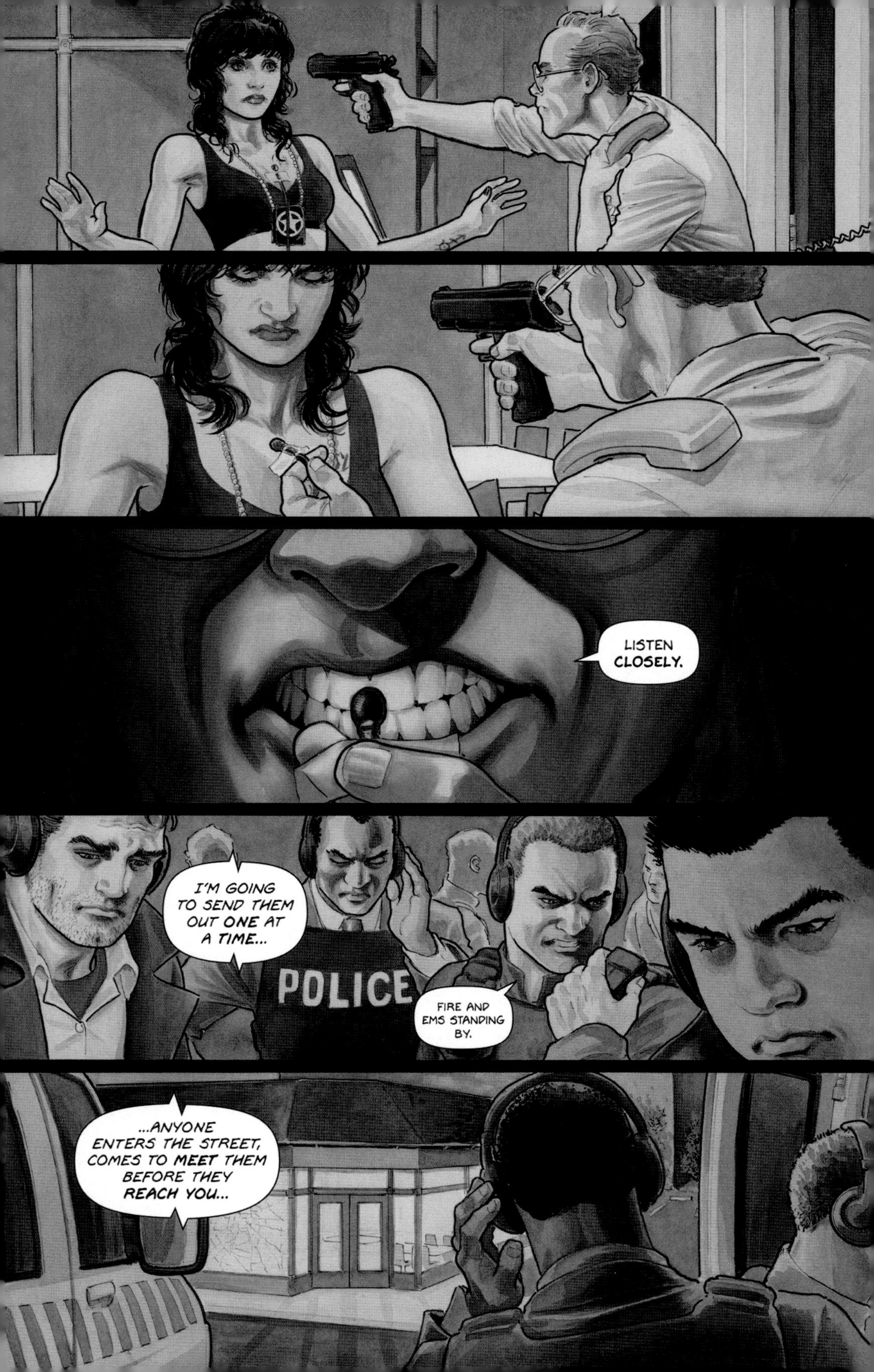
LISTEN CLOSELY.
I'M GOING TO SEND THEM OUT ONE AT A TIME...
FIRE AND EMS STANDING BY.
...ANYONE ENTERS THE STREET, COMES TO MEET THEM BEFORE THEY REACH YOU...

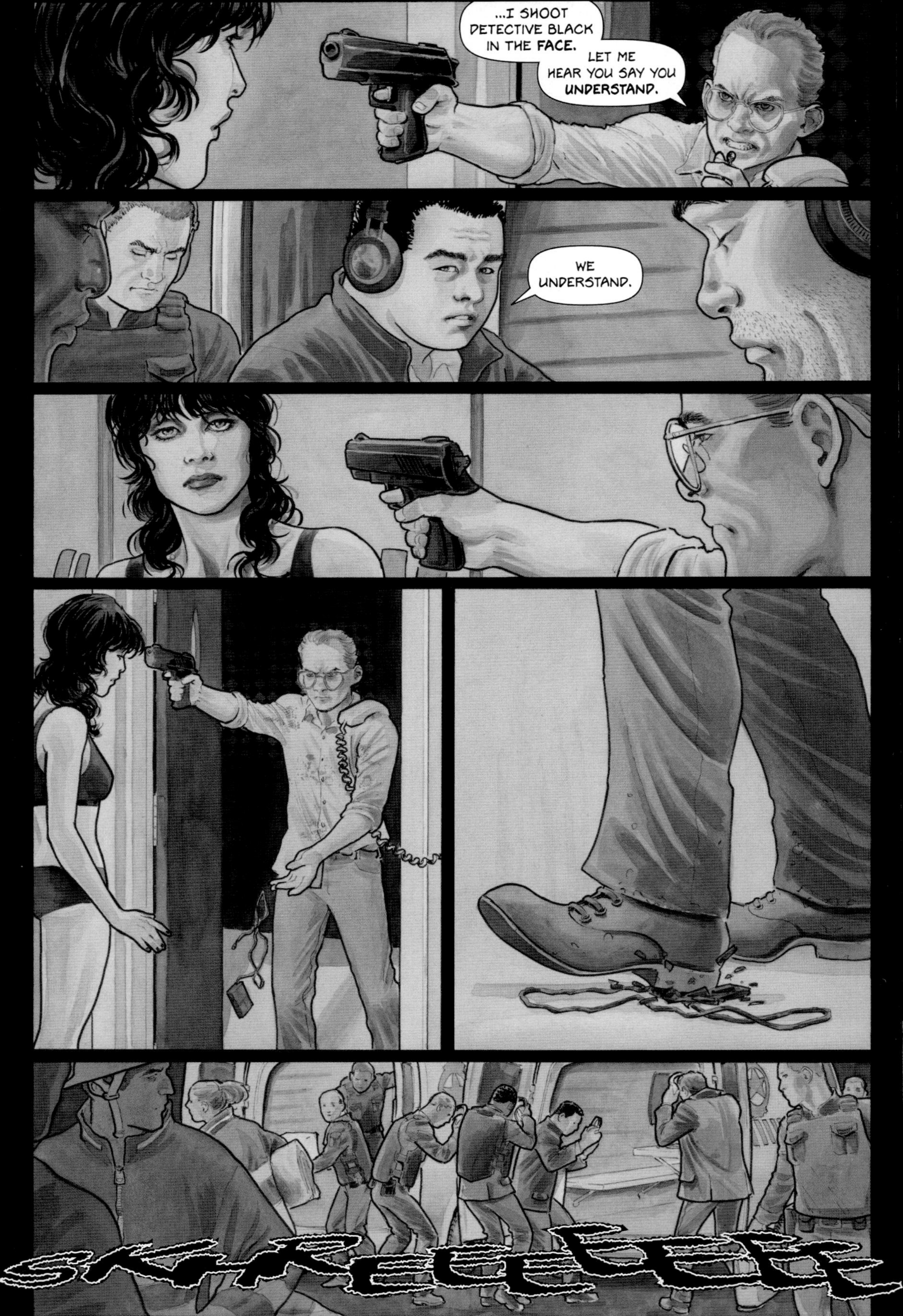
...I SHOOT DETECTIVE BLACK IN THE FACE.
LET ME HEAR YOU SAY YOU UNDERSTAND.
WE UNDERSTAND.

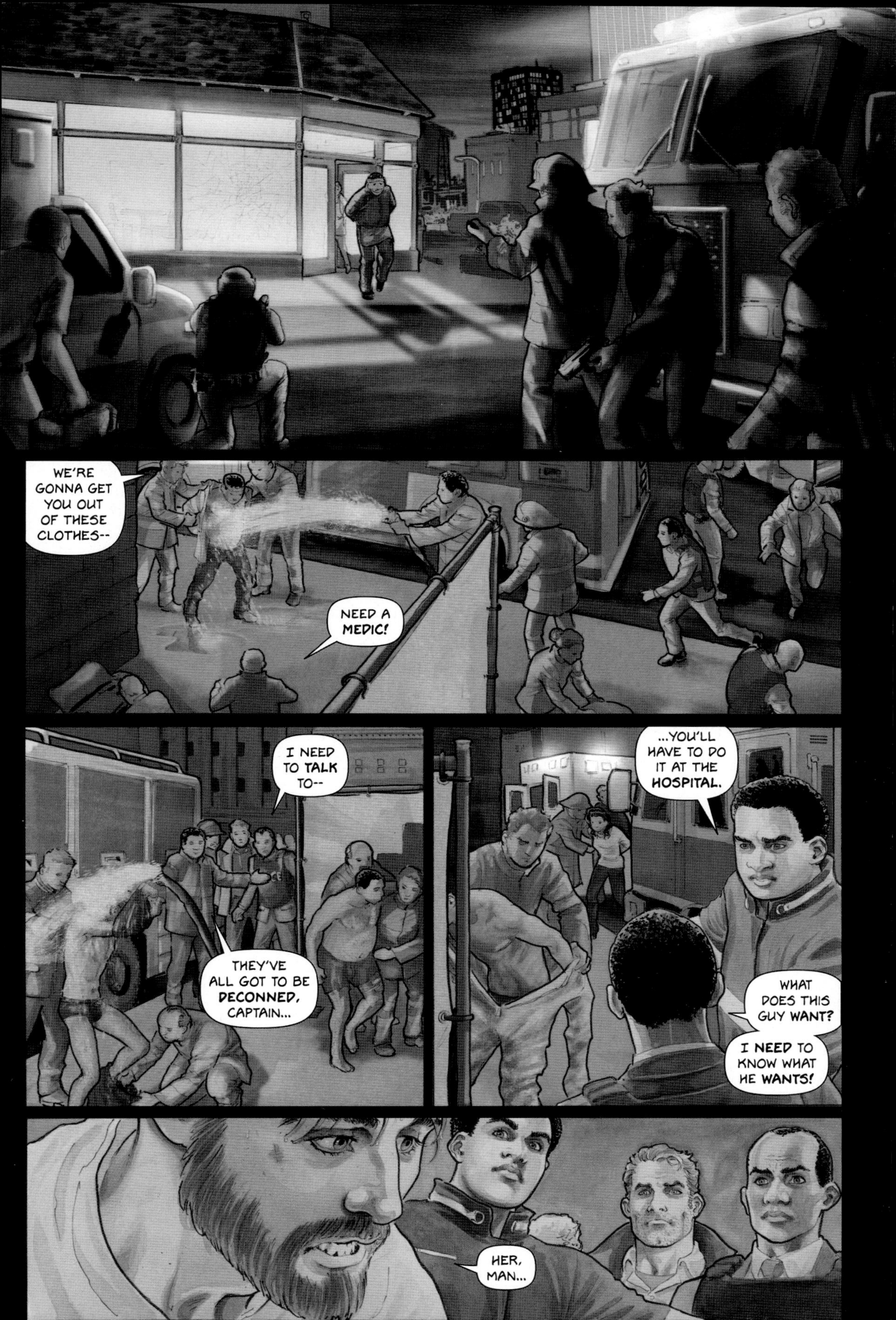
WE'RE GONNA GET YOU OUT OF THESE CLOTHES--
NEED A MEDIC!
I NEED TO TALK TO--
THEY'VE ALL GOT TO BE DECONNED, CAPTAIN...
...YOU'LL HAVE TO DO IT AT THE HOSPITAL.
WHAT DOES THIS GUY WANT?
I NEED TO KNOW WHAT HE WANTS!
HER, MAN...

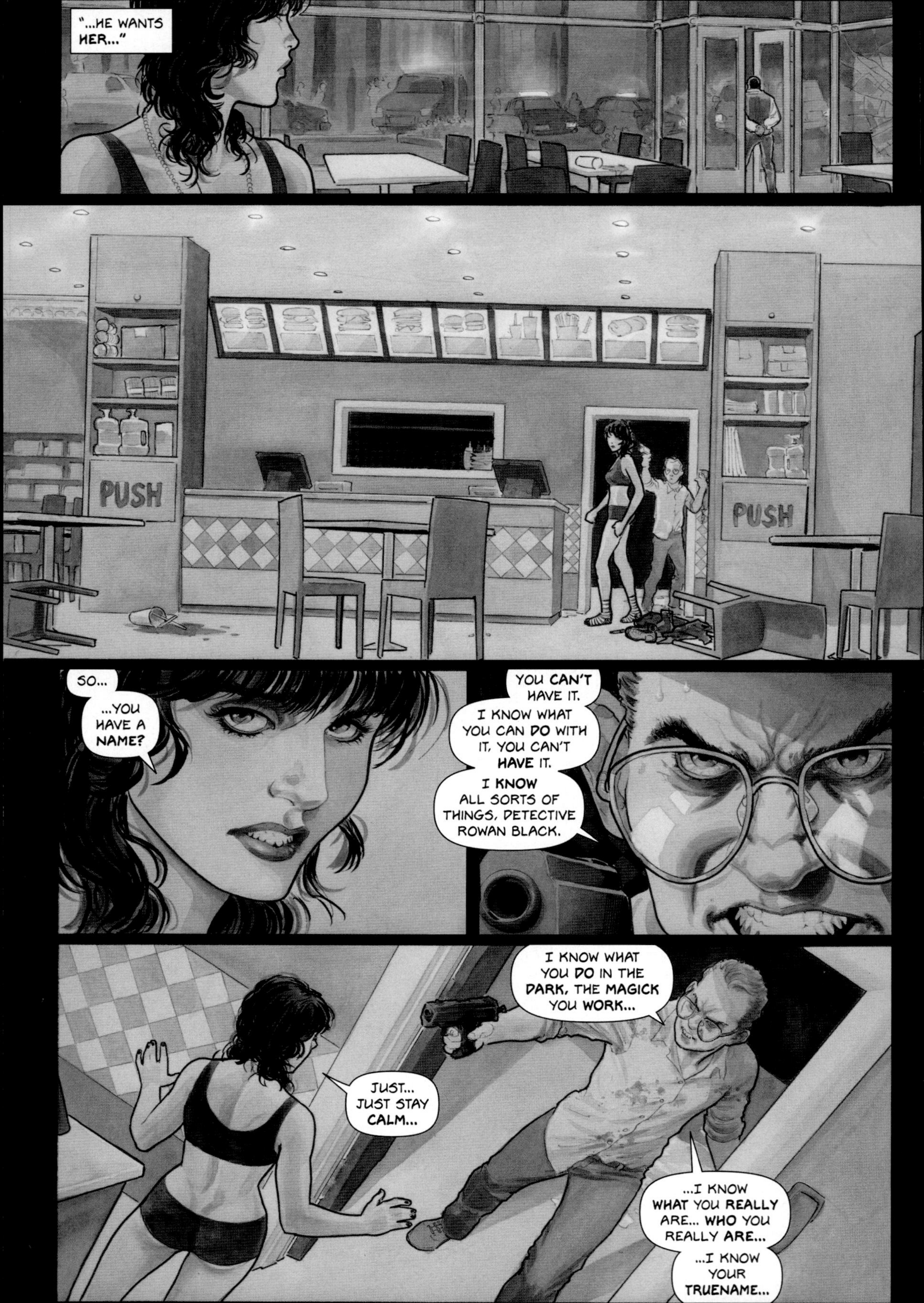
"...HE WANTS HER..."
SO...
...YOU HAVE A NAME?
YOU CAN'T HAVE IT.
I KNOW WHAT YOU CAN DO WITH IT, YOU CAN'T HAVE IT.
I KNOW ALL SORTS OF THINGS, DETECTIVE ROWAN BLACK.
I KNOW WHAT YOU DO IN THE DARK, THE MAGICK YOU WORK...
JUST... JUST STAY CALM...
...I KNOW WHAT YOU REALLY ARE... WHO YOU REALLY ARE...
...I KNOW YOUR TRUENAME...

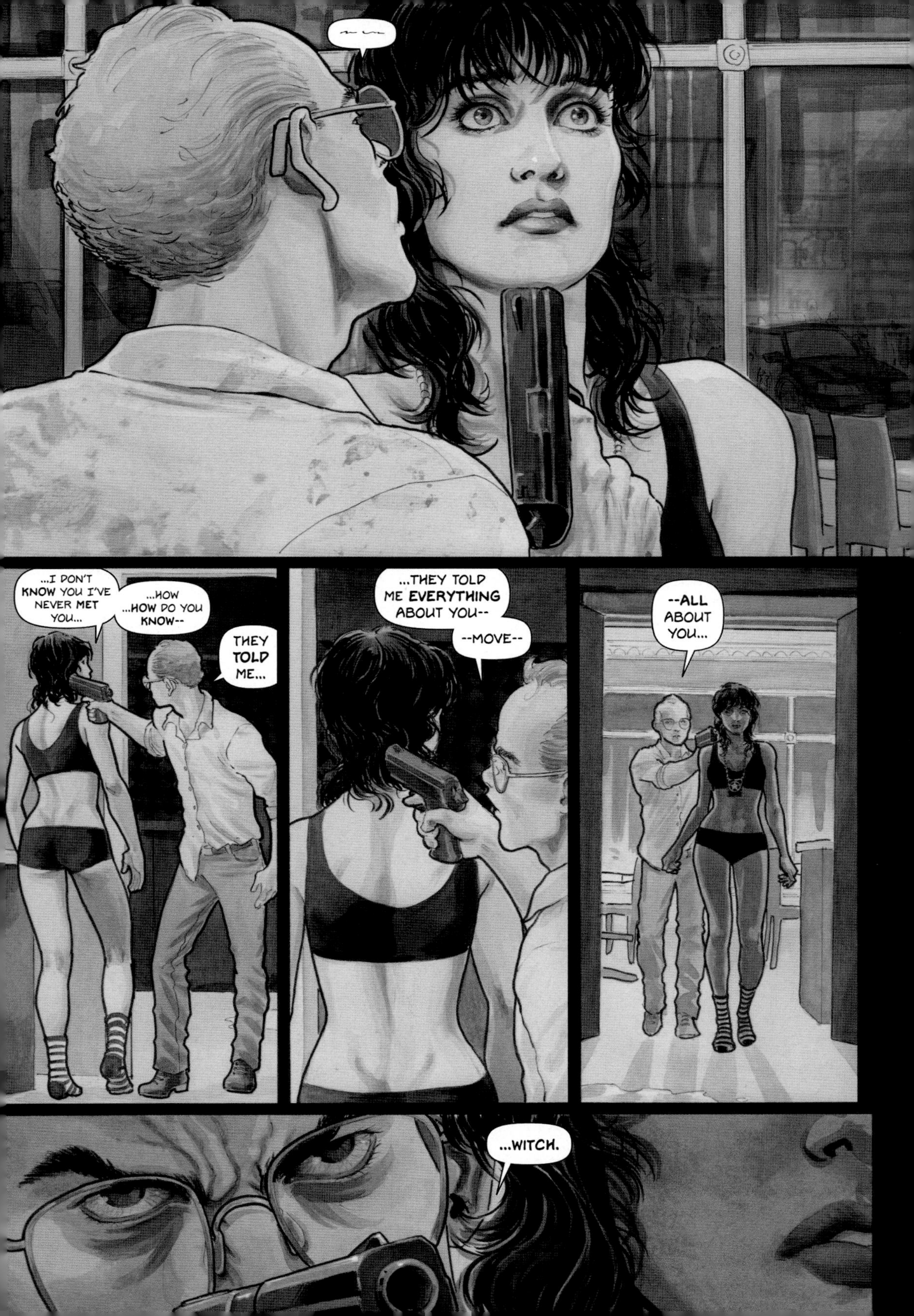
...I DON'T KNOW YOU I'VE NEVER MET YOU...
...HOW ...HOW DO YOU KNOW--
THEY TOLD ME...
...THEY TOLD ME EVERYTHING ABOUT YOU--
--MOVE--
--ALL ABOUT YOU...
...WITCH.

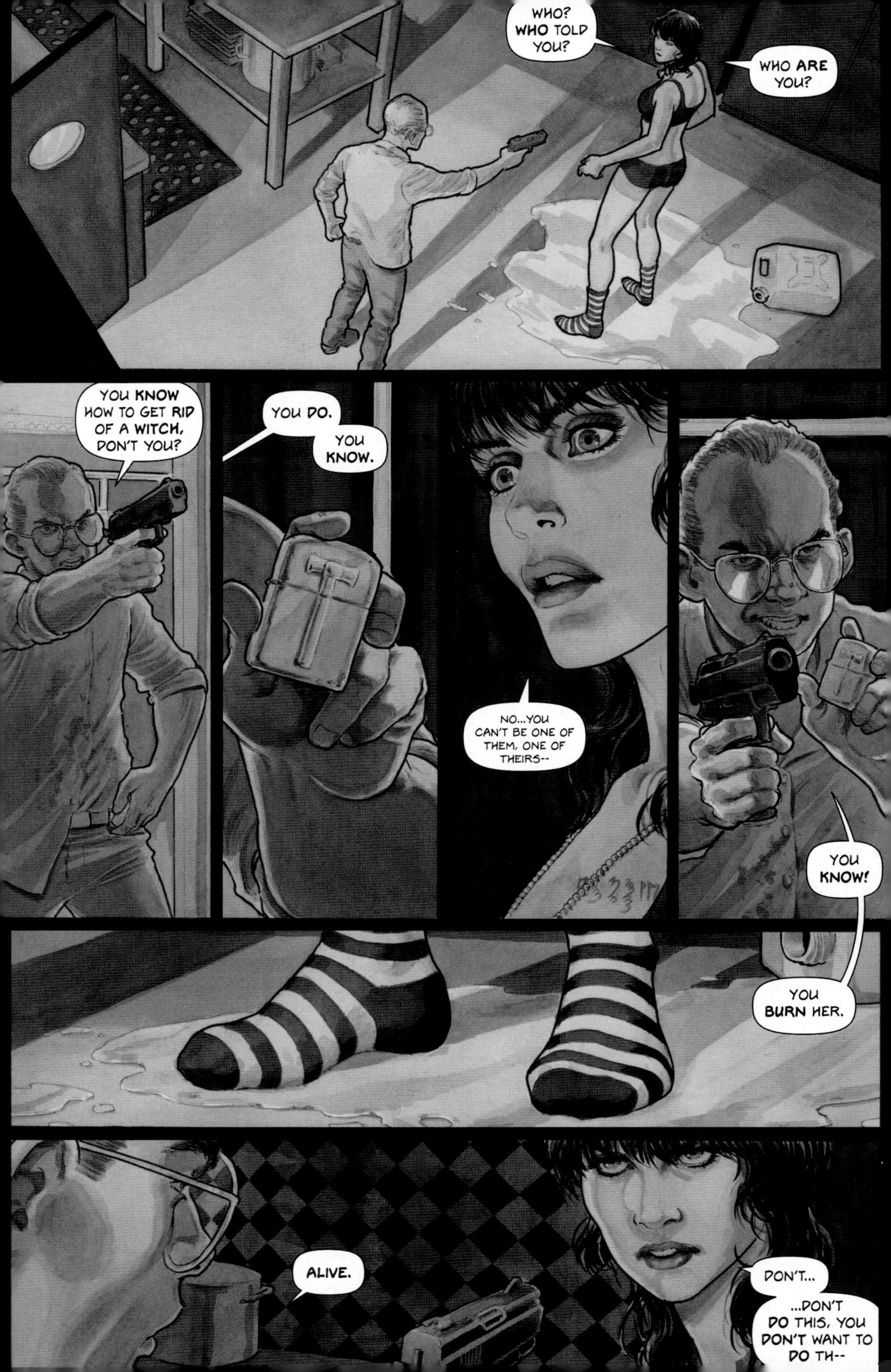
WHO? WHO TOLD YOU?
WHO ARE YOU?
YOU KNOW HOW TO GET RID OF A WITCH, DON'T YOU?
YOU DO.
YOU KNOW.
NO...YOU CAN'T BE ONE OF THEM, ONE OF THEIRS--
YOU KNOW!
YOU BURN HER.
ALIVE.
DON'T...
...DON'T DO THIS, YOU DON'T WANT TO DO TH--

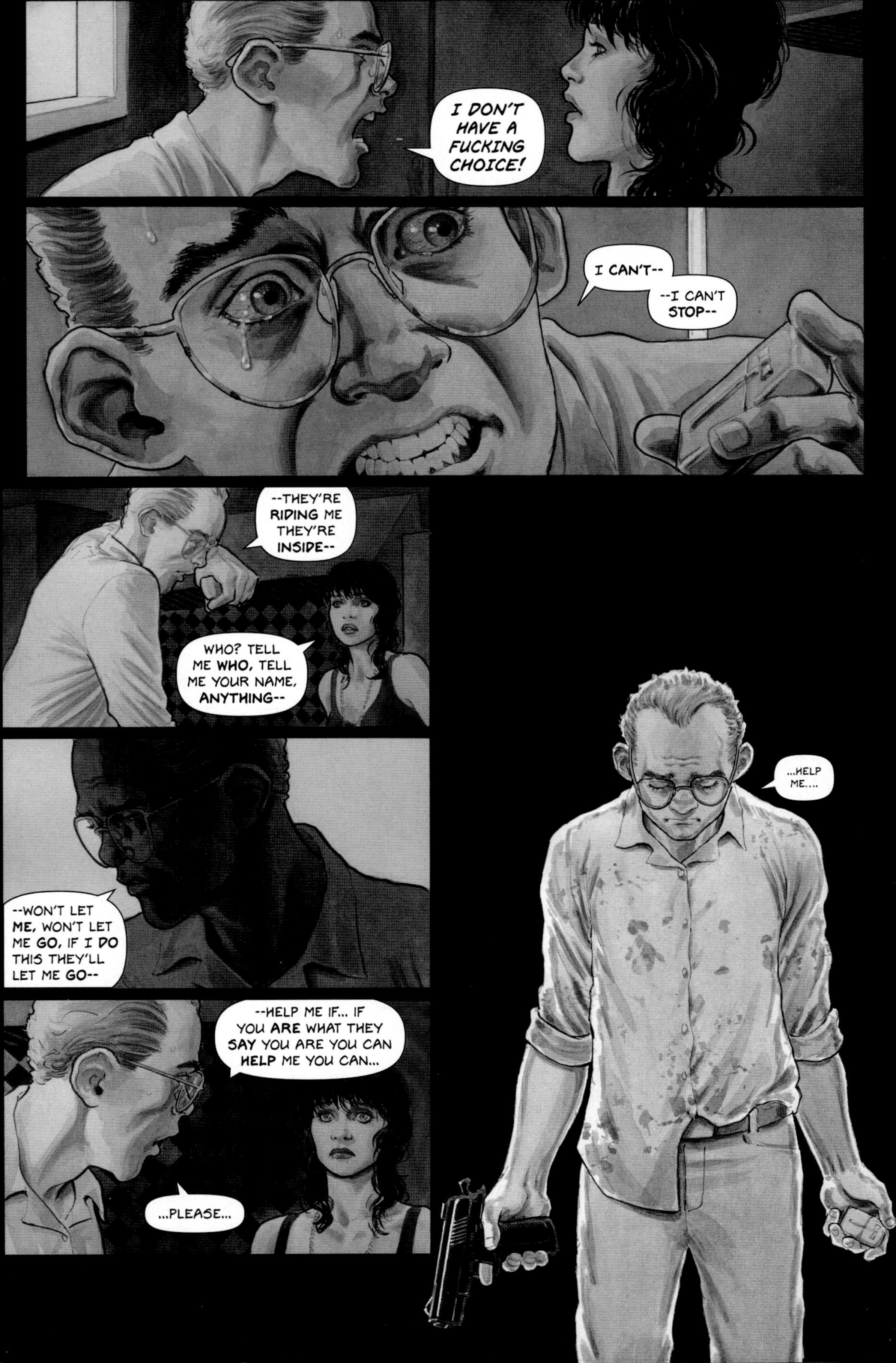
I DON'T HAVE A FUCKING CHOICE!
I CAN'T--
--I CAN'T STOP--
--THEY'RE RIDING ME THEY'RE INSIDE--
WHO? TELL ME WHO, TELL ME YOUR NAME, ANYTHING--
--WON'T LET ME, WON'T LET ME GO, IF I DO THIS THEY'LL LET ME GO--
--HELP ME IF... IF YOU ARE WHAT THEY SAY YOU ARE YOU CAN HELP ME YOU CAN...
...PLEASE...
...HELP ME....

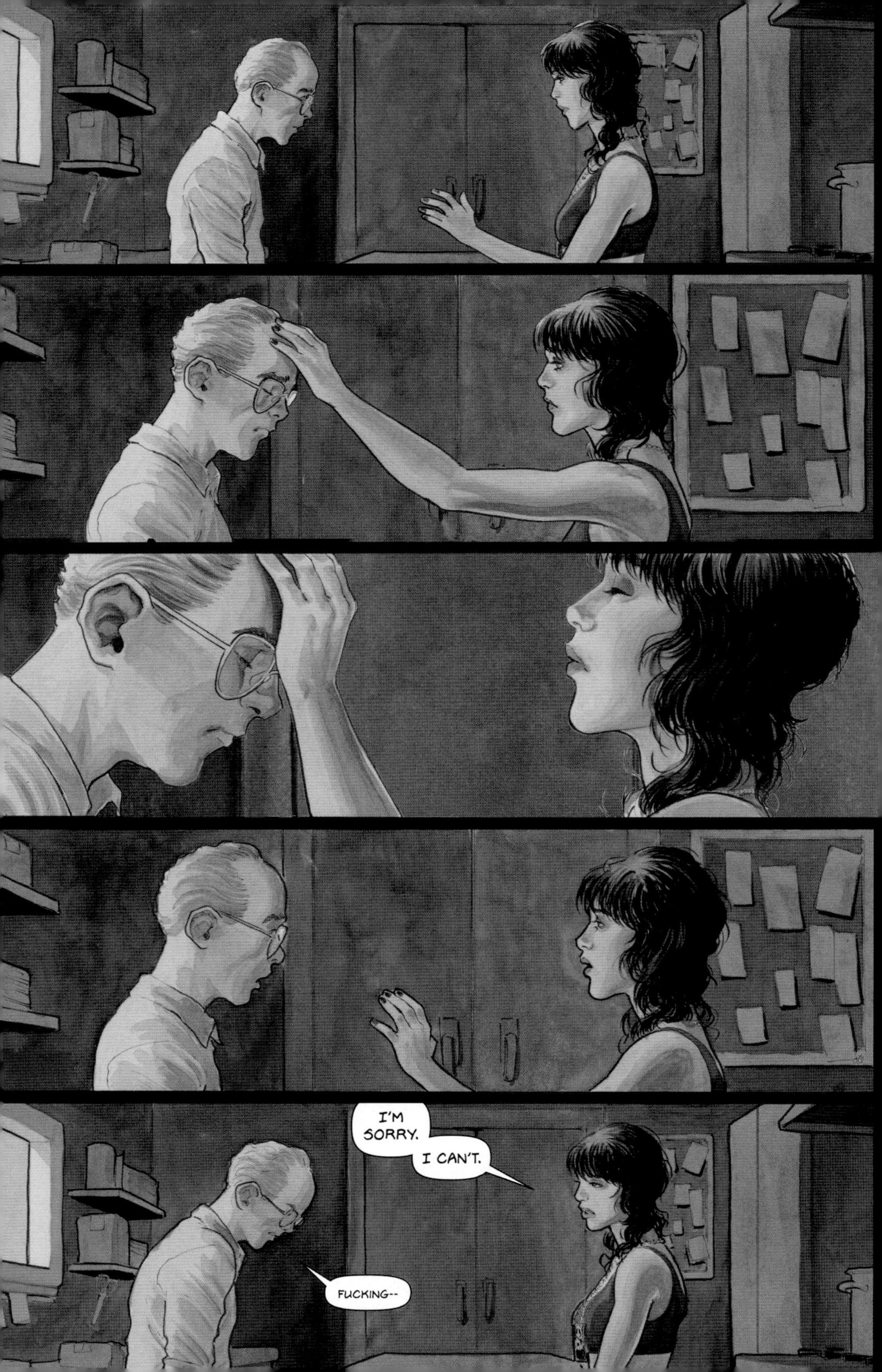
I'M SORRY.
I CAN'T.
FUCKING--

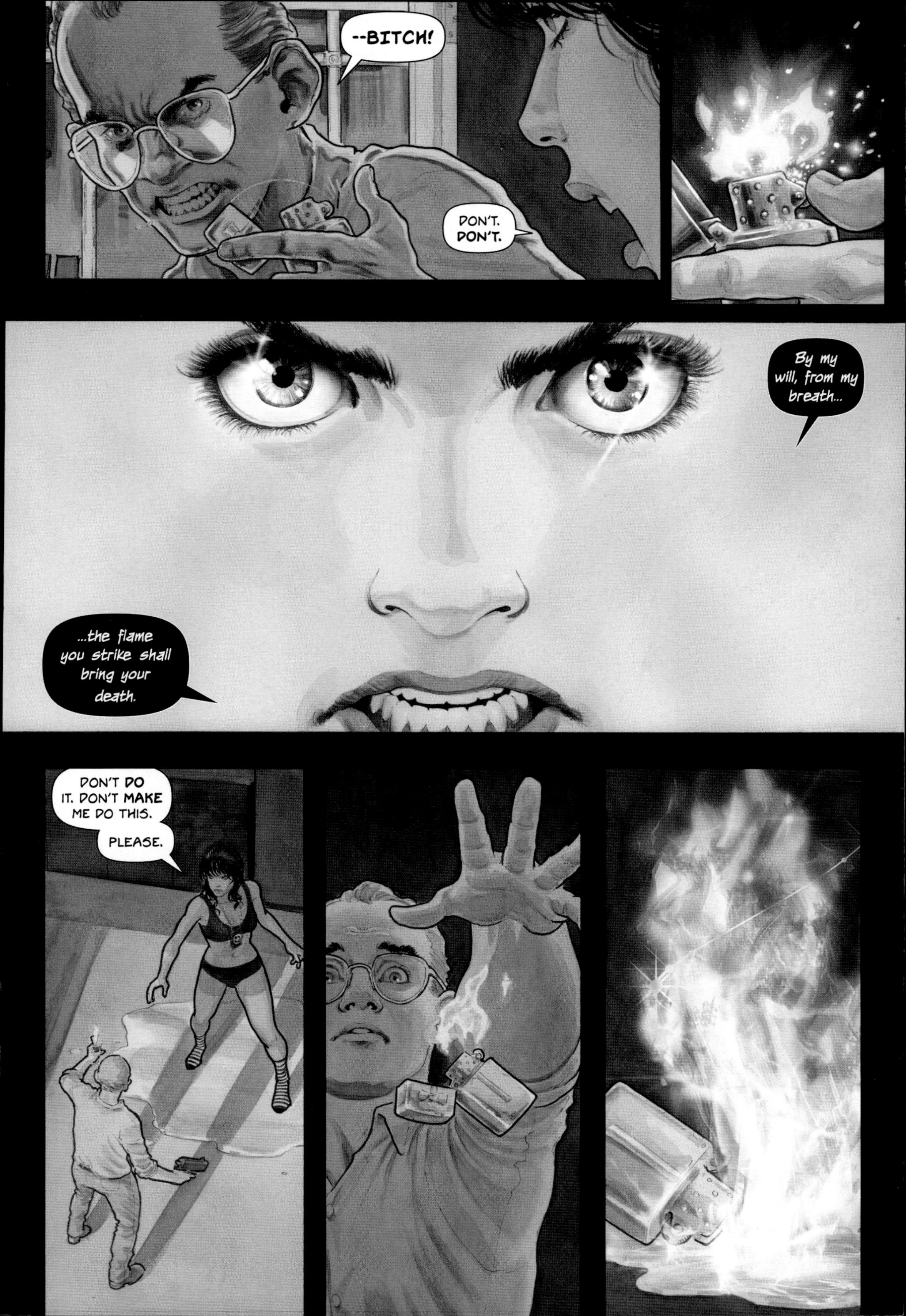
--BITCH!
DON'T. DON'T.
By my will, from my breath...
...the flame you strike shall bring your death.
DON'T DO IT. DON'T MAKE ME DO THIS.
PLEASE.

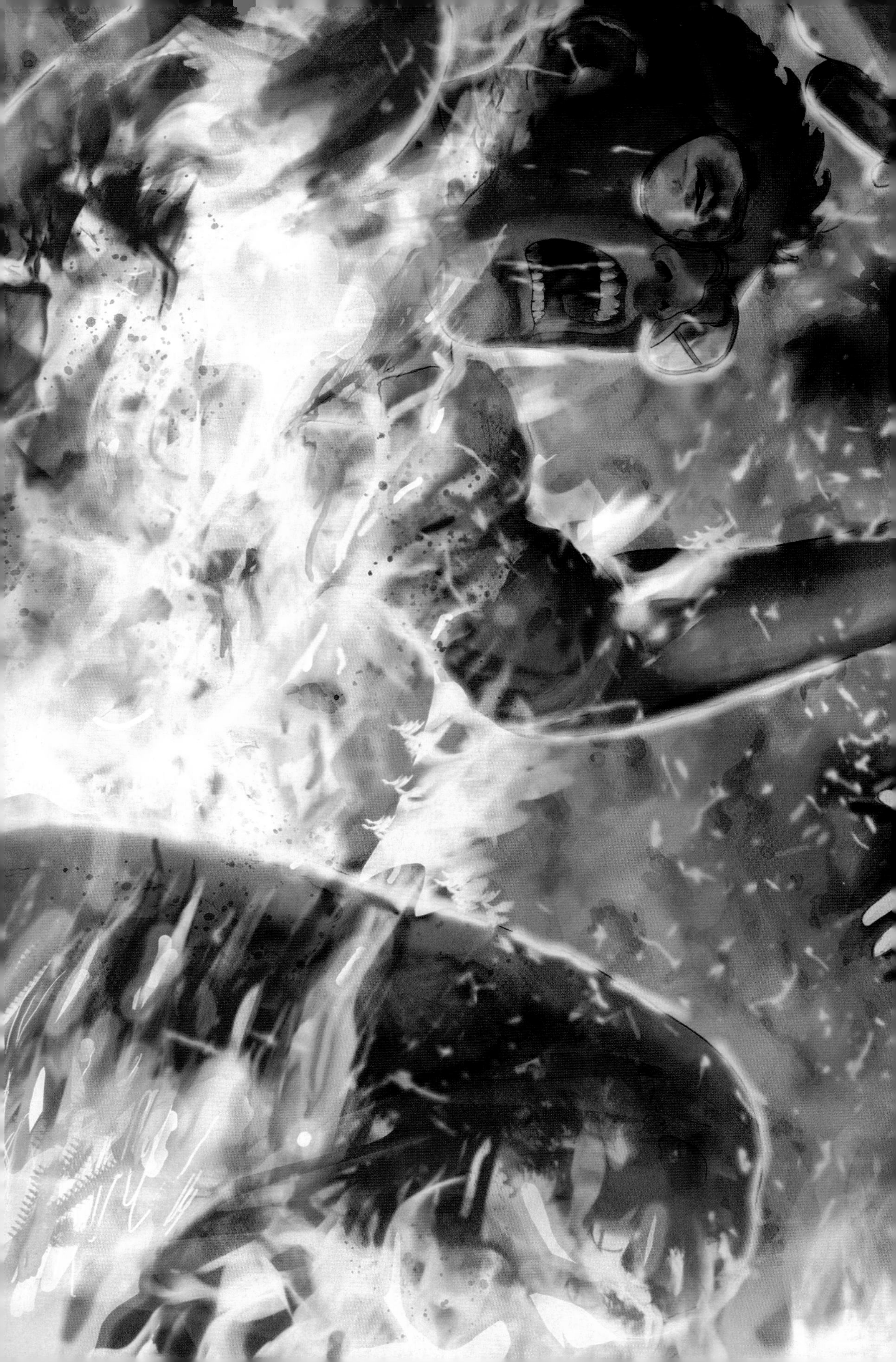

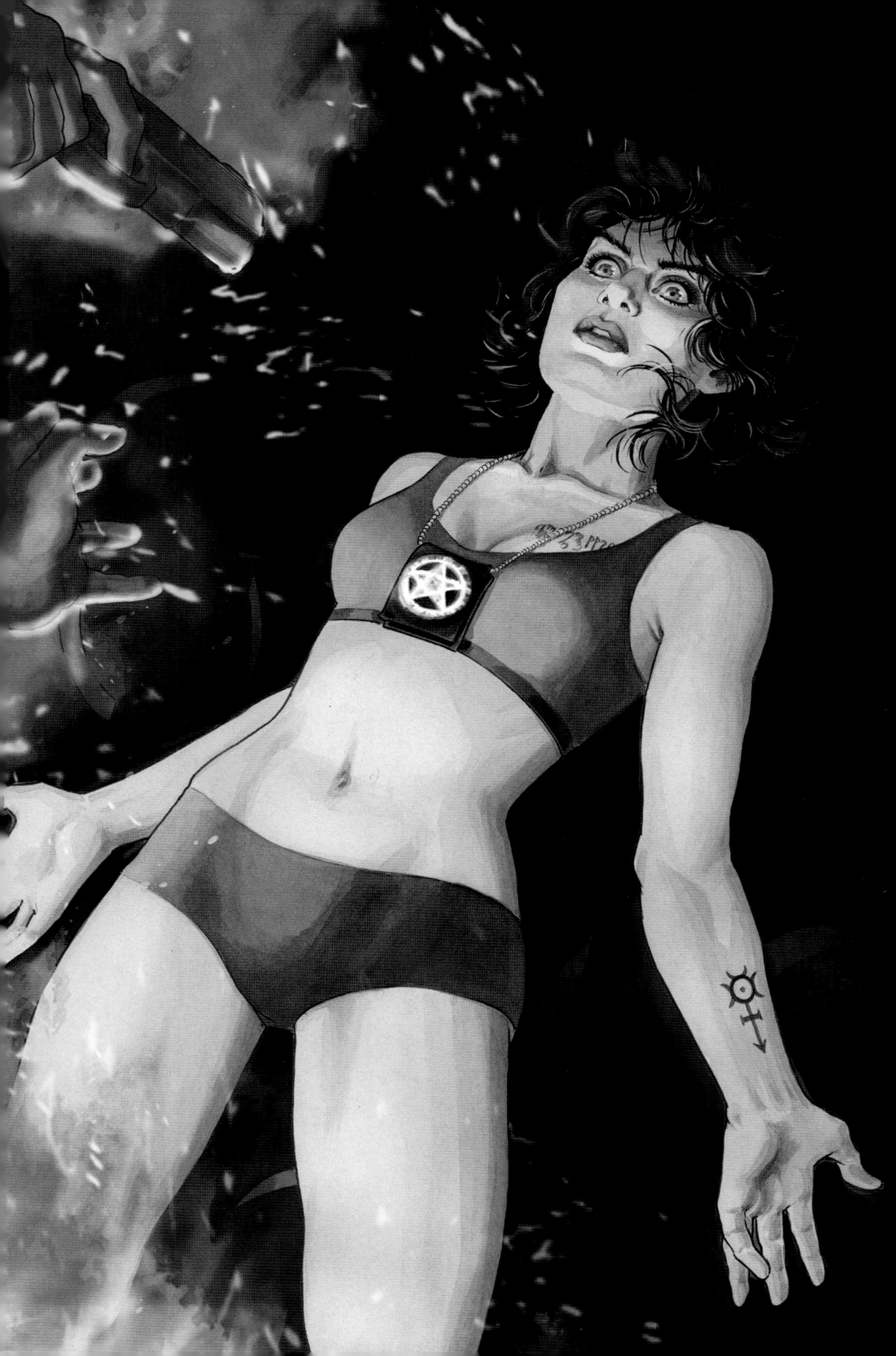

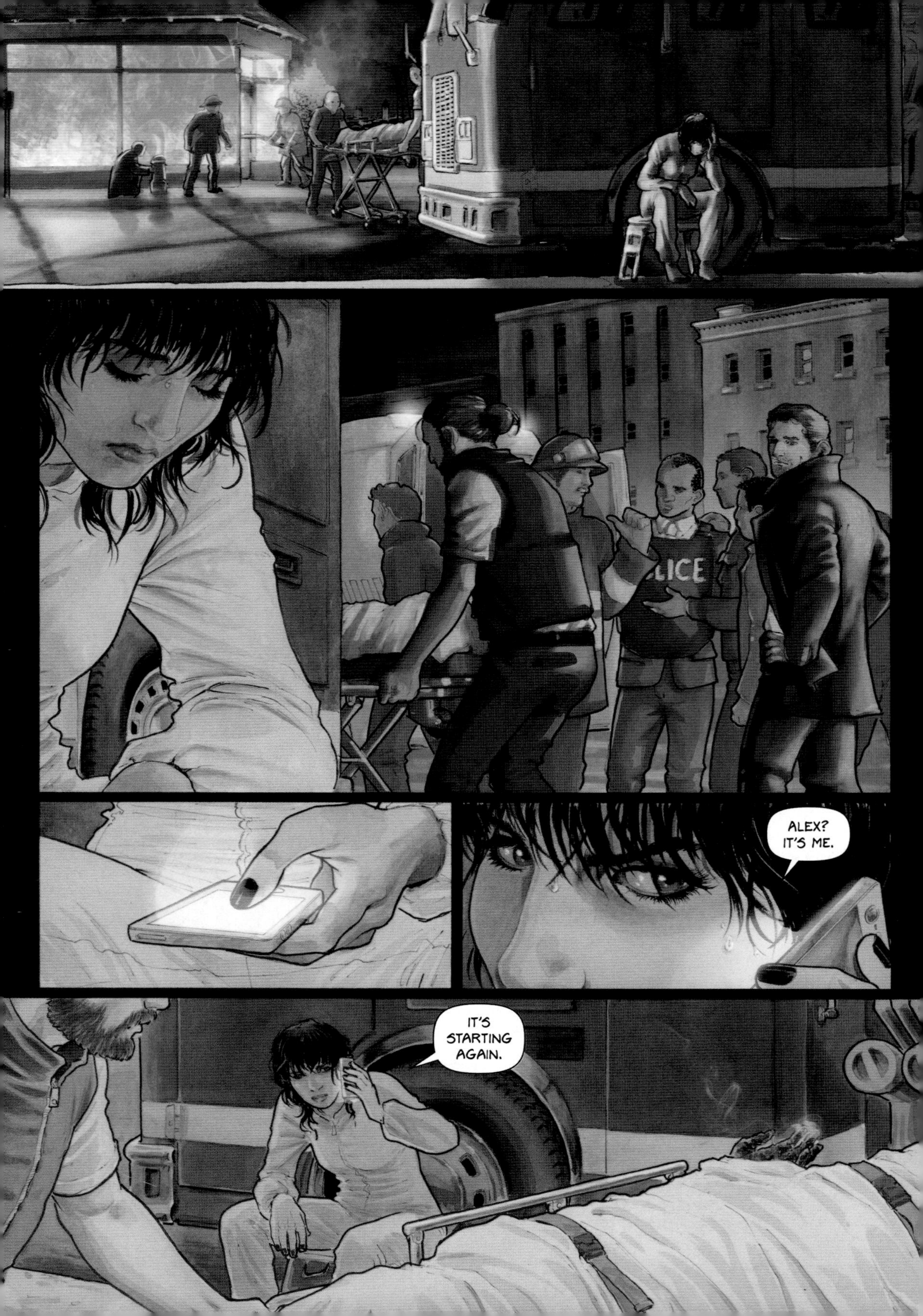
LICE
ALEX? IT'S ME.
IT'S STARTING AGAIN.

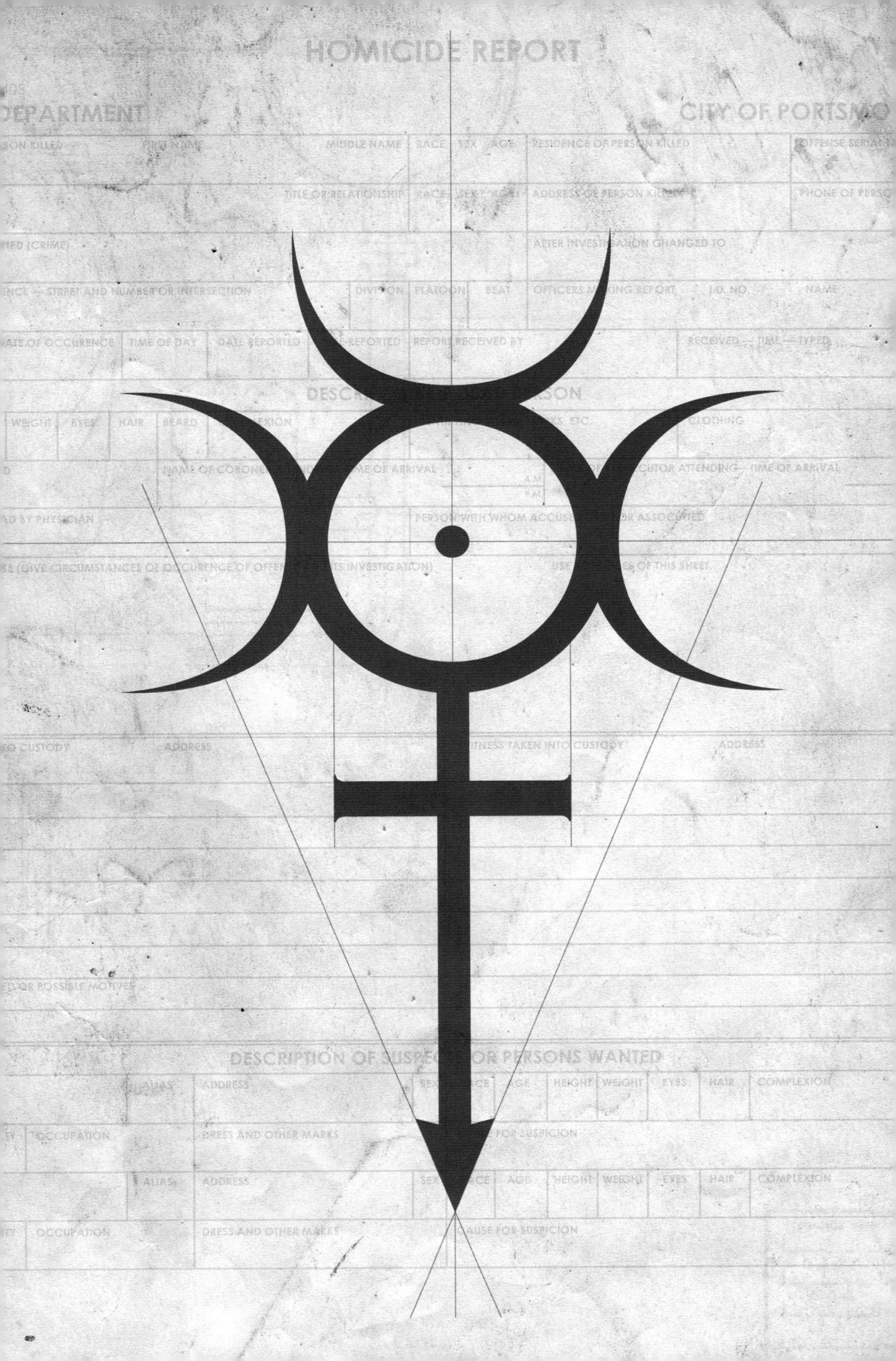
HOMICIDE REPORT
DEPARTMENT
CITY OF PORTSMO
DESCRIPTION OF SUSPEC OR PERSONS WANTED

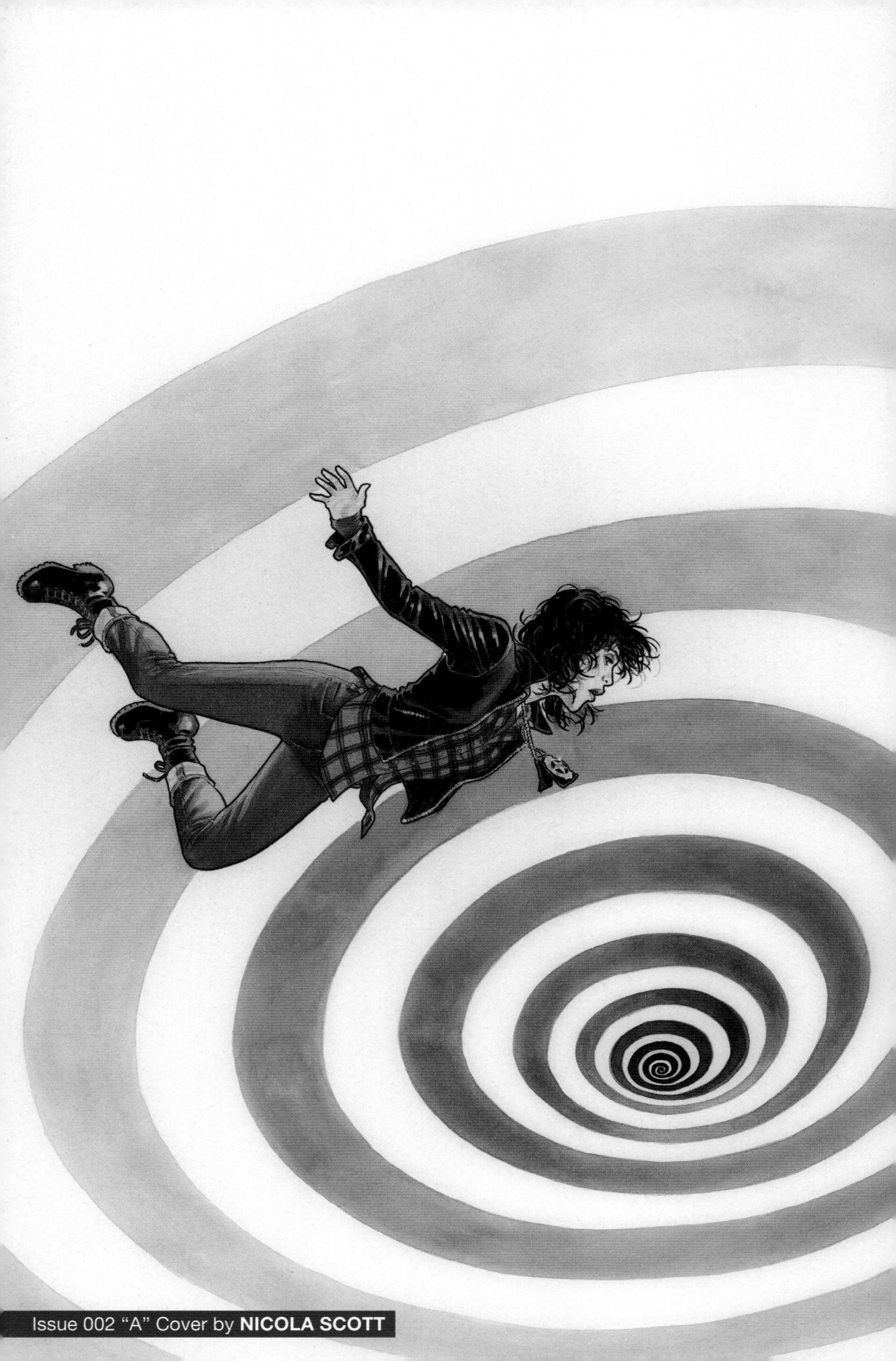

Issue 002 “A” Cover by **NICOLA SCOTT**

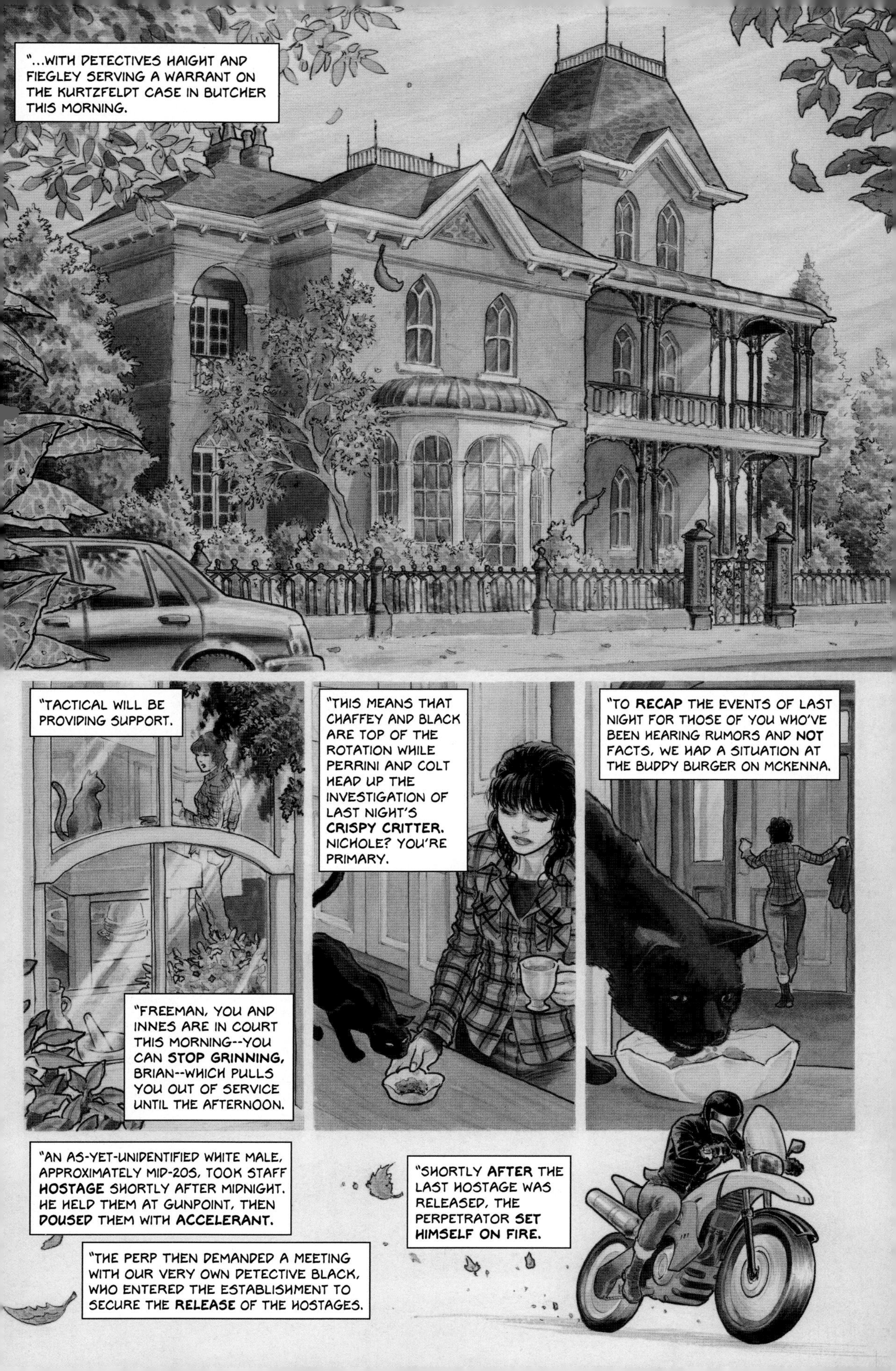
"...WITH DETECTIVES HAIGHT AND FIEGLEY SERVING A WARRANT ON THE KURTZFELDT CASE IN BUTCHER THIS MORNING.
"TACTICAL WILL BE PROVIDING SUPPORT.
"FREEMAN, YOU AND INNES ARE IN COURT THIS MORNING--YOU CAN STOP GRINNING, BRIAN--WHICH PULLS YOU OUT OF SERVICE UNTIL THE AFTERNOON.
"THIS MEANS THAT CHAFFEY AND BLACK ARE TOP OF THE ROTATION WHILE PERRINI AND COLT HEAD UP THE INVESTIGATION OF LAST NIGHT'S CRISPY CRITTER. NICHOLE? YOU'RE PRIMARY.
"TO RECAP THE EVENTS OF LAST NIGHT FOR THOSE OF YOU WHO'VE BEEN HEARING RUMORS AND NOT FACTS, WE HAD A SITUATION AT THE BUDDY BURGER ON MCKENNA.
"AN AS-YET-UNIDENTIFIED WHITE MALE, APPROXIMATELY MID-20S, TOOK STAFF HOSTAGE SHORTLY AFTER MIDNIGHT. HE HELD THEM AT GUNPOINT, THEN DOUSED THEM WITH ACCELERANT.
"THE PERP THEN DEMANDED A MEETING WITH OUR VERY OWN DETECTIVE BLACK, WHO ENTERED THE ESTABLISHMENT TO SECURE THE RELEASE OF THE HOSTAGES.
"SHORTLY AFTER THE LAST HOSTAGE WAS RELEASED, THE PERPETRATOR SET HIMSELF ON FIRE.

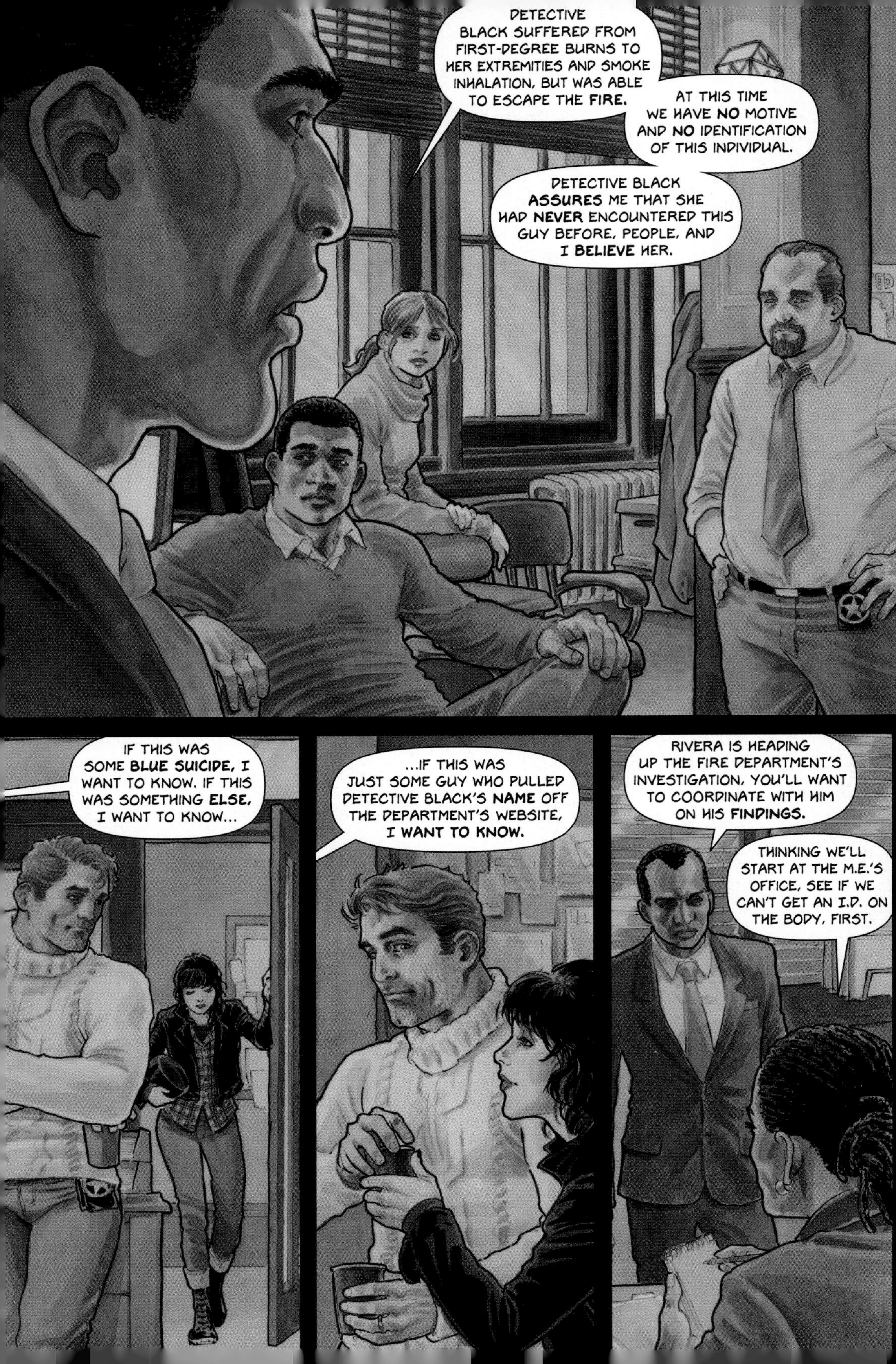
DETECTIVE BLACK SUFFERED FROM FIRST-DEGREE BURNS TO HER EXTREMITIES AND SMOKE INHALATION, BUT WAS ABLE TO ESCAPE THE **FIRE.**
AT THIS TIME WE HAVE **NO** MOTIVE AND **NO** IDENTIFICATION OF THIS INDIVIDUAL.
DETECTIVE BLACK **ASSURES** ME THAT SHE HAD **NEVER** ENCOUNTERED THIS GUY BEFORE, PEOPLE, AND **I BELIEVE** HER.
IF THIS WAS SOME **BLUE SUICIDE,** I WANT TO KNOW. IF THIS WAS SOMETHING **ELSE,** I WANT TO KNOW...
...IF THIS WAS JUST SOME GUY WHO PULLED DETECTIVE BLACK'S **NAME** OFF THE DEPARTMENT'S WEBSITE, **I WANT TO KNOW.**
RIVERA IS HEADING UP THE FIRE DEPARTMENT'S INVESTIGATION, YOU'LL WANT TO COORDINATE WITH HIM ON HIS **FINDINGS.**
THINKING WE'LL START AT THE M.E.'S OFFICE, SEE IF WE CAN'T GET AN I.D. ON THE BODY, FIRST.

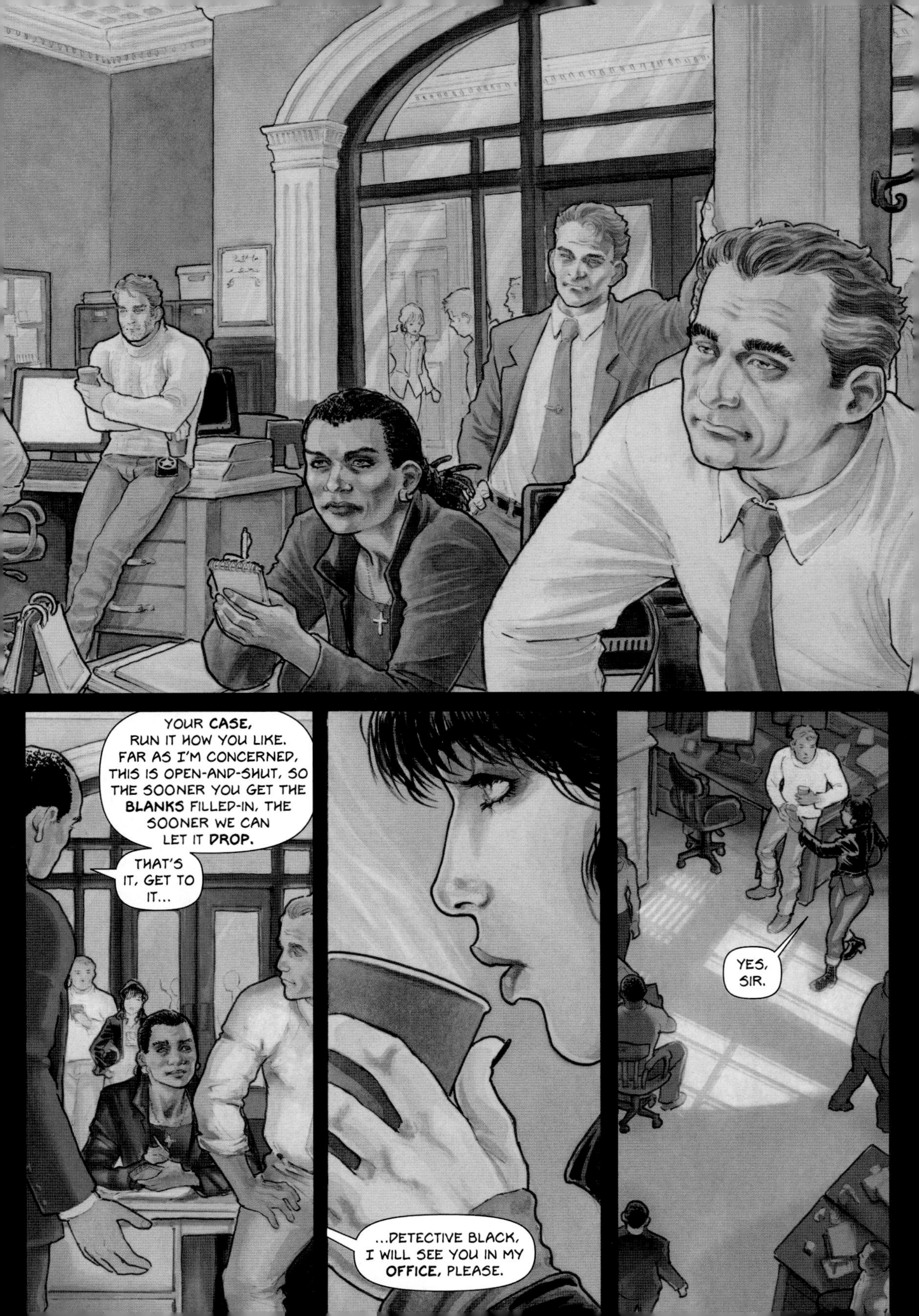
YOUR CASE, RUN IT HOW YOU LIKE. FAR AS I'M CONCERNED, THIS IS OPEN-AND-SHUT, SO THE SOONER YOU GET THE BLANKS FILLED-IN, THE SOONER WE CAN LET IT DROP.
THAT'S IT, GET TO IT...
...DETECTIVE BLACK, I WILL SEE YOU IN MY OFFICE, PLEASE.
YES, SIR.

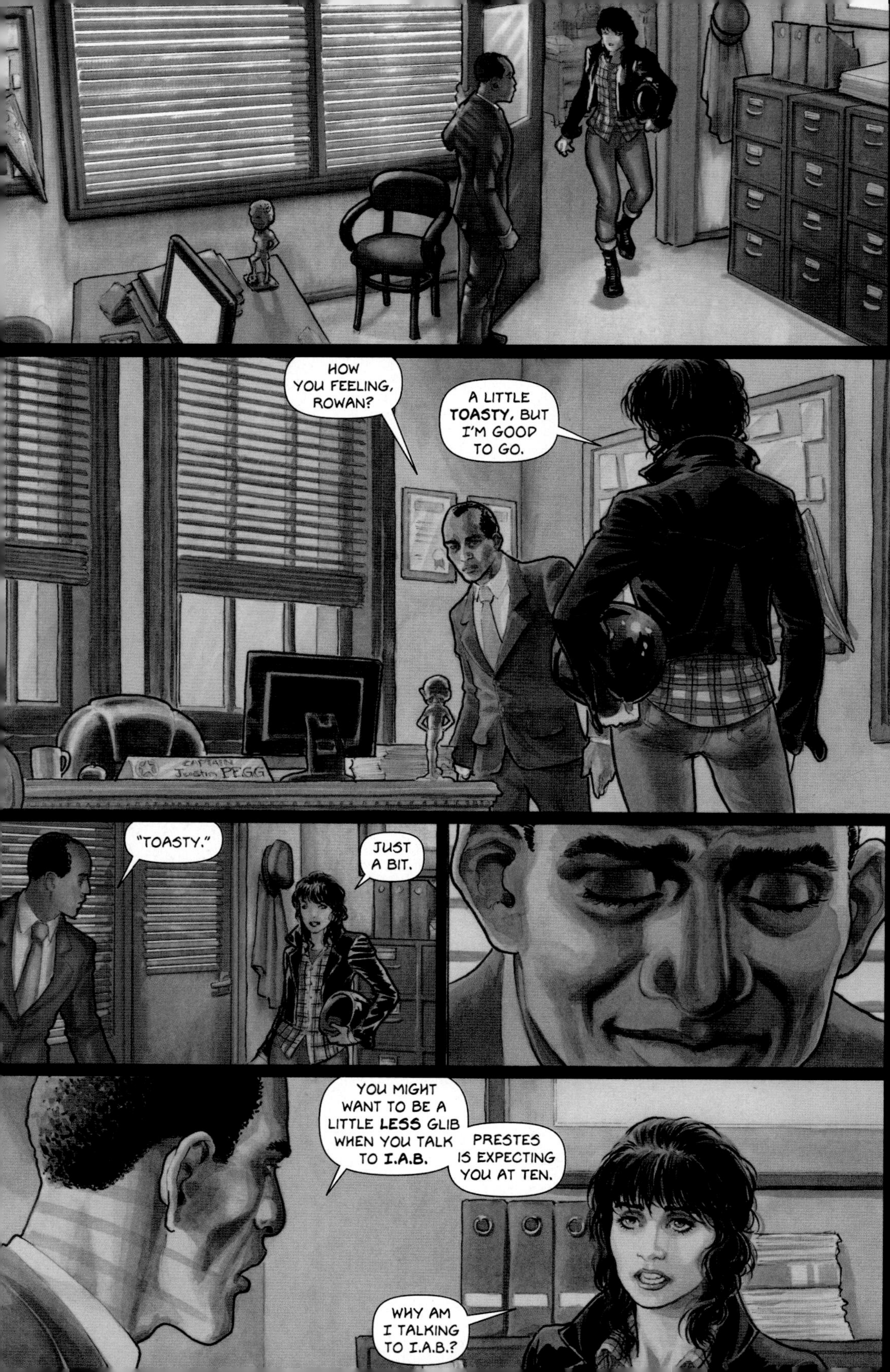
HOW YOU FEELING, ROWAN?
A LITTLE TOASTY, BUT I'M GOOD TO GO.
CAPTAIN Justin PEGG
"TOASTY."
JUST A BIT.
YOU MIGHT WANT TO BE A LITTLE LESS GLIB WHEN YOU TALK TO I.A.B.
PRESTES IS EXPECTING YOU AT TEN.
WHY AM I TALKING TO I.A.B.?

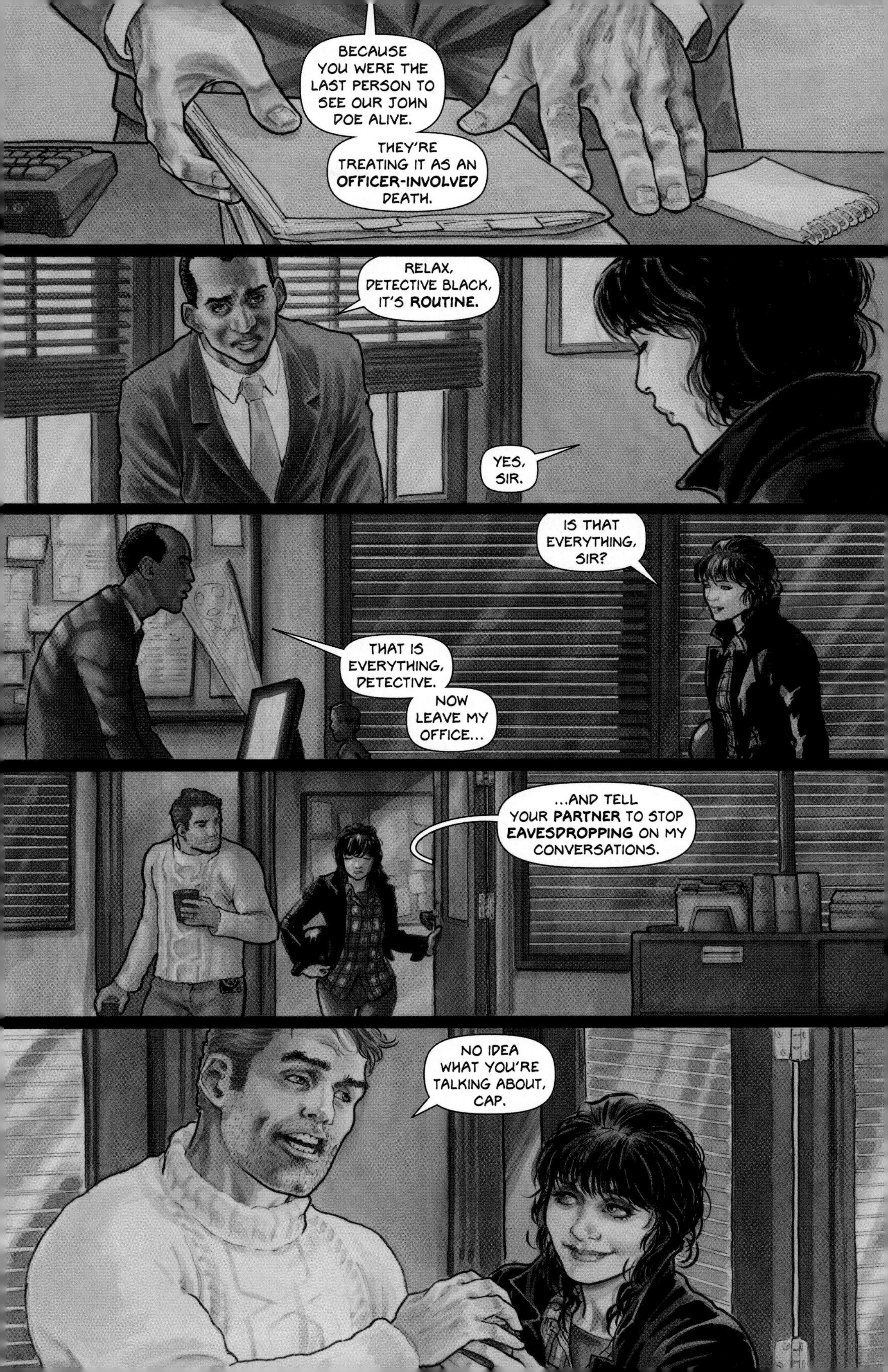
BECAUSE YOU WERE THE LAST PERSON TO SEE OUR JOHN DOE ALIVE.
THEY'RE TREATING IT AS AN **OFFICER-INVOLVED** DEATH.
RELAX, DETECTIVE BLACK, IT'S **ROUTINE.**
YES, SIR.
IS THAT EVERYTHING, SIR?
THAT IS EVERYTHING, DETECTIVE.
NOW LEAVE MY OFFICE...
...AND TELL YOUR **PARTNER** TO STOP **EAVESDROPPING** ON MY CONVERSATIONS.
NO IDEA WHAT YOU'RE TALKING ABOUT, CAP.

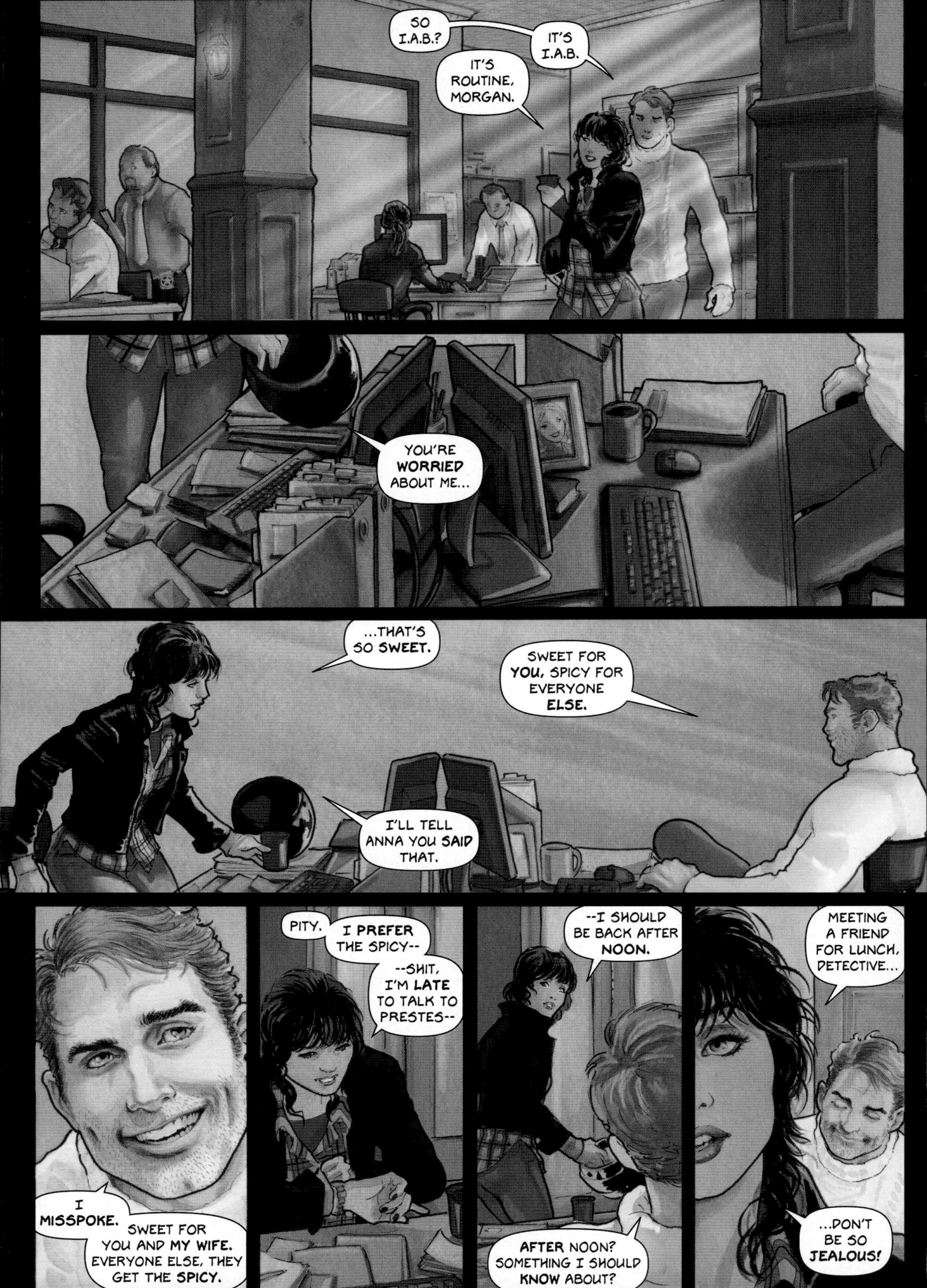
SO I.A.B.?
IT'S I.A.B.
IT'S ROUTINE, MORGAN.
YOU'RE WORRIED ABOUT ME...
...THAT'S SO SWEET.
SWEET FOR YOU, SPICY FOR EVERYONE ELSE.
I'LL TELL ANNA YOU SAID THAT.
I MISSPOKE.
SWEET FOR YOU AND MY WIFE. EVERYONE ELSE, THEY GET THE SPICY.
PITY.
I PREFER THE SPICY--
--SHIT, I'M LATE TO TALK TO PRESTES--
--I SHOULD BE BACK AFTER NOON.
AFTER NOON? SOMETHING I SHOULD KNOW ABOUT?
MEETING A FRIEND FOR LUNCH, DETECTIVE...
...DON'T BE SO JEALOUS!

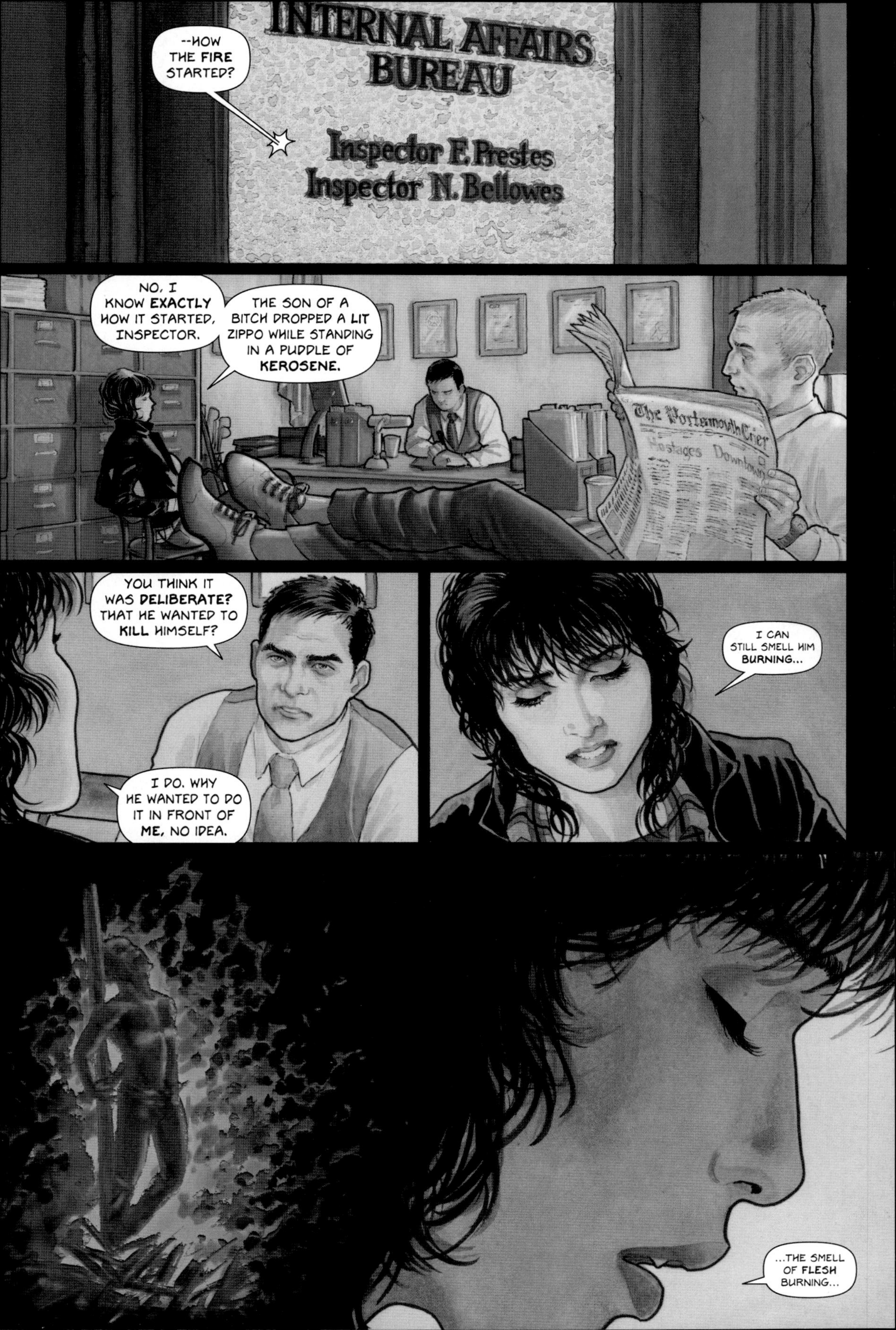
INTERNAL AFFAIRS BUREAU
Inspector F. Prestes
Inspector N. Bellowes
--HOW THE FIRE STARTED?
NO, I KNOW EXACTLY HOW IT STARTED, INSPECTOR.
THE SON OF A BITCH DROPPED A LIT ZIPPO WHILE STANDING IN A PUDDLE OF KEROSENE.
Hostages Downtown
YOU THINK IT WAS DELIBERATE? THAT HE WANTED TO KILL HIMSELF?
I DO. WHY HE WANTED TO DO IT IN FRONT OF ME, NO IDEA.
I CAN STILL SMELL HIM BURNING...
...THE SMELL OF FLESH BURNING...

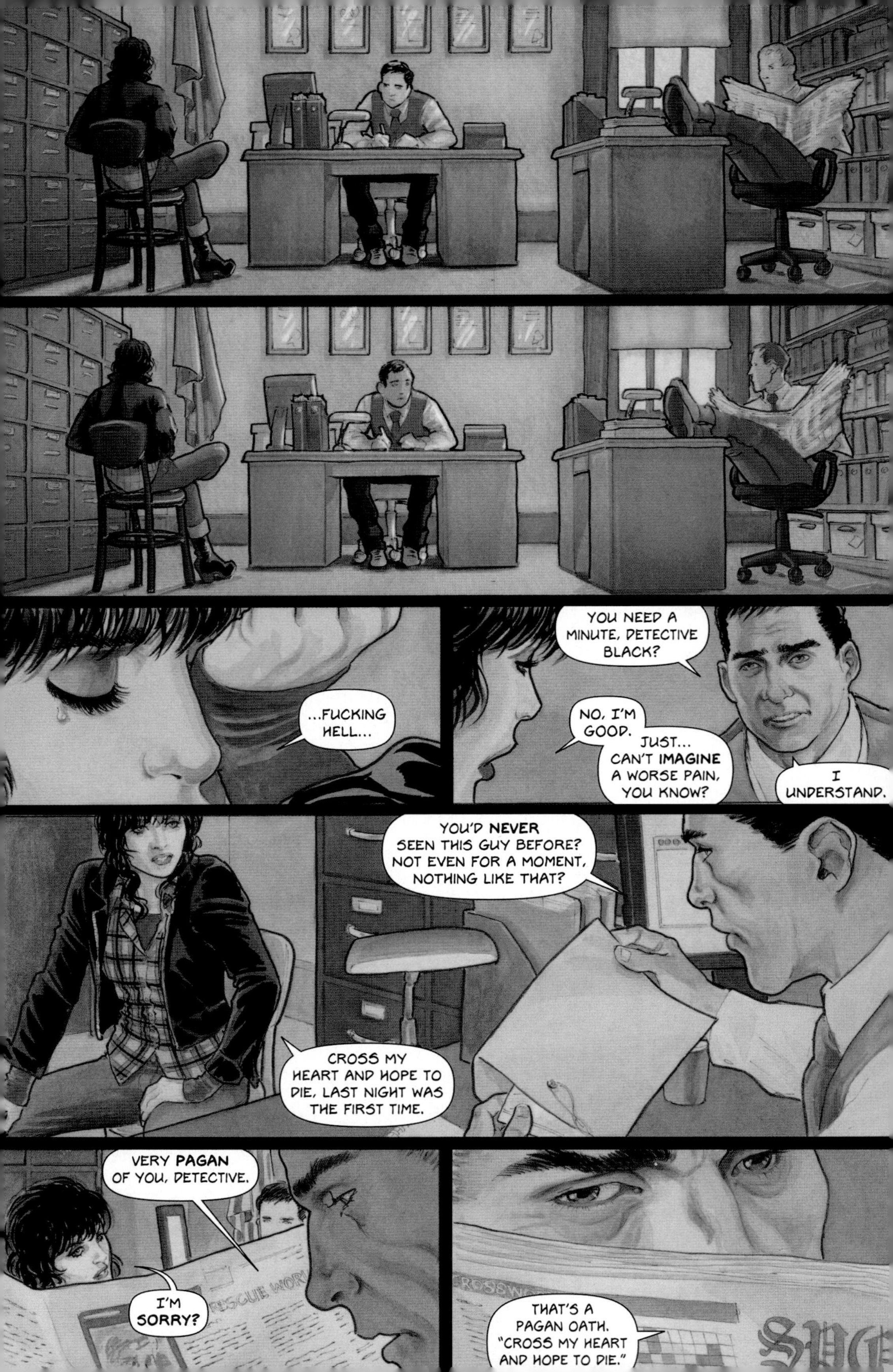
...FUCKING HELL...
YOU NEED A MINUTE, DETECTIVE BLACK?
NO, I'M GOOD.
JUST... CAN'T IMAGINE A WORSE PAIN, YOU KNOW?
I UNDERSTAND.
YOU'D NEVER SEEN THIS GUY BEFORE? NOT EVEN FOR A MOMENT, NOTHING LIKE THAT?
CROSS MY HEART AND HOPE TO DIE, LAST NIGHT WAS THE FIRST TIME.
VERY PAGAN OF YOU, DETECTIVE.
I'M SORRY?
THAT'S A PAGAN OATH. "CROSS MY HEART AND HOPE TO DIE."

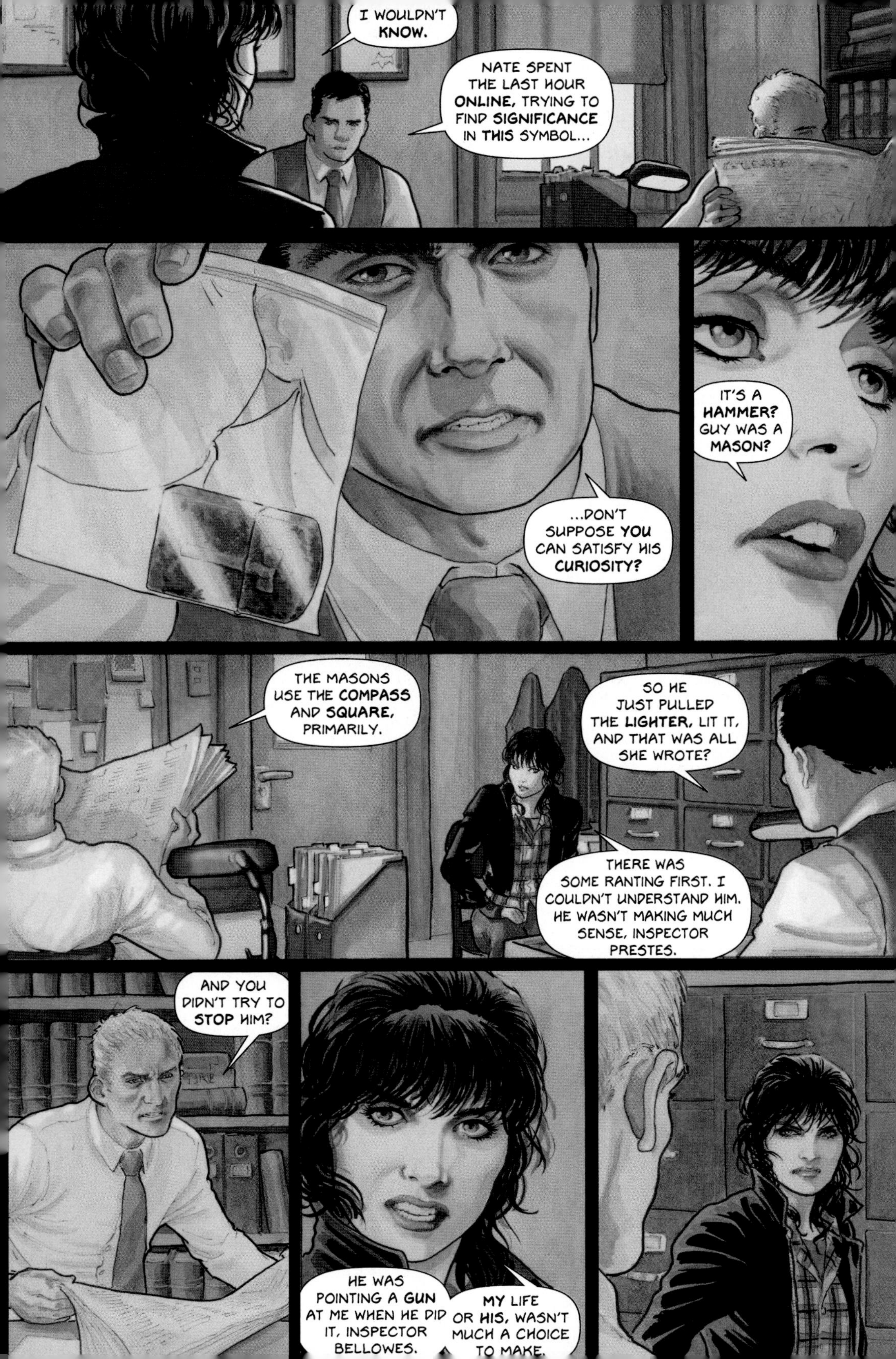
I WOULDN'T KNOW.
NATE SPENT THE LAST HOUR ONLINE, TRYING TO FIND SIGNIFICANCE IN THIS SYMBOL...
...DON'T SUPPOSE YOU CAN SATISFY HIS CURIOSITY?
IT'S A HAMMER? GUY WAS A MASON?
THE MASONS USE THE COMPASS AND SQUARE, PRIMARILY.
SO HE JUST PULLED THE LIGHTER, LIT IT, AND THAT WAS ALL SHE WROTE?
THERE WAS SOME RANTING FIRST. I COULDN'T UNDERSTAND HIM. HE WASN'T MAKING MUCH SENSE, INSPECTOR PRESTES.
AND YOU DIDN'T TRY TO STOP HIM?
HE WAS POINTING A GUN AT ME WHEN HE DID IT, INSPECTOR BELLOWES.
MY LIFE OR HIS, WASN'T MUCH A CHOICE TO MAKE.

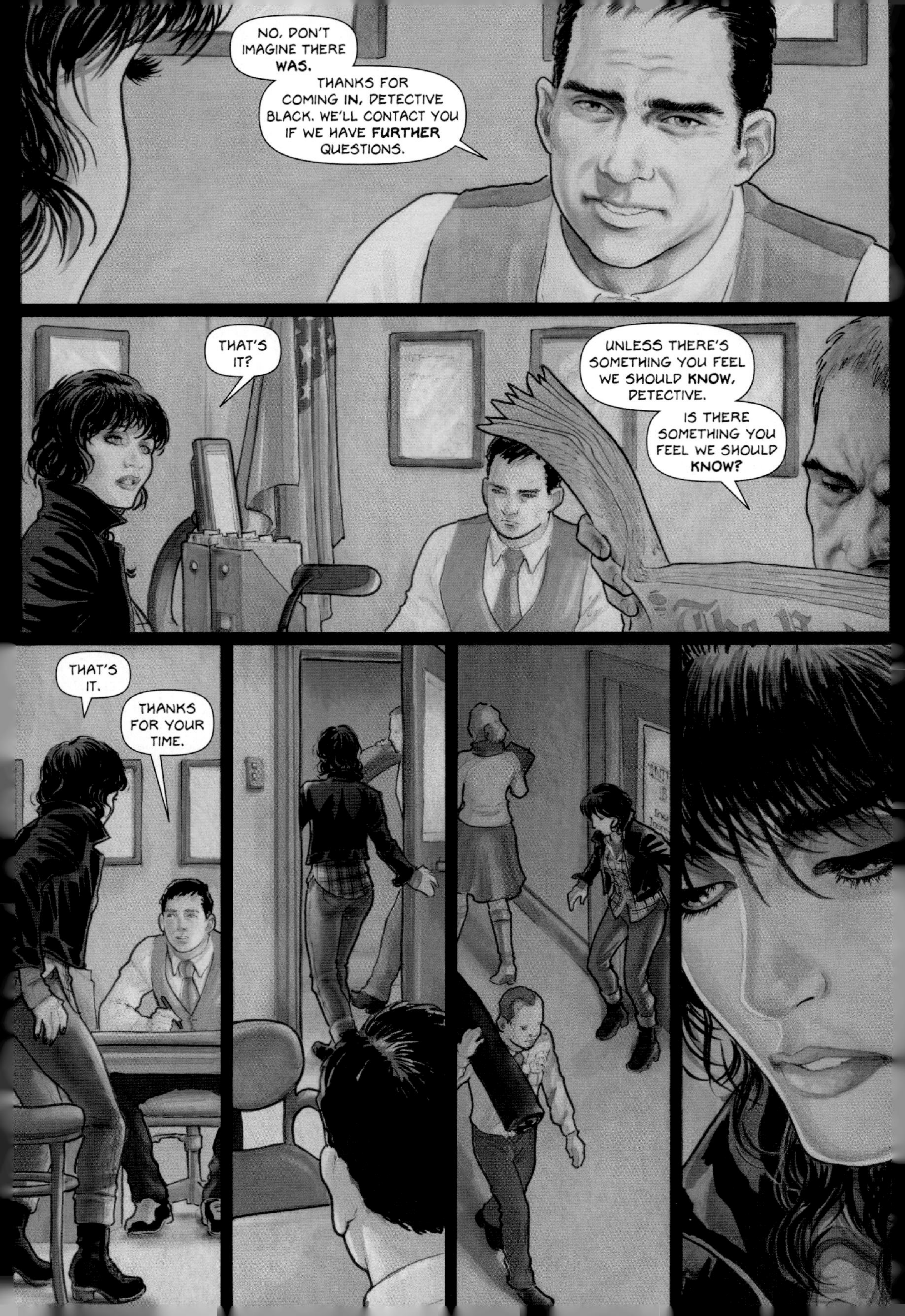
NO, DON'T IMAGINE THERE WAS.
THANKS FOR COMING IN, DETECTIVE BLACK. WE'LL CONTACT YOU IF WE HAVE FURTHER QUESTIONS.
THAT'S IT?
UNLESS THERE'S SOMETHING YOU FEEL WE SHOULD KNOW, DETECTIVE.
IS THERE SOMETHING YOU FEEL WE SHOULD KNOW?
THAT'S IT.
THANKS FOR YOUR TIME.

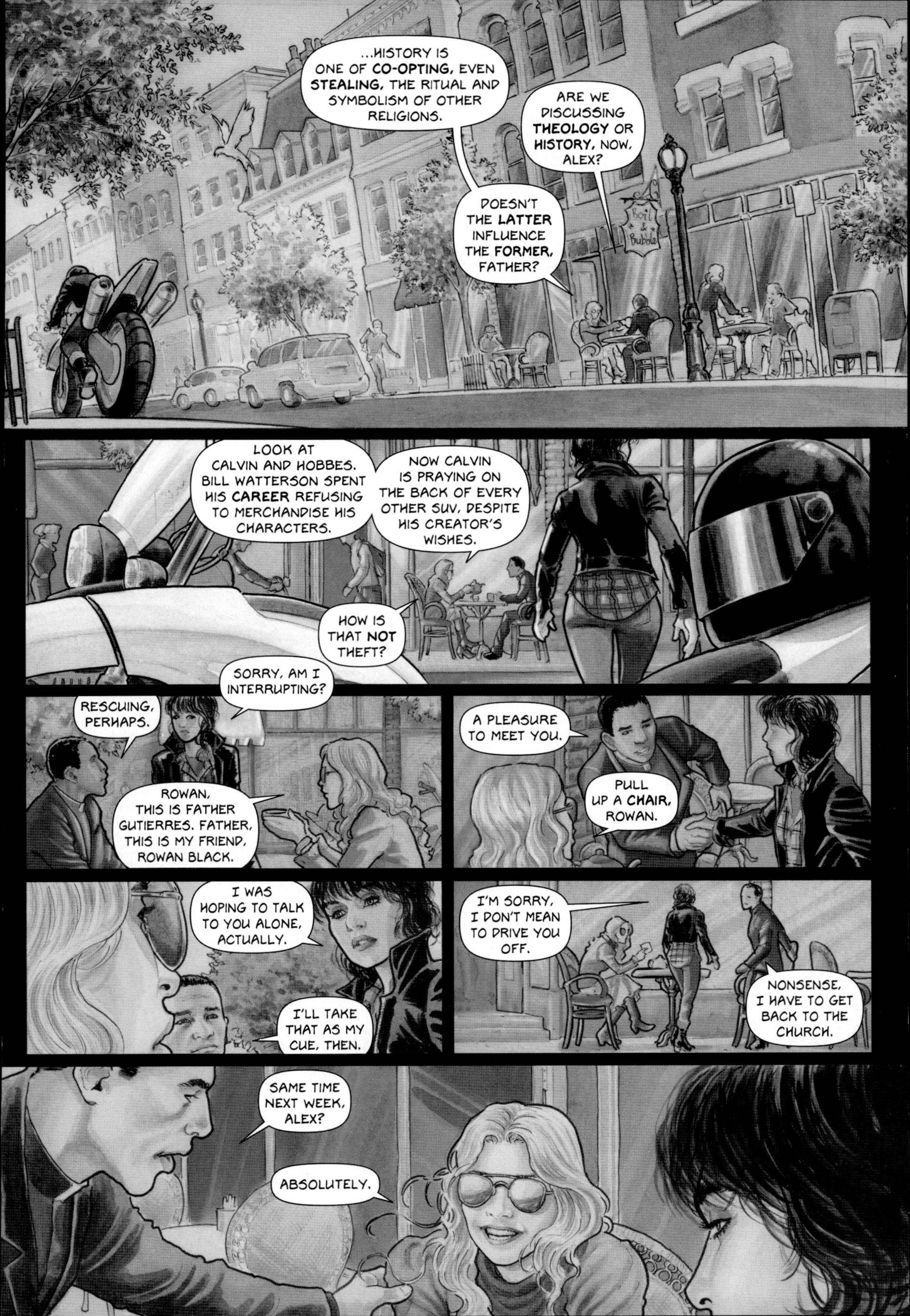
...HISTORY IS ONE OF CO-OPTING, EVEN STEALING, THE RITUAL AND SYMBOLISM OF OTHER RELIGIONS.
ARE WE DISCUSSING THEOLOGY OR HISTORY, NOW, ALEX?
DOESN'T THE LATTER INFLUENCE THE FORMER, FATHER?
Boil & Bubble
LOOK AT CALVIN AND HOBBES. BILL WATTERSON SPENT HIS CAREER REFUSING TO MERCHANDISE HIS CHARACTERS.
NOW CALVIN IS PRAYING ON THE BACK OF EVERY OTHER SUV, DESPITE HIS CREATOR'S WISHES.
HOW IS THAT NOT THEFT?
SORRY, AM I INTERRUPTING?
RESCUING, PERHAPS.
ROWAN, THIS IS FATHER GUTIERRES. FATHER, THIS IS MY FRIEND, ROWAN BLACK.
A PLEASURE TO MEET YOU.
PULL UP A CHAIR, ROWAN.
I WAS HOPING TO TALK TO YOU ALONE, ACTUALLY.
I'LL TAKE THAT AS MY CUE, THEN.
I'M SORRY, I DON'T MEAN TO DRIVE YOU OFF.
NONSENSE, I HAVE TO GET BACK TO THE CHURCH.
SAME TIME NEXT WEEK, ALEX?
ABSOLUTELY.

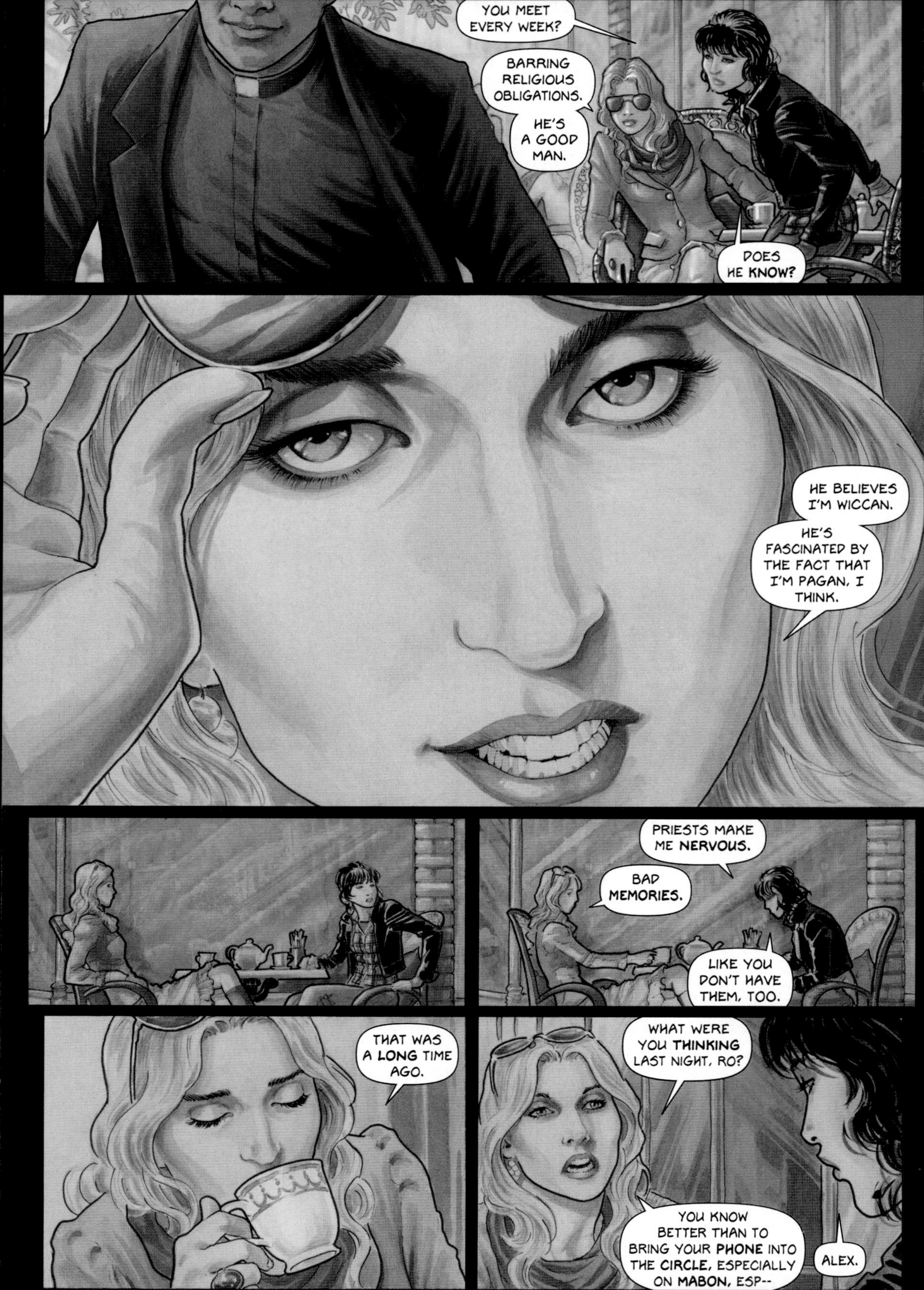
YOU MEET EVERY WEEK?
BARRING RELIGIOUS OBLIGATIONS.
HE'S A GOOD MAN.
DOES HE KNOW?
HE BELIEVES I'M WICCAN.
HE'S FASCINATED BY THE FACT THAT I'M PAGAN, I THINK.
PRIESTS MAKE ME NERVOUS.
BAD MEMORIES.
LIKE YOU DON'T HAVE THEM, TOO.
THAT WAS A LONG TIME AGO.
WHAT WERE YOU THINKING LAST NIGHT, RO?
YOU KNOW BETTER THAN TO BRING YOUR PHONE INTO THE CIRCLE, ESPECIALLY ON MABON, ESP--
ALEX.

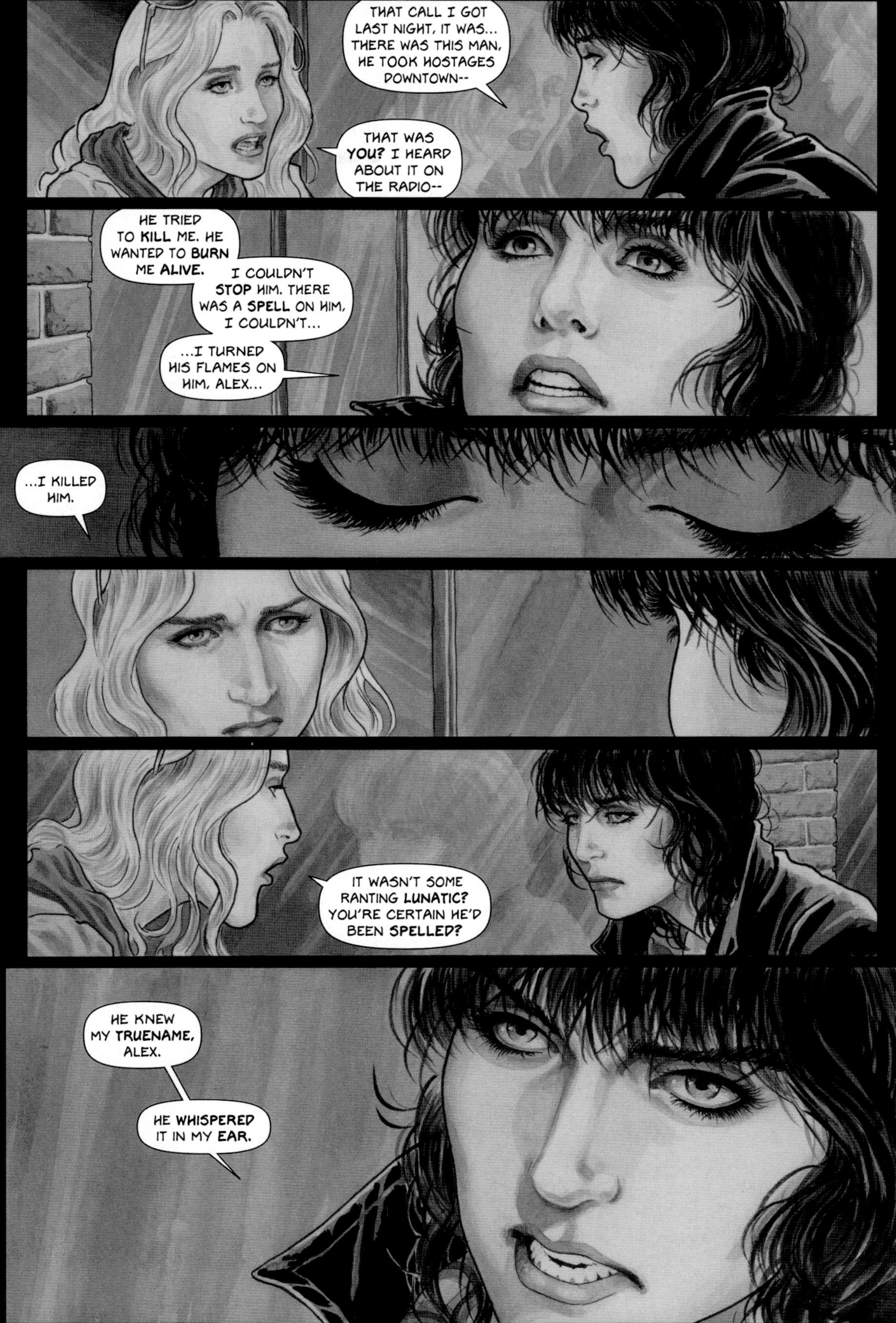
THAT CALL I GOT LAST NIGHT, IT WAS... THERE WAS THIS MAN, HE TOOK HOSTAGES DOWNTOWN--
THAT WAS YOU? I HEARD ABOUT IT ON THE RADIO--
HE TRIED TO KILL ME. HE WANTED TO BURN ME ALIVE.
I COULDN'T STOP HIM. THERE WAS A SPELL ON HIM, I COULDN'T...
...I TURNED HIS FLAMES ON HIM, ALEX...
...I KILLED HIM.
IT WASN'T SOME RANTING LUNATIC? YOU'RE CERTAIN HE'D BEEN SPELLED?
HE KNEW MY TRUENAME, ALEX.
HE WHISPERED IT IN MY EAR.

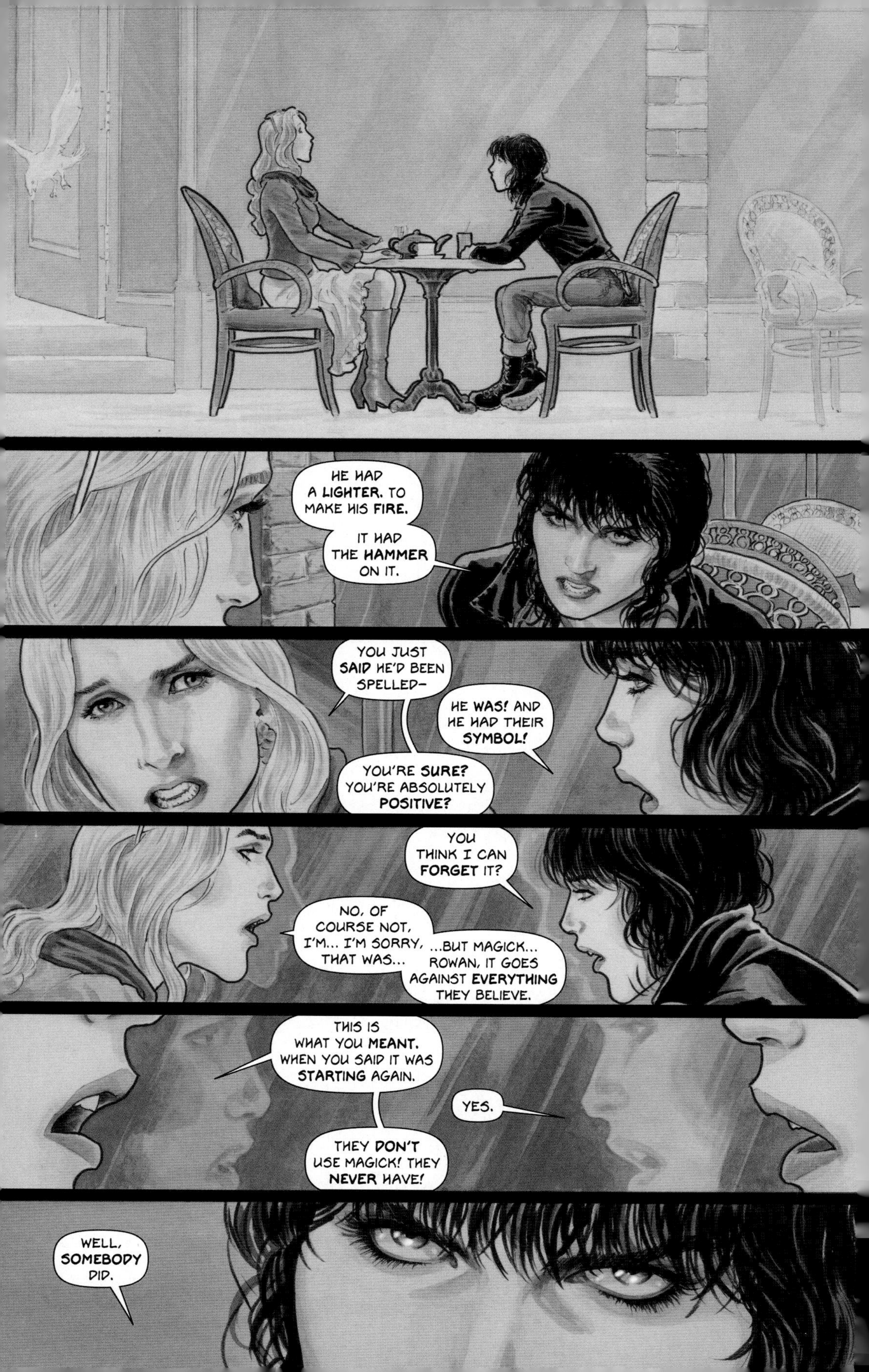
HE HAD A LIGHTER. TO MAKE HIS FIRE.
IT HAD THE HAMMER ON IT.
YOU JUST SAID HE'D BEEN SPELLED–
HE WAS! AND HE HAD THEIR SYMBOL!
YOU'RE SURE? YOU'RE ABSOLUTELY POSITIVE?
YOU THINK I CAN FORGET IT?
NO, OF COURSE NOT, I'M... I'M SORRY, THAT WAS...
...BUT MAGICK... ROWAN, IT GOES AGAINST EVERYTHING THEY BELIEVE.
THIS IS WHAT YOU MEANT. WHEN YOU SAID IT WAS STARTING AGAIN.
YES.
THEY DON'T USE MAGICK! THEY NEVER HAVE!
WELL, SOMEBODY DID.

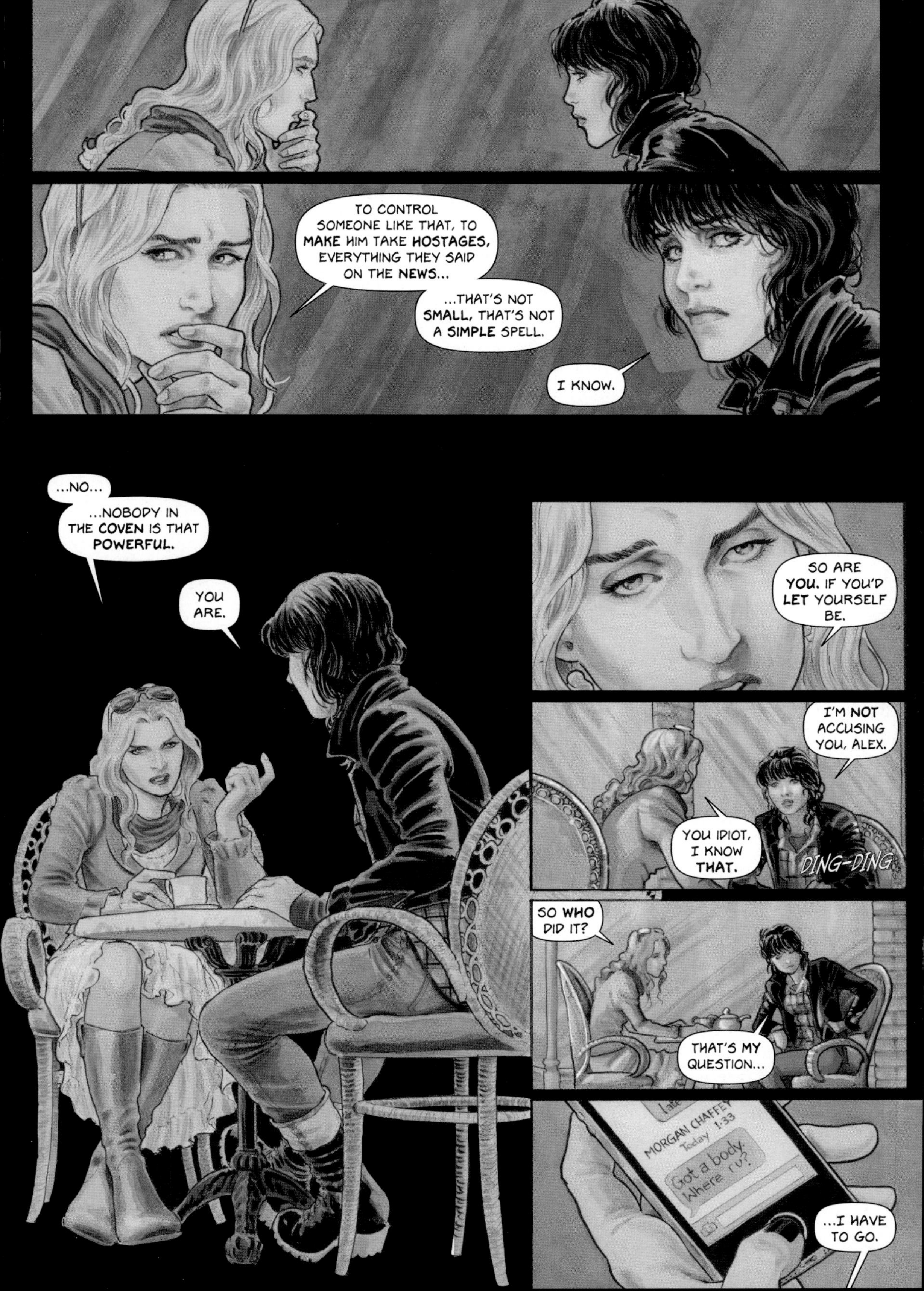
TO CONTROL SOMEONE LIKE THAT, TO MAKE HIM TAKE HOSTAGES, EVERYTHING THEY SAID ON THE NEWS...
...THAT'S NOT SMALL, THAT'S NOT A SIMPLE SPELL.
I KNOW.
...NO...
...NOBODY IN THE COVEN IS THAT POWERFUL.
YOU ARE.
SO ARE YOU. IF YOU'D LET YOURSELF BE.
I'M NOT ACCUSING YOU, ALEX.
YOU IDIOT, I KNOW THAT.
DING-DING
SO WHO DID IT?
THAT'S MY QUESTION...
MORGAN CHAFFEY
Today 1:33
Got a body. Where r u?
...I HAVE TO GO.

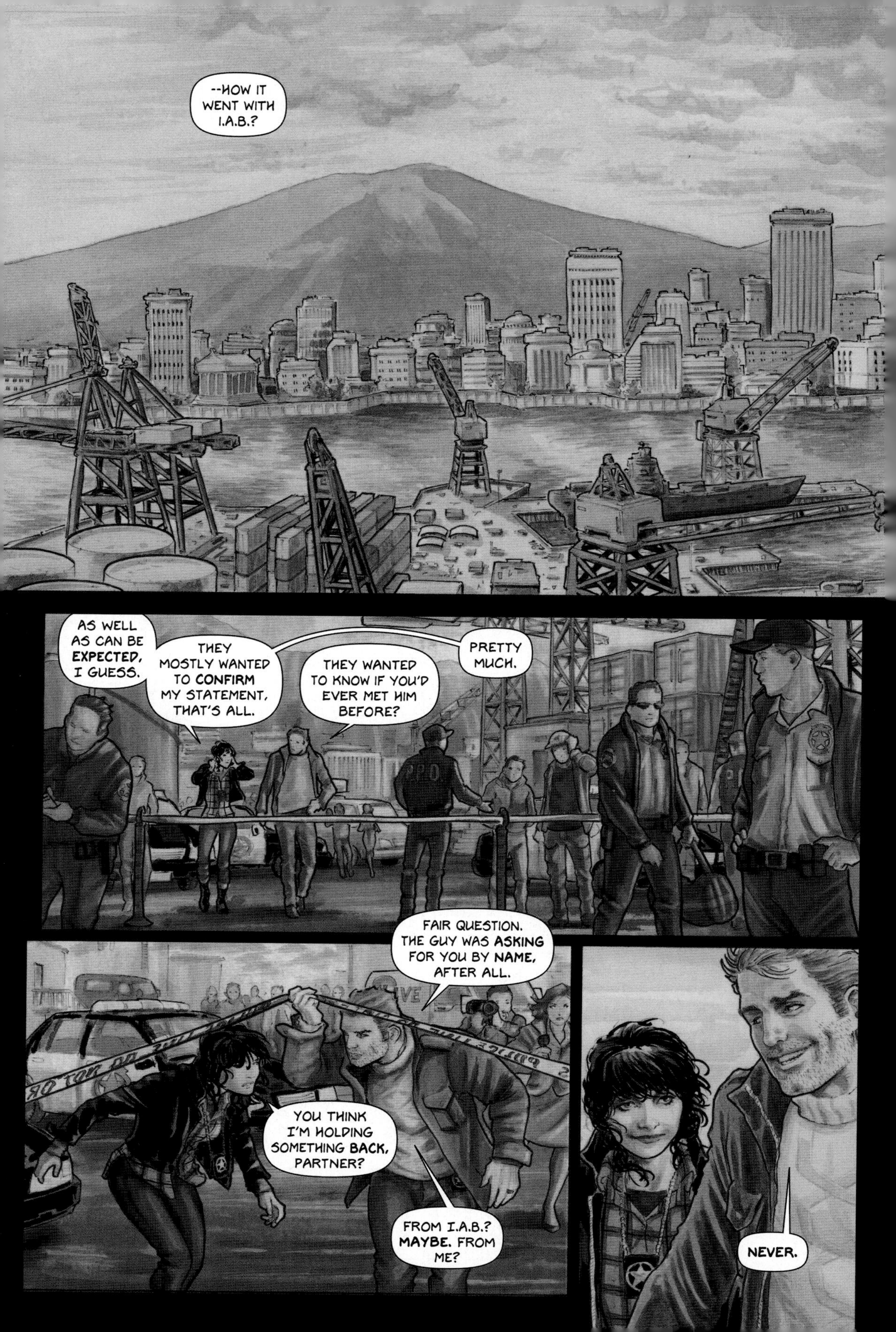
--HOW IT WENT WITH I.A.B.?
AS WELL AS CAN BE **EXPECTED**, I GUESS.
THEY MOSTLY WANTED TO **CONFIRM** MY STATEMENT, THAT'S ALL.
THEY WANTED TO KNOW IF YOU'D EVER MET HIM BEFORE?
PRETTY MUCH.
FAIR QUESTION. THE GUY WAS **ASKING** FOR YOU BY **NAME**, AFTER ALL.
YOU THINK I'M HOLDING SOMETHING **BACK**, PARTNER?
FROM I.A.B.? **MAYBE**. FROM ME?
NEVER.

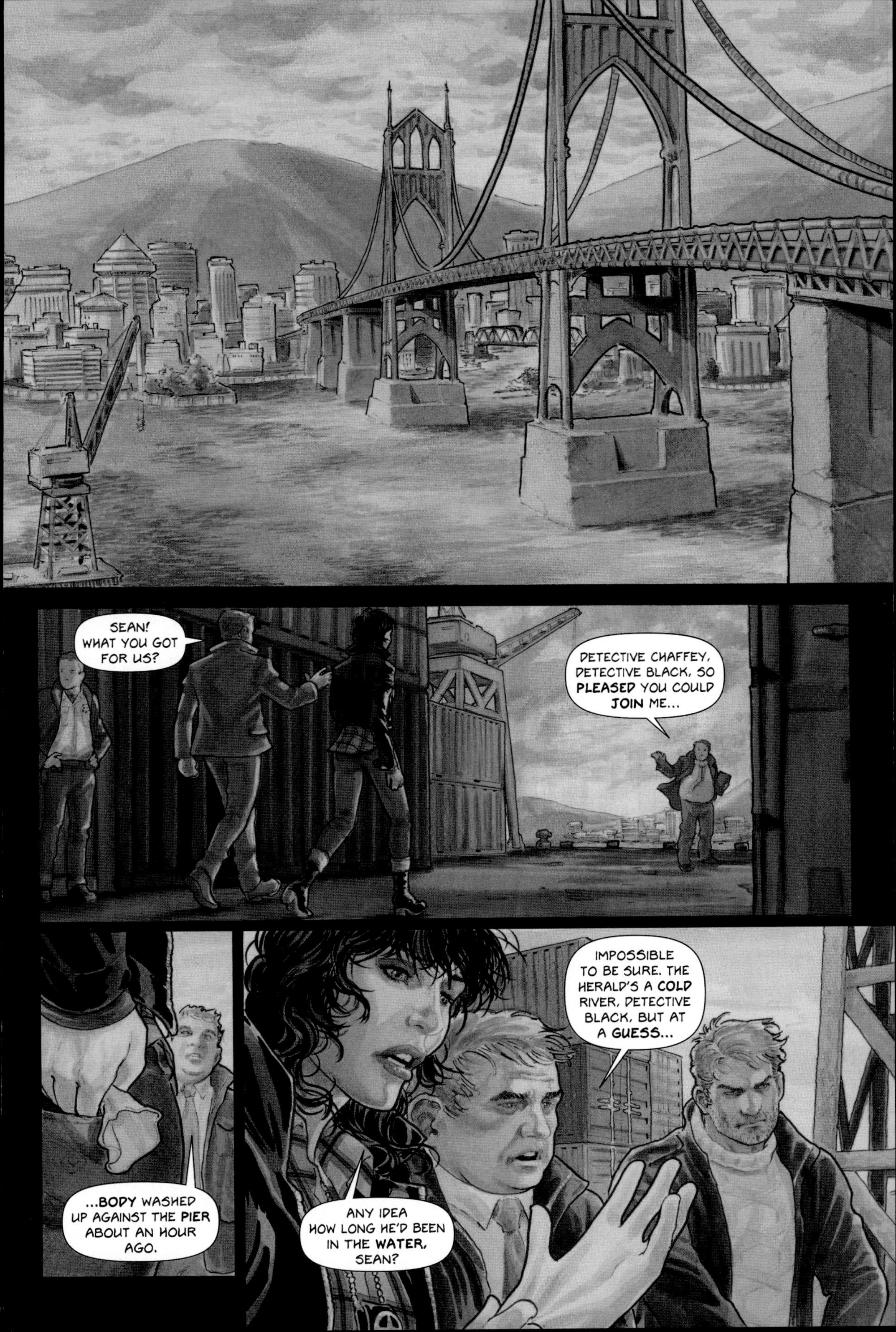
SEAN! WHAT YOU GOT FOR US?
DETECTIVE CHAFFEY, DETECTIVE BLACK, SO PLEASED YOU COULD JOIN ME...
...BODY WASHED UP AGAINST THE PIER ABOUT AN HOUR AGO.
ANY IDEA HOW LONG HE'D BEEN IN THE WATER, SEAN?
IMPOSSIBLE TO BE SURE. THE HERALD'S A COLD RIVER, DETECTIVE BLACK, BUT AT A GUESS...

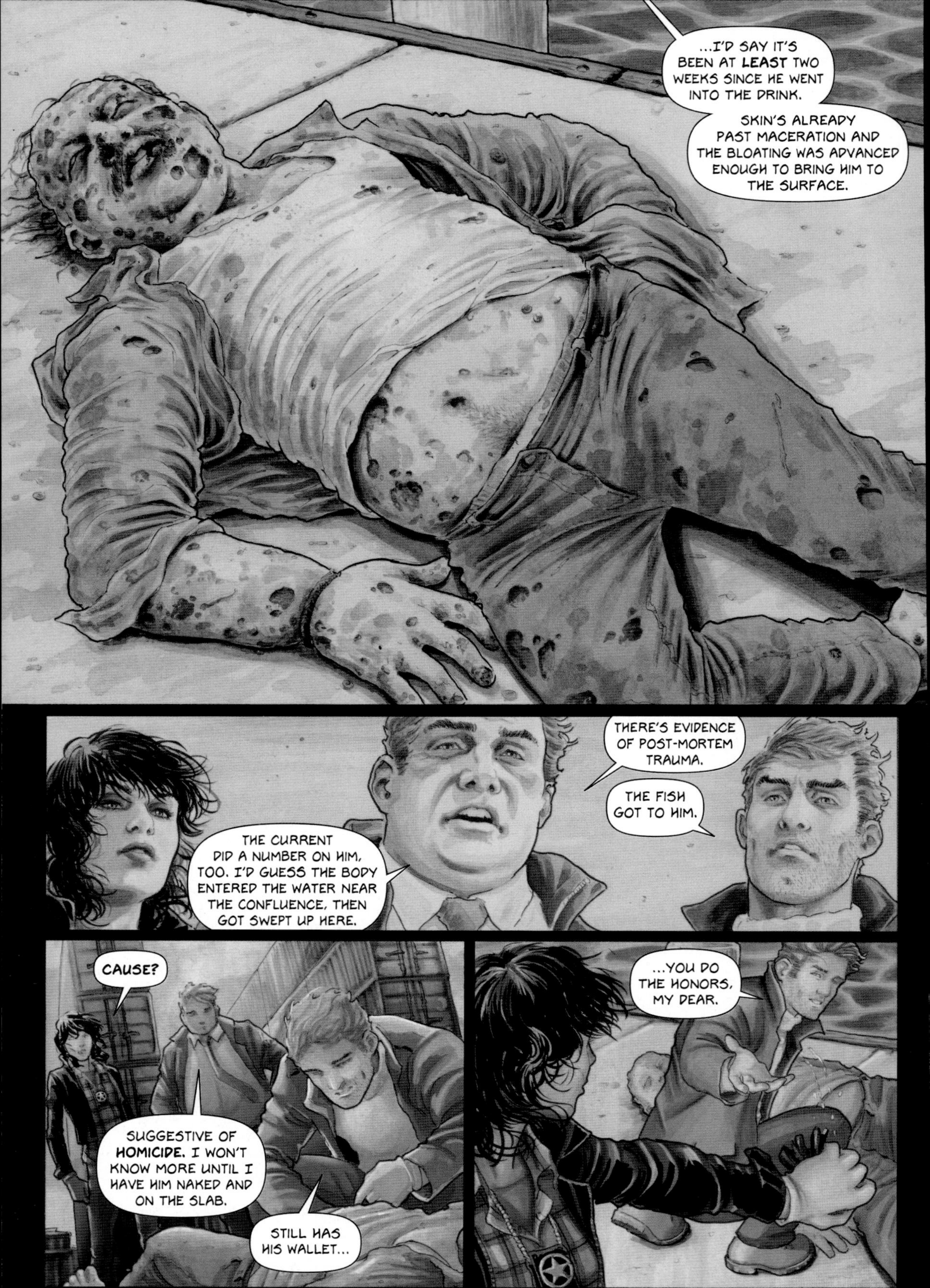
...I'D SAY IT'S BEEN AT **LEAST** TWO WEEKS SINCE HE WENT INTO THE DRINK.
SKIN'S ALREADY PAST MACERATION AND THE BLOATING WAS ADVANCED ENOUGH TO BRING HIM TO THE SURFACE.
THERE'S EVIDENCE OF POST-MORTEM TRAUMA.
THE FISH GOT TO HIM.
THE CURRENT DID A NUMBER ON HIM, TOO. I'D GUESS THE BODY ENTERED THE WATER NEAR THE CONFLUENCE, THEN GOT SWEPT UP HERE.
CAUSE?
SUGGESTIVE OF **HOMICIDE.** I WON'T KNOW MORE UNTIL I HAVE HIM NAKED AND ON THE SLAB.
STILL HAS HIS WALLET...
...YOU DO THE HONORS, MY DEAR.

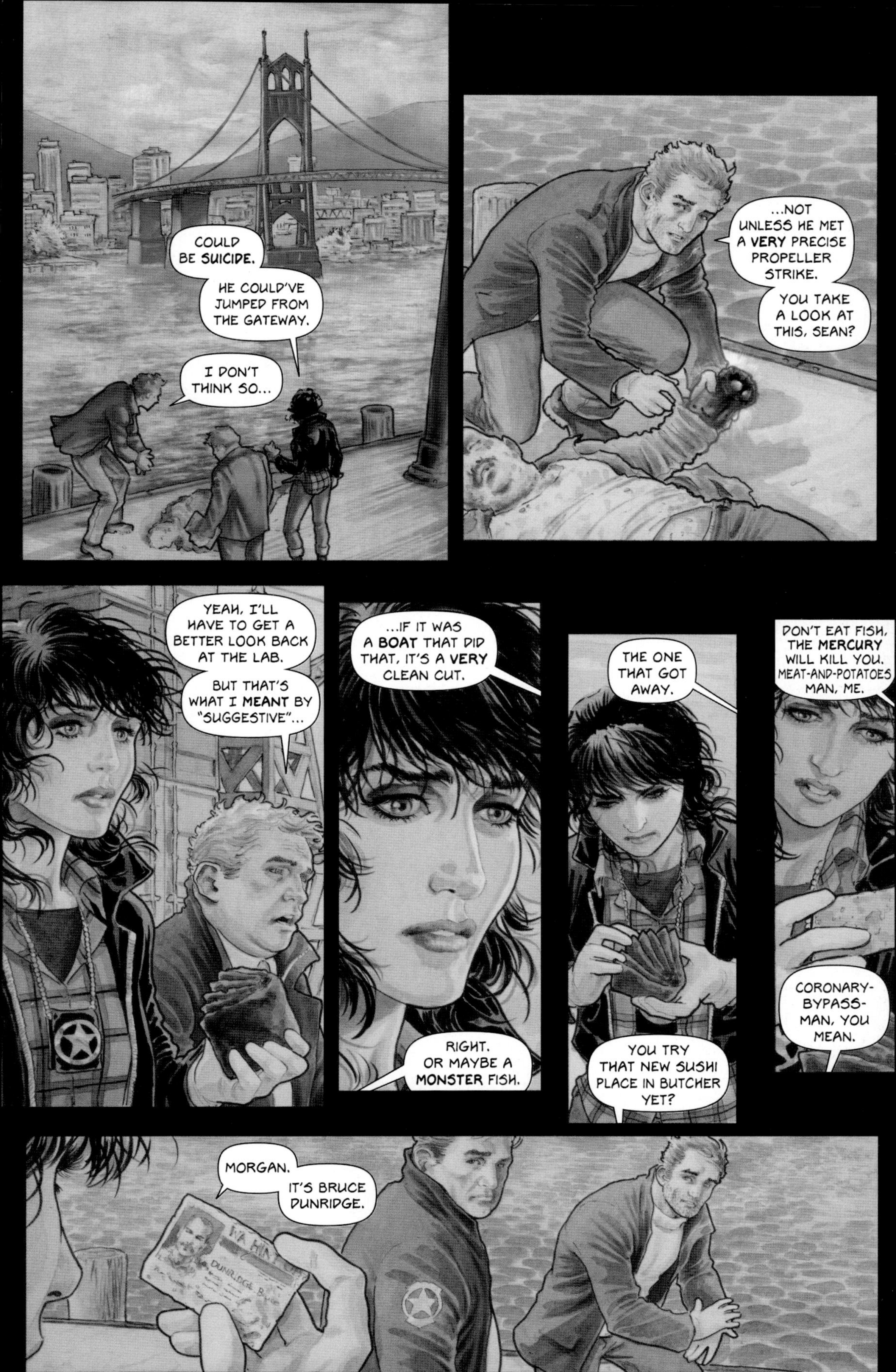
COULD BE SUICIDE.
HE COULD'VE JUMPED FROM THE GATEWAY.
I DON'T THINK SO...
...NOT UNLESS HE MET A VERY PRECISE PROPELLER STRIKE.
YOU TAKE A LOOK AT THIS, SEAN?
YEAH, I'LL HAVE TO GET A BETTER LOOK BACK AT THE LAB.
BUT THAT'S WHAT I MEANT BY "SUGGESTIVE"...
...IF IT WAS A BOAT THAT DID THAT, IT'S A VERY CLEAN CUT.
RIGHT. OR MAYBE A MONSTER FISH.
THE ONE THAT GOT AWAY.
YOU TRY THAT NEW SUSHI PLACE IN BUTCHER YET?
DON'T EAT FISH, THE MERCURY WILL KILL YOU. MEAT-AND-POTATOES MAN, ME.
CORONARY-BYPASS-MAN, YOU MEAN.
MORGAN.
IT'S BRUCE DUNRIDGE.

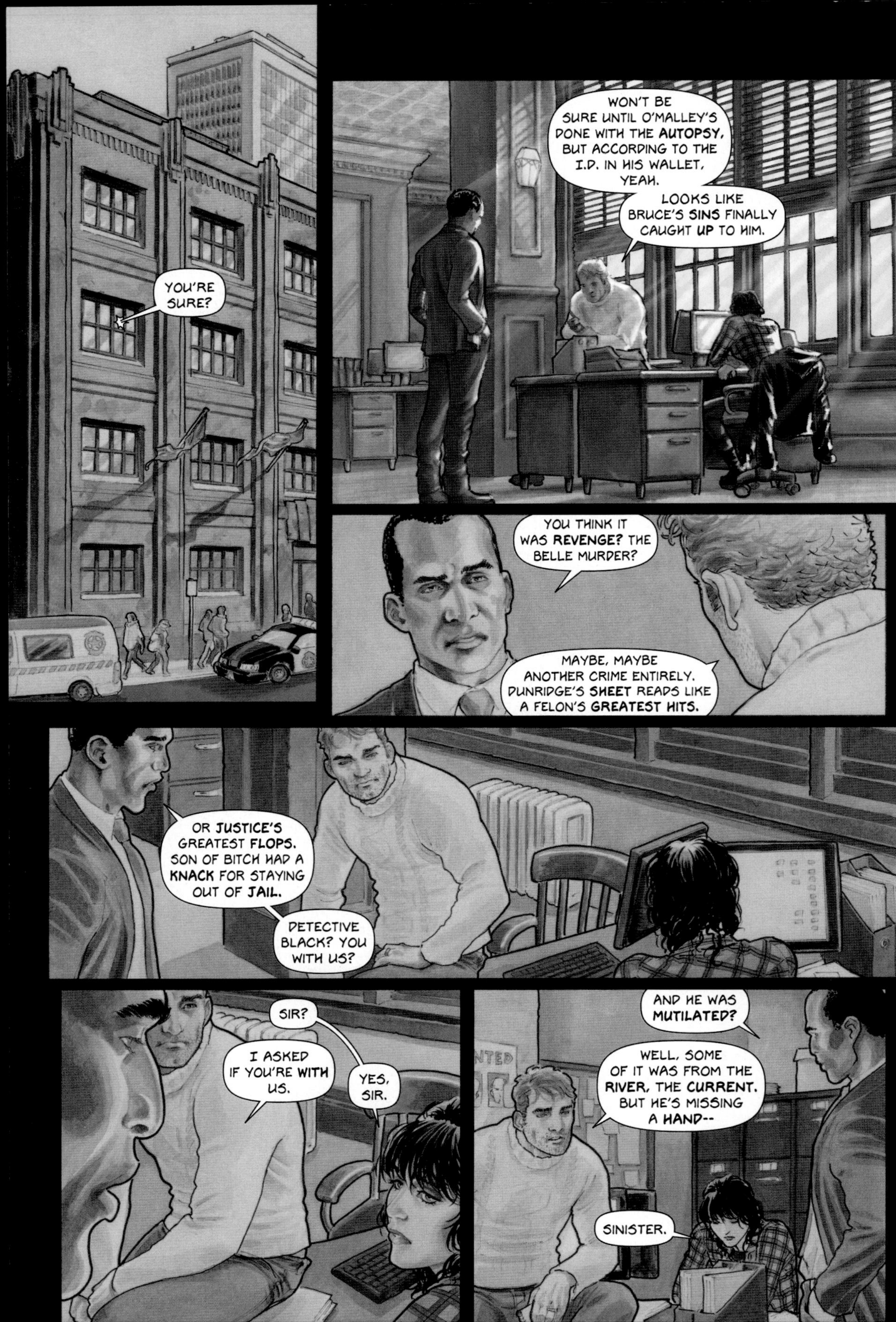
YOU'RE SURE?
WON'T BE SURE UNTIL O'MALLEY'S DONE WITH THE AUTOPSY, BUT ACCORDING TO THE I.D. IN HIS WALLET, YEAH.
LOOKS LIKE BRUCE'S SINS FINALLY CAUGHT UP TO HIM.
YOU THINK IT WAS REVENGE? THE BELLE MURDER?
MAYBE, MAYBE ANOTHER CRIME ENTIRELY. DUNRIDGE'S SHEET READS LIKE A FELON'S GREATEST HITS.
OR JUSTICE'S GREATEST FLOPS. SON OF BITCH HAD A KNACK FOR STAYING OUT OF JAIL.
DETECTIVE BLACK? YOU WITH US?
SIR?
I ASKED IF YOU'RE WITH US.
YES, SIR.
AND HE WAS MUTILATED?
WELL, SOME OF IT WAS FROM THE RIVER, THE CURRENT. BUT HE'S MISSING A HAND--
SINISTER.

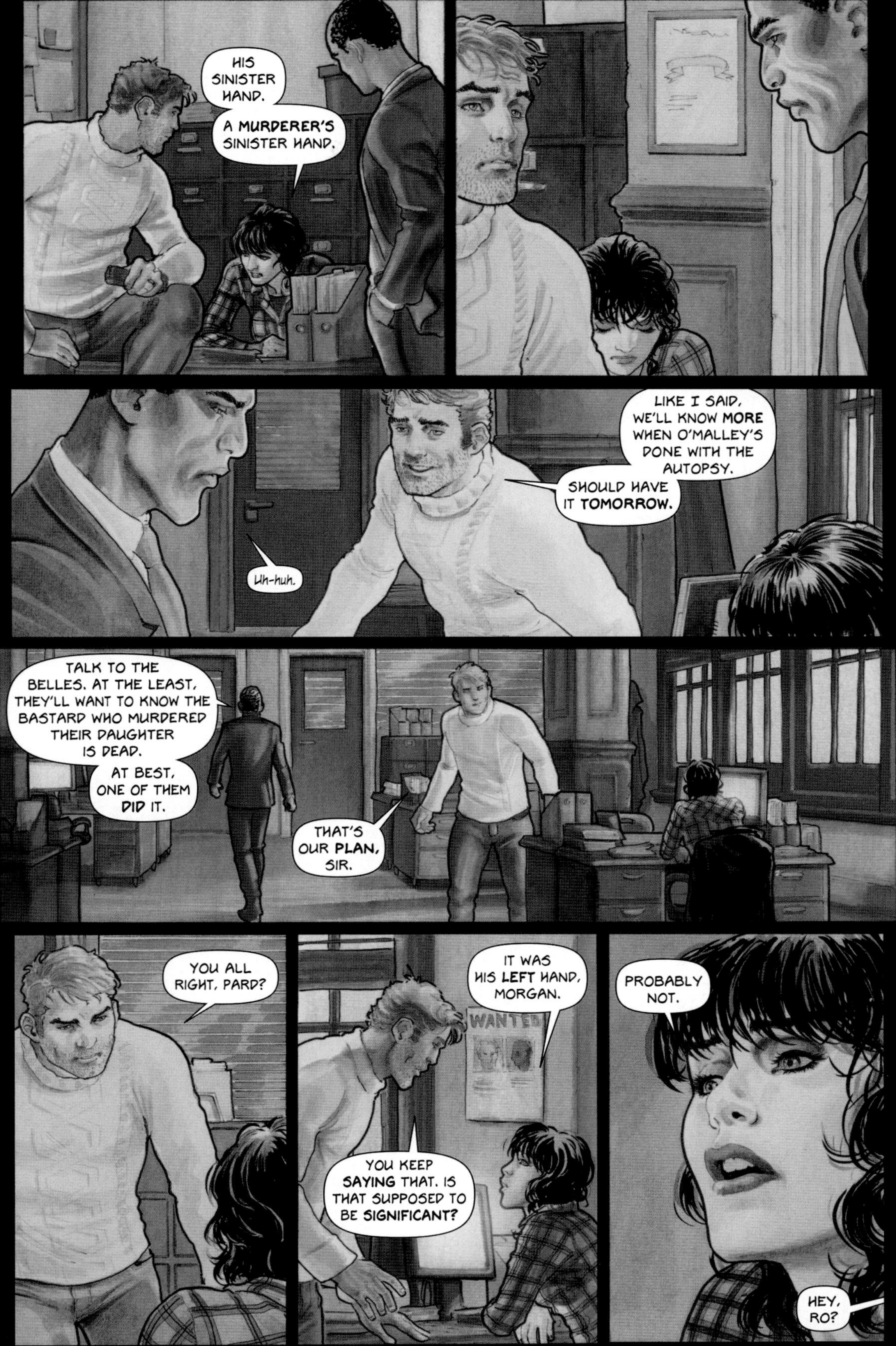
HIS SINISTER HAND.
A MURDERER'S SINISTER HAND.
LIKE I SAID, WE'LL KNOW MORE WHEN O'MALLEY'S DONE WITH THE AUTOPSY.
SHOULD HAVE IT TOMORROW.
Uh-huh.
TALK TO THE BELLES. AT THE LEAST, THEY'LL WANT TO KNOW THE BASTARD WHO MURDERED THEIR DAUGHTER IS DEAD.
AT BEST, ONE OF THEM DID IT.
THAT'S OUR PLAN, SIR.
YOU ALL RIGHT, PARD?
IT WAS HIS LEFT HAND, MORGAN.
WANTED
YOU KEEP SAYING THAT. IS THAT SUPPOSED TO BE SIGNIFICANT?
PROBABLY NOT.
HEY, RO?

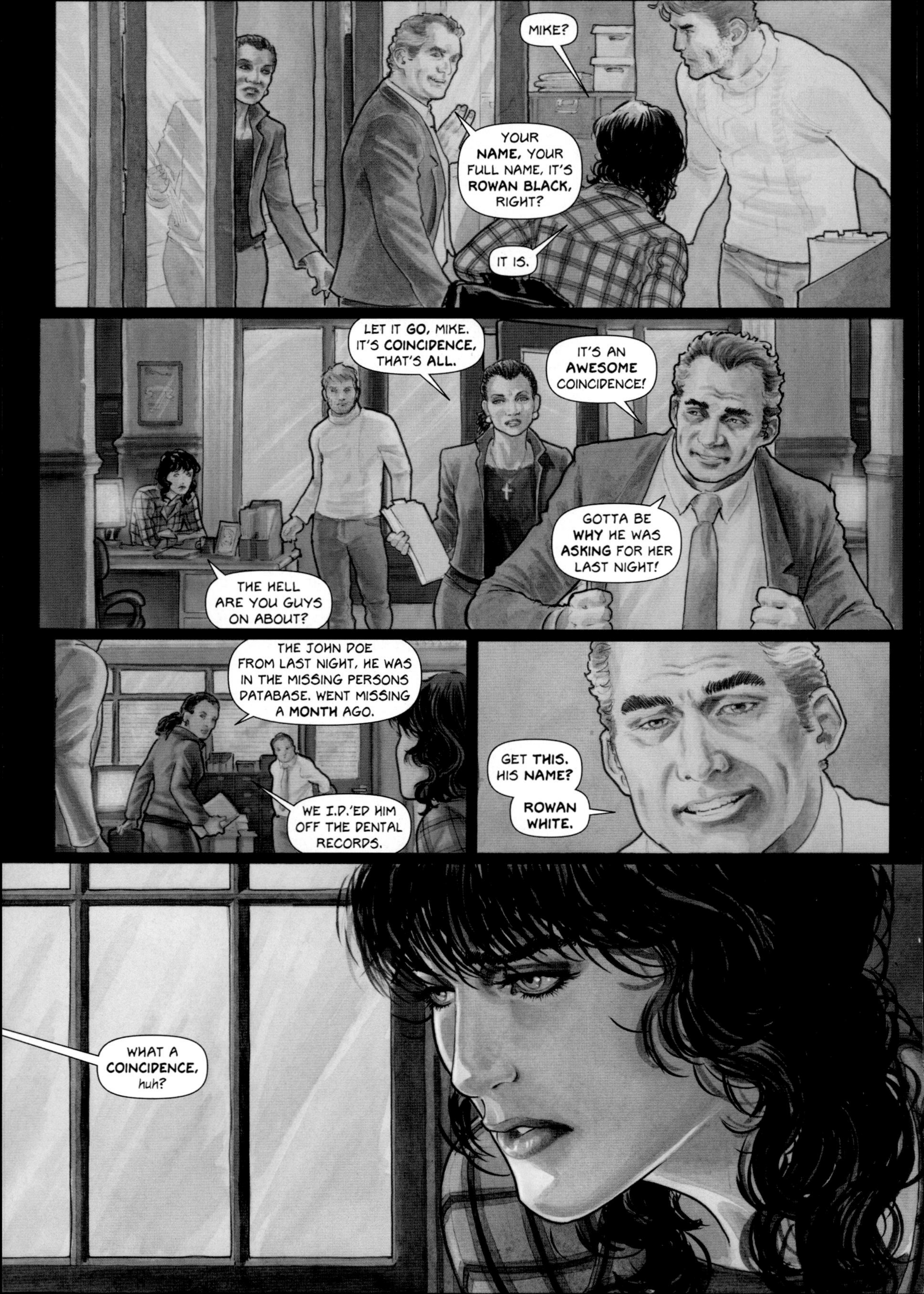
MIKE?
YOUR NAME, YOUR FULL NAME, IT'S ROWAN BLACK, RIGHT?
IT IS.
LET IT GO, MIKE. IT'S COINCIDENCE, THAT'S ALL.
IT'S AN AWESOME COINCIDENCE!
GOTTA BE WHY HE WAS ASKING FOR HER LAST NIGHT!
THE HELL ARE YOU GUYS ON ABOUT?
THE JOHN DOE FROM LAST NIGHT. HE WAS IN THE MISSING PERSONS DATABASE. WENT MISSING A MONTH AGO.
WE I.D.'ED HIM OFF THE DENTAL RECORDS.
GET THIS. HIS NAME?
ROWAN WHITE.
WHAT A COINCIDENCE, huh?

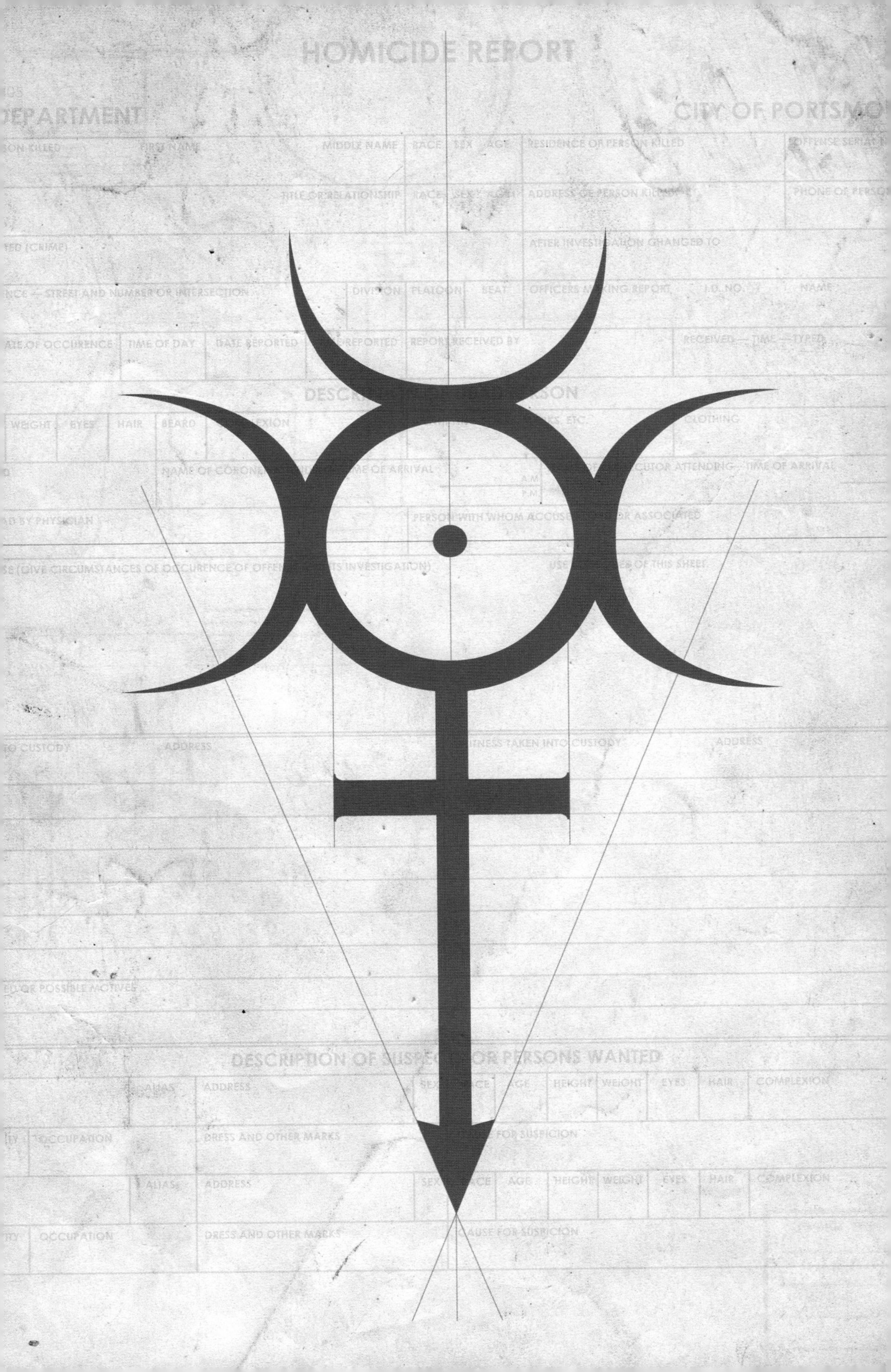
HOMICIDE REPORT
DEPARTMENT
MIDDLE NAME
RACE
SEX
AGE
TITLE OR RELATIONSHIP
AFTER INVESTIGATION CHANGED TO
DIVISION
PLATOON
BEAT
TIME OF DAY
DATE REPORTED
CLOTHING
ADDRESS
COMPLEXION
HEIGHT
WEIGHT
EYES
HAIR
OCCUPATION
DRESS AND OTHER MARKS

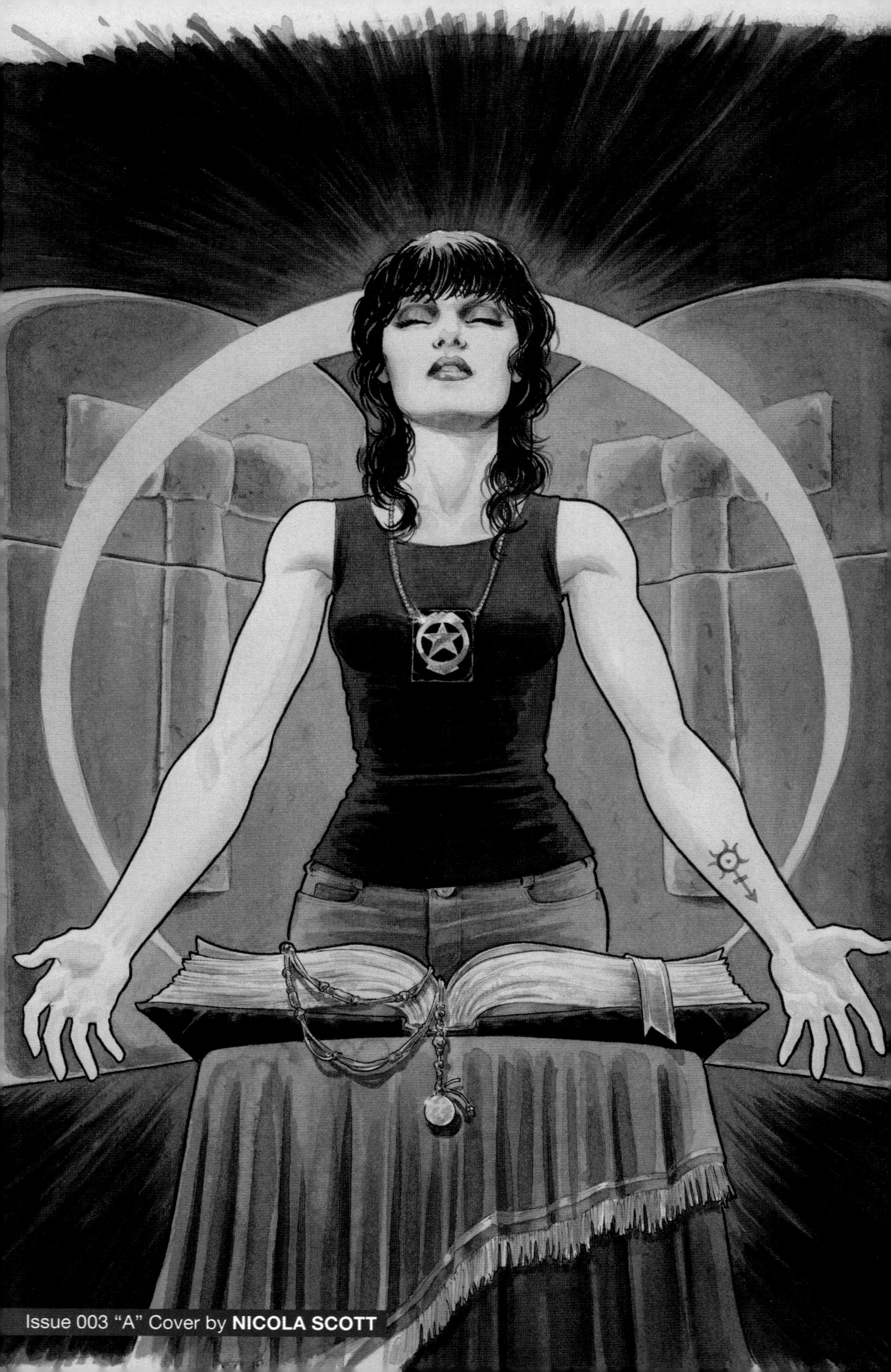
Issue 003 "A" Cover by **NICOLA SCOTT**

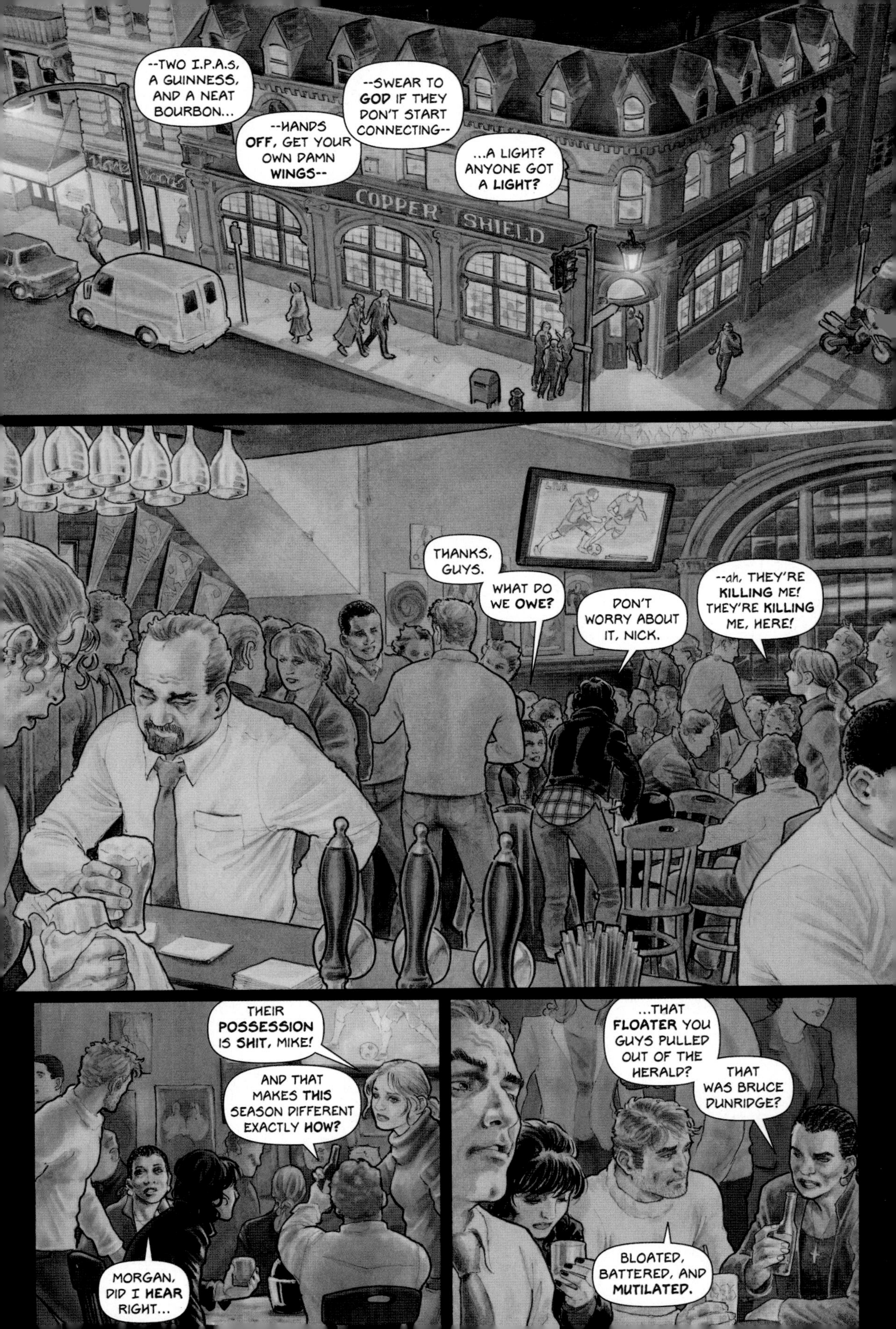
--TWO I.P.A.s, A GUINNESS, AND A NEAT BOURBON...
--HANDS **OFF**, GET YOUR OWN DAMN **WINGS**--
--SWEAR TO **GOD** IF THEY DON'T START CONNECTING--
...A LIGHT? ANYONE GOT A **LIGHT?**
COPPER SHIELD
THANKS, GUYS.
WHAT DO WE **OWE?**
DON'T WORRY ABOUT IT, NICK.
--*ah*, THEY'RE **KILLING** ME! THEY'RE **KILLING** ME, HERE!
THEIR **POSSESSION** IS **SHIT**, MIKE!
AND THAT MAKES **THIS** SEASON DIFFERENT EXACTLY **HOW?**
MORGAN, DID I **HEAR** RIGHT...
...THAT **FLOATER** YOU GUYS PULLED OUT OF THE HERALD?
THAT WAS BRUCE DUNRIDGE?
BLOATED, BATTERED, AND **MUTILATED.**

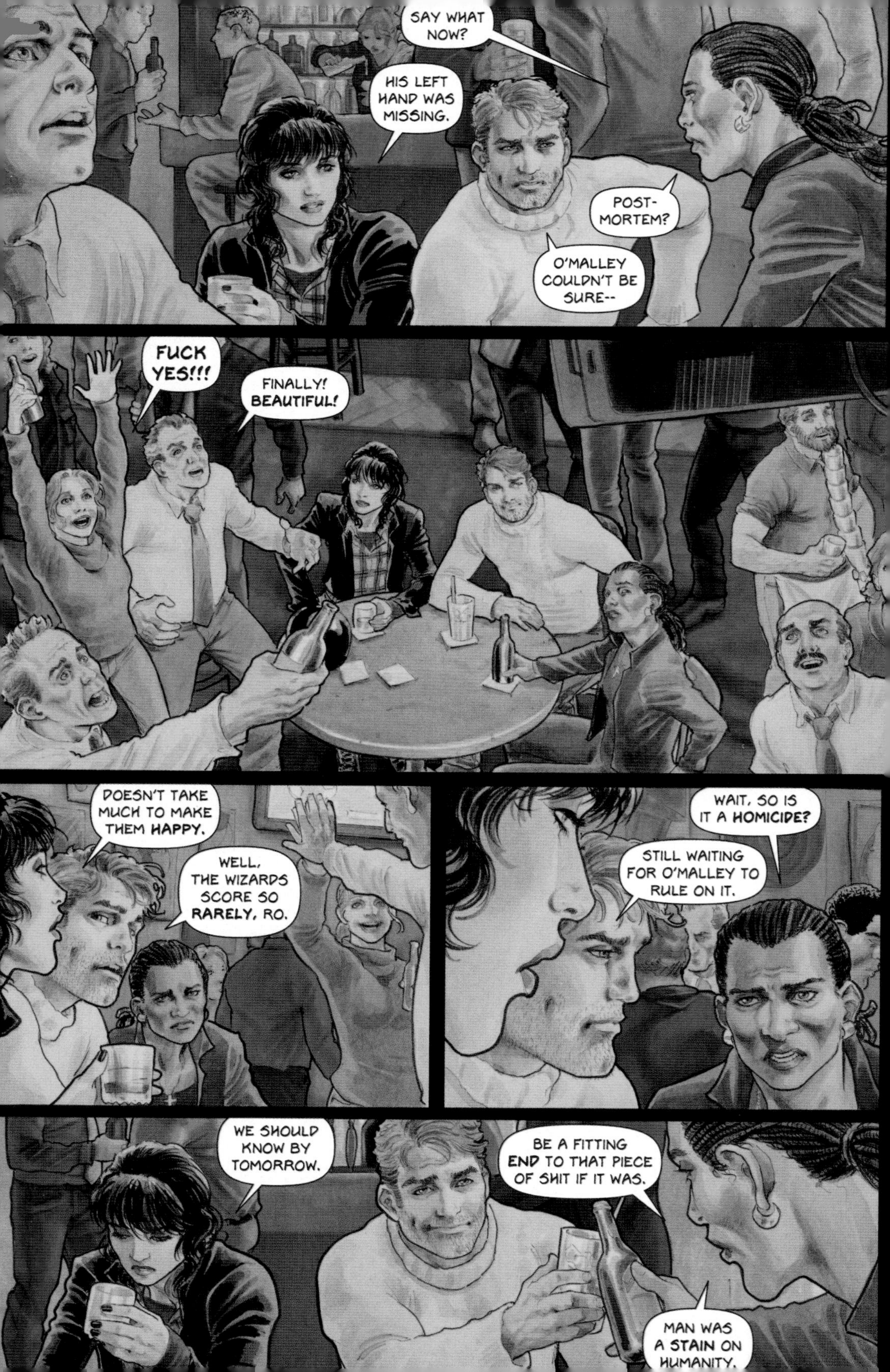
SAY WHAT NOW?
HIS LEFT HAND WAS MISSING.
POST-MORTEM?
O'MALLEY COULDN'T BE SURE--
FUCK YES!!!
FINALLY! BEAUTIFUL!
DOESN'T TAKE MUCH TO MAKE THEM HAPPY.
WELL, THE WIZARDS SCORE SO RARELY, RO.
WAIT, SO IS IT A HOMICIDE?
STILL WAITING FOR O'MALLEY TO RULE ON IT.
WE SHOULD KNOW BY TOMORROW.
BE A FITTING END TO THAT PIECE OF SHIT IF IT WAS.
MAN WAS A STAIN ON HUMANITY.

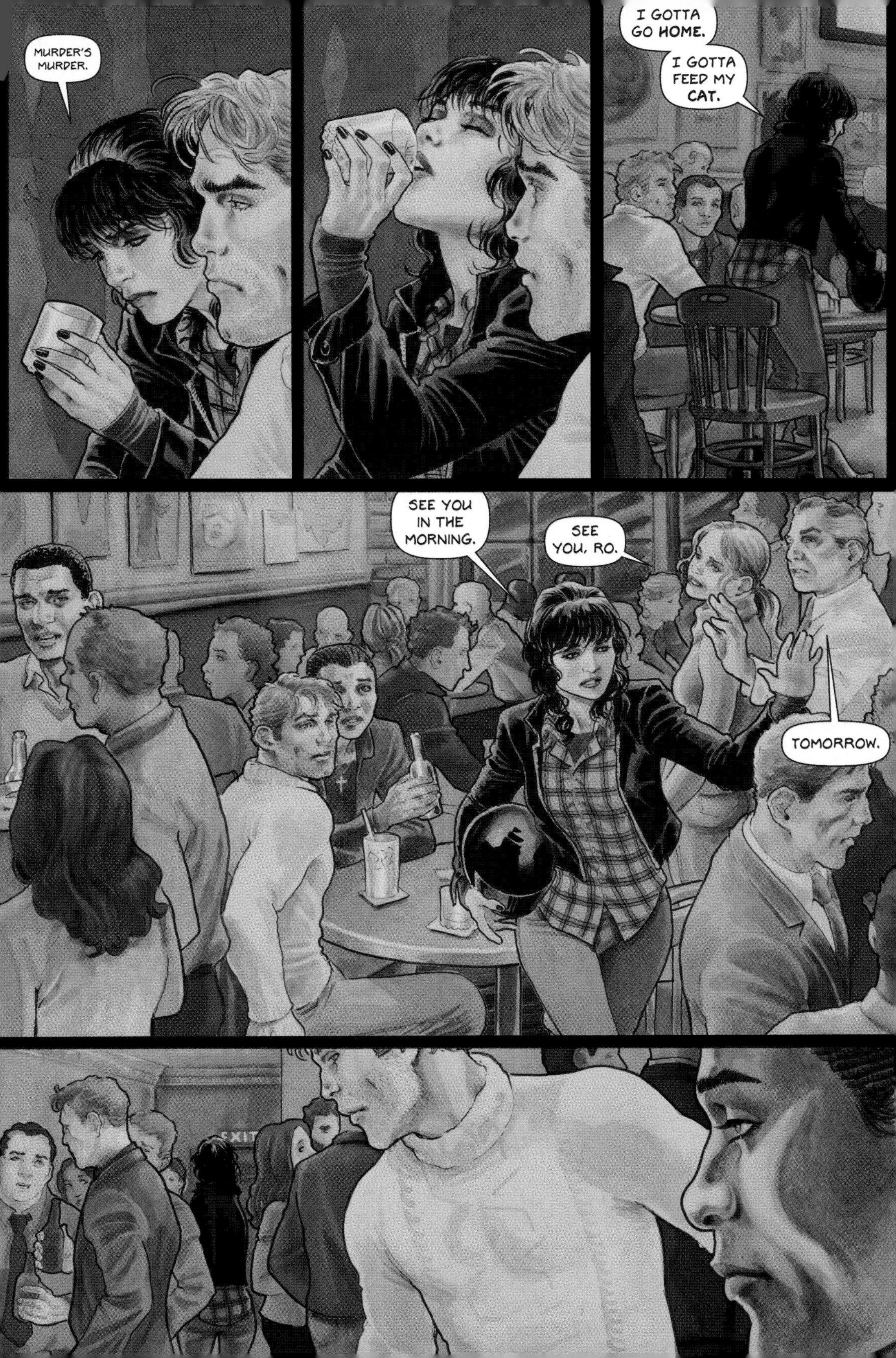
MURDER'S MURDER.
I GOTTA GO HOME.
I GOTTA FEED MY CAT.
SEE YOU IN THE MORNING.
SEE YOU, RO.
TOMORROW.

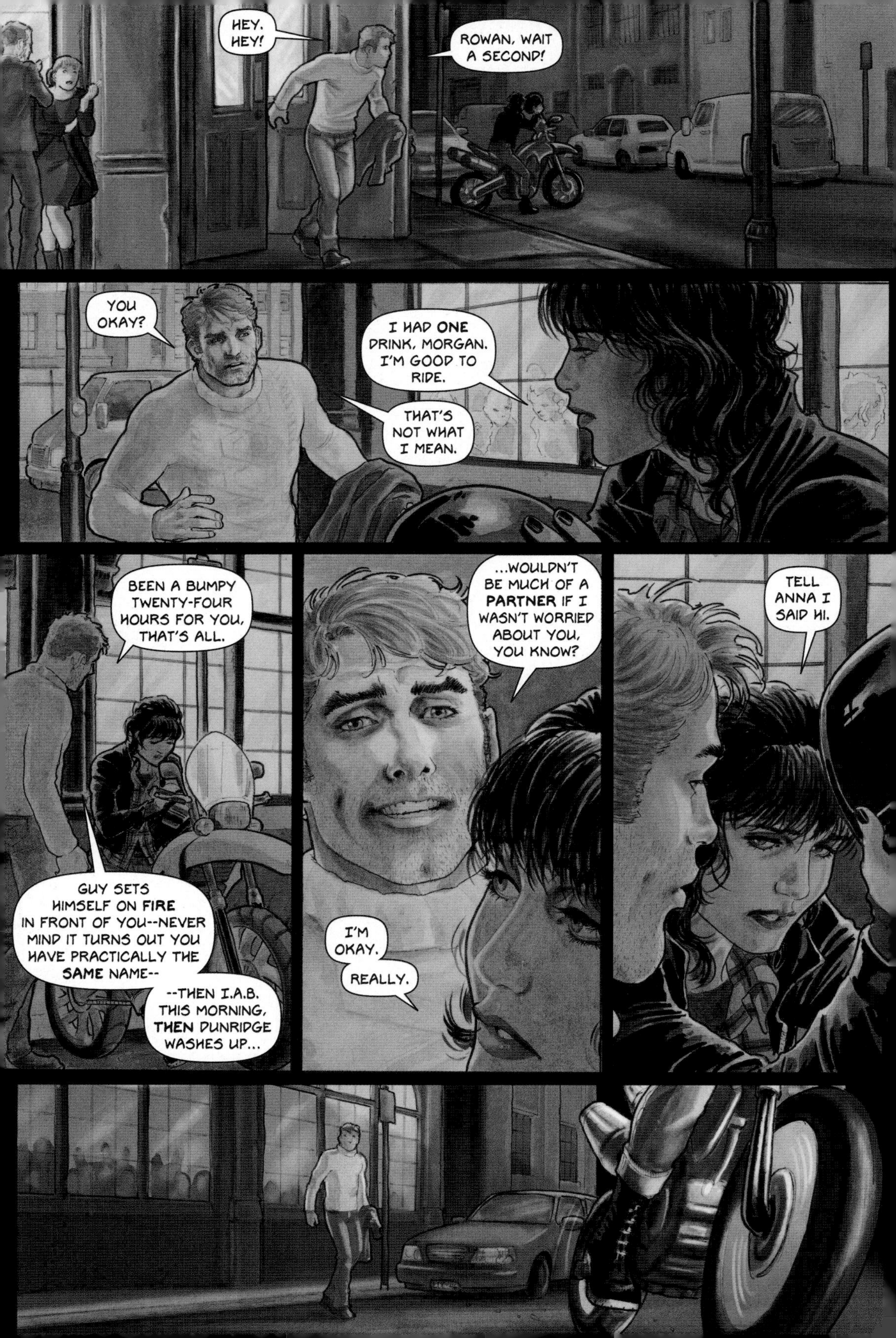
HEY. HEY!
ROWAN, WAIT A SECOND!
YOU OKAY?
I HAD ONE DRINK, MORGAN. I'M GOOD TO RIDE.
THAT'S NOT WHAT I MEAN.
BEEN A BUMPY TWENTY-FOUR HOURS FOR YOU, THAT'S ALL.
GUY SETS HIMSELF ON FIRE IN FRONT OF YOU--NEVER MIND IT TURNS OUT YOU HAVE PRACTICALLY THE SAME NAME--
--THEN I.A.B. THIS MORNING, THEN DUNRIDGE WASHES UP...
...WOULDN'T BE MUCH OF A PARTNER IF I WASN'T WORRIED ABOUT YOU, YOU KNOW?
I'M OKAY.
REALLY.
TELL ANNA I SAID HI.

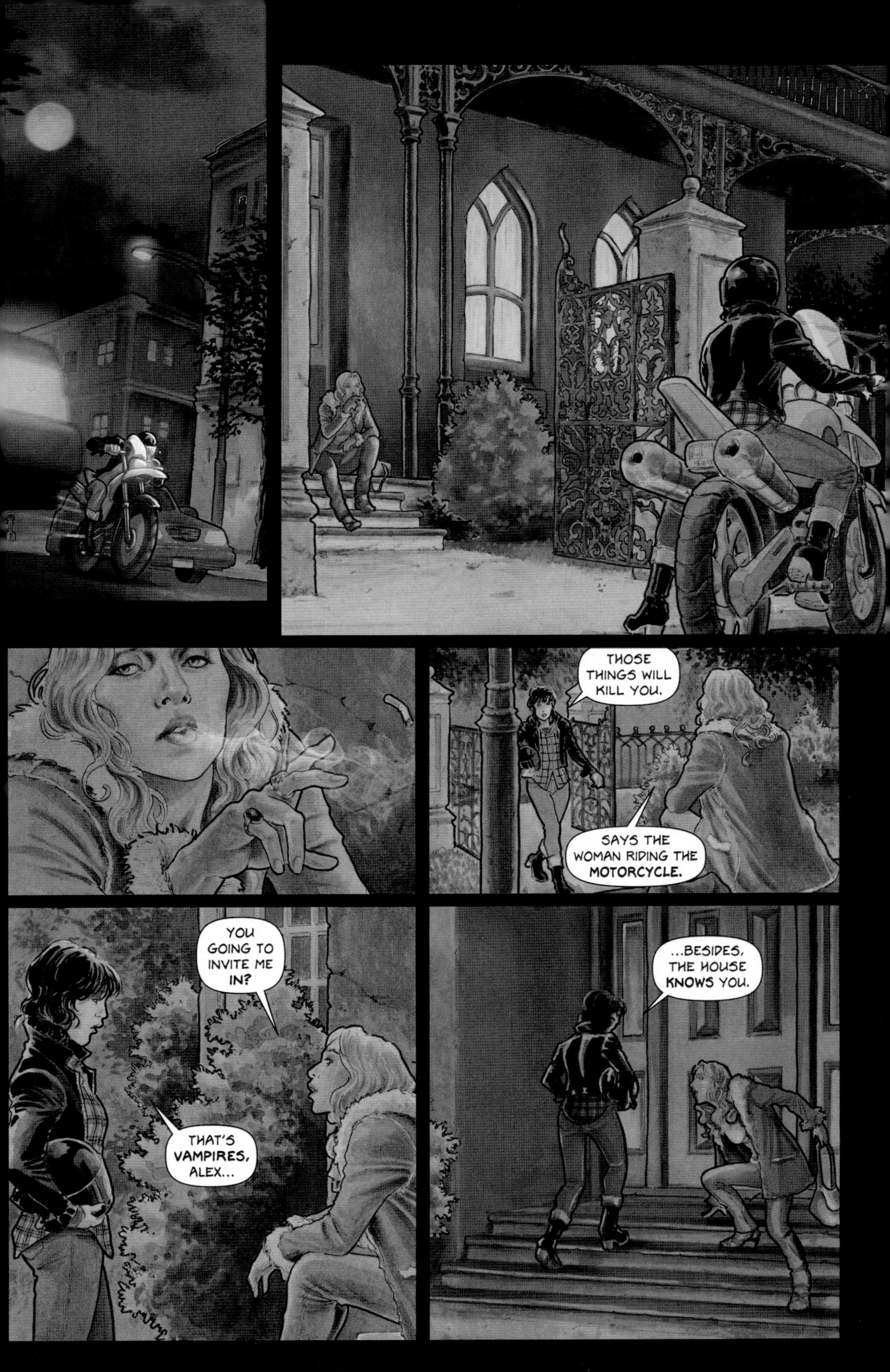
THOSE THINGS WILL KILL YOU.
SAYS THE WOMAN RIDING THE **MOTORCYCLE.**
YOU GOING TO INVITE ME **IN?**
THAT'S **VAMPIRES,** ALEX...
...BESIDES, THE HOUSE **KNOWS** YOU.

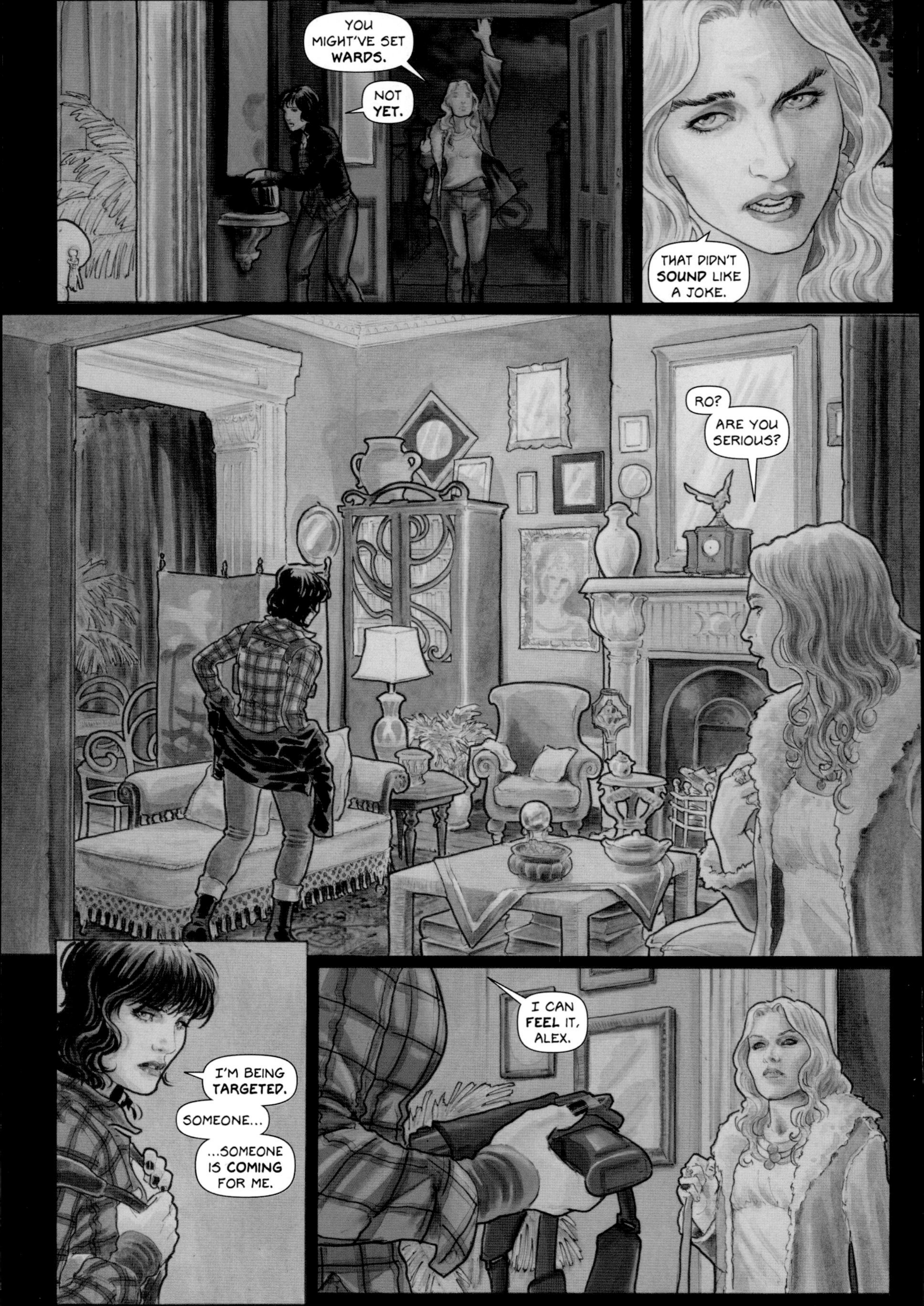

YOU MIGHT'VE SET WARDS.
NOT YET.
THAT DIDN'T SOUND LIKE A JOKE.
RO?
ARE YOU SERIOUS?
I'M BEING TARGETED.
SOMEONE...
...SOMEONE IS COMING FOR ME.
I CAN FEEL IT, ALEX.

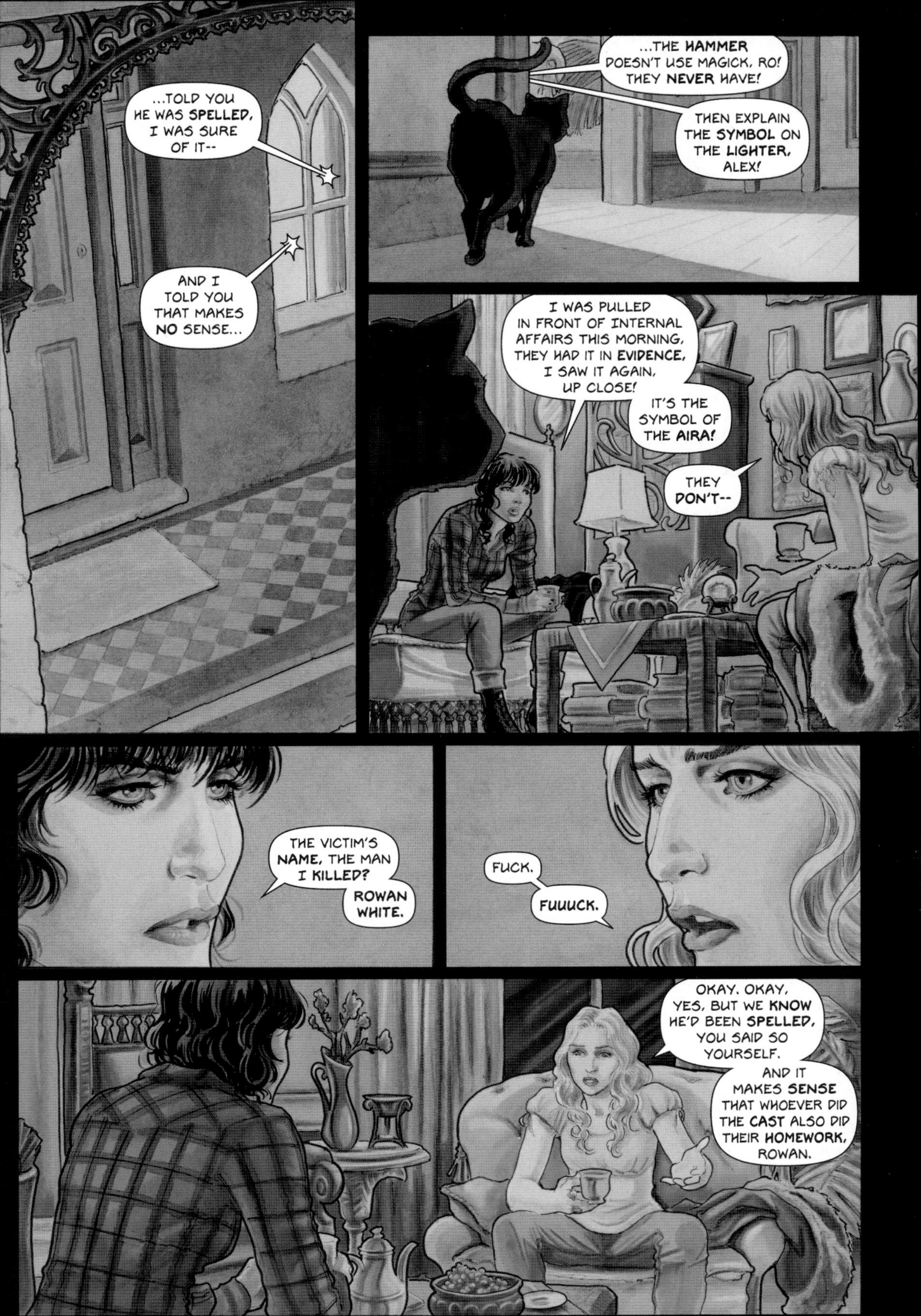
...TOLD YOU HE WAS SPELLED, I WAS SURE OF IT--
AND I TOLD YOU THAT MAKES NO SENSE...
...THE HAMMER DOESN'T USE MAGICK, RO! THEY NEVER HAVE!
THEN EXPLAIN THE SYMBOL ON THE LIGHTER, ALEX!
I WAS PULLED IN FRONT OF INTERNAL AFFAIRS THIS MORNING, THEY HAD IT IN EVIDENCE, I SAW IT AGAIN, UP CLOSE!
IT'S THE SYMBOL OF THE AIRA!
THEY DON'T--
THE VICTIM'S NAME, THE MAN I KILLED?
ROWAN WHITE.
FUCK.
FUUUCK.
OKAY. OKAY, YES, BUT WE KNOW HE'D BEEN SPELLED, YOU SAID SO YOURSELF.
AND IT MAKES SENSE THAT WHOEVER DID THE CAST ALSO DID THEIR HOMEWORK, ROWAN.

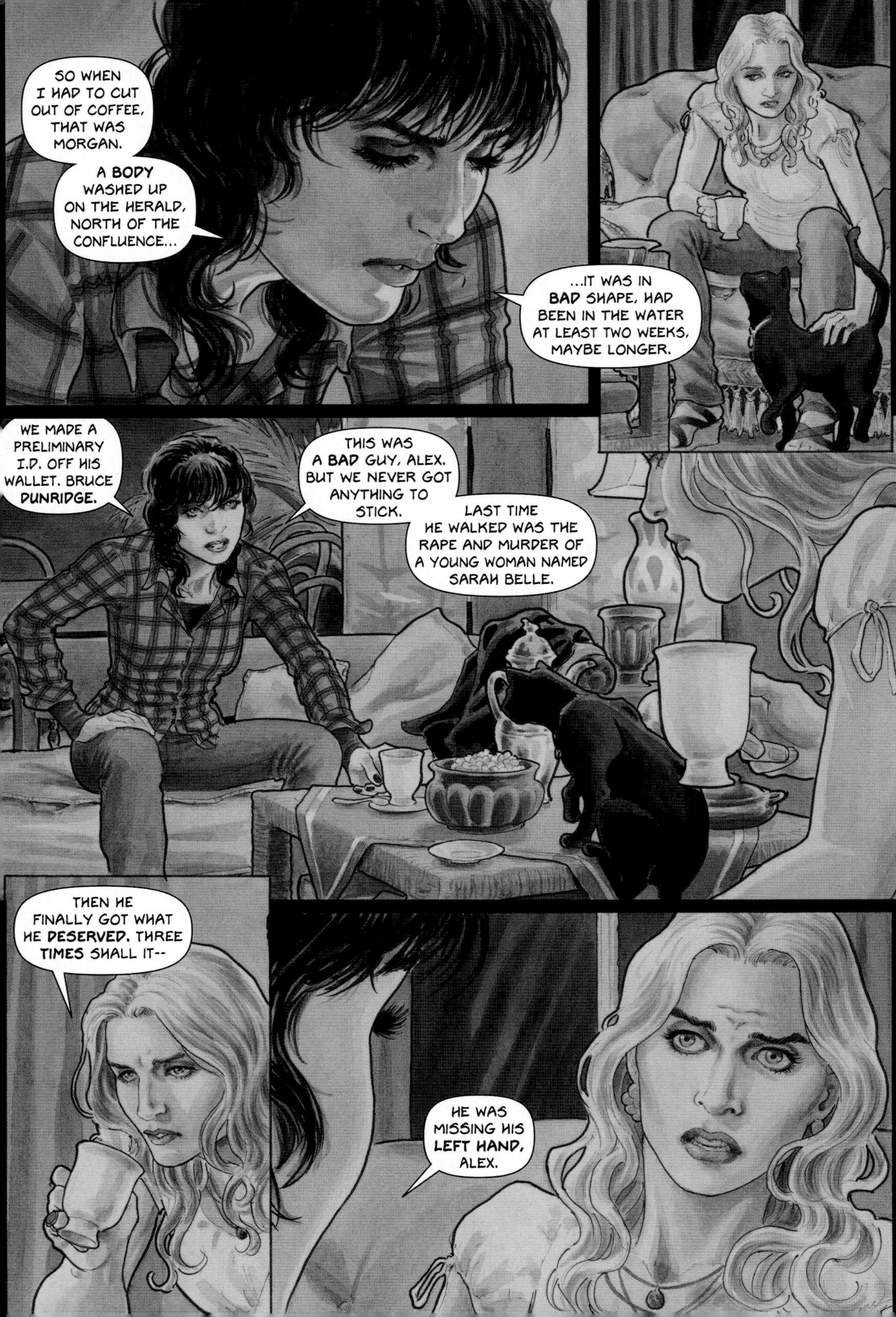
SO WHEN I HAD TO CUT OUT OF COFFEE, THAT WAS MORGAN.
A BODY WASHED UP ON THE HERALD, NORTH OF THE CONFLUENCE...
...IT WAS IN BAD SHAPE, HAD BEEN IN THE WATER AT LEAST TWO WEEKS, MAYBE LONGER.
WE MADE A PRELIMINARY I.D. OFF HIS WALLET. BRUCE DUNRIDGE.
THIS WAS A BAD GUY, ALEX. BUT WE NEVER GOT ANYTHING TO STICK.
LAST TIME HE WALKED WAS THE RAPE AND MURDER OF A YOUNG WOMAN NAMED SARAH BELLE.
THEN HE FINALLY GOT WHAT HE DESERVED. THREE TIMES SHALL IT--
HE WAS MISSING HIS LEFT HAND, ALEX.

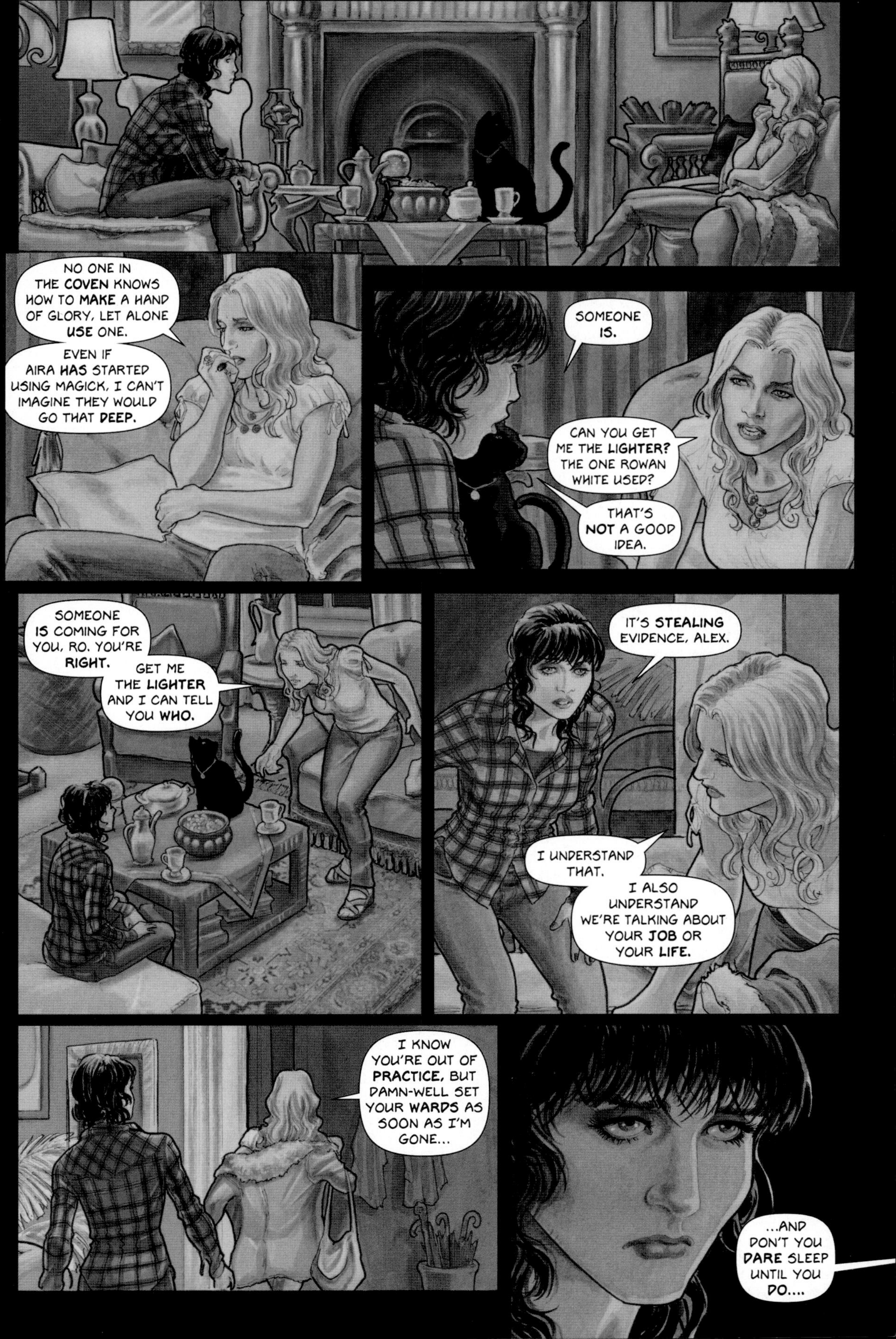
NO ONE IN THE COVEN KNOWS HOW TO MAKE A HAND OF GLORY, LET ALONE USE ONE.
EVEN IF AIRA HAS STARTED USING MAGICK, I CAN'T IMAGINE THEY WOULD GO THAT DEEP.
SOMEONE IS.
CAN YOU GET ME THE LIGHTER? THE ONE ROWAN WHITE USED?
THAT'S NOT A GOOD IDEA.
SOMEONE IS COMING FOR YOU, RO. YOU'RE RIGHT.
GET ME THE LIGHTER AND I CAN TELL YOU WHO.
IT'S STEALING EVIDENCE, ALEX.
I UNDERSTAND THAT.
I ALSO UNDERSTAND WE'RE TALKING ABOUT YOUR JOB OR YOUR LIFE.
I KNOW YOU'RE OUT OF PRACTICE, BUT DAMN-WELL SET YOUR WARDS AS SOON AS I'M GONE...
...AND DON'T YOU DARE SLEEP UNTIL YOU DO....

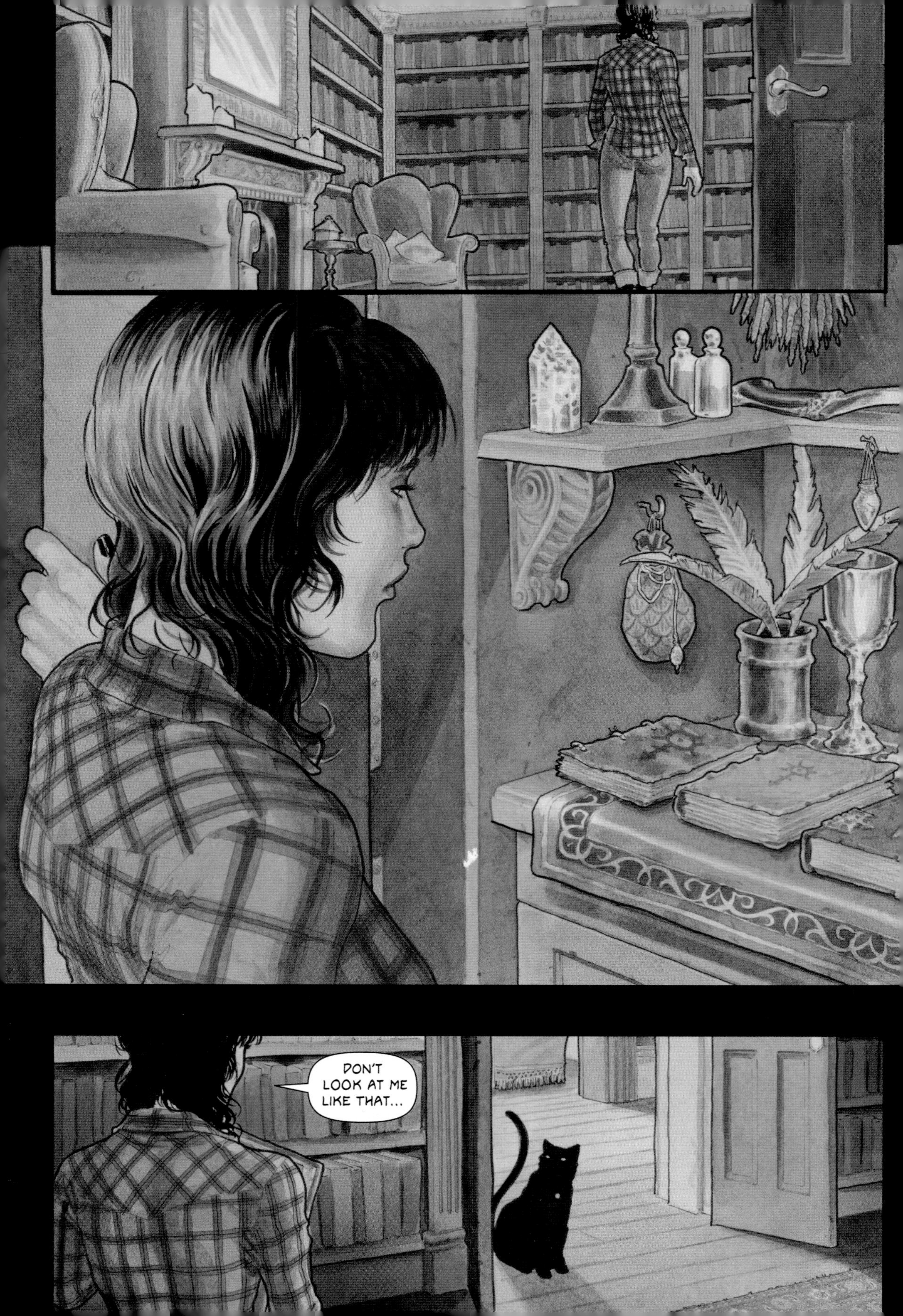
DON'T LOOK AT ME LIKE THAT...

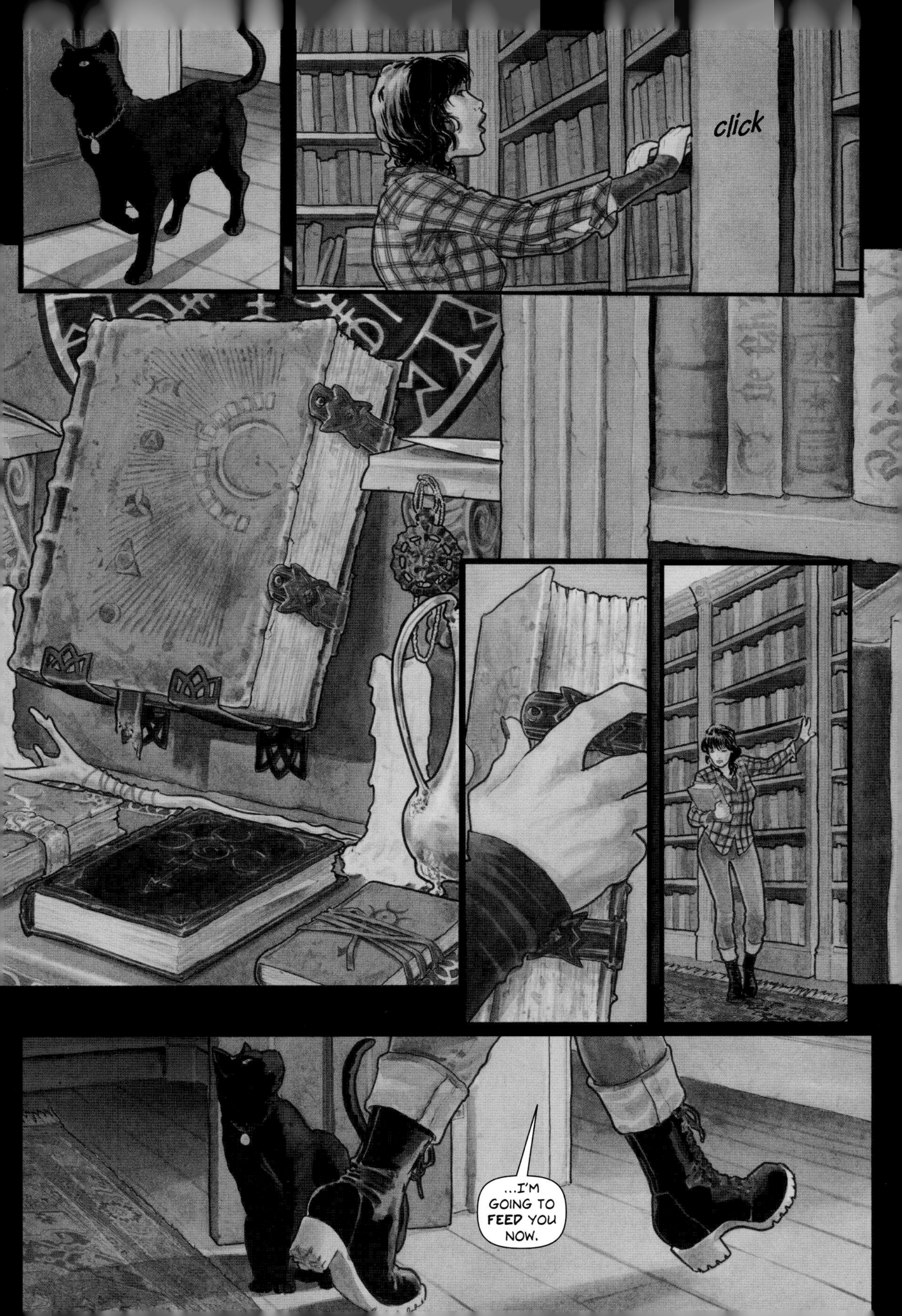
click
...I'M GOING TO FEED YOU NOW.

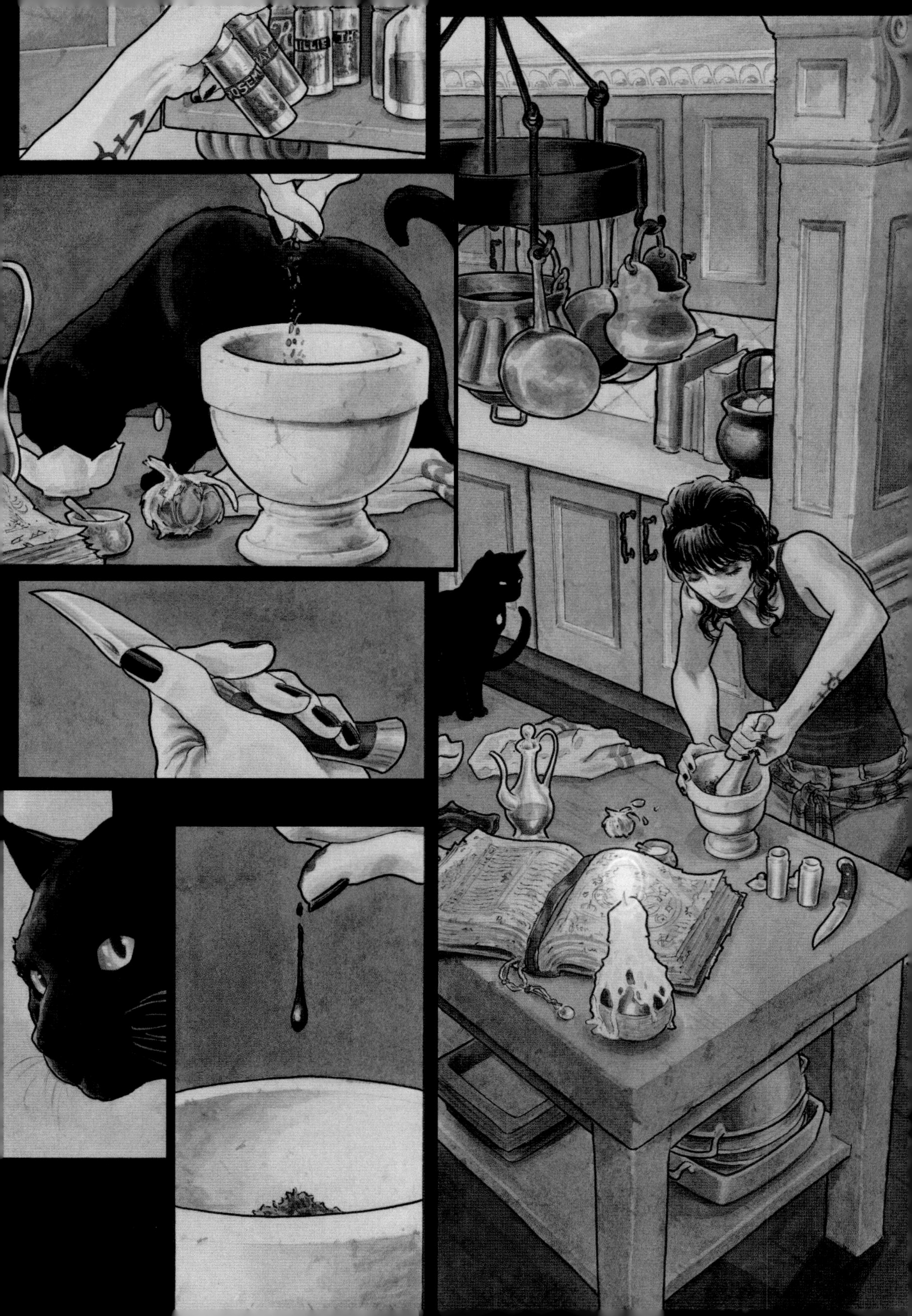

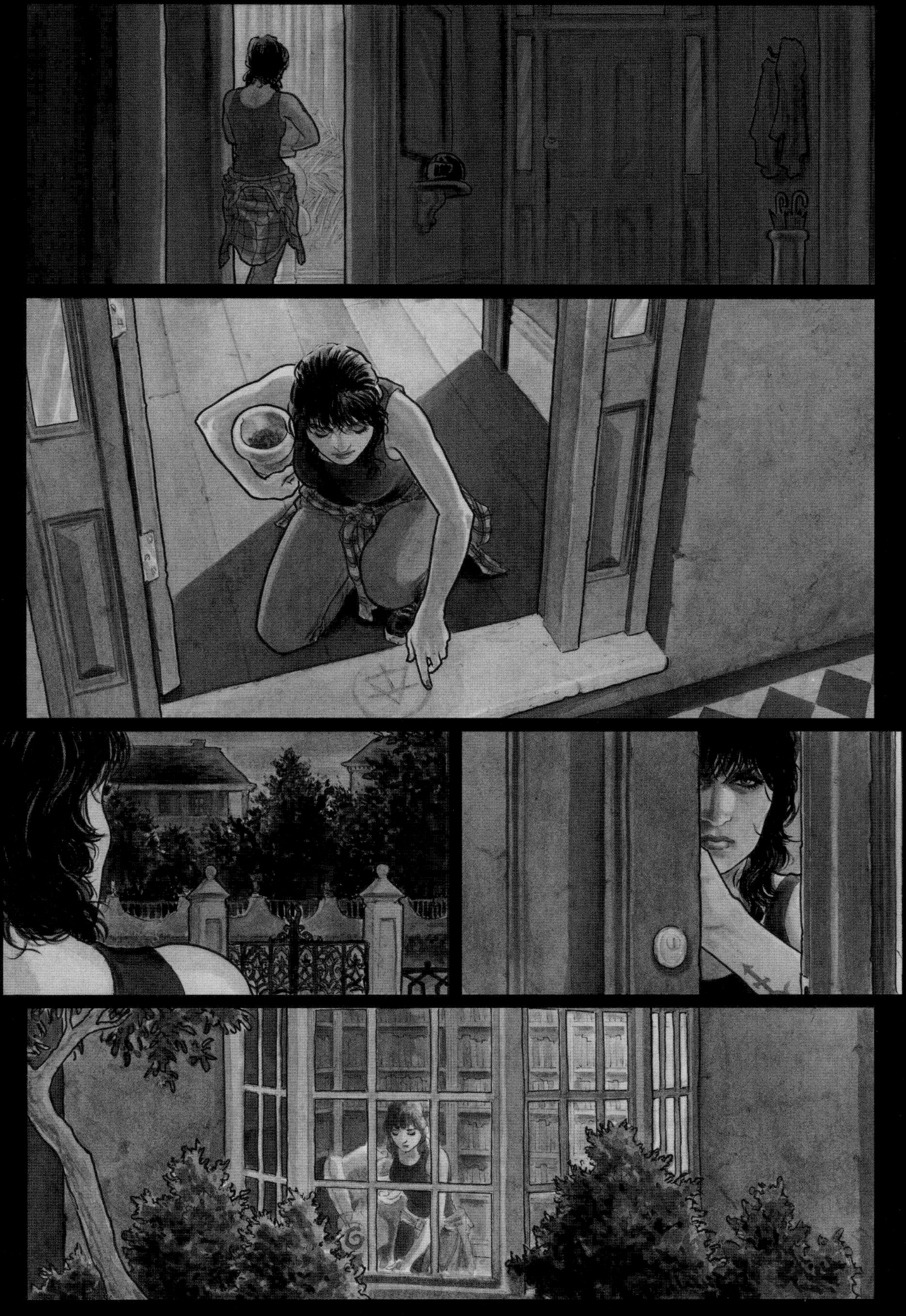

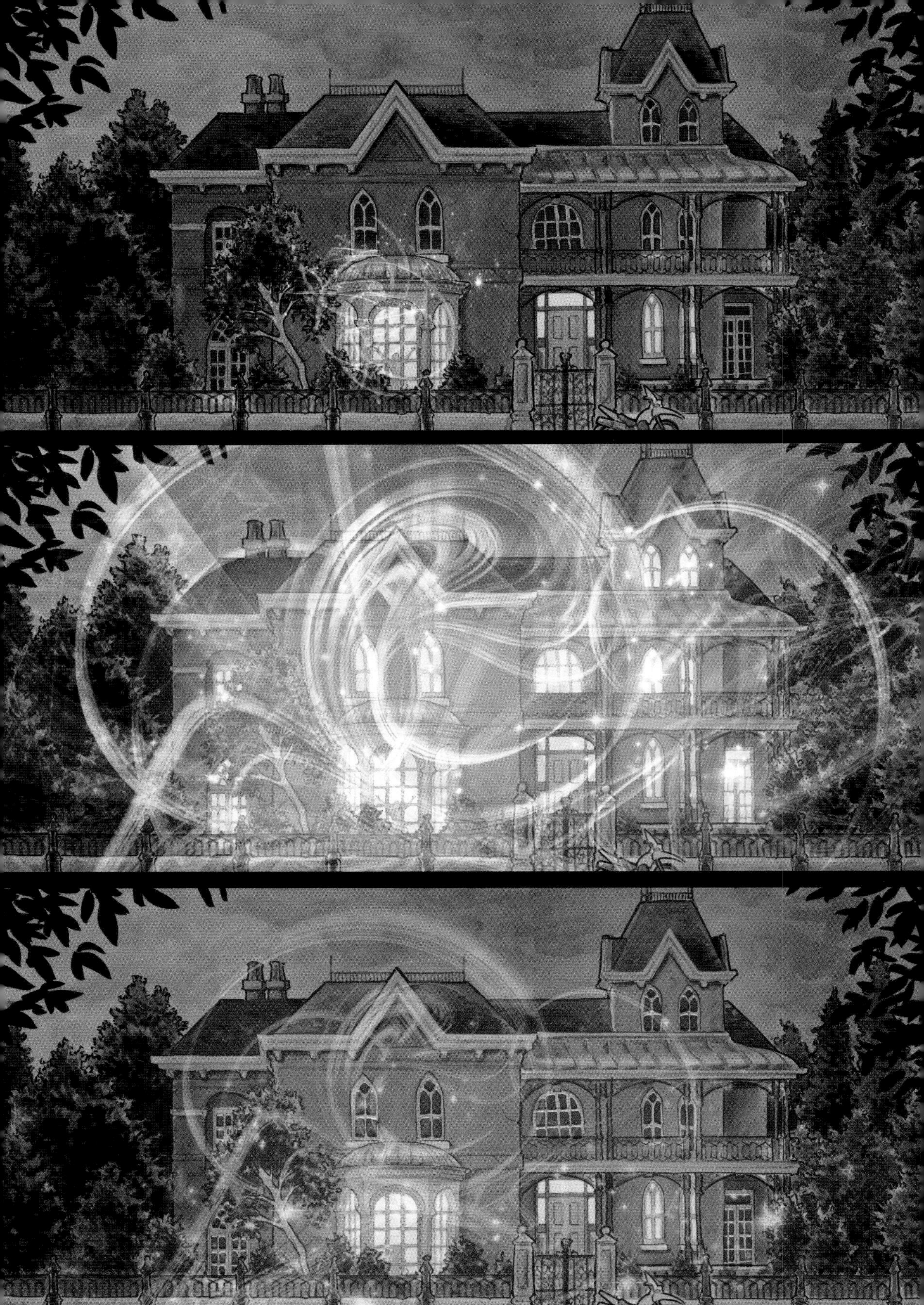

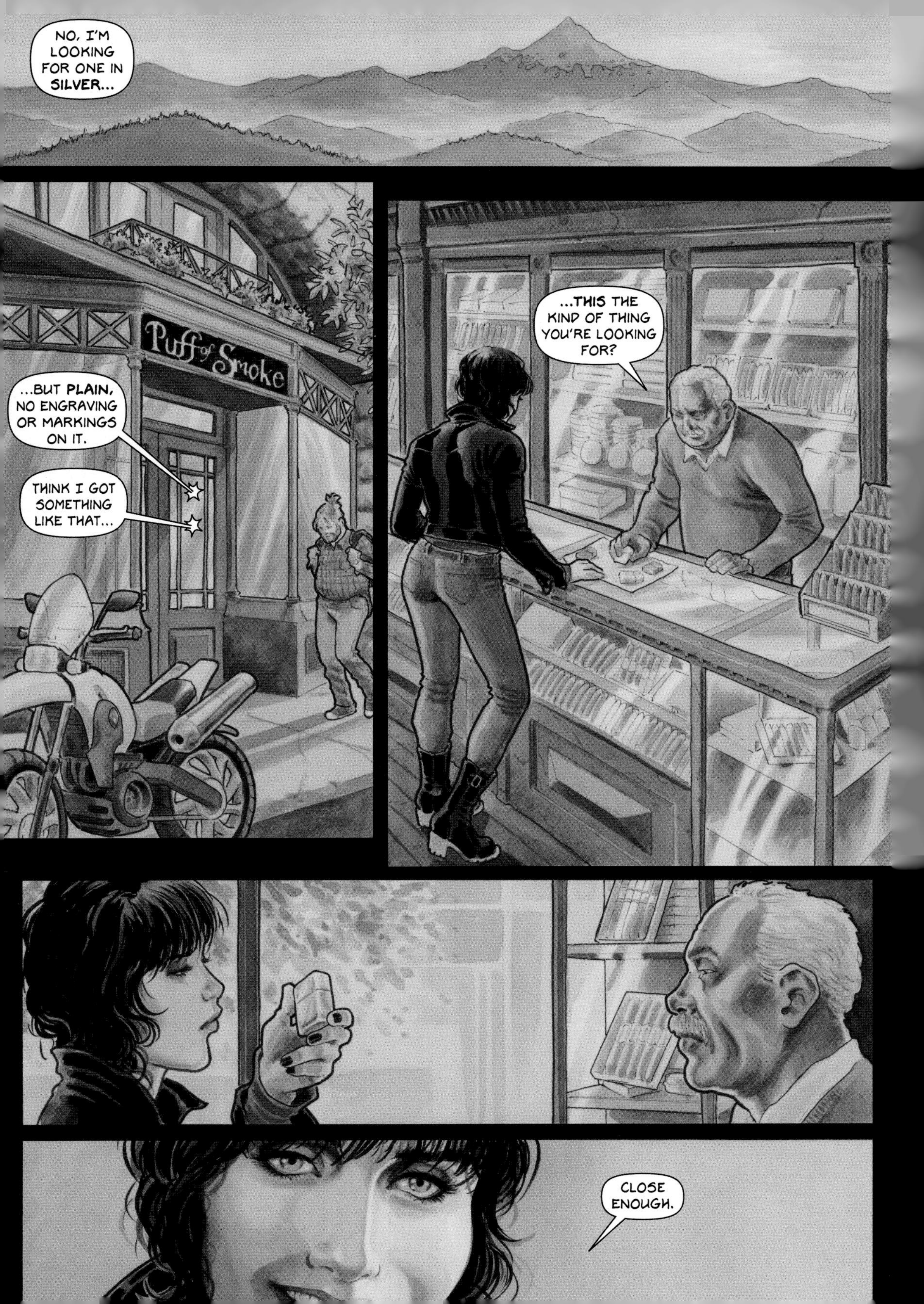
NO, I'M LOOKING FOR ONE IN SILVER...
...BUT PLAIN, NO ENGRAVING OR MARKINGS ON IT.
THINK I GOT SOMETHING LIKE THAT...
Puff of Smoke
...THIS THE KIND OF THING YOU'RE LOOKING FOR?
CLOSE ENOUGH.

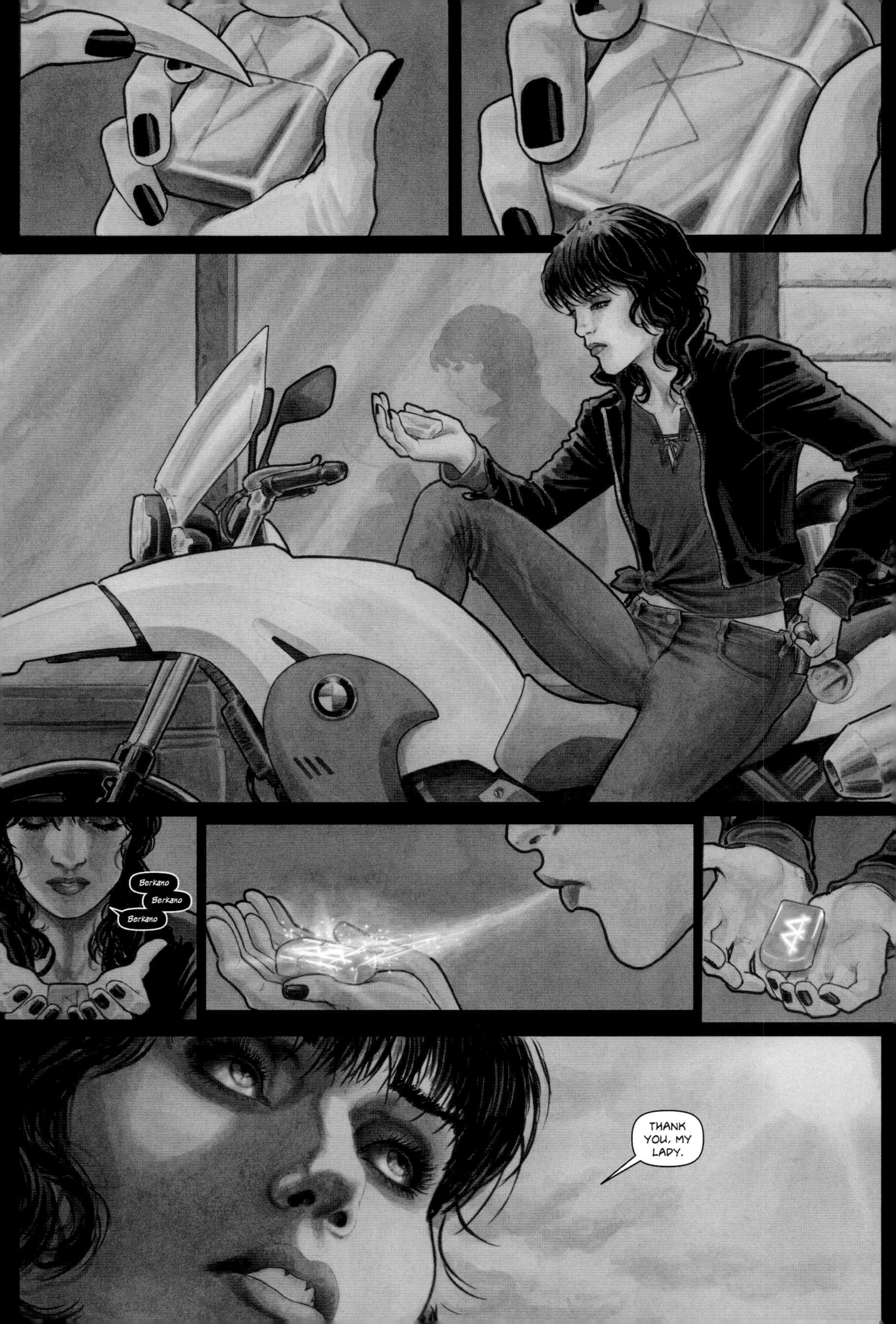
Berkano
Berkano
Berkano
THANK YOU, MY LADY.

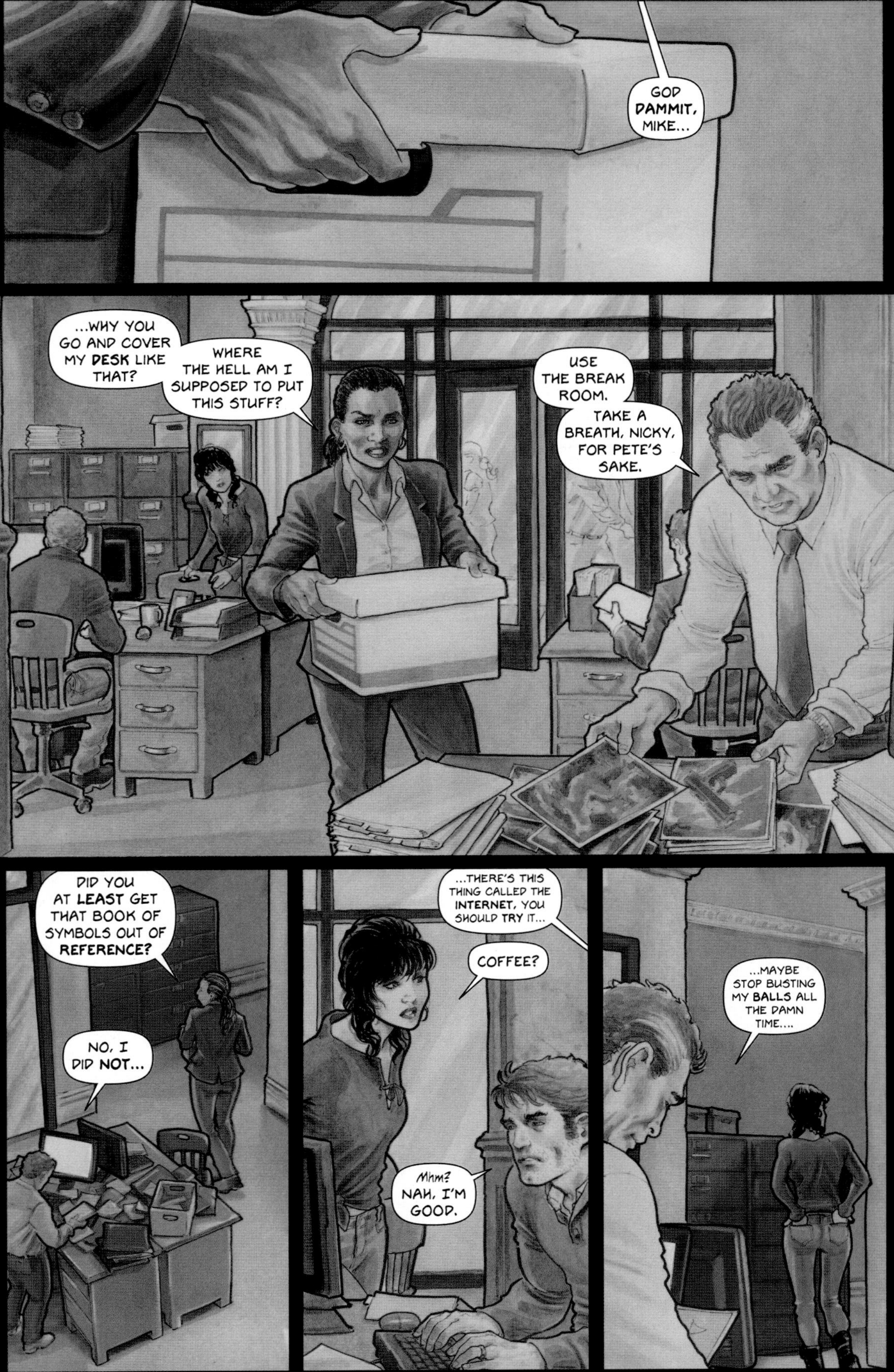
GOD **DAMMIT,** MIKE...
...WHY YOU GO AND COVER MY **DESK** LIKE THAT?
WHERE THE HELL AM I SUPPOSED TO PUT THIS STUFF?
USE THE BREAK ROOM.
TAKE A BREATH, NICKY, FOR PETE'S SAKE.
DID YOU AT **LEAST** GET THAT BOOK OF SYMBOLS OUT OF **REFERENCE?**
NO, I DID **NOT...**
...THERE'S THIS THING CALLED THE **INTERNET,** YOU SHOULD **TRY** IT...
COFFEE?
Mhm? NAH, I'M GOOD.
...MAYBE STOP BUSTING MY **BALLS** ALL THE DAMN TIME....

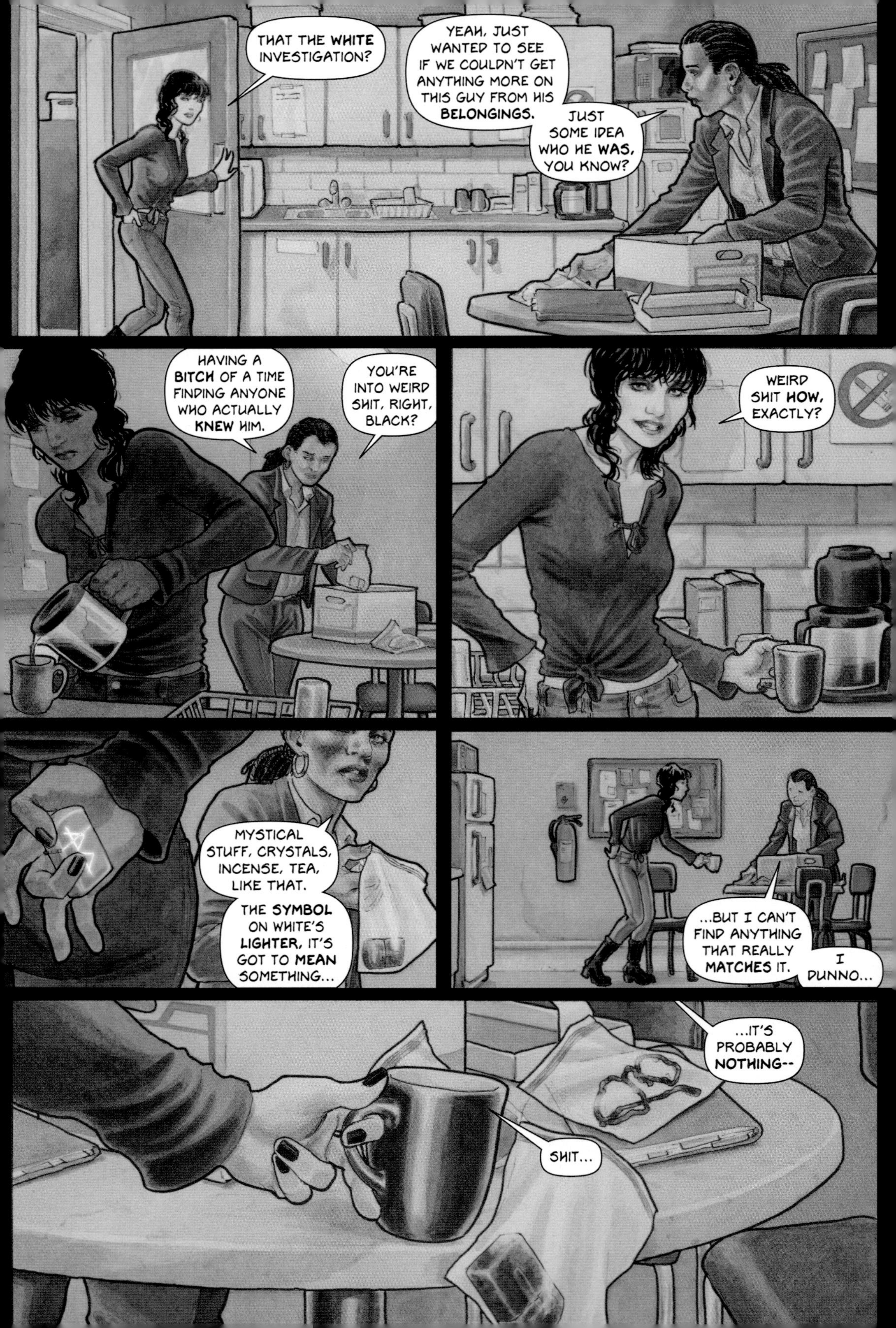
THAT THE WHITE INVESTIGATION?
YEAH, JUST WANTED TO SEE IF WE COULDN'T GET ANYTHING MORE ON THIS GUY FROM HIS BELONGINGS.
JUST SOME IDEA WHO HE WAS, YOU KNOW?
HAVING A BITCH OF A TIME FINDING ANYONE WHO ACTUALLY KNEW HIM.
YOU'RE INTO WEIRD SHIT, RIGHT, BLACK?
WEIRD SHIT HOW, EXACTLY?
MYSTICAL STUFF, CRYSTALS, INCENSE, TEA, LIKE THAT.
THE SYMBOL ON WHITE'S LIGHTER, IT'S GOT TO MEAN SOMETHING...
...BUT I CAN'T FIND ANYTHING THAT REALLY MATCHES IT.
I DUNNO...
...IT'S PROBABLY NOTHING--
SHIT...

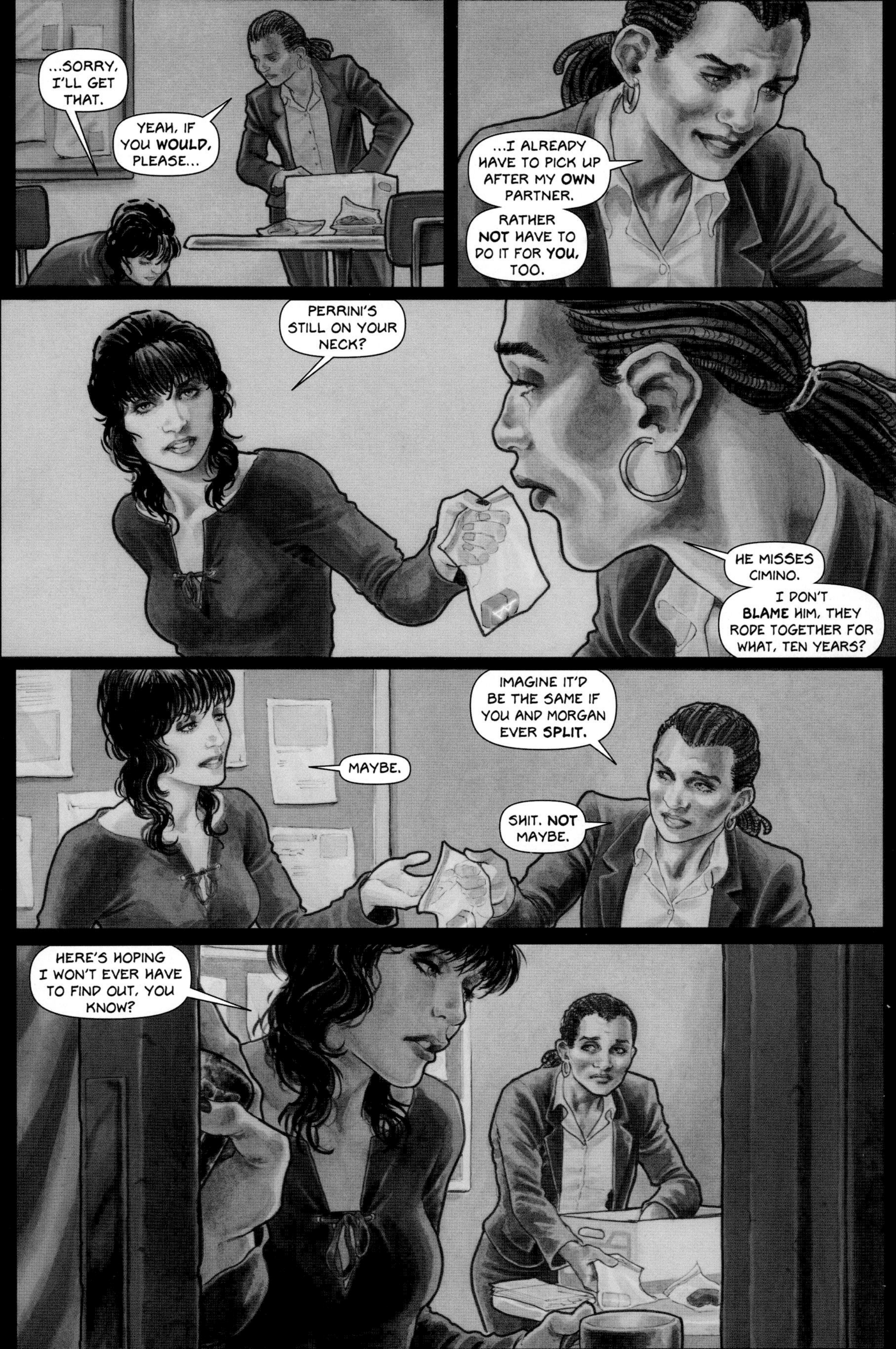
...SORRY, I'LL GET THAT.
YEAH, IF YOU **WOULD**, PLEASE...
...I ALREADY HAVE TO PICK UP AFTER MY **OWN** PARTNER.
RATHER **NOT** HAVE TO DO IT FOR **YOU**, TOO.
PERRINI'S STILL ON YOUR NECK?
HE MISSES CIMINO.
I DON'T **BLAME** HIM, THEY RODE TOGETHER FOR WHAT, TEN YEARS?
IMAGINE IT'D BE THE SAME IF YOU AND MORGAN EVER **SPLIT**.
MAYBE.
SHIT. **NOT** MAYBE.
HERE'S HOPING I WON'T EVER HAVE TO FIND OUT, YOU KNOW?

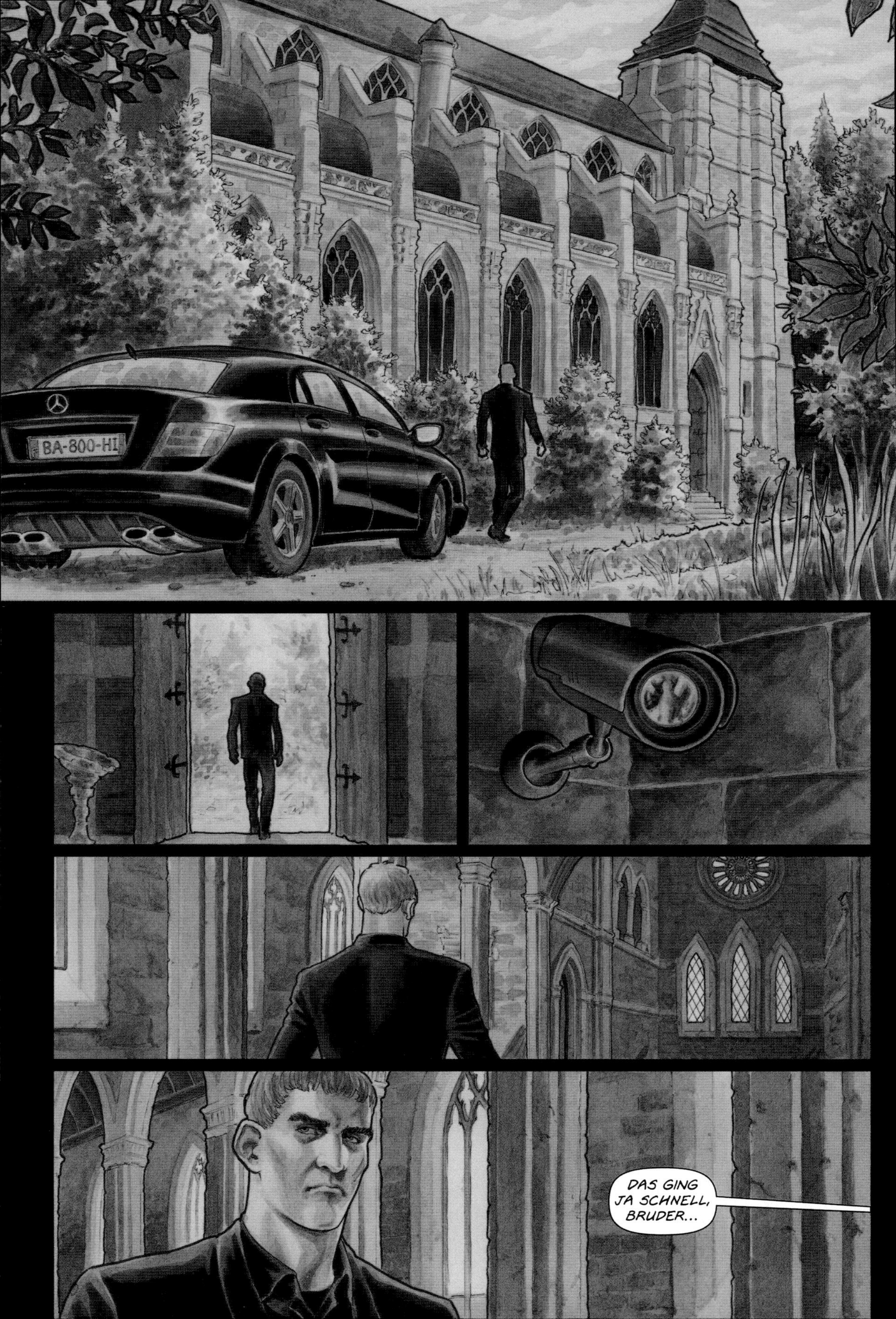
BA-800-HI
DAS GING JA SCHNELL, BRUDER...

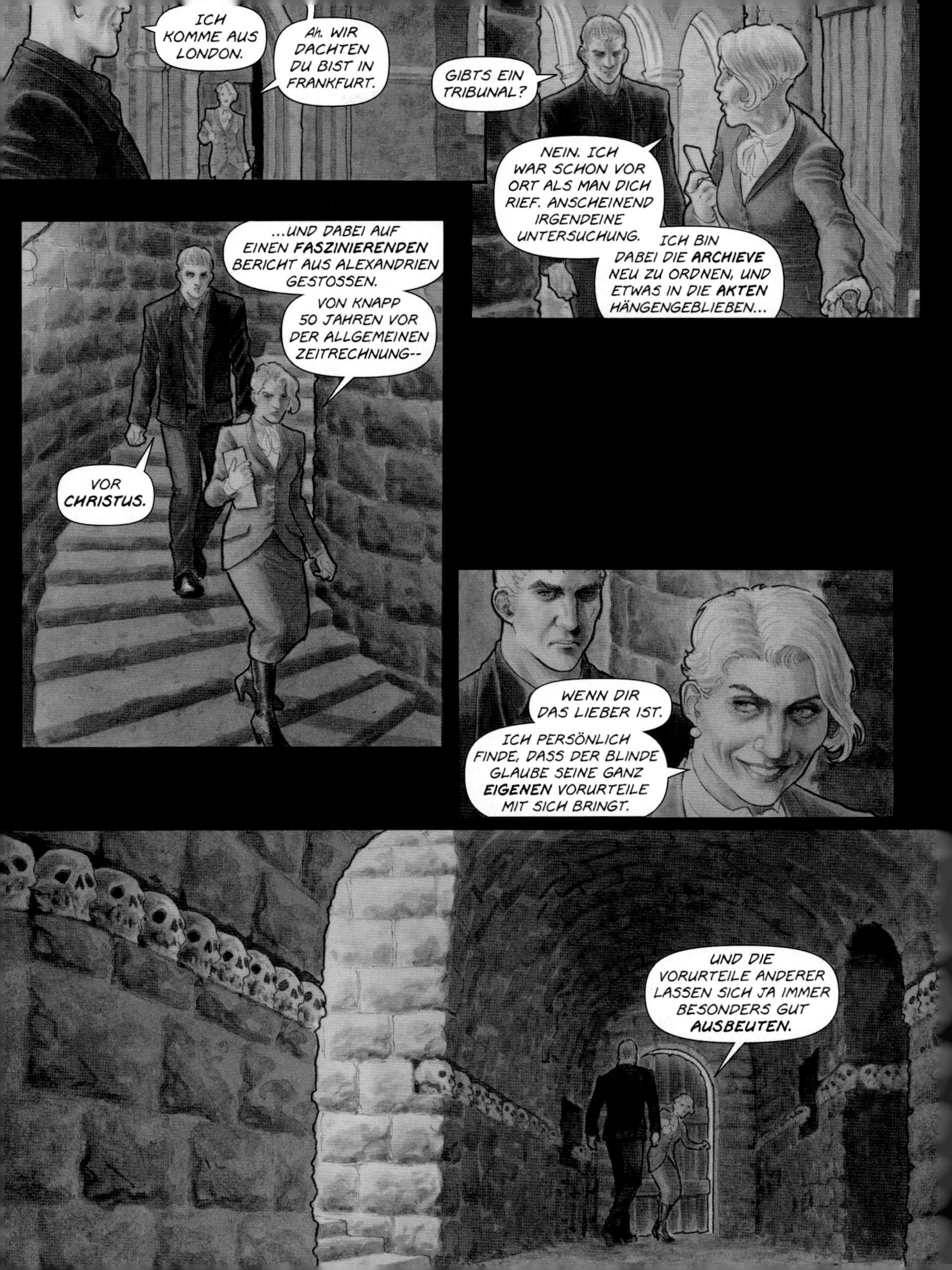
ICH KOMME AUS LONDON.
Ah. WIR DACHTEN DU BIST IN FRANKFURT.
GIBTS EIN TRIBUNAL?
NEIN. ICH WAR SCHON VOR ORT ALS MAN DICH RIEF. ANSCHEINEND IRGENDEINE UNTERSUCHUNG.
ICH BIN DABEI DIE ARCHIEVE NEU ZU ORDNEN, UND ETWAS IN DIE AKTEN HÄNGENGEBLIEBEN...
...UND DABEI AUF EINEN FASZINIERENDEN BERICHT AUS ALEXANDRIEN GESTOSSEN.
VON KNAPP 50 JAHREN VOR DER ALLGEMEINEN ZEITRECHNUNG--
VOR CHRISTUS.
WENN DIR DAS LIEBER IST.
ICH PERSÖNLICH FINDE, DASS DER BLINDE GLAUBE SEINE GANZ EIGENEN VORURTEILE MIT SICH BRINGT.
UND DIE VORURTEILE ANDERER LASSEN SICH JA IMMER BESONDERS GUT AUSBEUTEN.

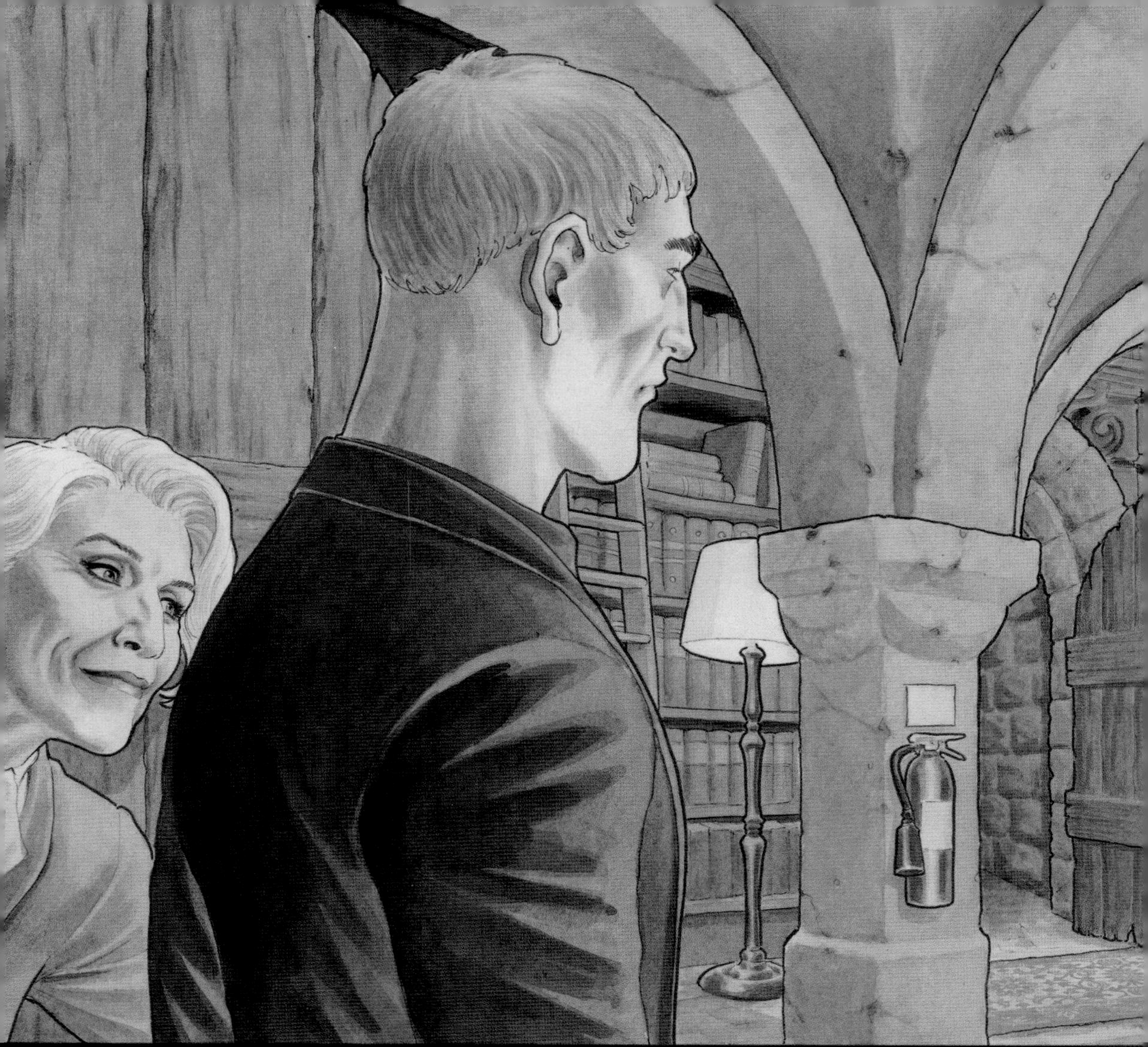

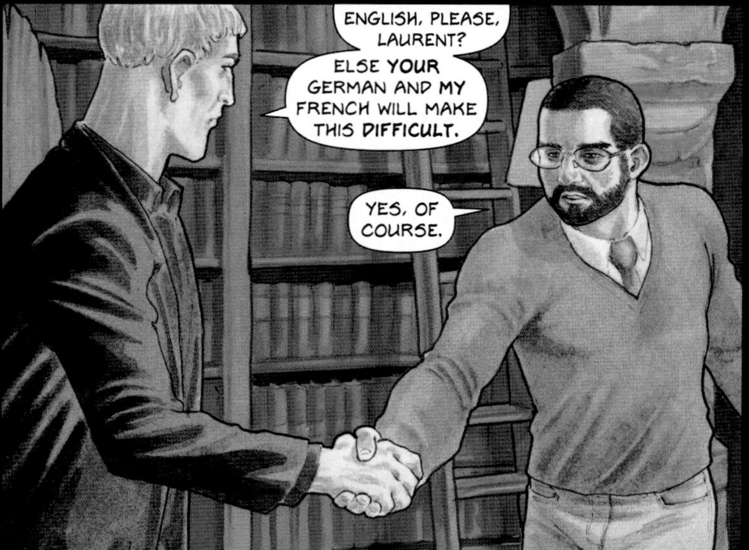
ENGLISH, PLEASE, LAURENT?
ELSE **YOUR** GERMAN AND **MY** FRENCH WILL MAKE THIS **DIFFICULT**.
YES, OF COURSE.

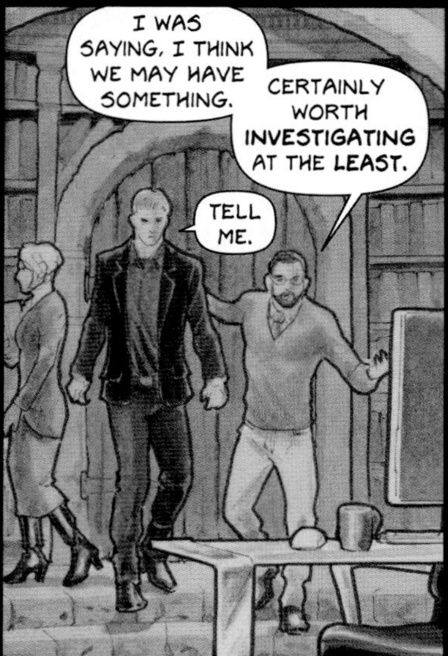
I WAS SAYING, I THINK WE MAY HAVE SOMETHING.
CERTAINLY WORTH **INVESTIGATING** AT THE **LEAST**.
TELL ME.

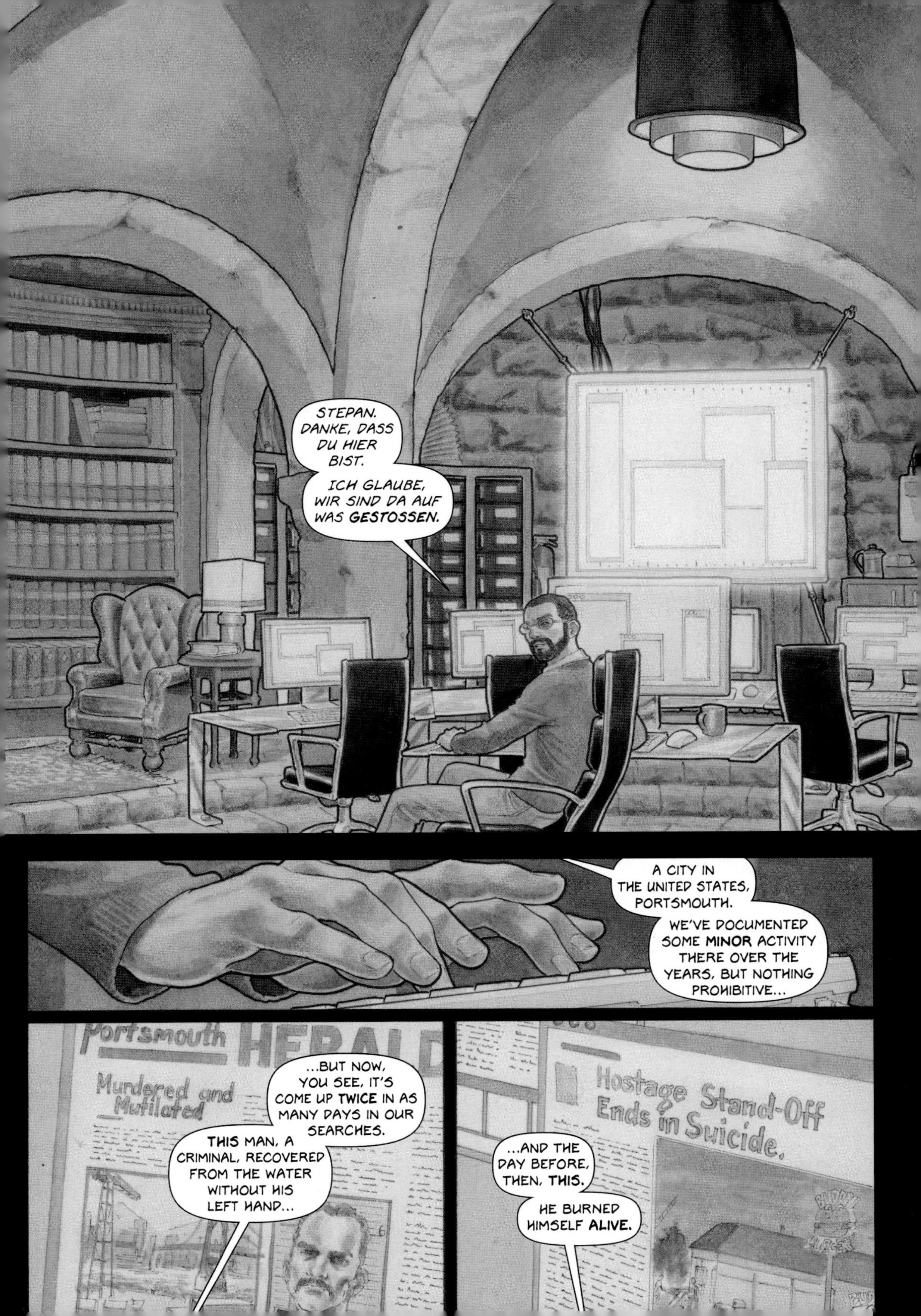
STEPAN. DANKE, DASS DU HIER BIST.
ICH GLAUBE, WIR SIND DA AUF WAS **GESTOSSEN.**
A CITY IN THE UNITED STATES, PORTSMOUTH.
WE'VE DOCUMENTED SOME **MINOR** ACTIVITY THERE OVER THE YEARS, BUT NOTHING PROHIBITIVE...
Murdered and Mutilated
...BUT NOW, YOU SEE, IT'S COME UP **TWICE** IN AS MANY DAYS IN OUR SEARCHES.
THIS MAN, A CRIMINAL, RECOVERED FROM THE WATER WITHOUT HIS LEFT HAND...
Hostage Stand-Off Ends in Suicide.
...AND THE DAY BEFORE, THEN, **THIS.**
HE BURNED HIMSELF **ALIVE.**

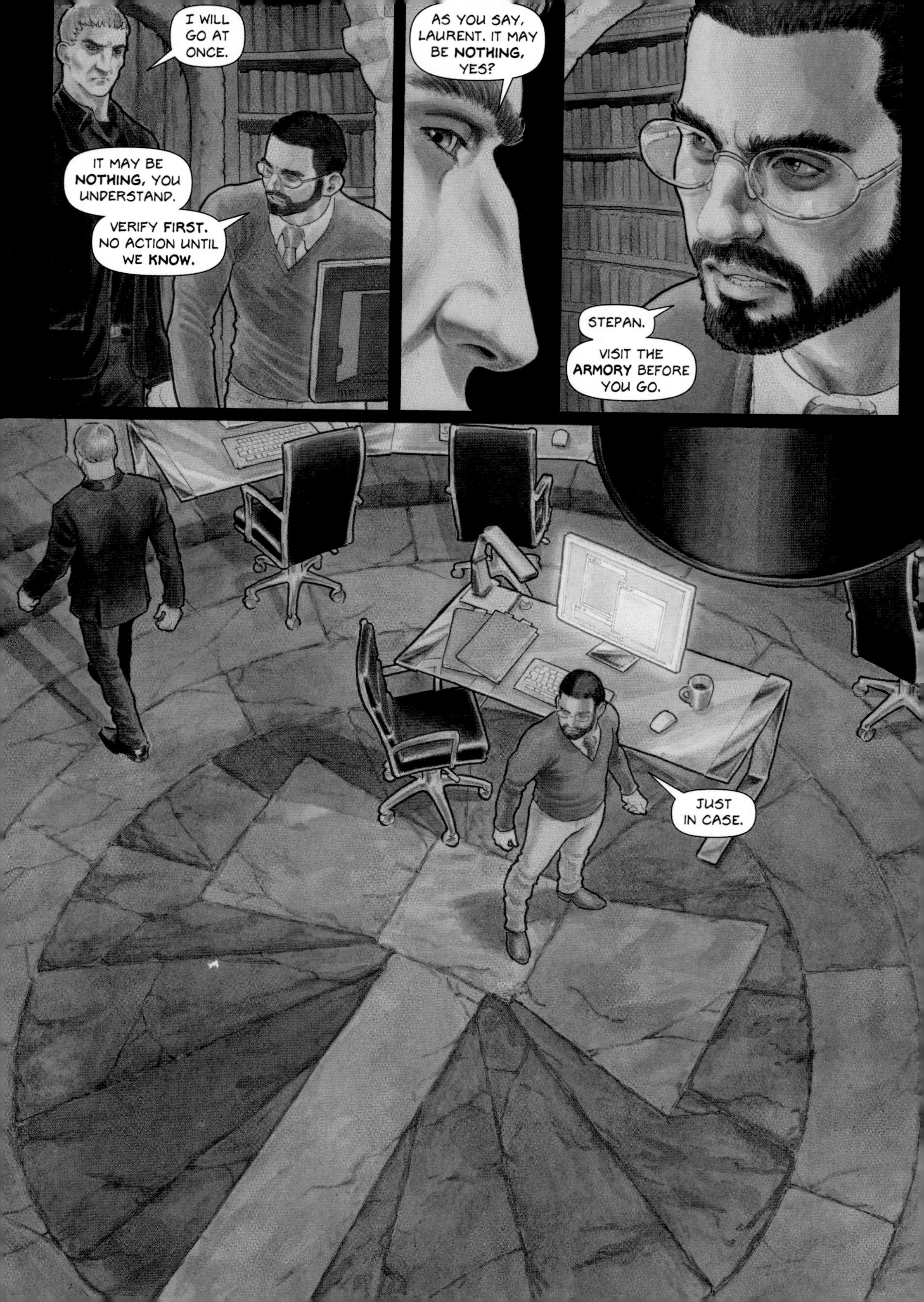
I WILL GO AT ONCE.
IT MAY BE **NOTHING,** YOU UNDERSTAND.
VERIFY **FIRST.** NO ACTION UNTIL WE **KNOW.**
AS YOU SAY, LAURENT. IT MAY BE **NOTHING,** YES?
STEPAN.
VISIT THE **ARMORY** BEFORE YOU GO.
JUST IN CASE.

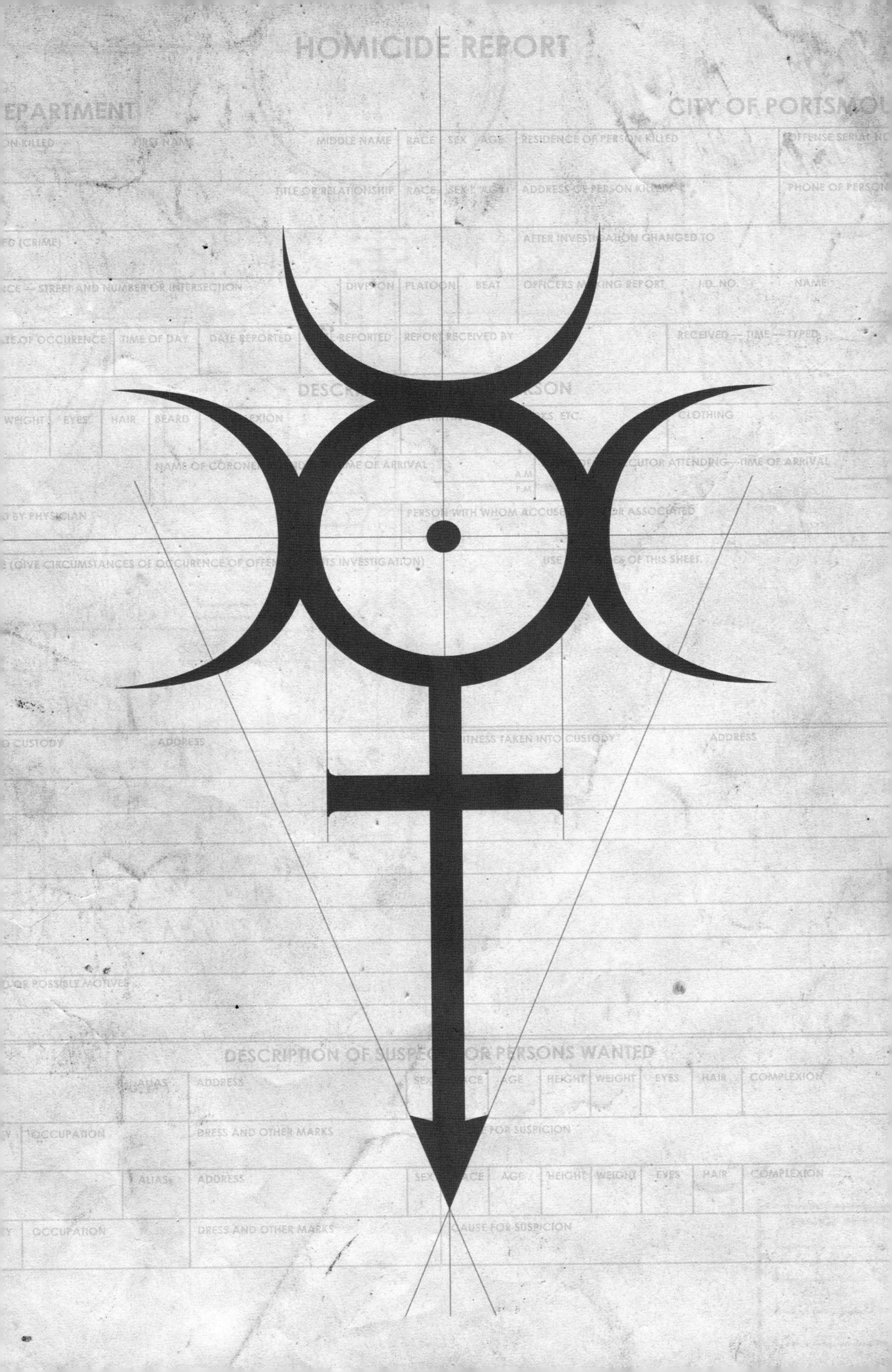
HOMICIDE REPORT
MIDDLE NAME
RACE
SEX
AGE
RESIDENCE OF PERSON KILLED
TITLE OR RELATIONSHIP
AFTER INVESTIGATION CHANGED TO
DIVISION
PLATOON
BEAT
TIME OF DAY
DATE REPORTED
CLOTHING
ADDRESS
HEIGHT
WEIGHT
EYES
HAIR
COMPLEXION
OCCUPATION
DRESS AND OTHER MARKS
CAUSE FOR SUSPICION

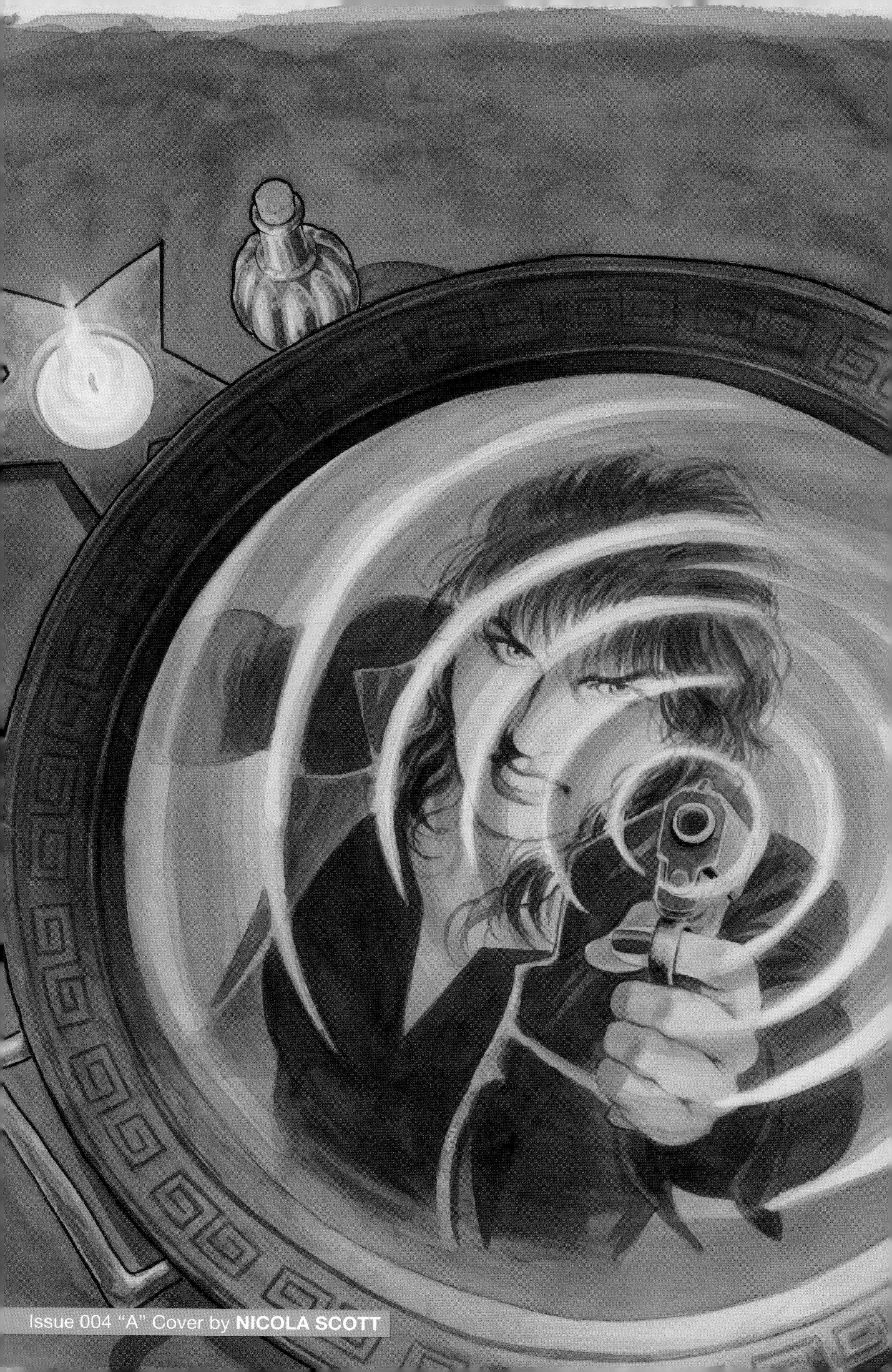

Issue 004 “A” Cover by **NICOLA SCOTT**

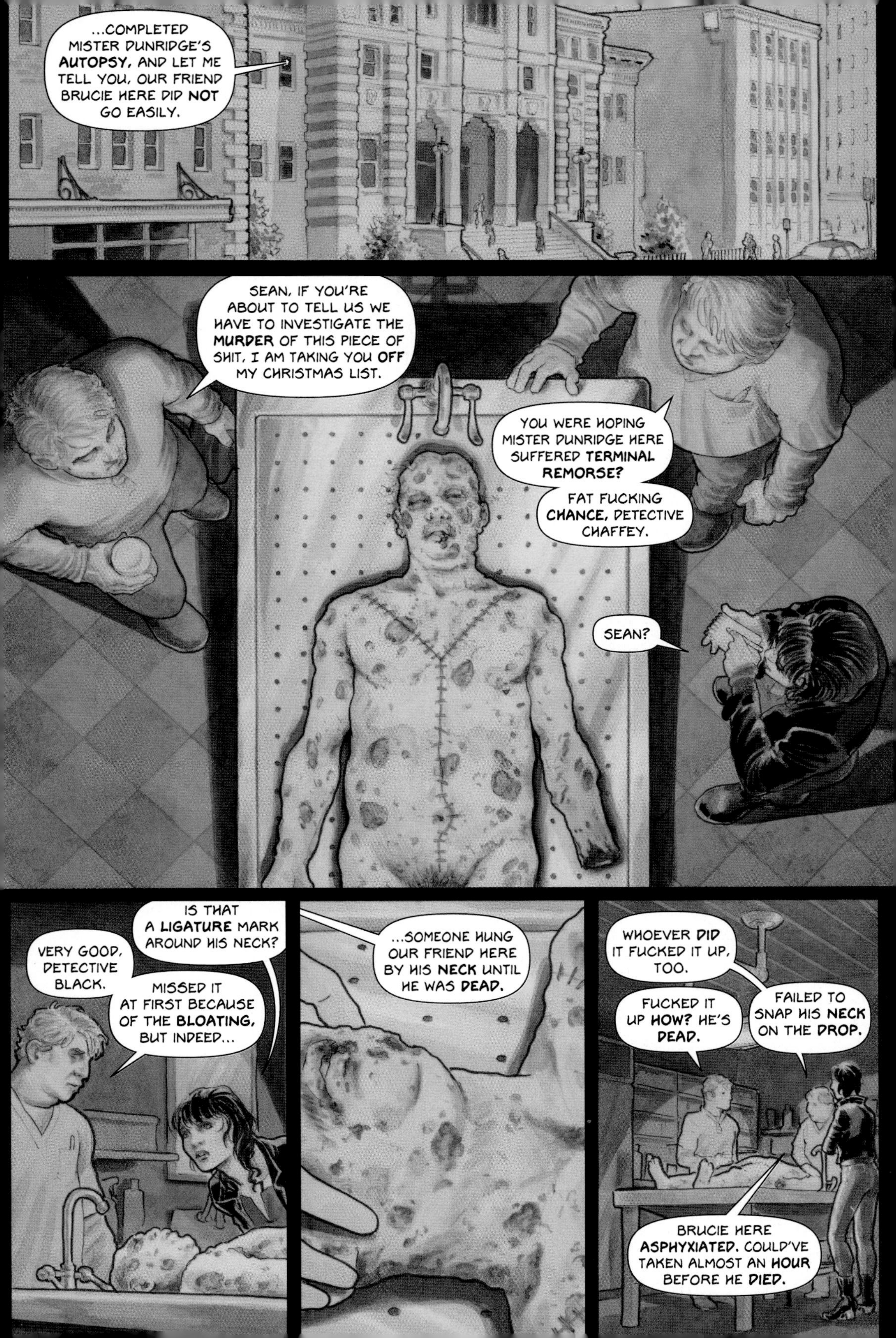
...COMPLETED MISTER DUNRIDGE'S AUTOPSY, AND LET ME TELL YOU, OUR FRIEND BRUCIE HERE DID NOT GO EASILY.
SEAN, IF YOU'RE ABOUT TO TELL US WE HAVE TO INVESTIGATE THE MURDER OF THIS PIECE OF SHIT, I AM TAKING YOU OFF MY CHRISTMAS LIST.
YOU WERE HOPING MISTER DUNRIDGE HERE SUFFERED TERMINAL REMORSE?
FAT FUCKING CHANCE, DETECTIVE CHAFFEY.
SEAN?
IS THAT A LIGATURE MARK AROUND HIS NECK?
VERY GOOD, DETECTIVE BLACK.
MISSED IT AT FIRST BECAUSE OF THE BLOATING, BUT INDEED...
...SOMEONE HUNG OUR FRIEND HERE BY HIS NECK UNTIL HE WAS DEAD.
WHOEVER DID IT FUCKED IT UP, TOO.
FUCKED IT UP HOW? HE'S DEAD.
FAILED TO SNAP HIS NECK ON THE DROP.
BRUCIE HERE ASPHYXIATED. COULD'VE TAKEN ALMOST AN HOUR BEFORE HE DIED.

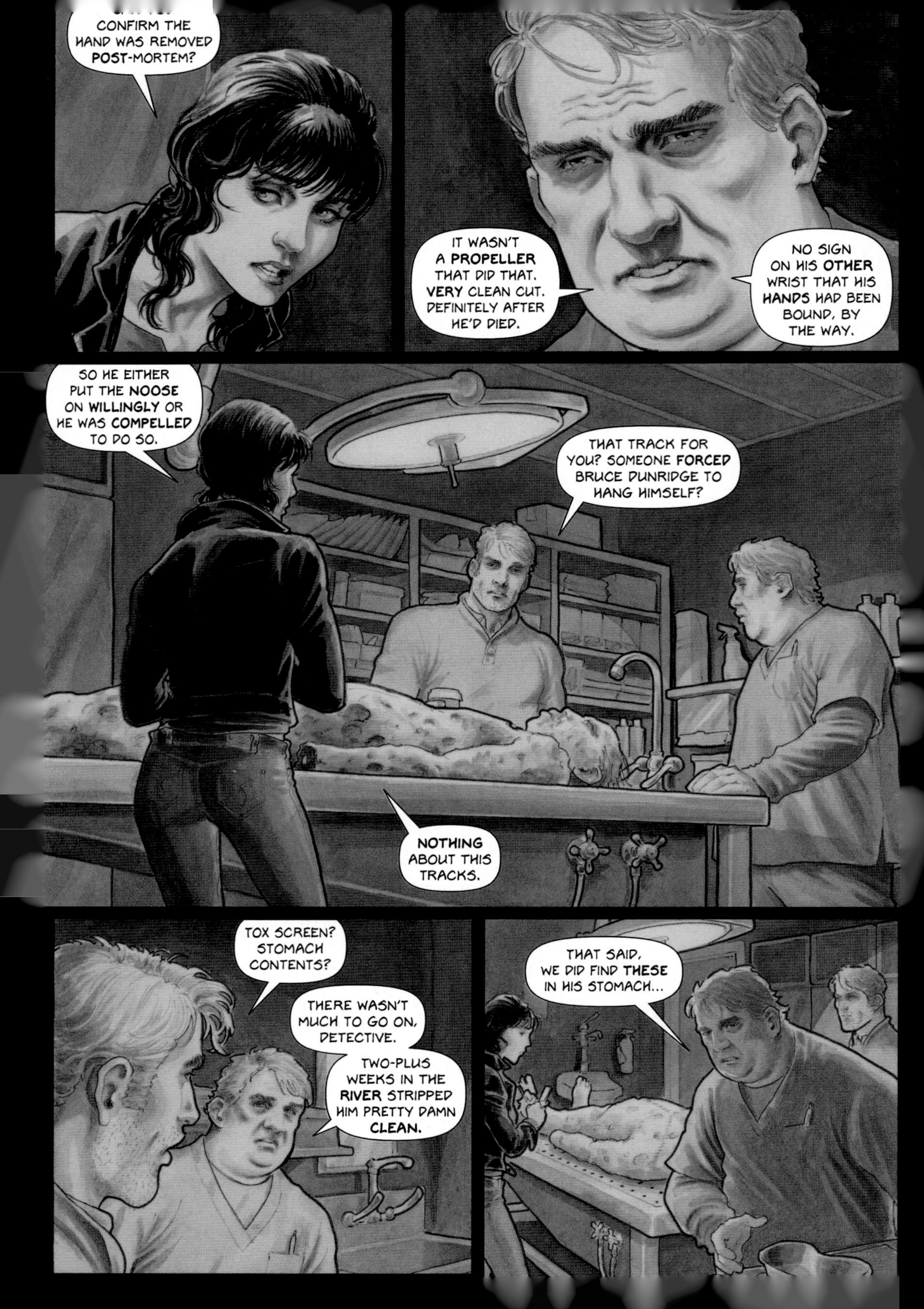
CONFIRM THE HAND WAS REMOVED POST-MORTEM?
IT WASN'T A PROPELLER THAT DID THAT. VERY CLEAN CUT. DEFINITELY AFTER HE'D DIED.
NO SIGN ON HIS OTHER WRIST THAT HIS HANDS HAD BEEN BOUND, BY THE WAY.
SO HE EITHER PUT THE NOOSE ON WILLINGLY OR HE WAS COMPELLED TO DO SO.
THAT TRACK FOR YOU? SOMEONE FORCED BRUCE DUNRIDGE TO HANG HIMSELF?
NOTHING ABOUT THIS TRACKS.
TOX SCREEN? STOMACH CONTENTS?
THERE WASN'T MUCH TO GO ON, DETECTIVE.
TWO-PLUS WEEKS IN THE RIVER STRIPPED HIM PRETTY DAMN CLEAN.
THAT SAID, WE DID FIND THESE IN HIS STOMACH...

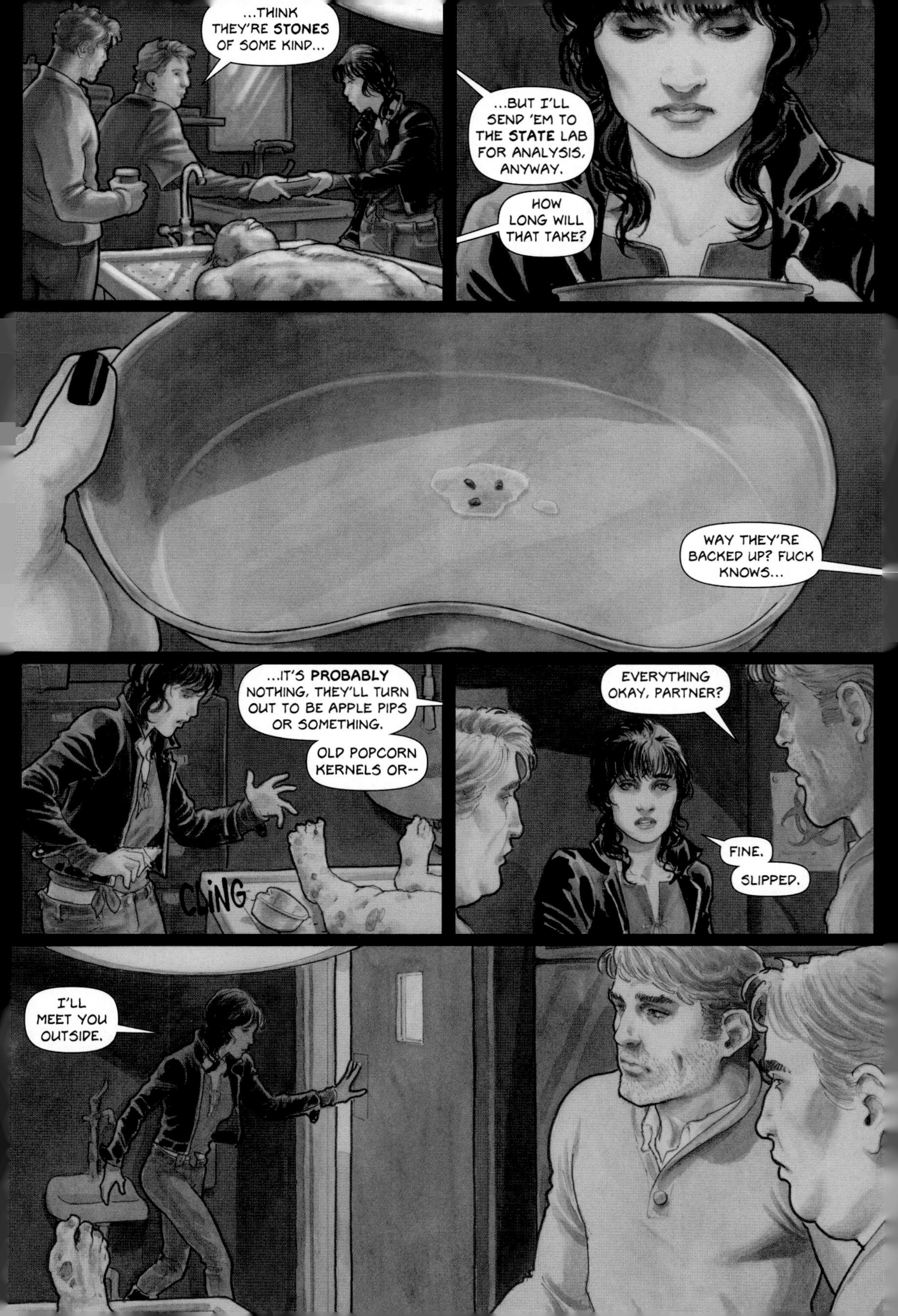
...THINK THEY'RE STONES OF SOME KIND...
...BUT I'LL SEND 'EM TO THE STATE LAB FOR ANALYSIS, ANYWAY.
HOW LONG WILL THAT TAKE?
WAY THEY'RE BACKED UP? FUCK KNOWS...
...IT'S PROBABLY NOTHING, THEY'LL TURN OUT TO BE APPLE PIPS OR SOMETHING.
OLD POPCORN KERNELS OR--
CLING
EVERYTHING OKAY, PARTNER?
FINE.
SLIPPED.
I'LL MEET YOU OUTSIDE.

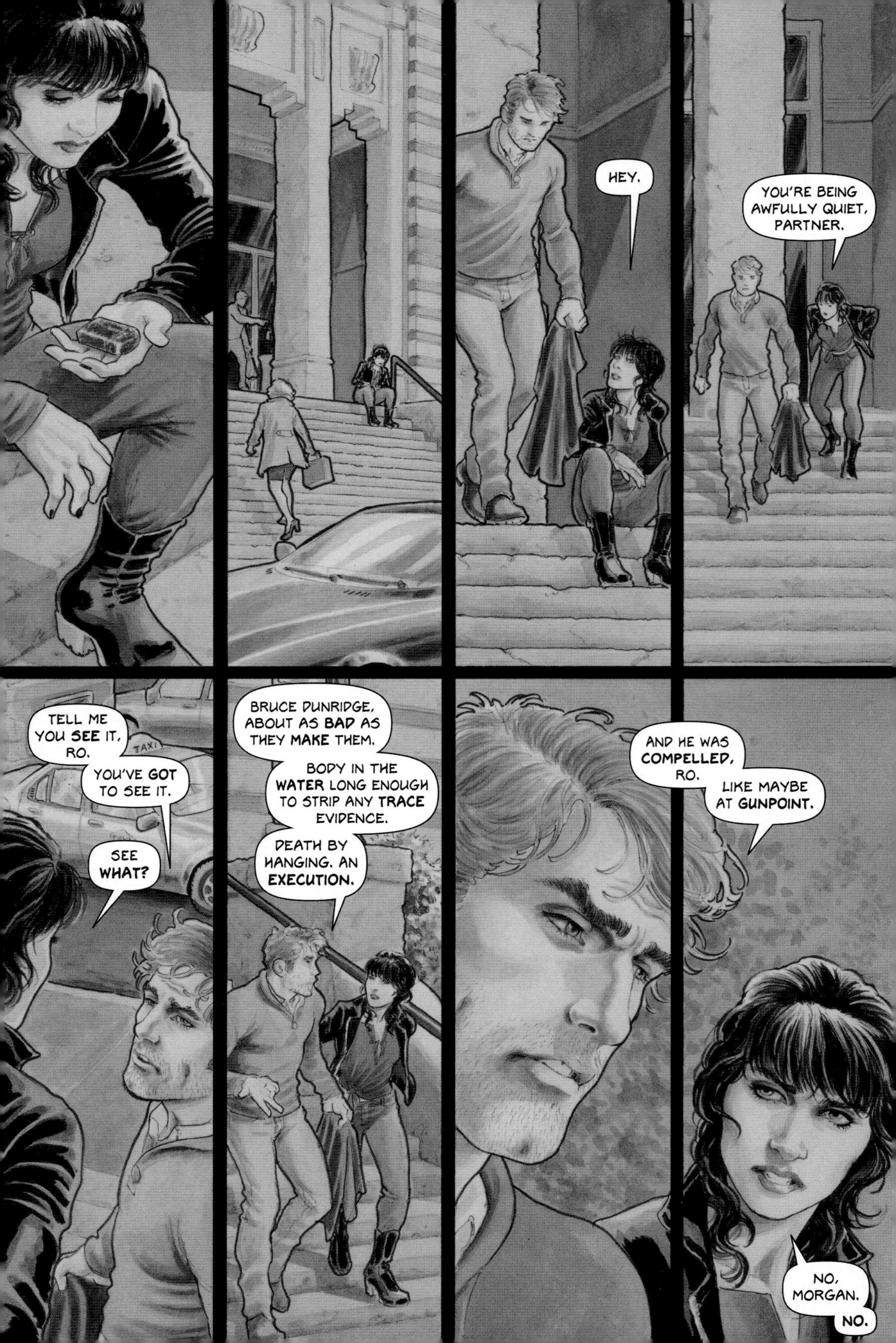
HEY.
YOU'RE BEING AWFULLY QUIET, PARTNER.
TELL ME YOU SEE IT, RO.
YOU'VE GOT TO SEE IT.
SEE WHAT?
BRUCE DUNRIDGE, ABOUT AS BAD AS THEY MAKE THEM.
BODY IN THE WATER LONG ENOUGH TO STRIP ANY TRACE EVIDENCE.
DEATH BY HANGING. AN EXECUTION.
AND HE WAS COMPELLED, RO.
LIKE MAYBE AT GUNPOINT.
NO, MORGAN.
NO.

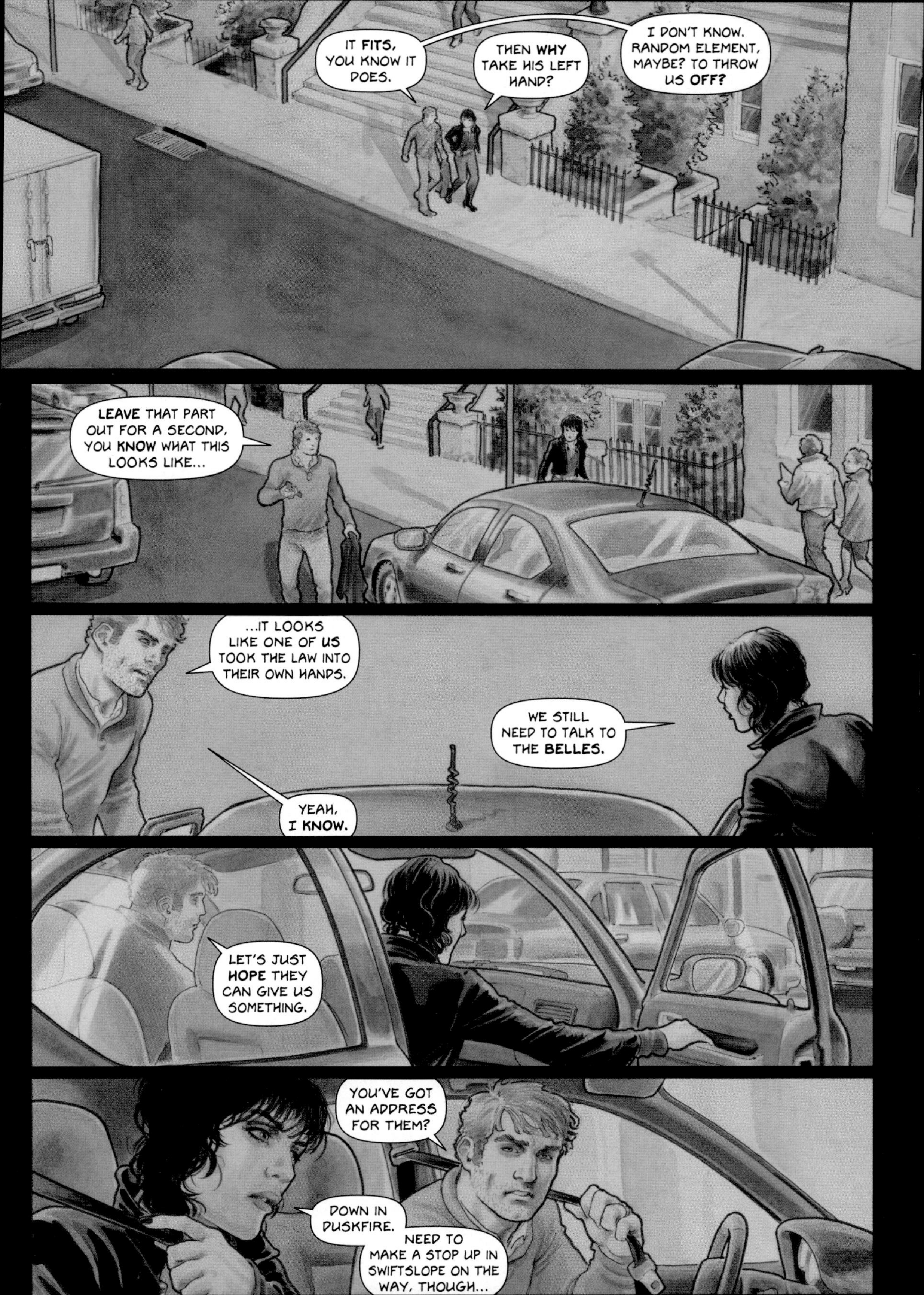
IT FITS, YOU KNOW IT DOES.
THEN WHY TAKE HIS LEFT HAND?
I DON'T KNOW. RANDOM ELEMENT, MAYBE? TO THROW US OFF?
LEAVE THAT PART OUT FOR A SECOND, YOU KNOW WHAT THIS LOOKS LIKE...
...IT LOOKS LIKE ONE OF US TOOK THE LAW INTO THEIR OWN HANDS.
WE STILL NEED TO TALK TO THE BELLES.
YEAH, I KNOW.
LET'S JUST HOPE THEY CAN GIVE US SOMETHING.
YOU'VE GOT AN ADDRESS FOR THEM?
DOWN IN DUSKFIRE.
NEED TO MAKE A STOP UP IN SWIFTSLOPE ON THE WAY, THOUGH...

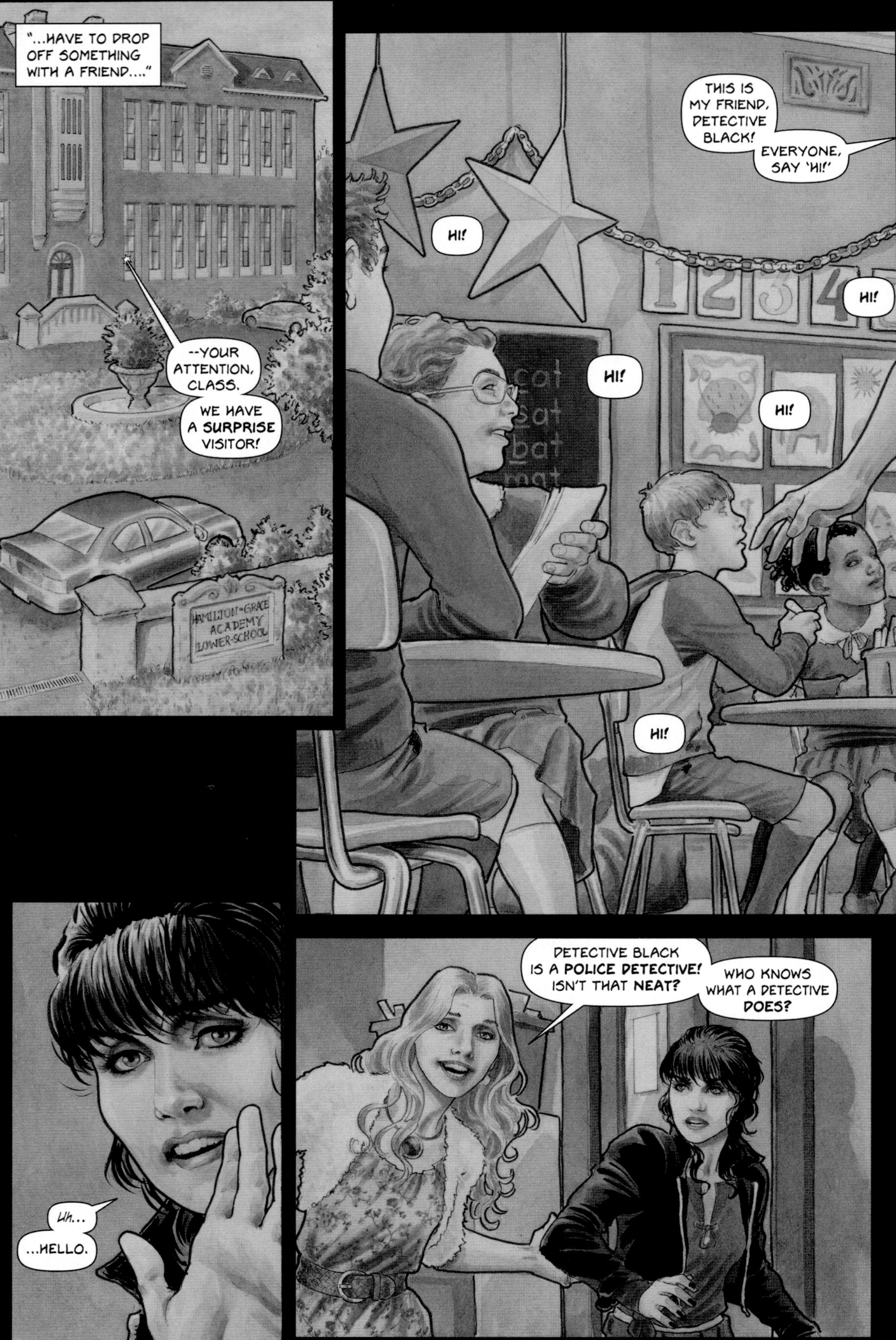
"...HAVE TO DROP OFF SOMETHING WITH A FRIEND...."
--YOUR ATTENTION, CLASS.
WE HAVE A **SURPRISE** VISITOR!
HAMILTON-GRACE ACADEMY LOWER-SCHOOL
THIS IS MY FRIEND, DETECTIVE BLACK!
EVERYONE, SAY 'HI!'
HI!
HI!
HI!
HI!
HI!
cat
sat
bat
Uh...
...HELLO.
DETECTIVE BLACK IS A **POLICE DETECTIVE!** ISN'T THAT **NEAT?**
WHO KNOWS WHAT A DETECTIVE **DOES?**

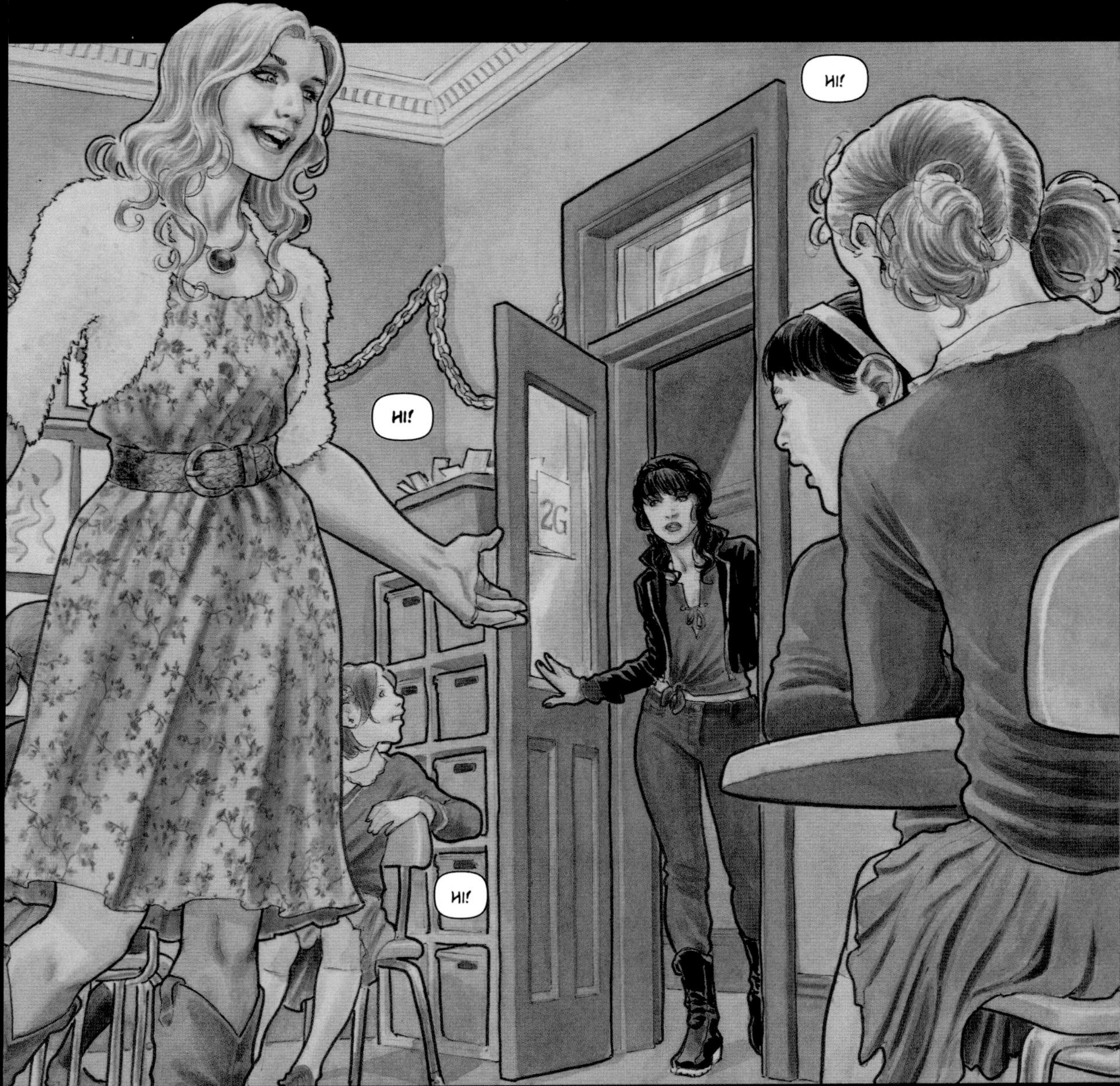
HI!
HI!
HI!

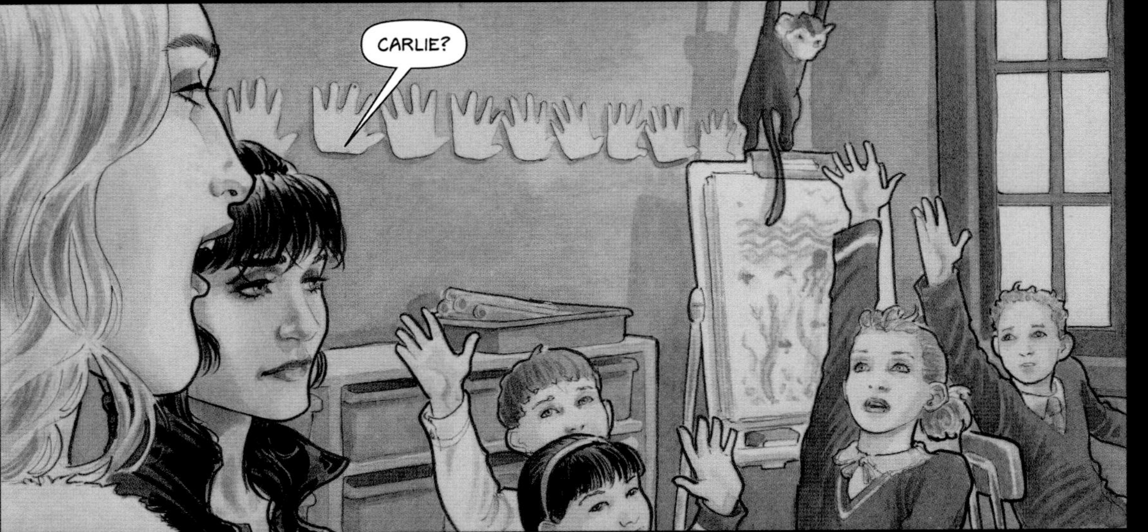
CARLIE?

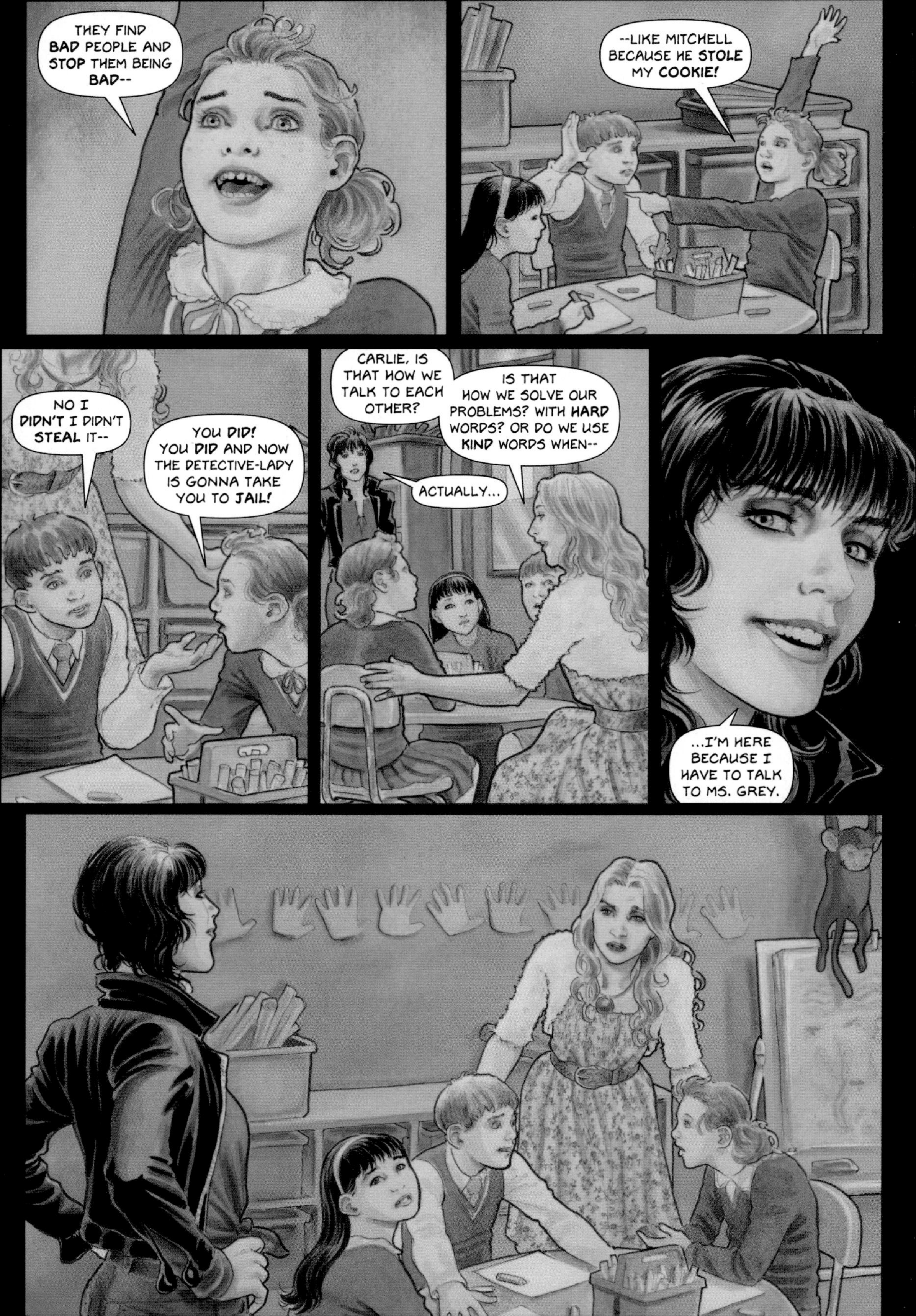
THEY FIND BAD PEOPLE AND STOP THEM BEING BAD--
--LIKE MITCHELL BECAUSE HE STOLE MY COOKIE!
NO I DIDN'T I DIDN'T STEAL IT--
YOU DID! YOU DID AND NOW THE DETECTIVE-LADY IS GONNA TAKE YOU TO JAIL!
CARLIE, IS THAT HOW WE TALK TO EACH OTHER?
IS THAT HOW WE SOLVE OUR PROBLEMS? WITH HARD WORDS? OR DO WE USE KIND WORDS WHEN--
ACTUALLY...
...I'M HERE BECAUSE I HAVE TO TALK TO MS. GREY.

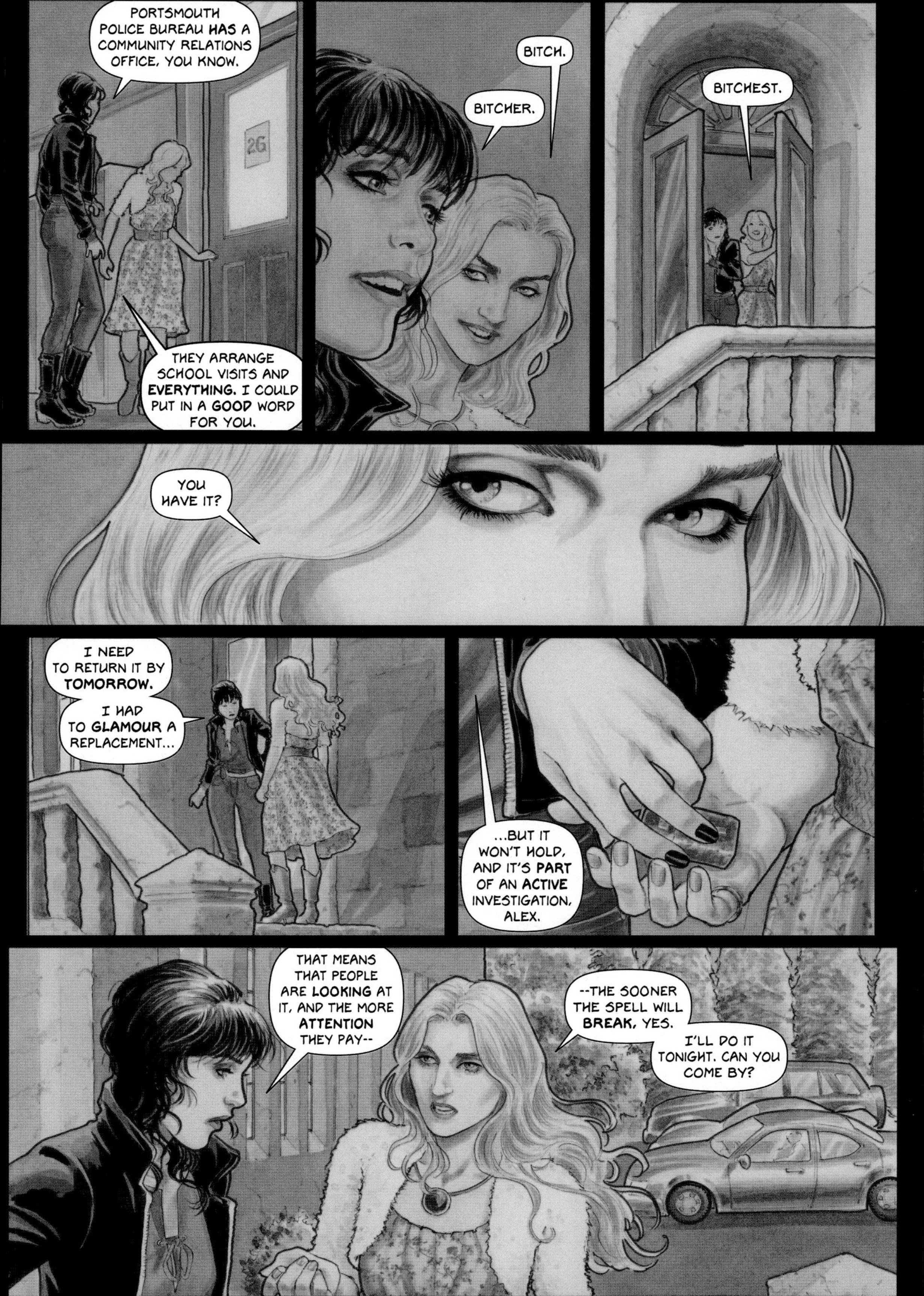
PORTSMOUTH POLICE BUREAU HAS A COMMUNITY RELATIONS OFFICE, YOU KNOW.
2G
THEY ARRANGE SCHOOL VISITS AND EVERYTHING. I COULD PUT IN A GOOD WORD FOR YOU.
BITCH.
BITCHER.
BITCHEST.
YOU HAVE IT?
I NEED TO RETURN IT BY TOMORROW.
I HAD TO GLAMOUR A REPLACEMENT...
...BUT IT WON'T HOLD, AND IT'S PART OF AN ACTIVE INVESTIGATION, ALEX.
THAT MEANS THAT PEOPLE ARE LOOKING AT IT, AND THE MORE ATTENTION THEY PAY--
--THE SOONER THE SPELL WILL BREAK, YES.
I'LL DO IT TONIGHT. CAN YOU COME BY?

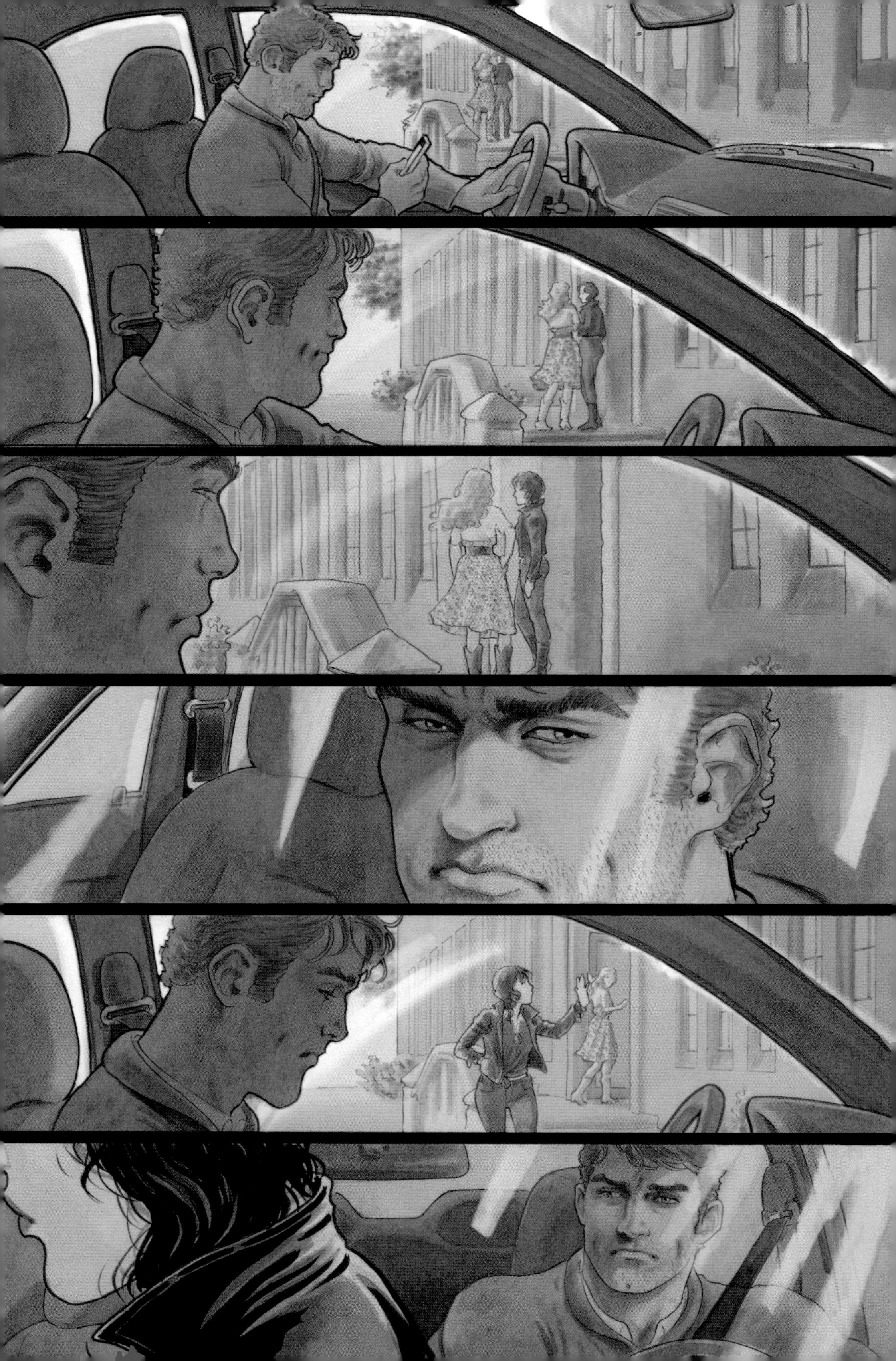

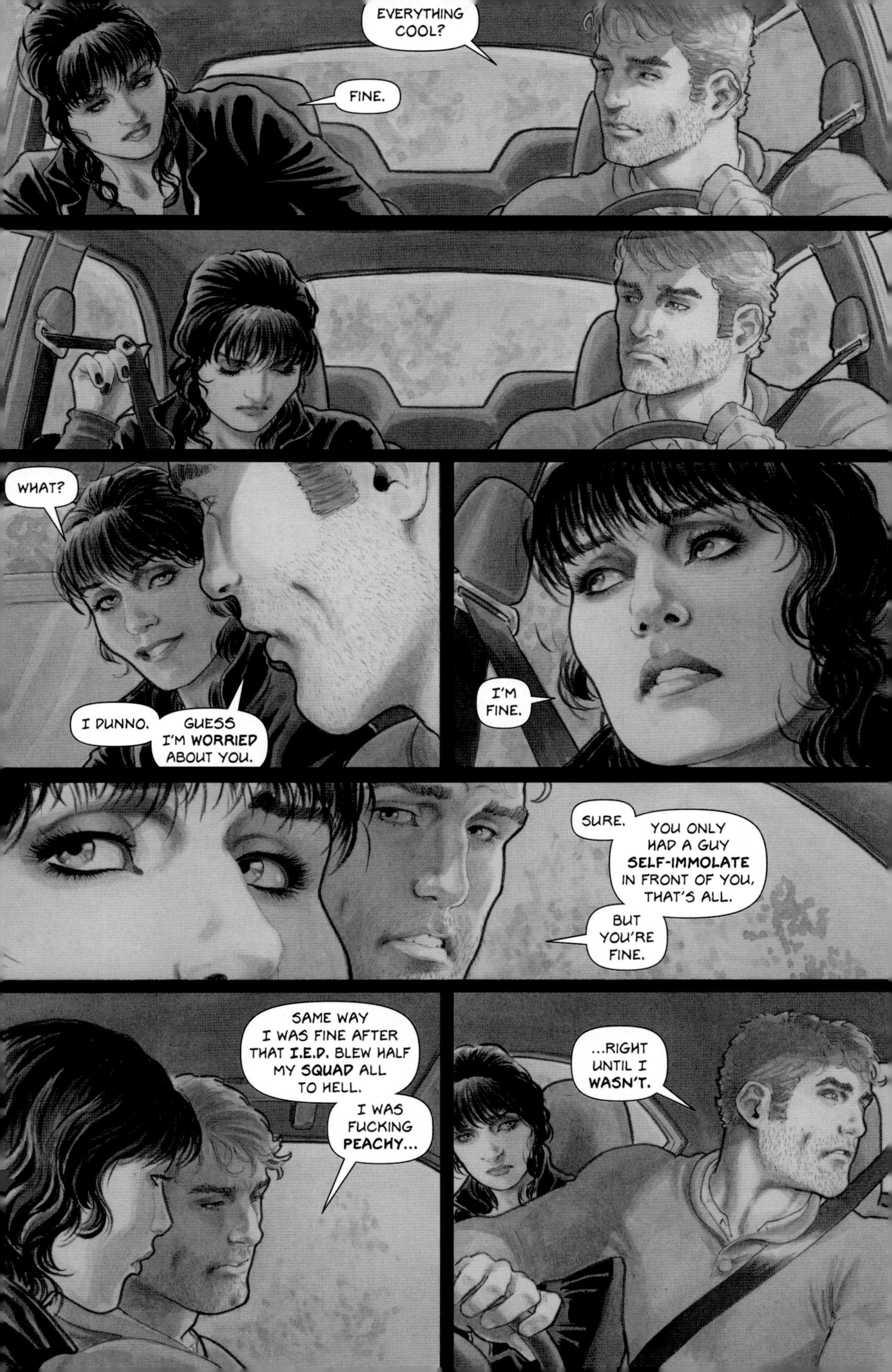
EVERYTHING COOL?
FINE.
WHAT?
I DUNNO.
GUESS I'M **WORRIED** ABOUT YOU.
I'M FINE.
SURE.
YOU ONLY HAD A GUY **SELF-IMMOLATE** IN FRONT OF YOU, THAT'S ALL.
BUT YOU'RE FINE.
SAME WAY I WAS FINE AFTER THAT **I.E.D.** BLEW HALF MY **SQUAD** ALL TO HELL.
I WAS FUCKING **PEACHY**...
...RIGHT UNTIL I **WASN'T.**

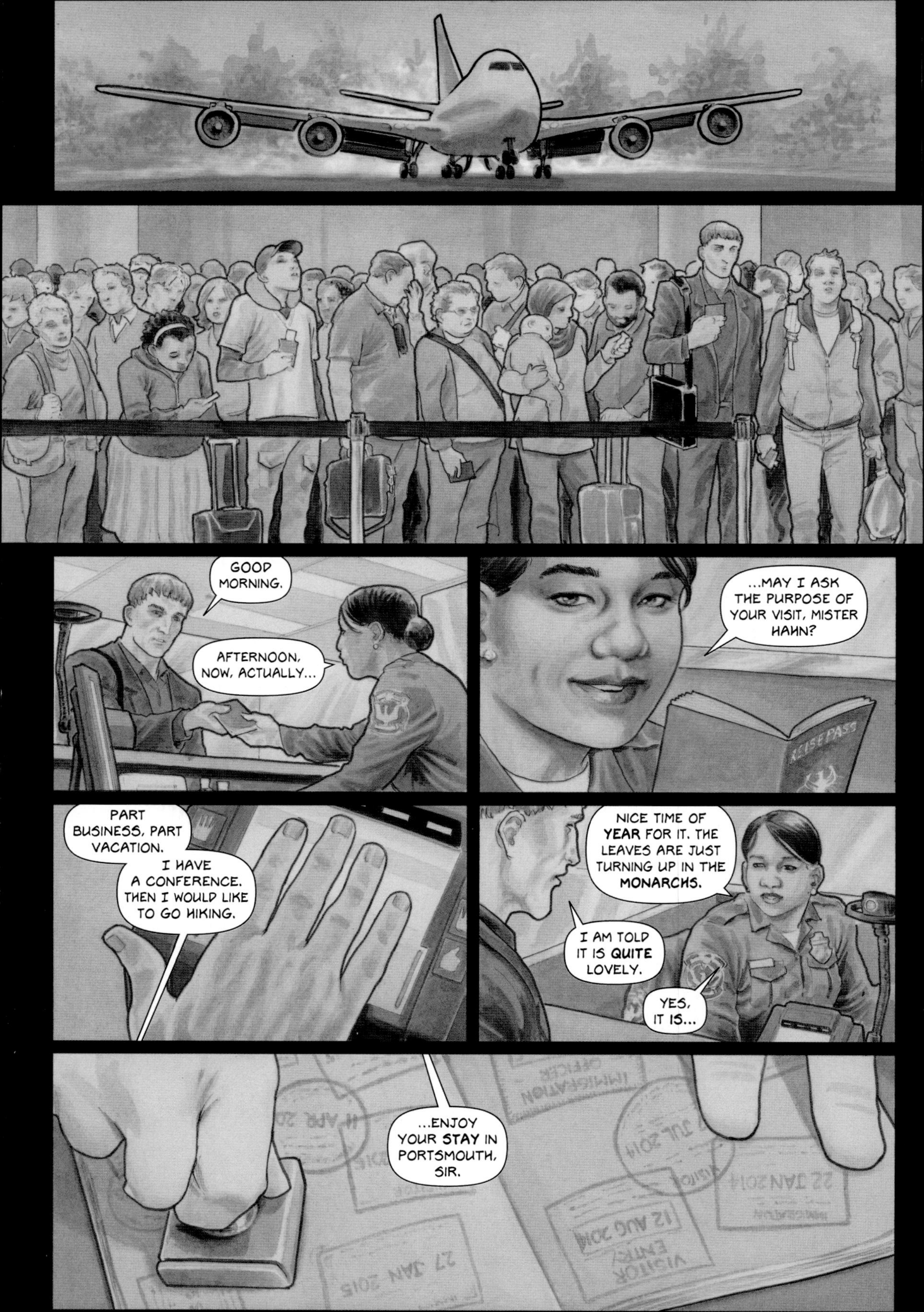
GOOD MORNING.
AFTERNOON, NOW, ACTUALLY...
...MAY I ASK THE PURPOSE OF YOUR VISIT, MISTER HAHN?
REISEPASS
PART BUSINESS, PART VACATION.
I HAVE A CONFERENCE. THEN I WOULD LIKE TO GO HIKING.
NICE TIME OF YEAR FOR IT. THE LEAVES ARE JUST TURNING UP IN THE MONARCHS.
I AM TOLD IT IS QUITE LOVELY.
YES, IT IS...
...ENJOY YOUR STAY IN PORTSMOUTH, SIR.
IMMIGRATION OFFICER
VISITOR ENTRY
12 AUG 2014
27 JAN 2015
22 JAN 2014

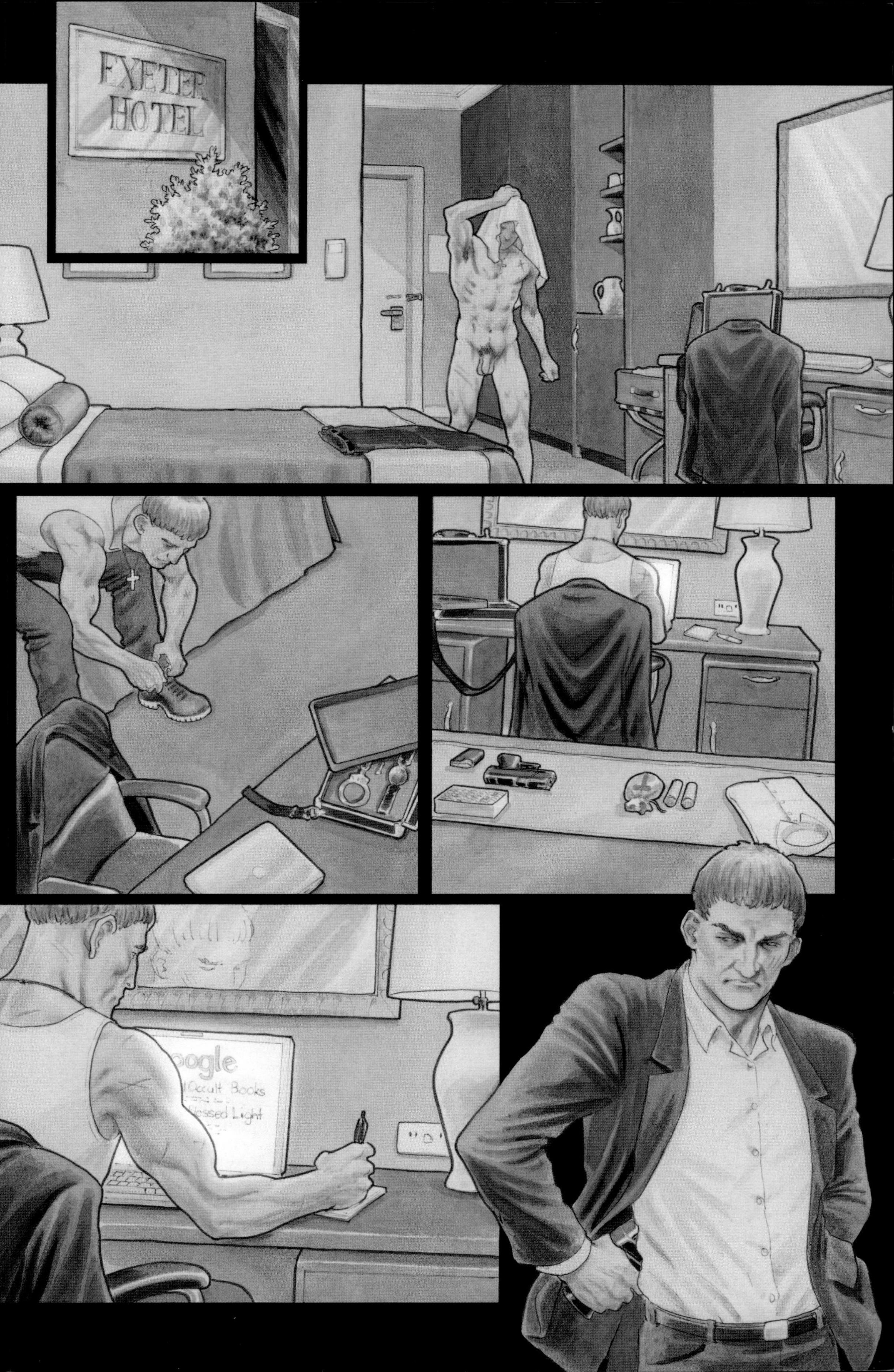
EXETER HOTEL
oogle
Occult Books
lessed Light

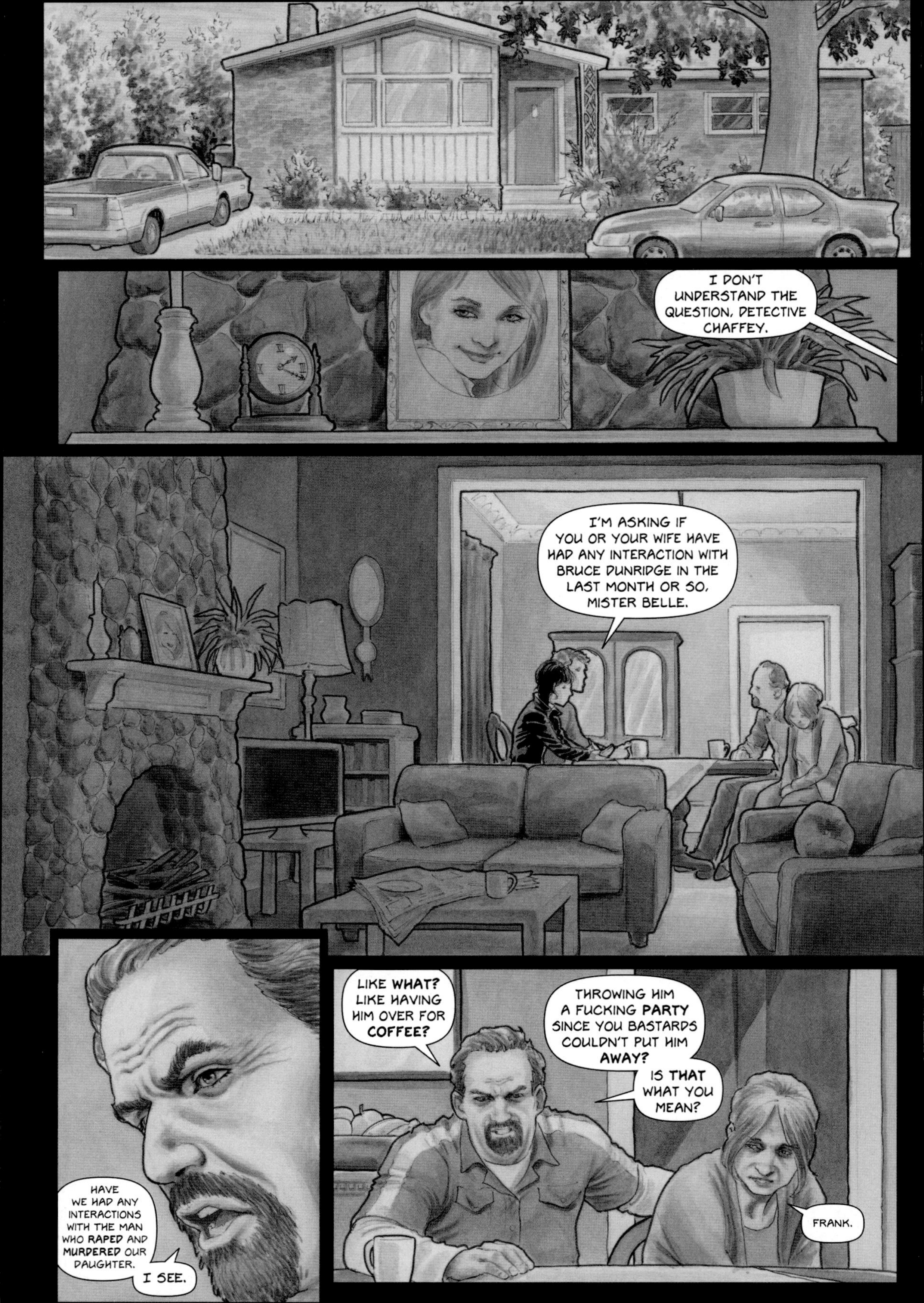
I DON'T UNDERSTAND THE QUESTION, DETECTIVE CHAFFEY.
I'M ASKING IF YOU OR YOUR WIFE HAVE HAD ANY INTERACTION WITH BRUCE DUNRIDGE IN THE LAST MONTH OR SO, MISTER BELLE.
HAVE WE HAD ANY INTERACTIONS WITH THE MAN WHO RAPED AND MURDERED OUR DAUGHTER.
I SEE.
LIKE WHAT? LIKE HAVING HIM OVER FOR COFFEE?
THROWING HIM A FUCKING PARTY SINCE YOU BASTARDS COULDN'T PUT HIM AWAY?
IS THAT WHAT YOU MEAN?
FRANK.

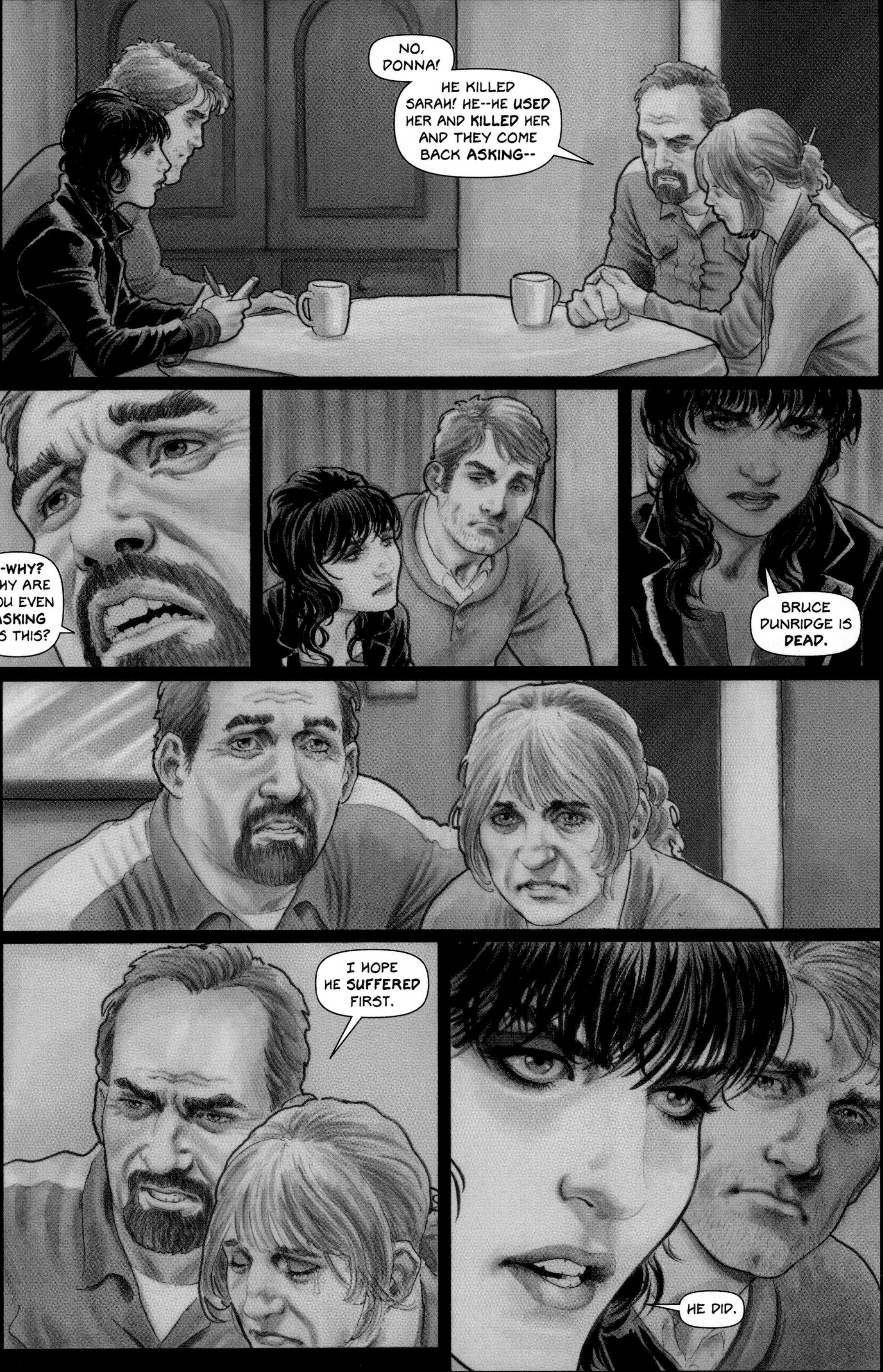
NO, DONNA!
HE KILLED SARAH! HE--HE USED HER AND KILLED HER AND THEY COME BACK ASKING--
--WHY? WHY ARE YOU EVEN ASKING US THIS?
BRUCE DUNRIDGE IS DEAD.
I HOPE HE SUFFERED FIRST.
HE DID.

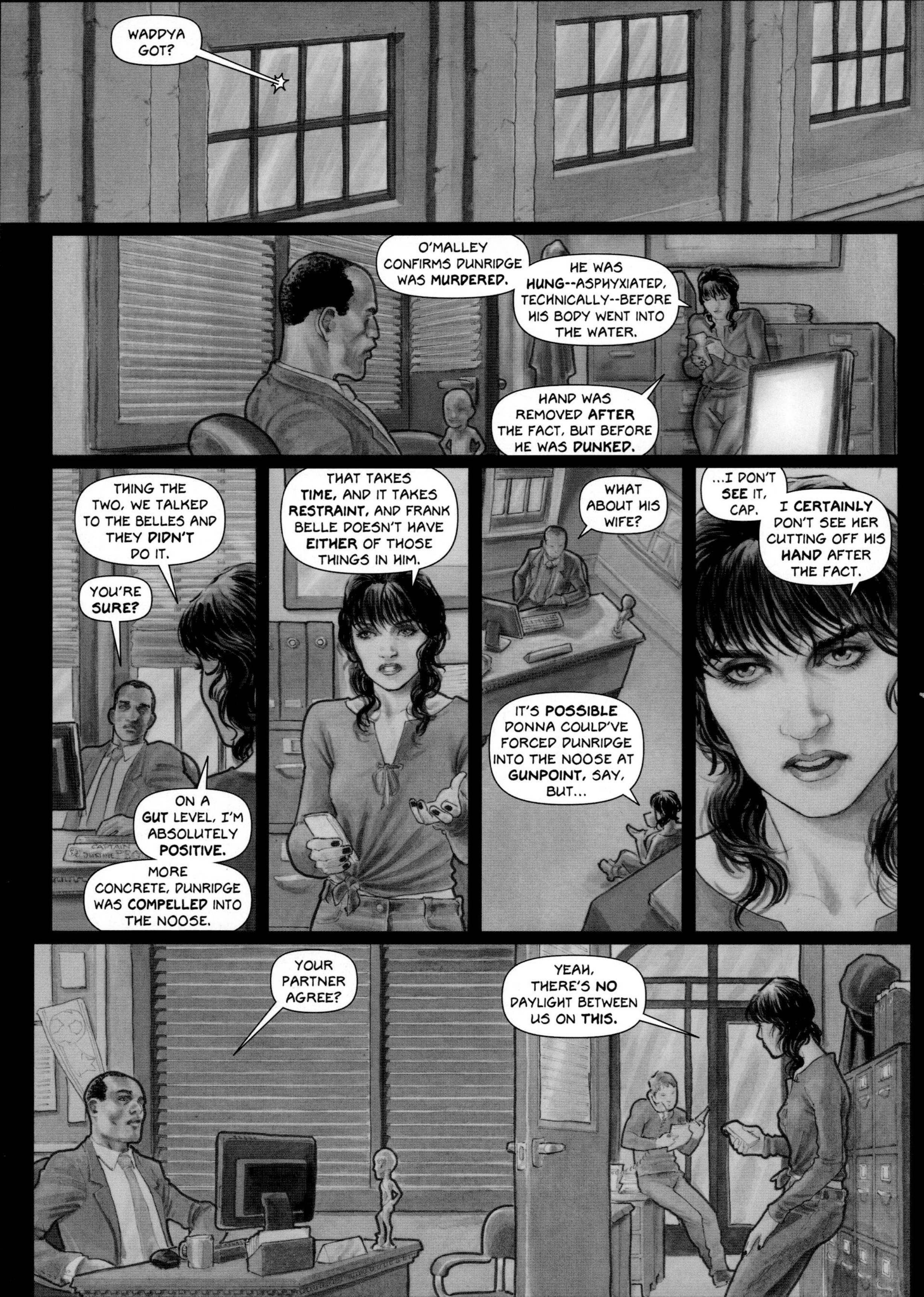
WADDYA GOT?
O'MALLEY CONFIRMS DUNRIDGE WAS **MURDERED.**
HE WAS **HUNG**--ASPHYXIATED, TECHNICALLY--BEFORE HIS BODY WENT INTO THE WATER.
HAND WAS REMOVED **AFTER** THE FACT, BUT BEFORE HE WAS **DUNKED.**
THING THE TWO, WE TALKED TO THE BELLES AND THEY **DIDN'T** DO IT.
YOU'RE **SURE?**
ON A **GUT** LEVEL, I'M ABSOLUTELY **POSITIVE.**
MORE CONCRETE, DUNRIDGE WAS **COMPELLED** INTO THE NOOSE.
THAT TAKES **TIME,** AND IT TAKES **RESTRAINT,** AND FRANK BELLE DOESN'T HAVE **EITHER** OF THOSE THINGS IN HIM.
WHAT ABOUT HIS WIFE?
IT'S **POSSIBLE** DONNA COULD'VE FORCED DUNRIDGE INTO THE NOOSE AT **GUNPOINT,** SAY, BUT...
...I DON'T **SEE** IT, CAP.
I CERTAINLY DON'T SEE HER CUTTING OFF HIS **HAND** AFTER THE FACT.
YOUR PARTNER AGREE?
YEAH, THERE'S **NO** DAYLIGHT BETWEEN US ON **THIS.**

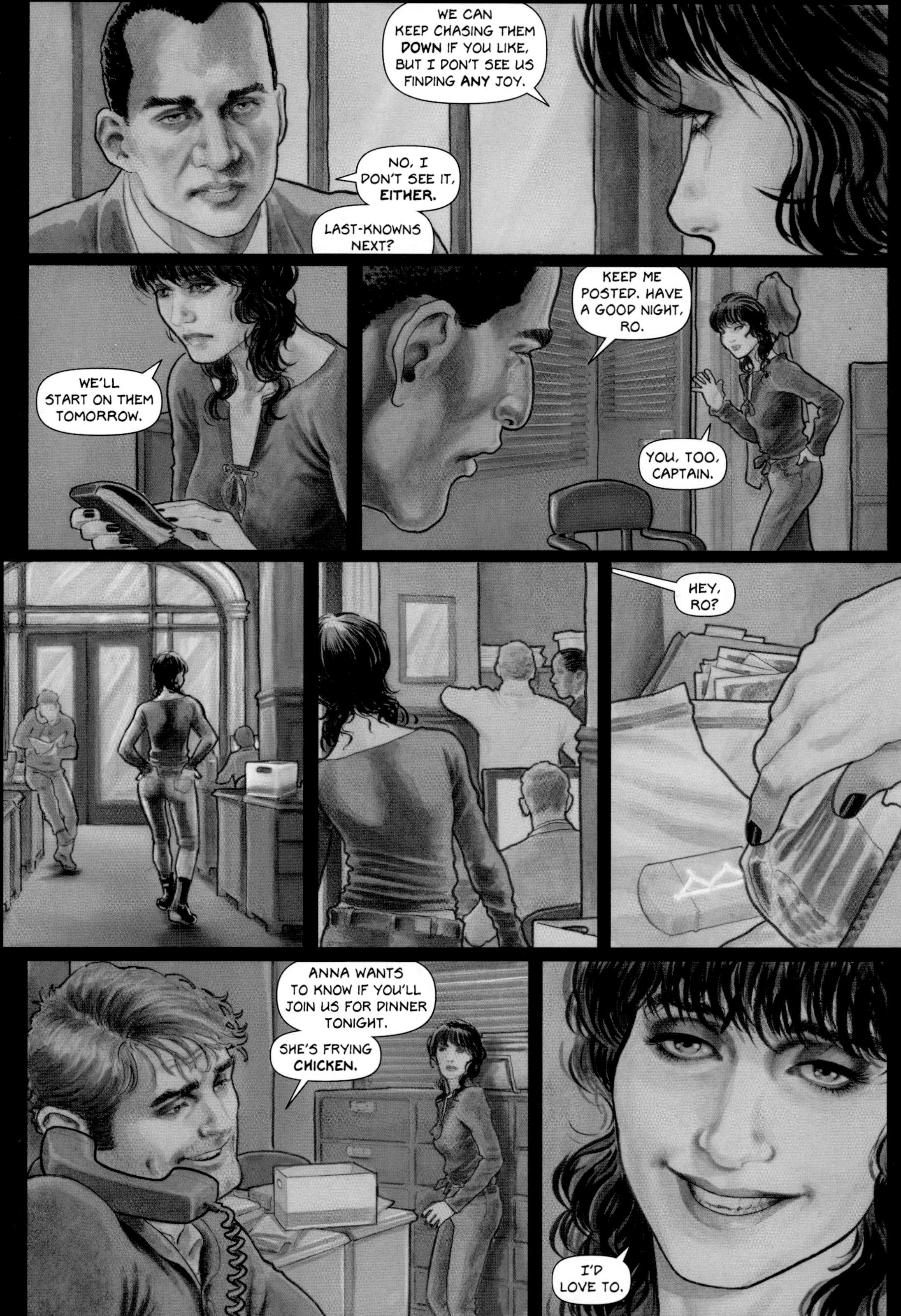
WE CAN KEEP CHASING THEM DOWN IF YOU LIKE, BUT I DON'T SEE US FINDING ANY JOY.
NO, I DON'T SEE IT, EITHER.
LAST-KNOWNS NEXT?
WE'LL START ON THEM TOMORROW.
KEEP ME POSTED. HAVE A GOOD NIGHT, RO.
YOU, TOO, CAPTAIN.
HEY, RO?
ANNA WANTS TO KNOW IF YOU'LL JOIN US FOR DINNER TONIGHT.
SHE'S FRYING CHICKEN.
I'D LOVE TO.

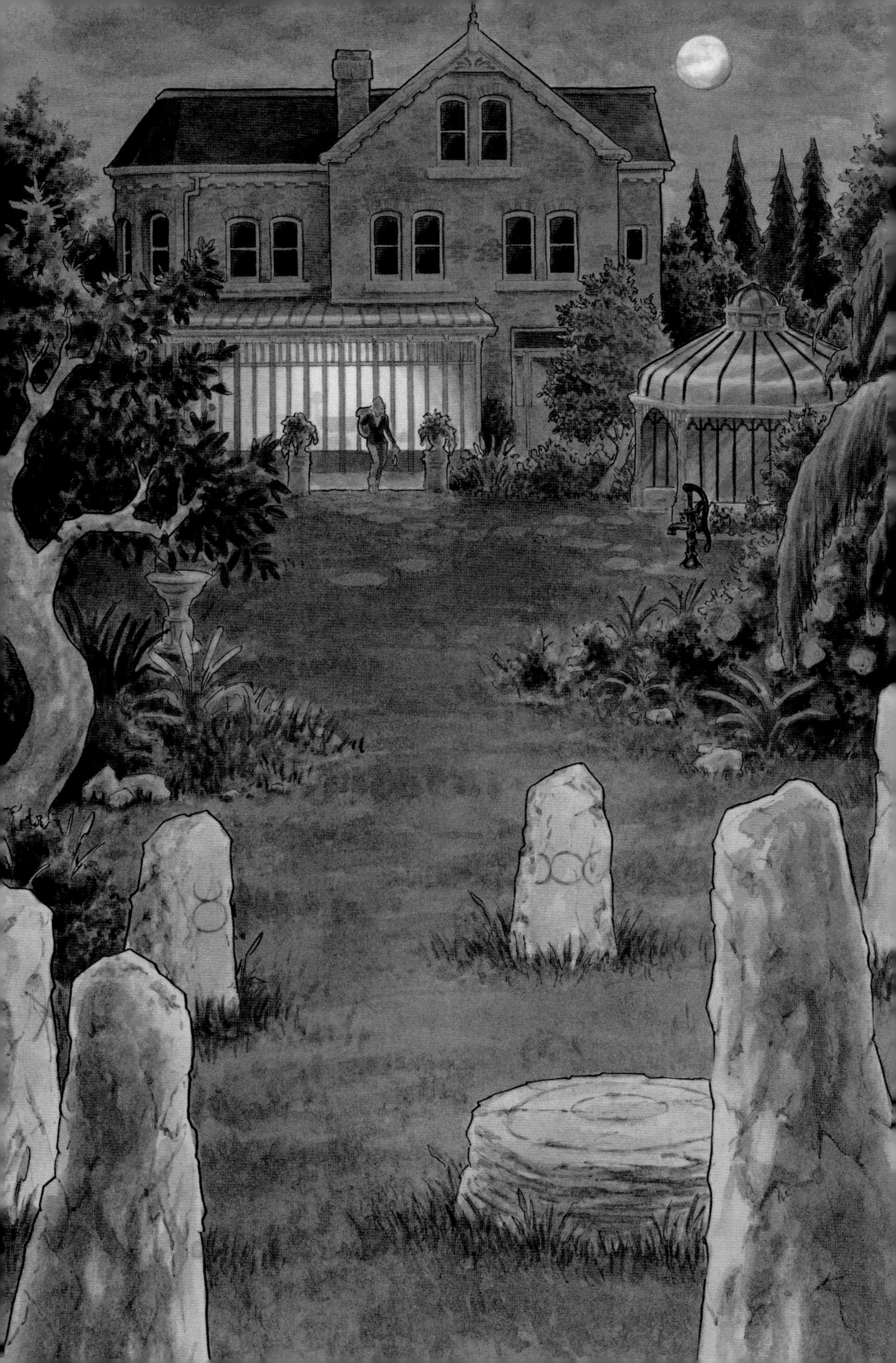

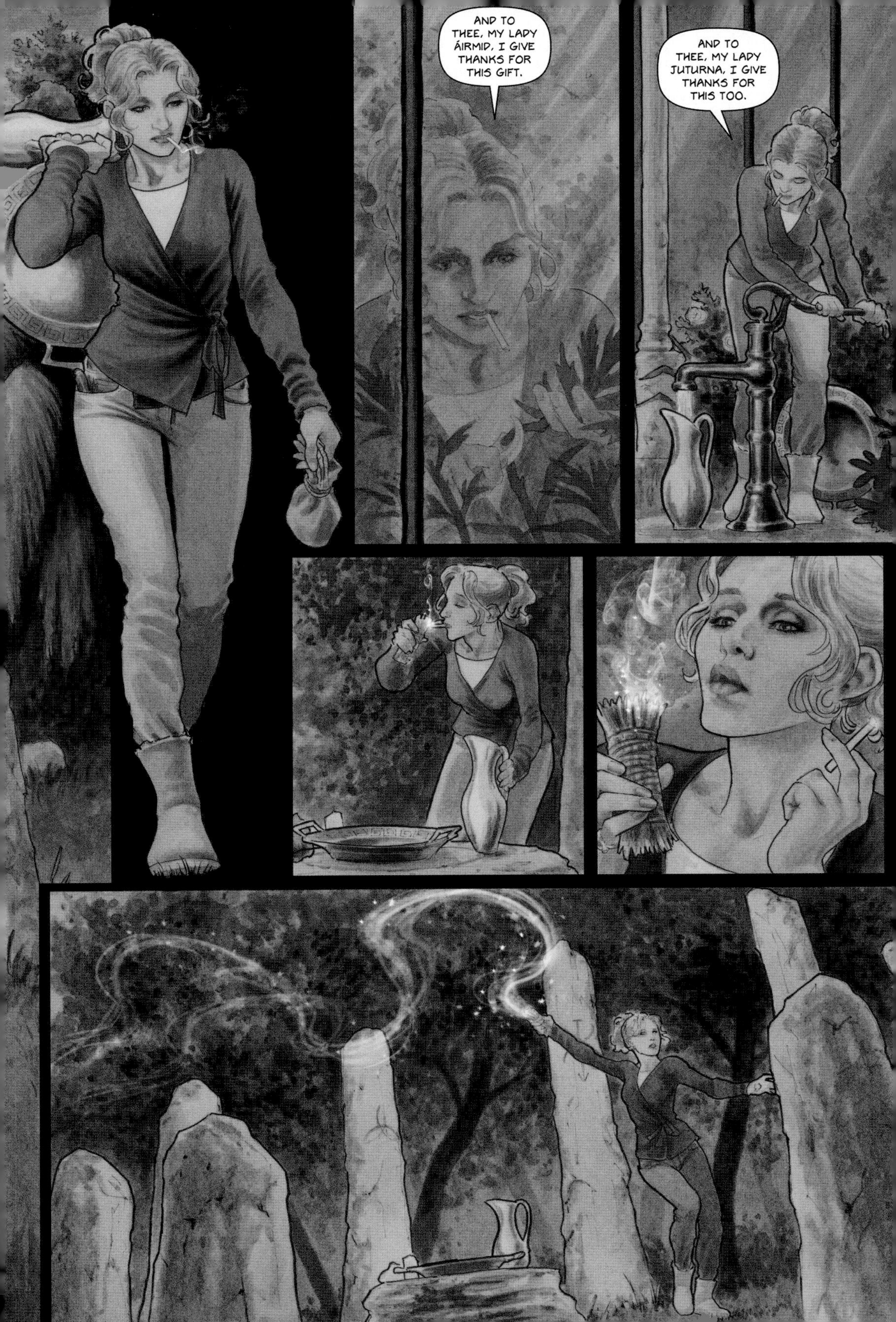
AND TO THEE, MY LADY ÁIRMID, I GIVE THANKS FOR THIS GIFT.
AND TO THEE, MY LADY JUTURNA, I GIVE THANKS FOR THIS TOO.

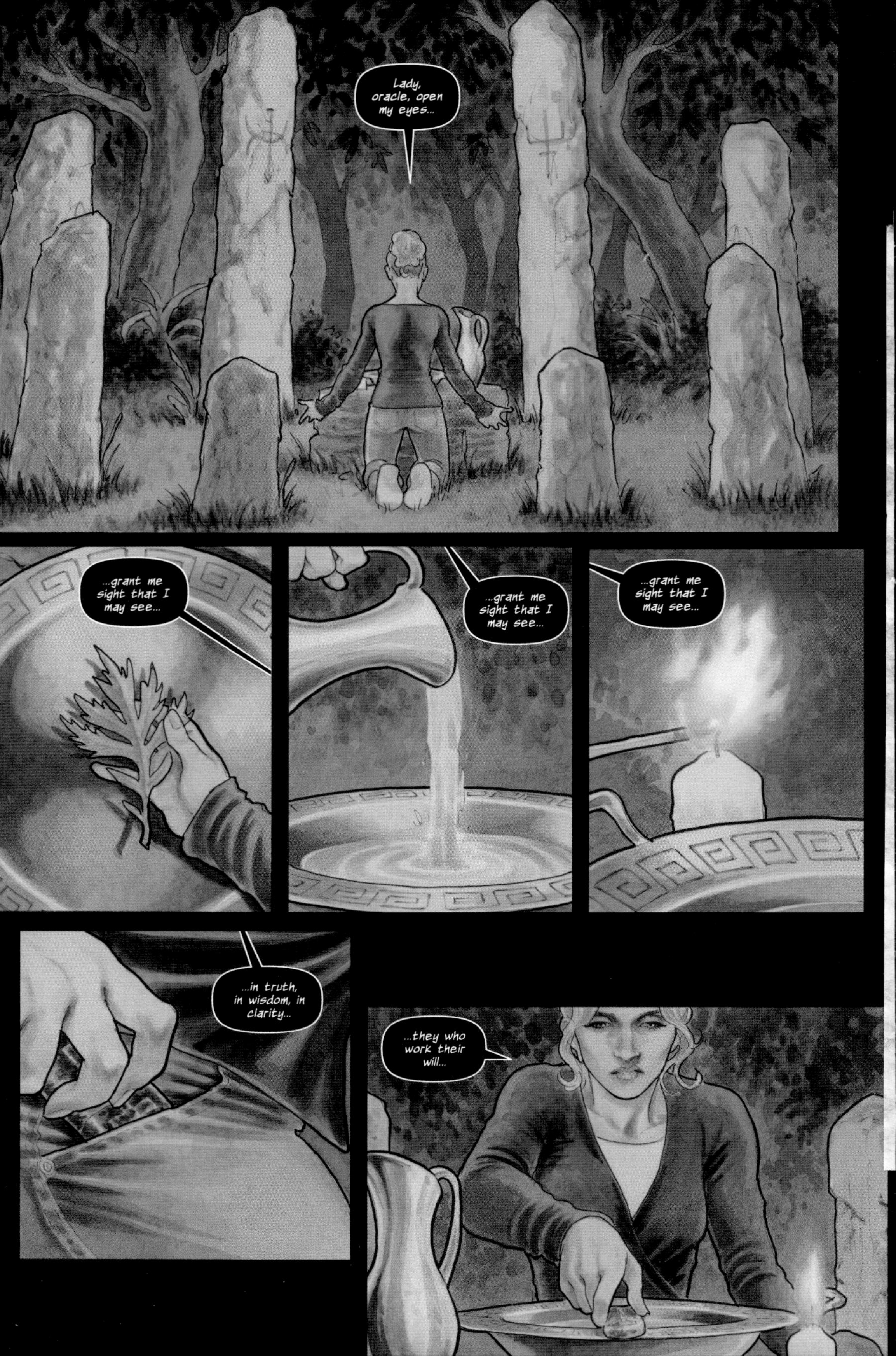
Lady, oracle, open my eyes...
...grant me sight that I may see...
...grant me sight that I may see...
...grant me sight that I may see...
...in truth, in wisdom, in clarity...
...they who work their will...

...against my sister, my mother, my daughter...

...against my bride, my lover, my husband...

...by my will...

...grant me sight...

...so mote it be.

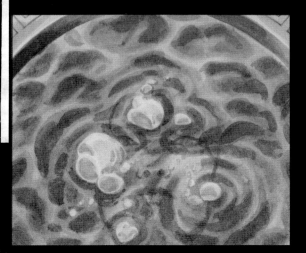

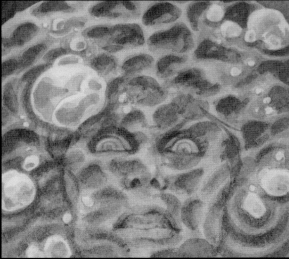

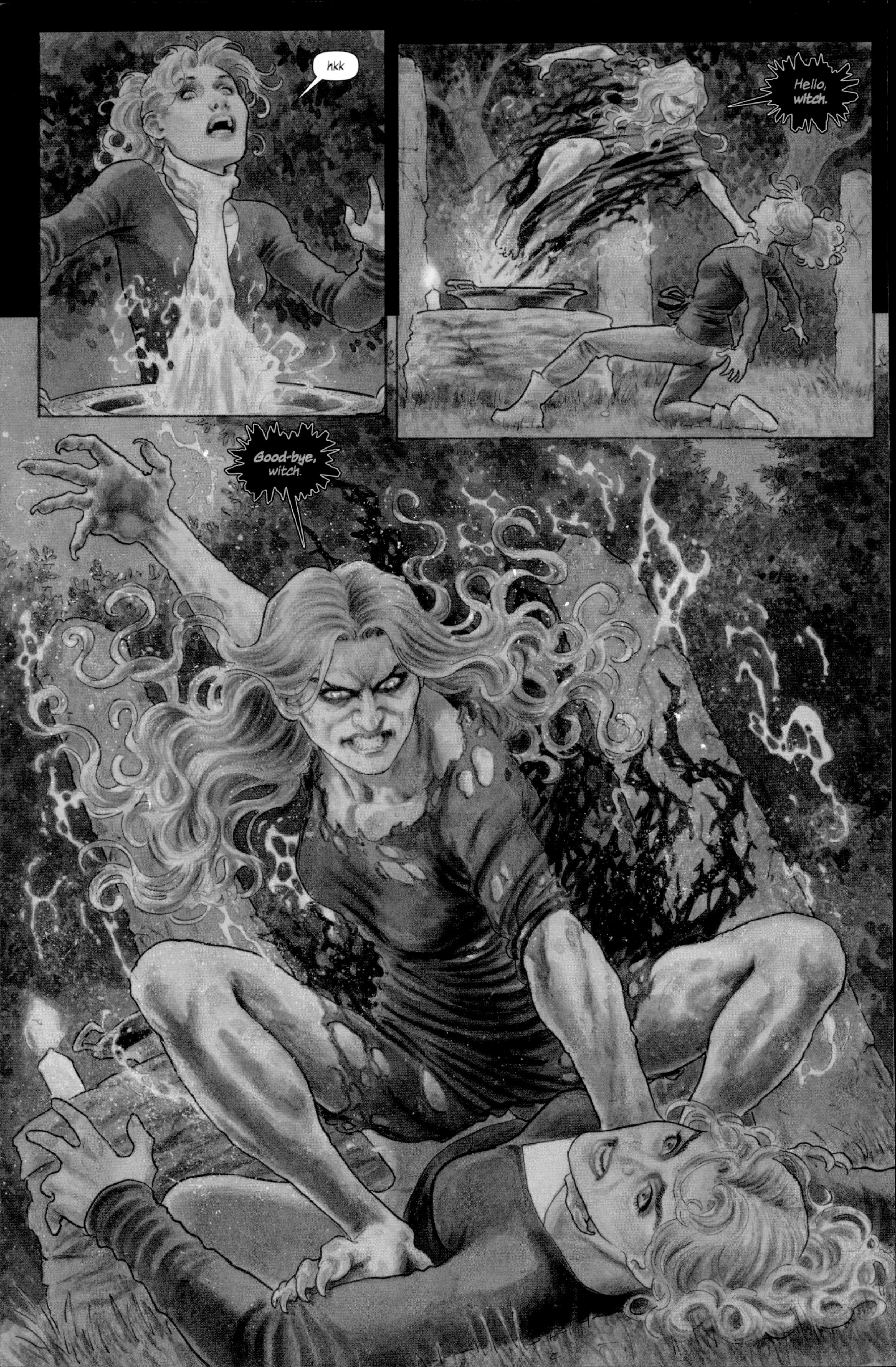
hkk
Hello, witch.
Good-bye, witch.

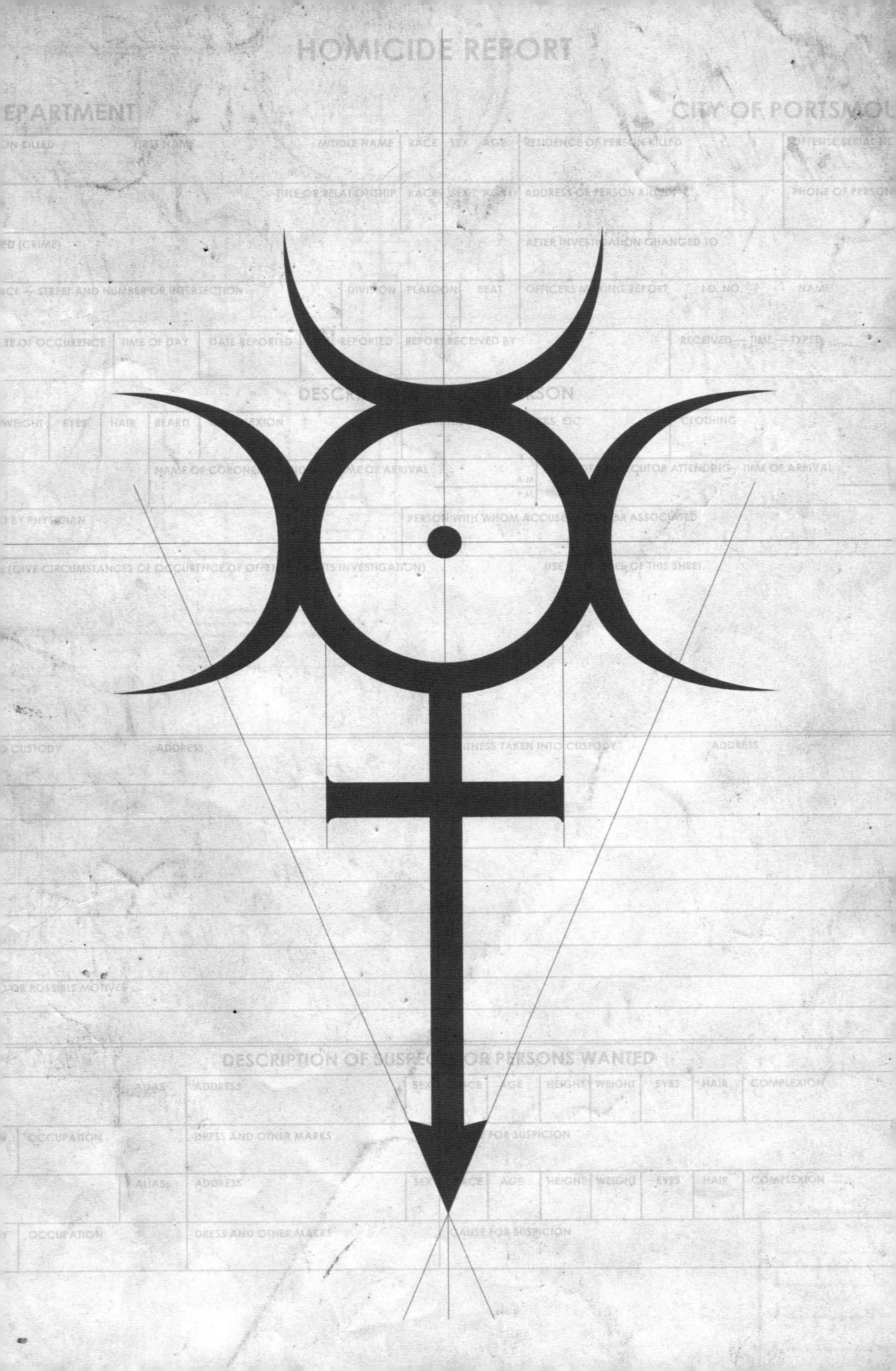
HOMICIDE REPORT
EPARTMENT
FIRST NAME
MIDDLE NAME
RACE
SEX
AGE
RESIDENCE OF PERSON KILLED
TITLE OR RELATIONSHIP
AFTER INVESTIGATION CHANGED TO
DIVISION
PLATOON
BEAT
I.D. NO.
NAME
TIME OF DAY
DATE REPORTED
RECEIVED — TIME — TYPED
WEIGHT
EYES
HAIR
BEARD
CLOTHING
A.M.
P.M.
ADDRESS
WITNESS TAKEN INTO CUSTODY
ALIAS
ADDRESS
HEIGHT
WEIGHT
EYES
HAIR
COMPLEXION
OCCUPATION
DRESS AND OTHER MARKS

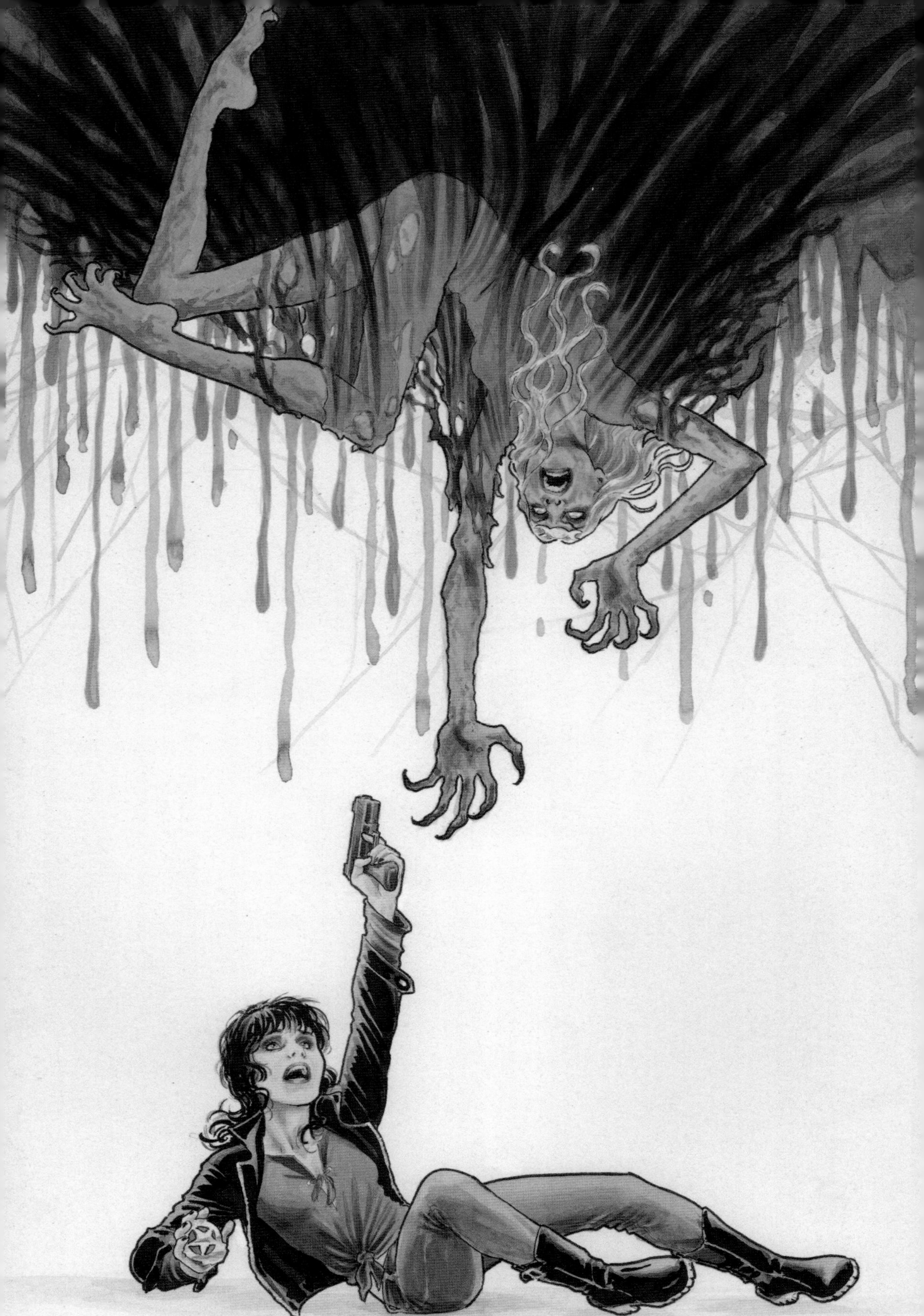
Issue 005 “A” Cover by **NICOLA SCOTT**

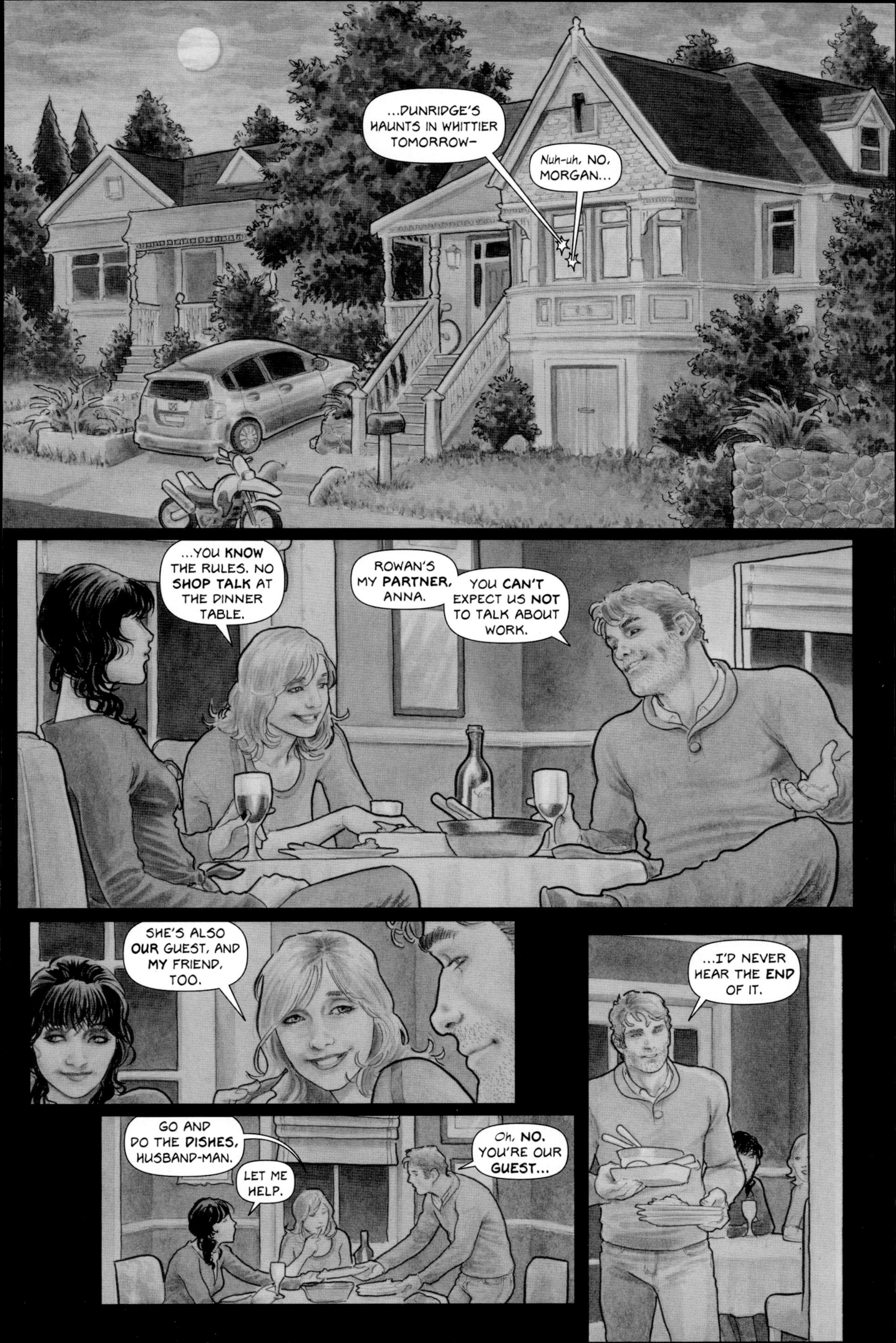
...DUNRIDGE'S HAUNTS IN WHITTIER TOMORROW–
Nuh-uh, NO, MORGAN...
...YOU KNOW THE RULES. NO SHOP TALK AT THE DINNER TABLE.
ROWAN'S MY PARTNER, ANNA.
YOU CAN'T EXPECT US NOT TO TALK ABOUT WORK.
SHE'S ALSO OUR GUEST, AND MY FRIEND, TOO.
...I'D NEVER HEAR THE END OF IT.
GO AND DO THE DISHES, HUSBAND-MAN.
LET ME HELP.
Oh, NO. YOU'RE OUR GUEST...

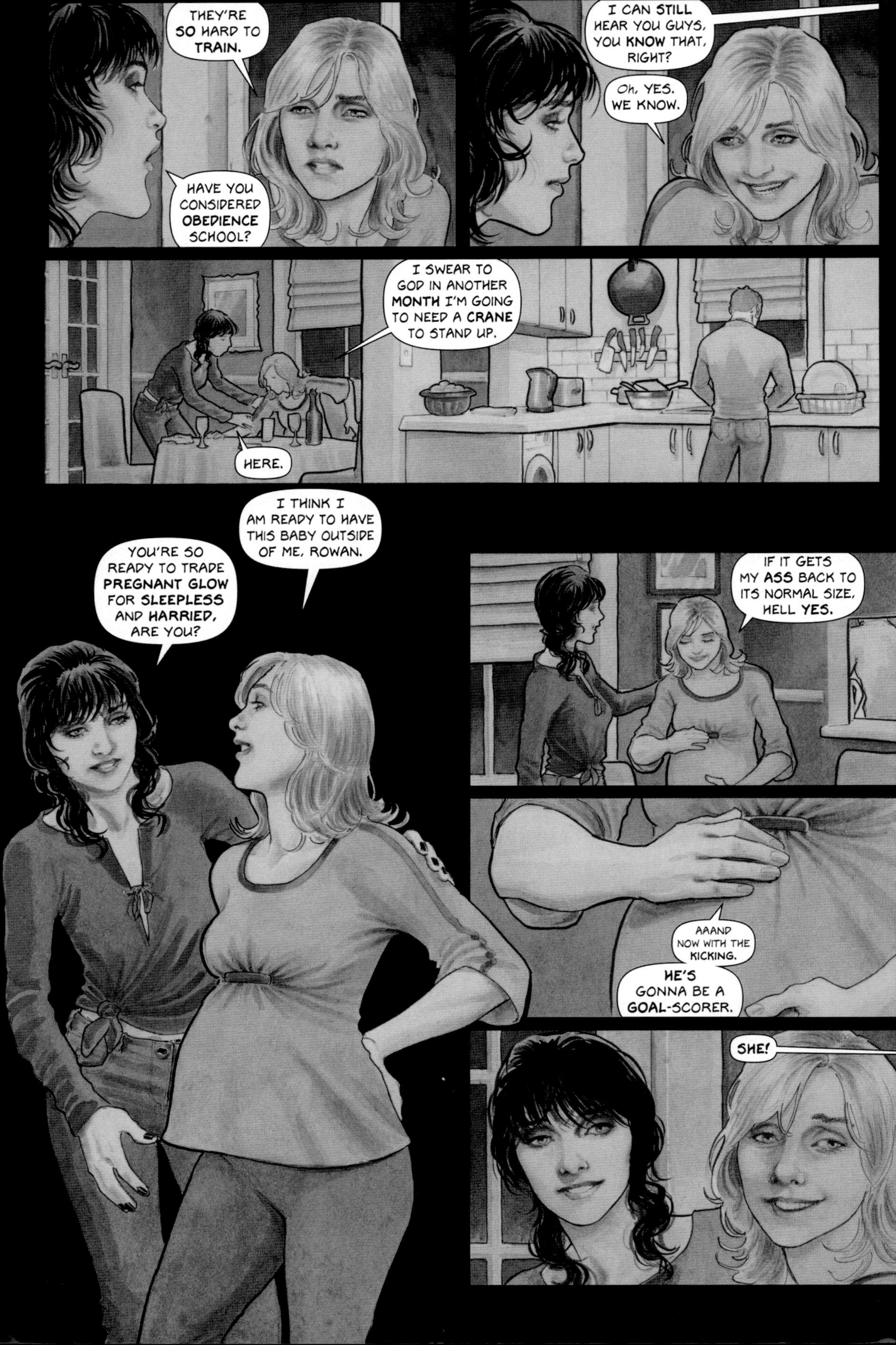

THEY'RE SO HARD TO TRAIN.
HAVE YOU CONSIDERED OBEDIENCE SCHOOL?
I CAN STILL HEAR YOU GUYS, YOU KNOW THAT, RIGHT?
Oh, YES. WE KNOW.
I SWEAR TO GOD IN ANOTHER MONTH I'M GOING TO NEED A CRANE TO STAND UP.
HERE.
I THINK I AM READY TO HAVE THIS BABY OUTSIDE OF ME, ROWAN.
YOU'RE SO READY TO TRADE PREGNANT GLOW FOR SLEEPLESS AND HARRIED, ARE YOU?
IF IT GETS MY ASS BACK TO ITS NORMAL SIZE, HELL YES.
AAAND NOW WITH THE KICKING.
HE'S GONNA BE A GOAL-SCORER.
SHE!

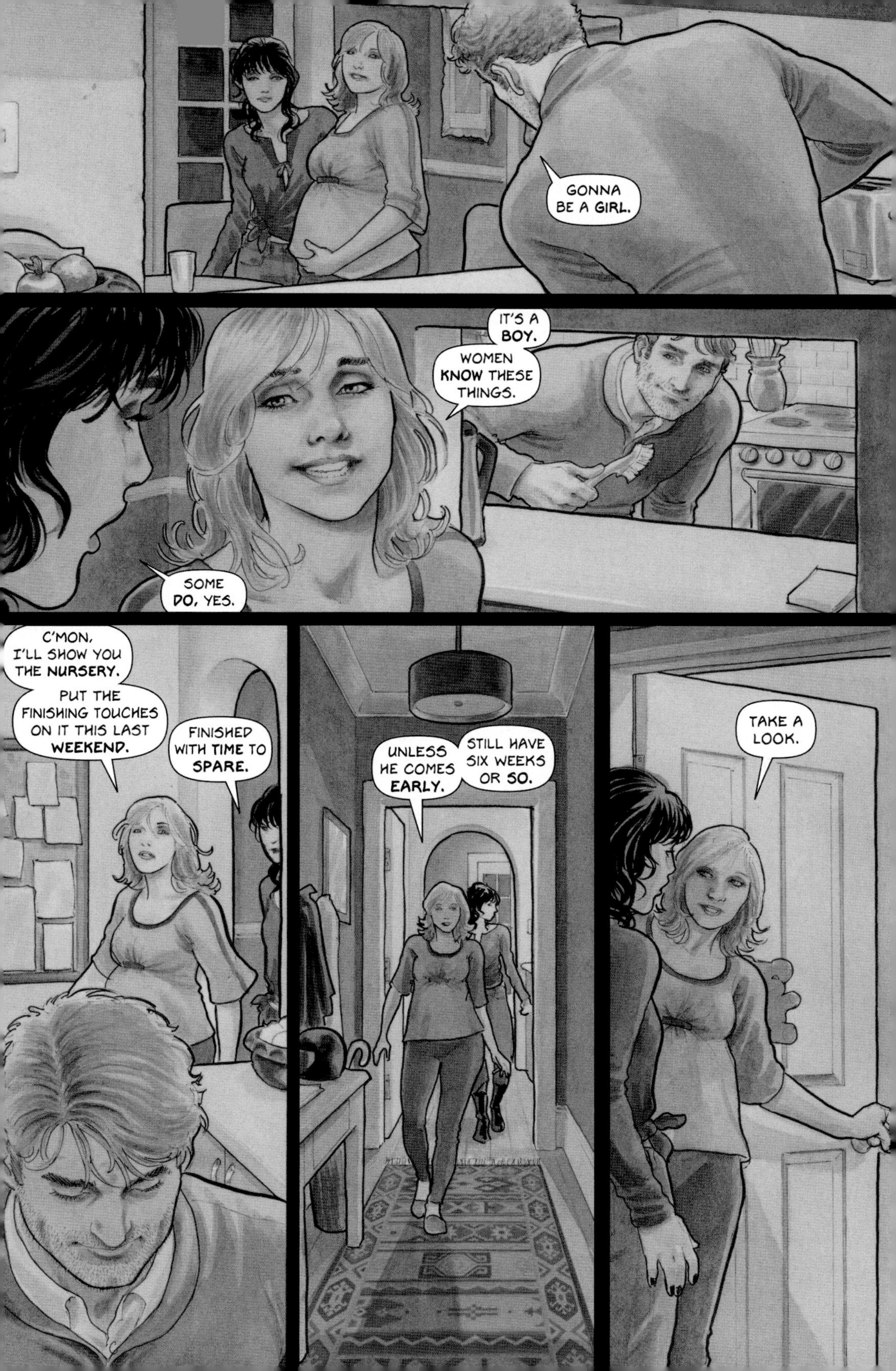
GONNA BE A GIRL.
IT'S A BOY.
WOMEN KNOW THESE THINGS.
SOME DO, YES.
C'MON, I'LL SHOW YOU THE NURSERY.
PUT THE FINISHING TOUCHES ON IT THIS LAST WEEKEND.
FINISHED WITH TIME TO SPARE.
STILL HAVE SIX WEEKS OR SO.
UNLESS HE COMES EARLY.
TAKE A LOOK.

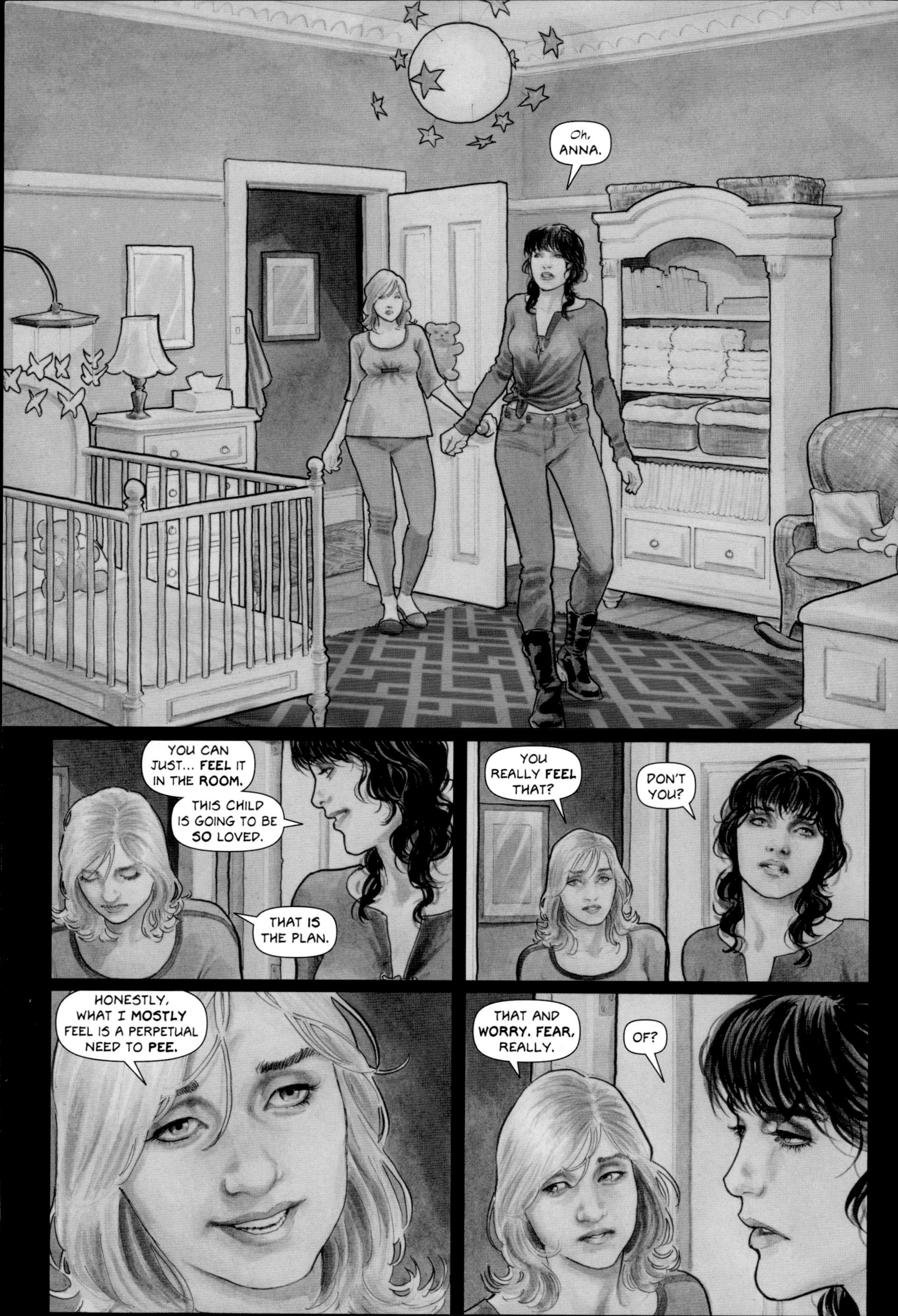
Oh, ANNA.
YOU CAN JUST... FEEL IT IN THE ROOM.
THIS CHILD IS GOING TO BE SO LOVED.
THAT IS THE PLAN.
YOU REALLY FEEL THAT?
DON'T YOU?
HONESTLY, WHAT I MOSTLY FEEL IS A PERPETUAL NEED TO PEE.
THAT AND WORRY. FEAR, REALLY.
OF?

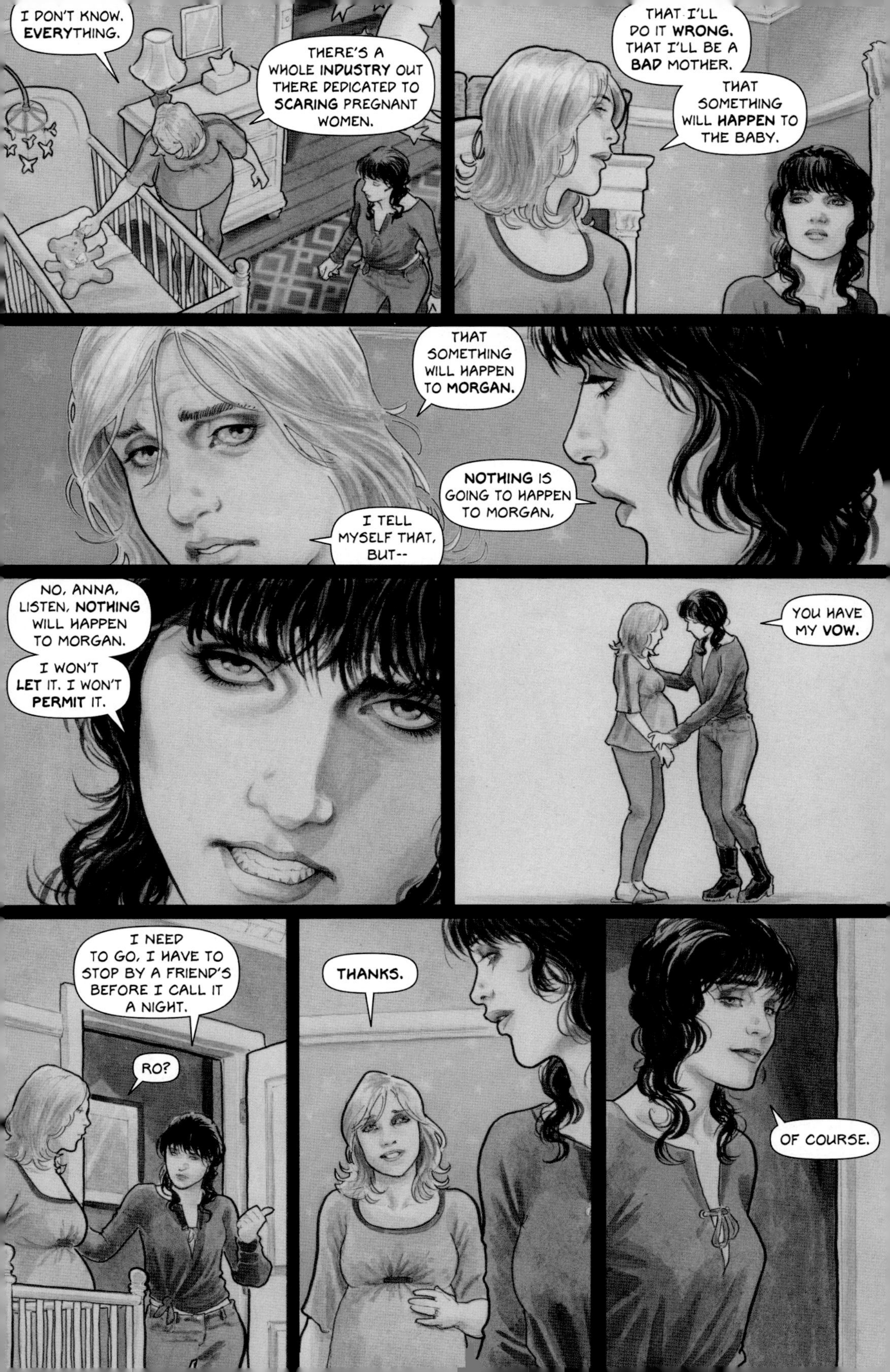
I DON'T KNOW. EVERYTHING.
THERE'S A WHOLE INDUSTRY OUT THERE DEDICATED TO SCARING PREGNANT WOMEN.
THAT I'LL DO IT WRONG. THAT I'LL BE A BAD MOTHER.
THAT SOMETHING WILL HAPPEN TO THE BABY.
THAT SOMETHING WILL HAPPEN TO MORGAN.
NOTHING IS GOING TO HAPPEN TO MORGAN.
I TELL MYSELF THAT, BUT--
NO, ANNA, LISTEN, NOTHING WILL HAPPEN TO MORGAN.
I WON'T LET IT. I WON'T PERMIT IT.
YOU HAVE MY VOW.
I NEED TO GO, I HAVE TO STOP BY A FRIEND'S BEFORE I CALL IT A NIGHT.
RO?
THANKS.
OF COURSE.

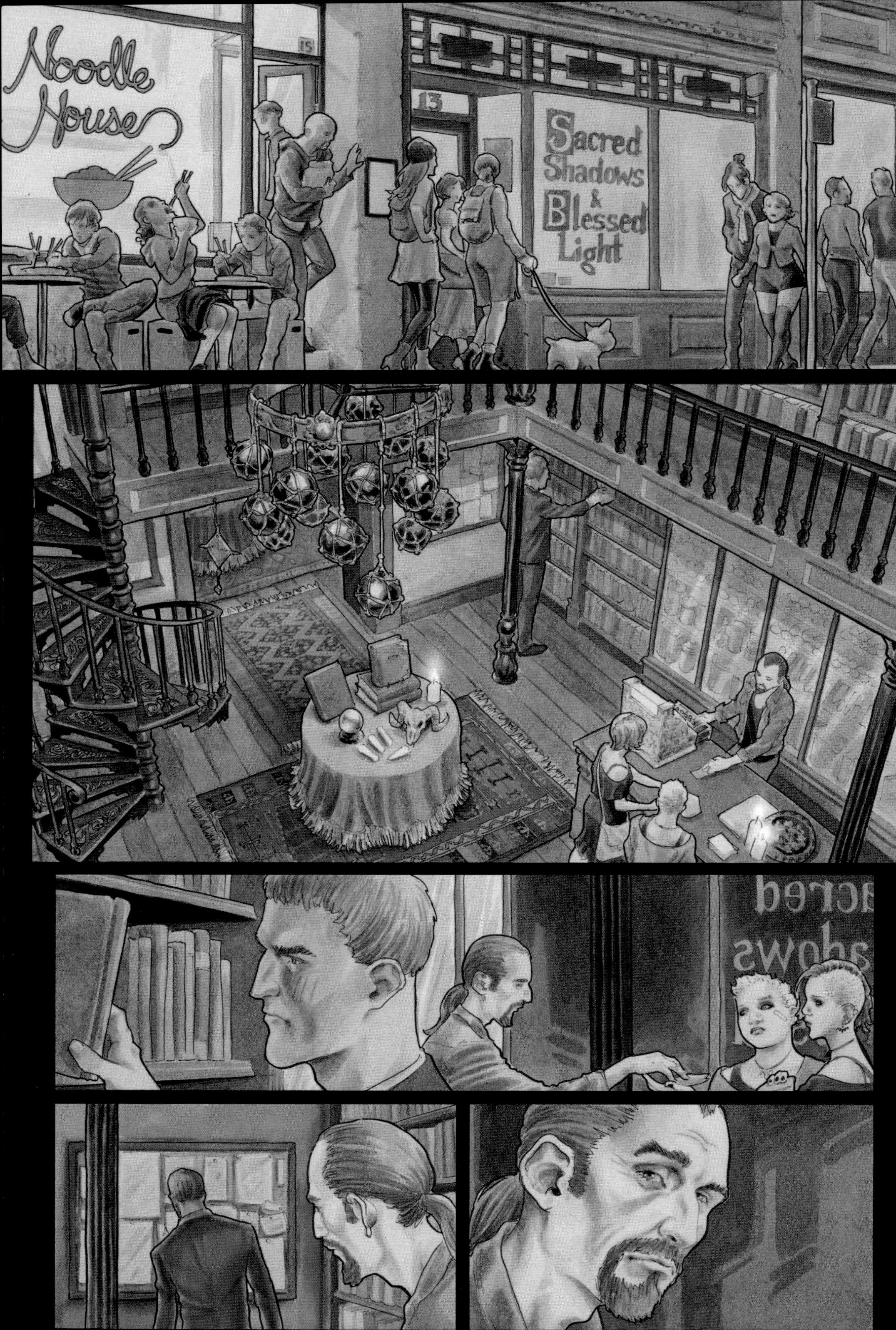
Noodle House
15
13
Sacred Shadows & Blessed Light

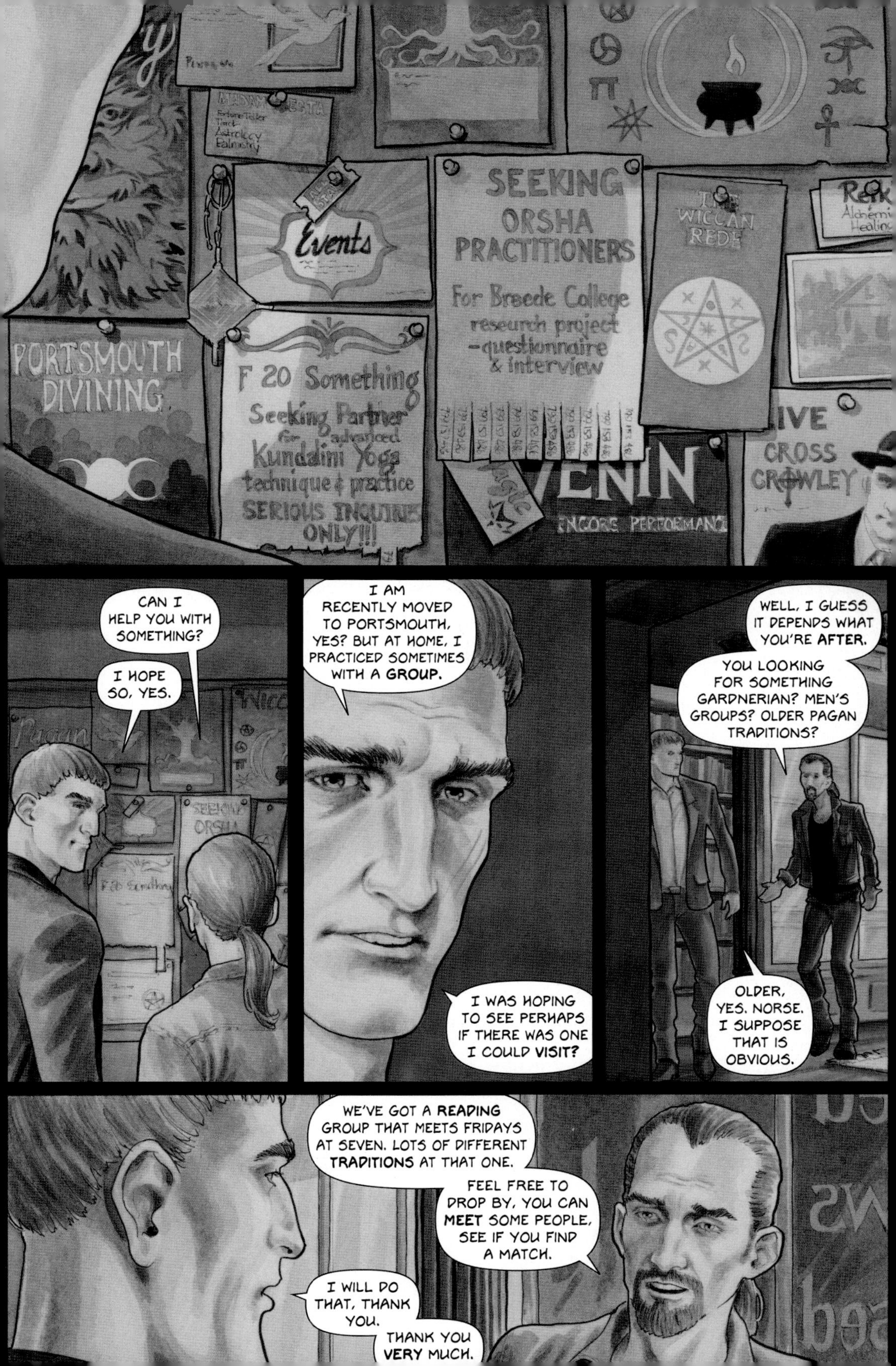
Events
SEEKING ORSHA PRACTITIONERS
For Breede College research project -questionnaire & interview
THE WICCAN REDE
PORTSMOUTH DIVINING
F 20 Something
Seeking Partner for advanced Kundalini Yoga technique & practice
ONLY!!!
CROSS CROWLEY
CAN I HELP YOU WITH SOMETHING?
I HOPE SO, YES.
I AM RECENTLY MOVED TO PORTSMOUTH, YES? BUT AT HOME, I PRACTICED SOMETIMES WITH A GROUP.
I WAS HOPING TO SEE PERHAPS IF THERE WAS ONE I COULD VISIT?
WELL, I GUESS IT DEPENDS WHAT YOU'RE AFTER.
YOU LOOKING FOR SOMETHING GARDNERIAN? MEN'S GROUPS? OLDER PAGAN TRADITIONS?
OLDER, YES. NORSE. I SUPPOSE THAT IS OBVIOUS.
WE'VE GOT A READING GROUP THAT MEETS FRIDAYS AT SEVEN. LOTS OF DIFFERENT TRADITIONS AT THAT ONE.
FEEL FREE TO DROP BY, YOU CAN MEET SOME PEOPLE, SEE IF YOU FIND A MATCH.
I WILL DO THAT, THANK YOU.
THANK YOU VERY MUCH.

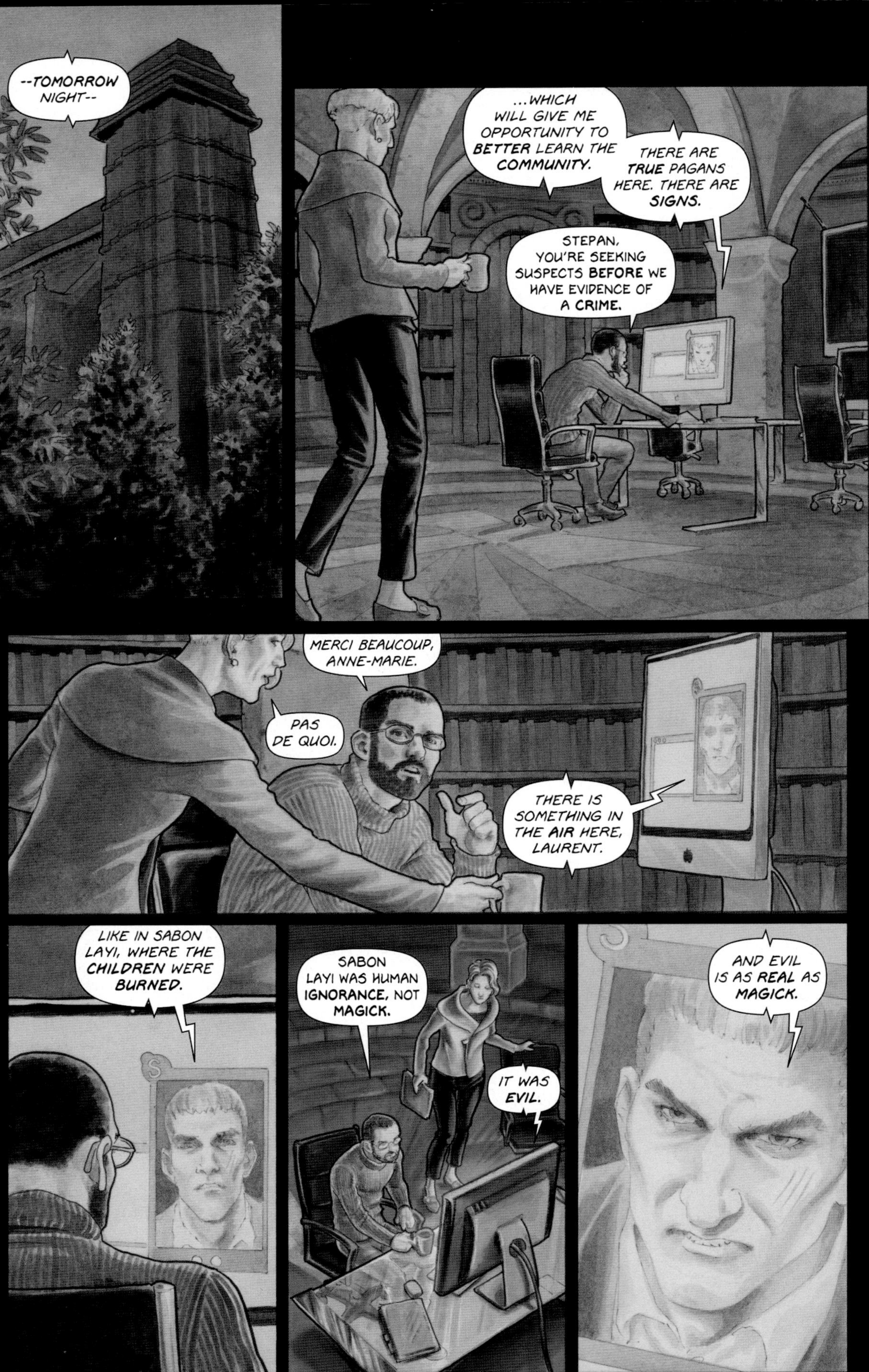
--TOMORROW NIGHT--
...WHICH WILL GIVE ME OPPORTUNITY TO BETTER LEARN THE COMMUNITY.
THERE ARE TRUE PAGANS HERE. THERE ARE SIGNS.
STEPAN, YOU'RE SEEKING SUSPECTS BEFORE WE HAVE EVIDENCE OF A CRIME.
MERCI BEAUCOUP, ANNE-MARIE.
PAS DE QUOI.
THERE IS SOMETHING IN THE AIR HERE, LAURENT.
LIKE IN SABON LAYI, WHERE THE CHILDREN WERE BURNED.
SABON LAYI WAS HUMAN IGNORANCE, NOT MAGICK.
IT WAS EVIL.
AND EVIL IS AS REAL AS MAGICK.

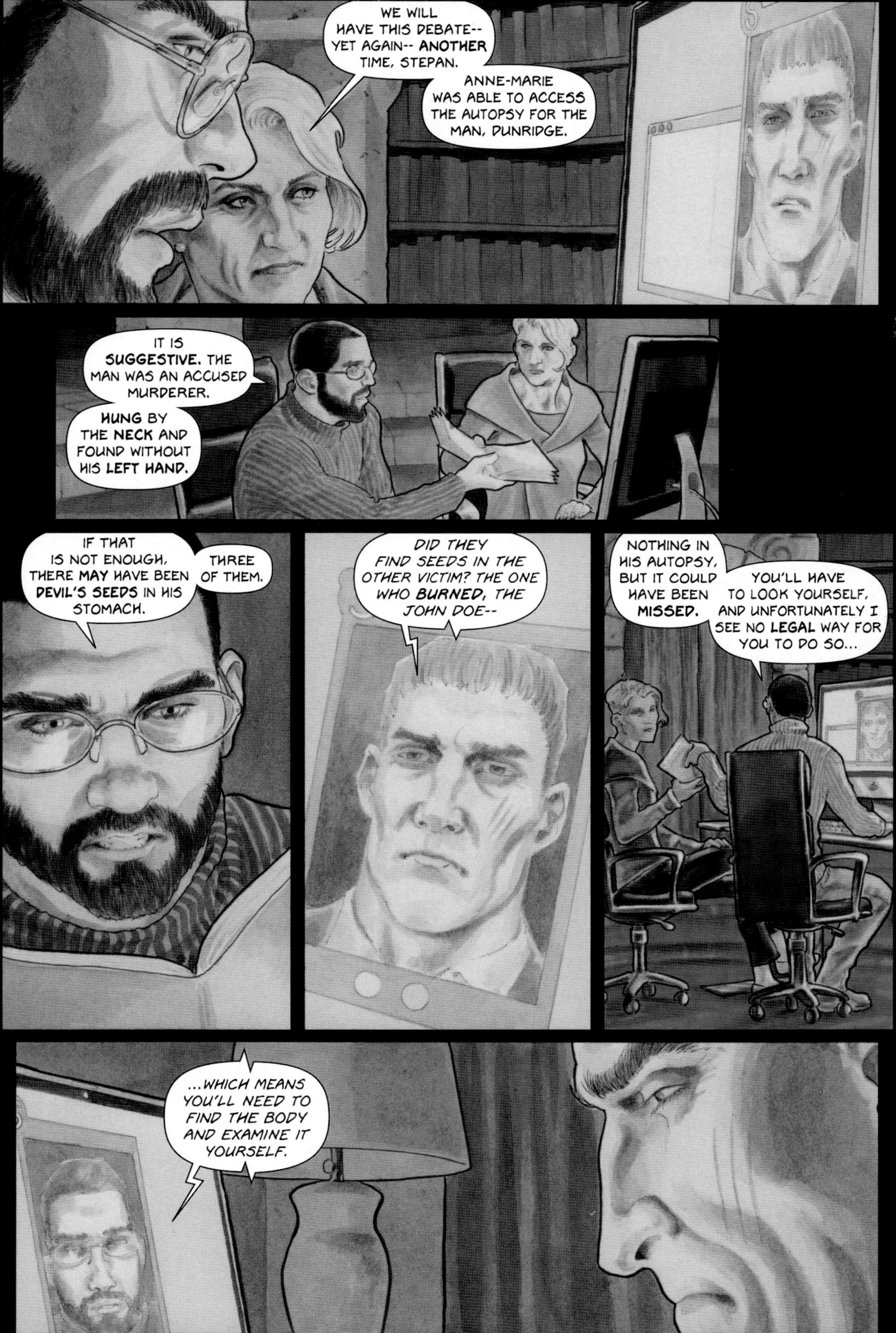

WE WILL HAVE THIS DEBATE-- YET AGAIN-- ANOTHER TIME, STEPAN.
ANNE-MARIE WAS ABLE TO ACCESS THE AUTOPSY FOR THE MAN, DUNRIDGE.
IT IS SUGGESTIVE. THE MAN WAS AN ACCUSED MURDERER.
HUNG BY THE NECK AND FOUND WITHOUT HIS LEFT HAND.
IF THAT IS NOT ENOUGH, THERE MAY HAVE BEEN DEVIL'S SEEDS IN HIS STOMACH.
THREE OF THEM.
DID THEY FIND SEEDS IN THE OTHER VICTIM? THE ONE WHO BURNED, THE JOHN DOE--
NOTHING IN HIS AUTOPSY, BUT IT COULD HAVE BEEN MISSED.
YOU'LL HAVE TO LOOK YOURSELF, AND UNFORTUNATELY I SEE NO LEGAL WAY FOR YOU TO DO SO...
...WHICH MEANS YOU'LL NEED TO FIND THE BODY AND EXAMINE IT YOURSELF.

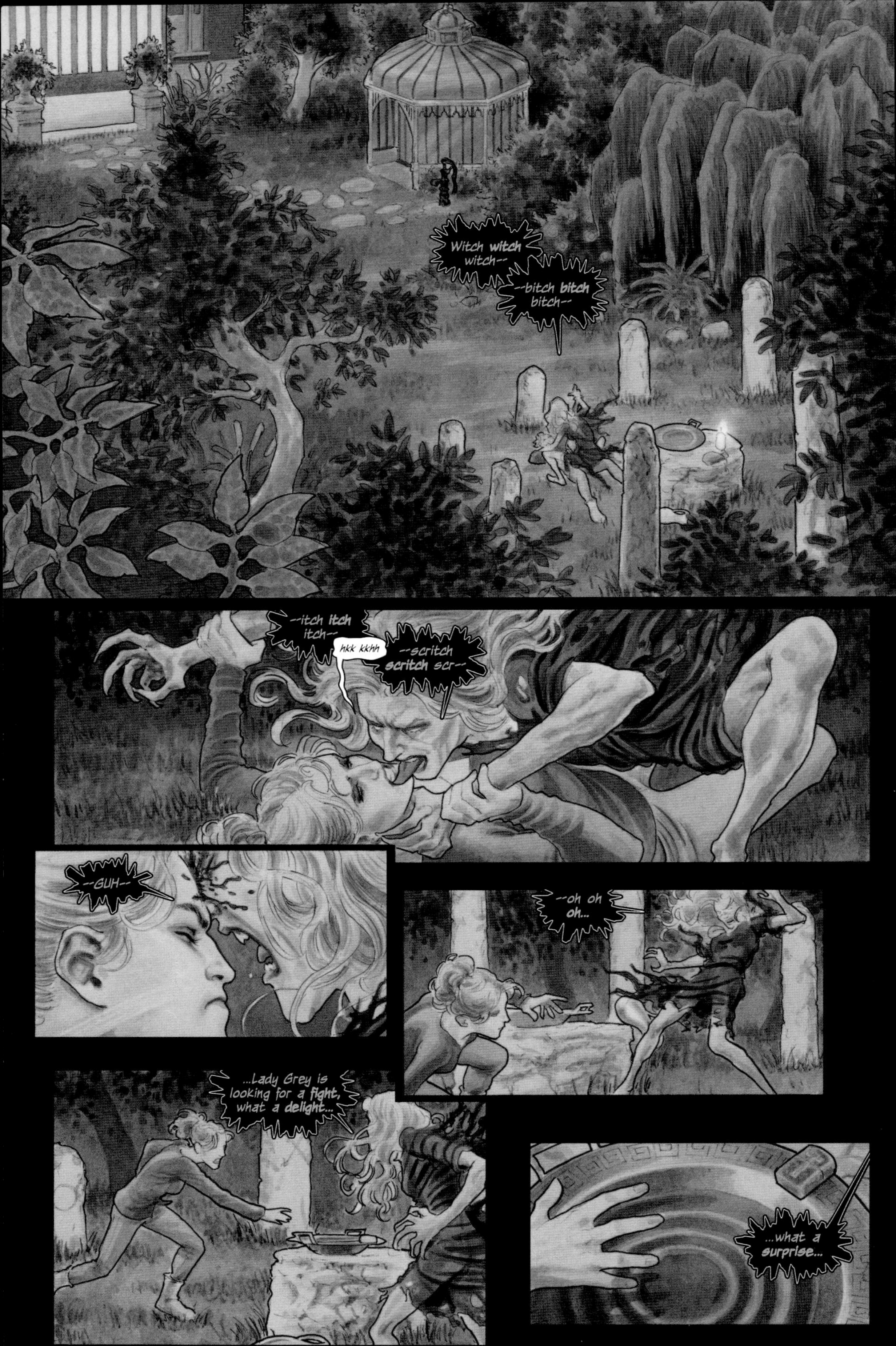
Witch witch witch--
--bitch bitch bitch--
--itch itch itch--
hkk kkhh
--scritch scritch scr--
--GUH--
--oh oh oh...
...Lady Grey is looking for a fight, what a delight...
...what a surprise...

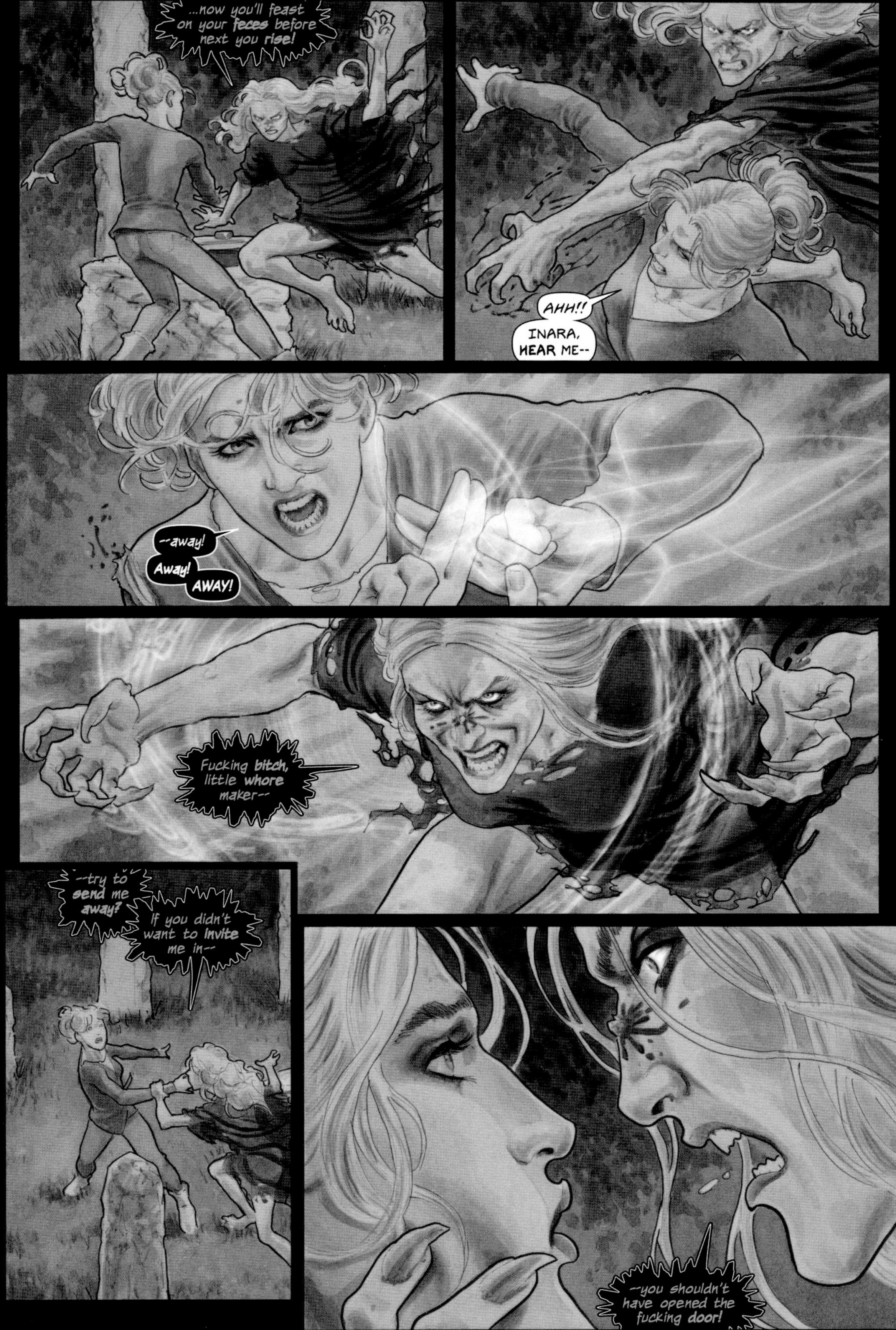
...now you'll feast on your feces before next you rise!
AHH!!
INARA, HEAR ME--
--away!
Away!
AWAY!
Fucking bitch, little whore maker--
--try to send me away?
If you didn't want to invite me in--
--you shouldn't have opened the fucking door!

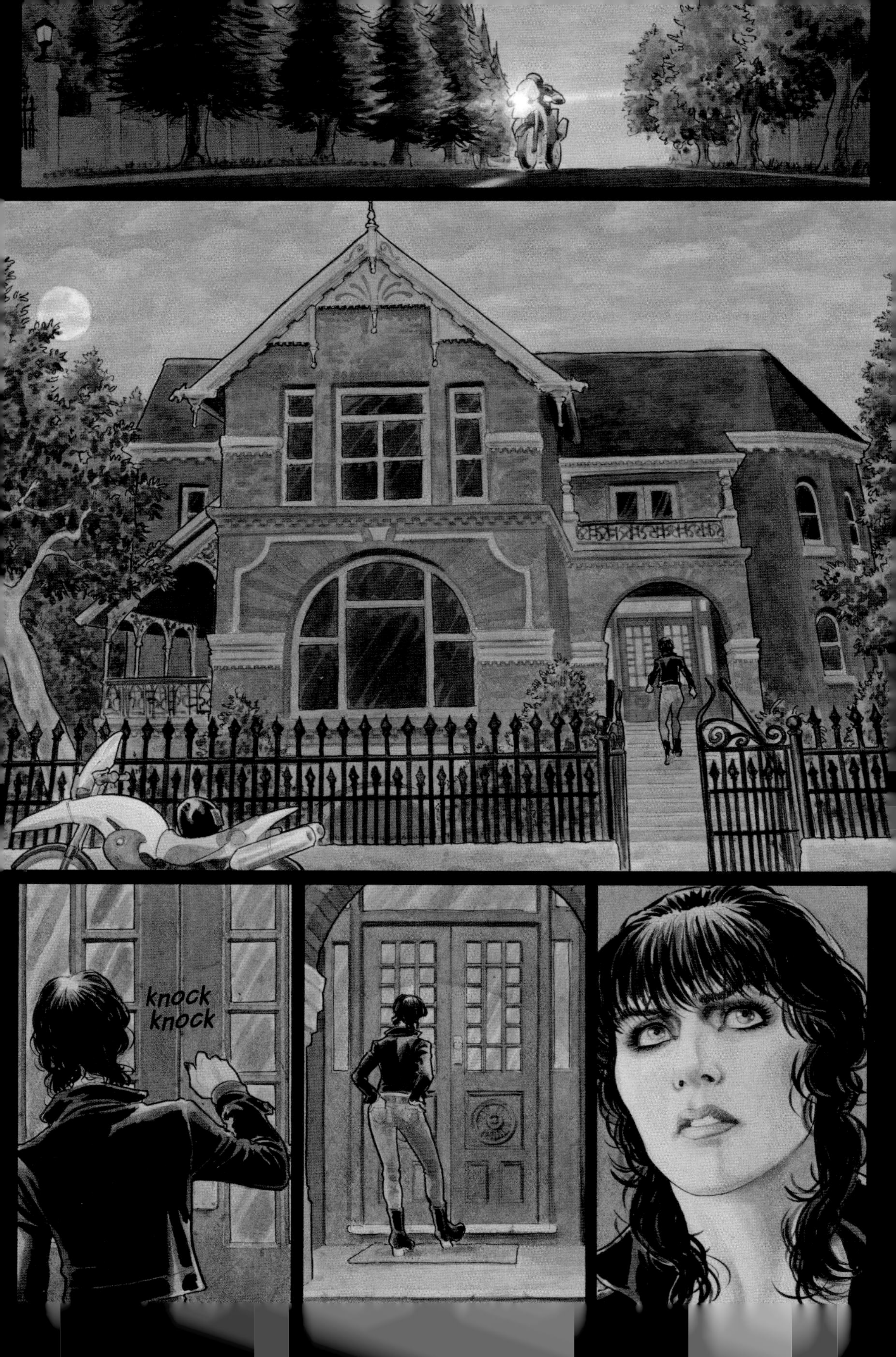
knock
knock

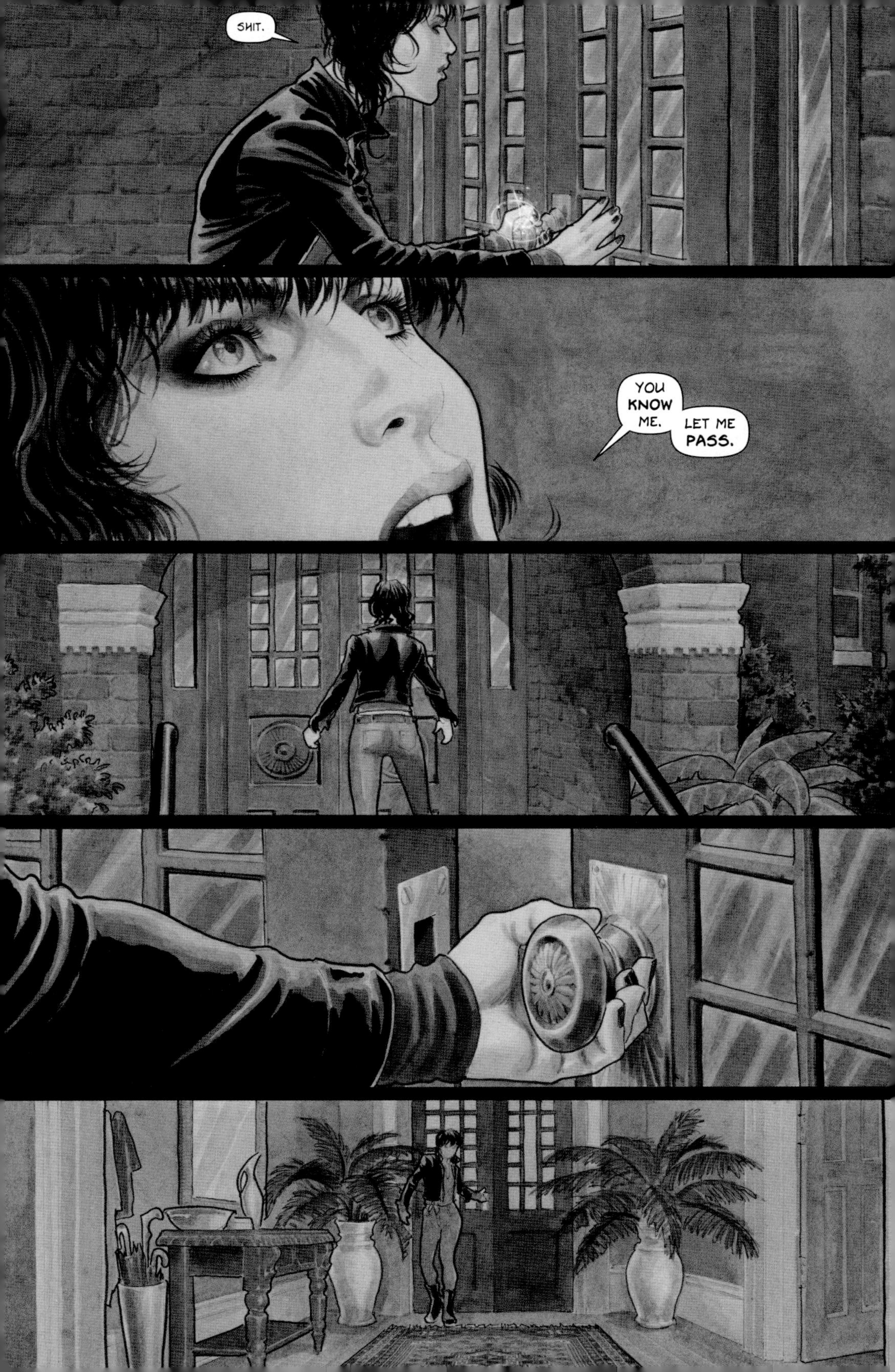
SHIT.
YOU KNOW ME.
LET ME PASS.

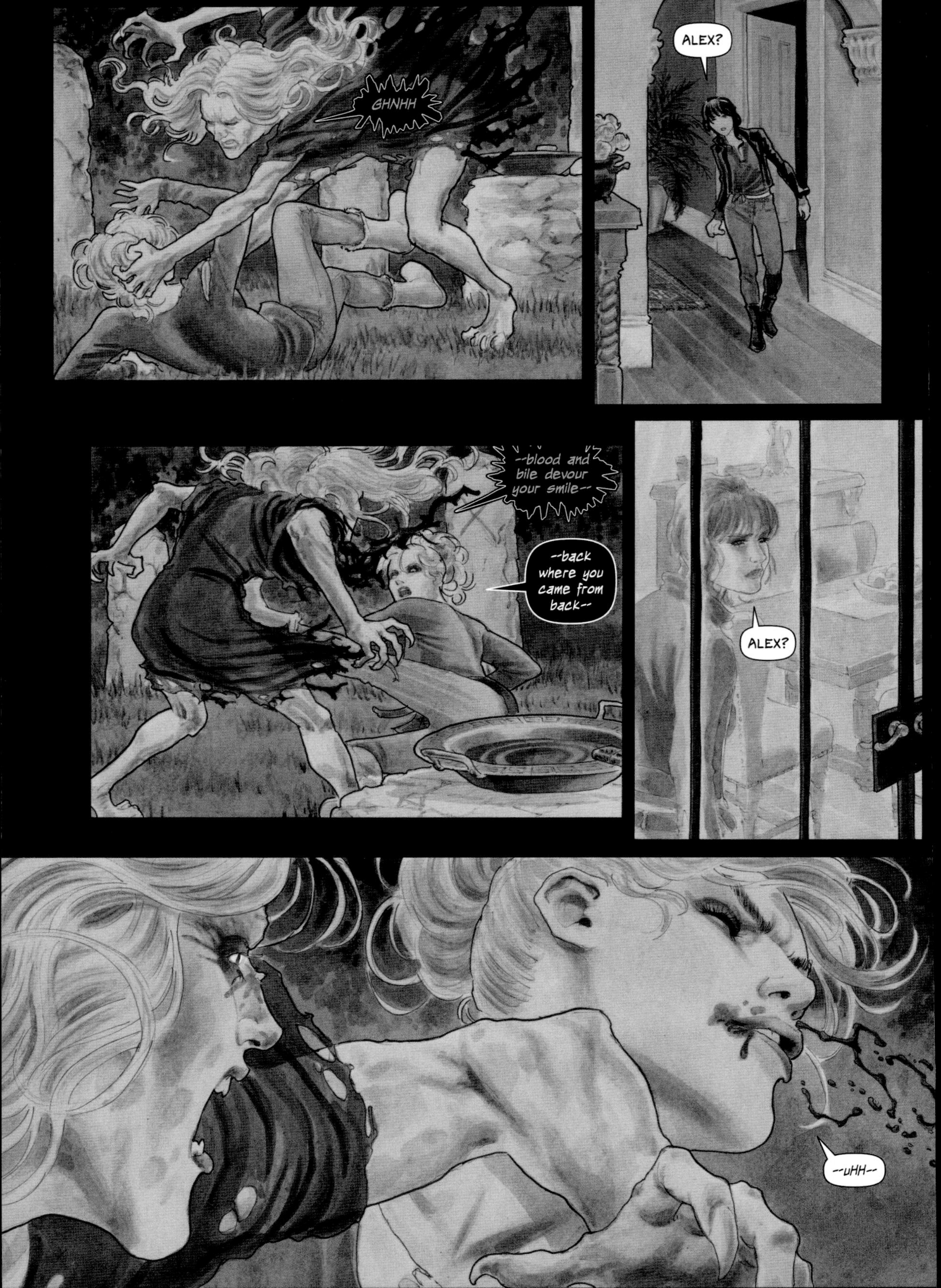
GHNHH
ALEX?
--blood and bile devour your smile--
--back where you came from back--
ALEX?
--uHH--

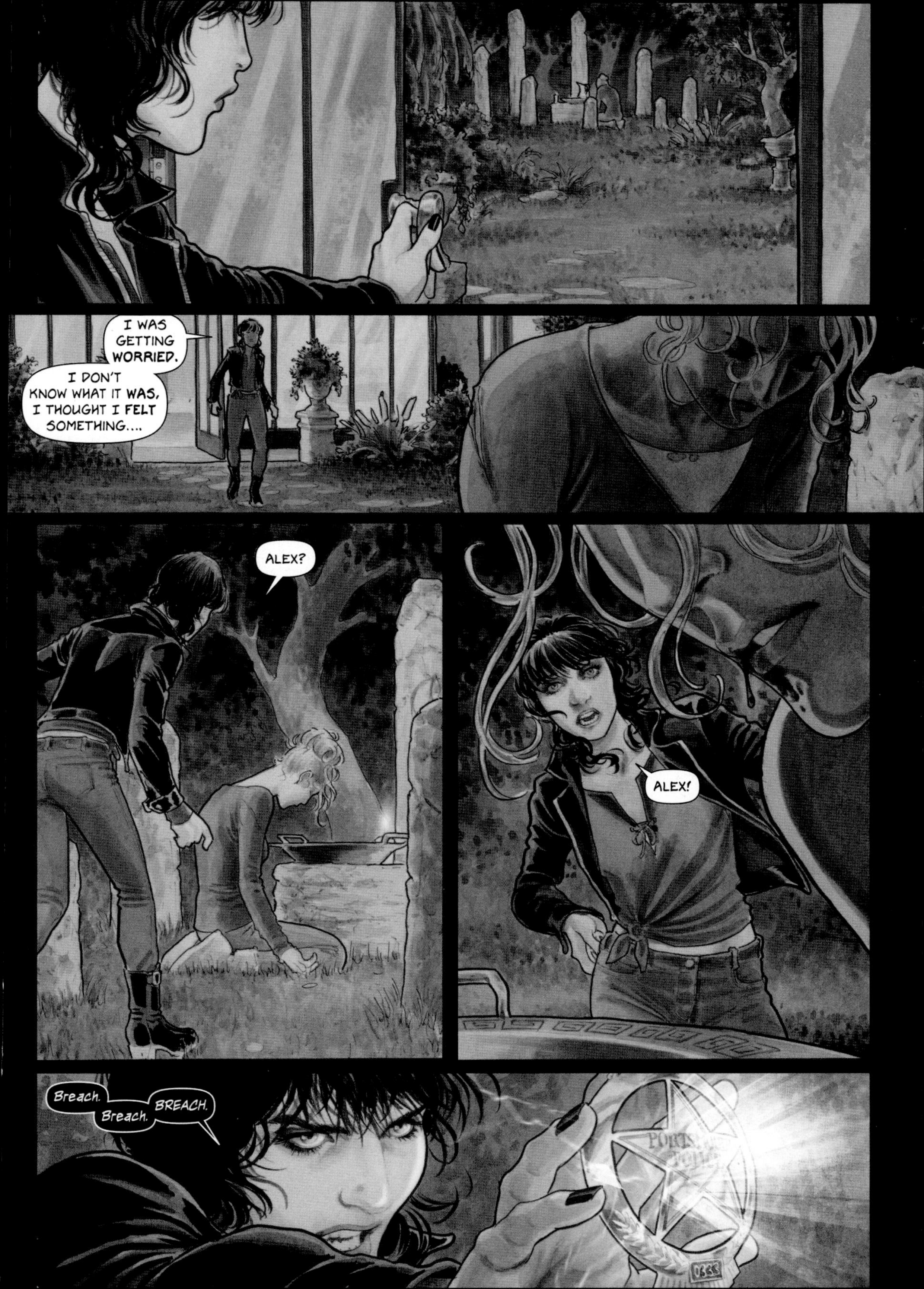
I WAS GETTING WORRIED.
I DON'T KNOW WHAT IT WAS, I THOUGHT I FELT SOMETHING....
ALEX?
ALEX!
Breach. Breach. BREACH.

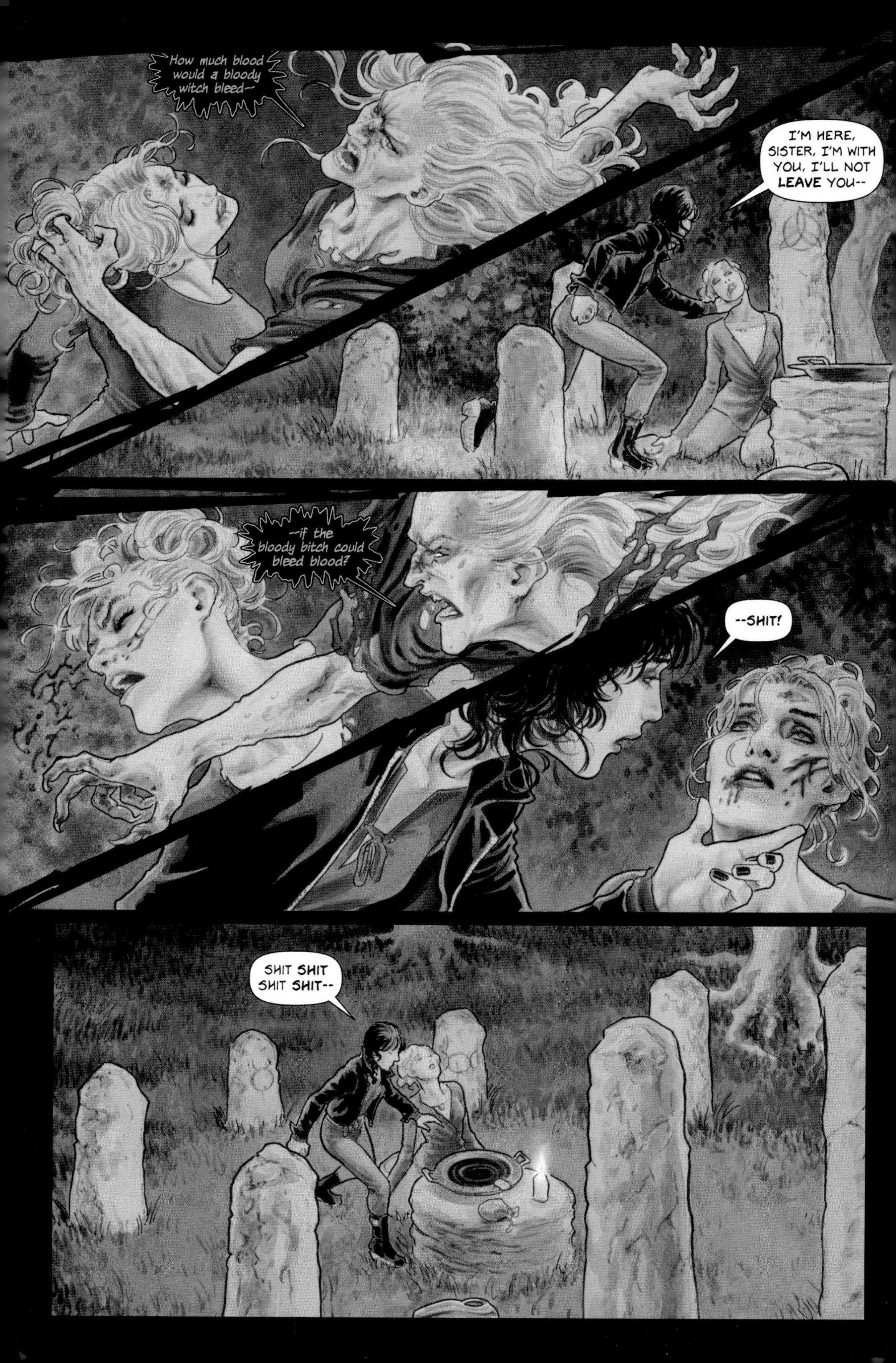
How much blood would a bloody witch bleed--
I'M HERE, SISTER, I'M WITH YOU, I'LL NOT LEAVE YOU--
--if the bloody bitch could bleed blood?
--SHIT!
SHIT SHIT SHIT SHIT--

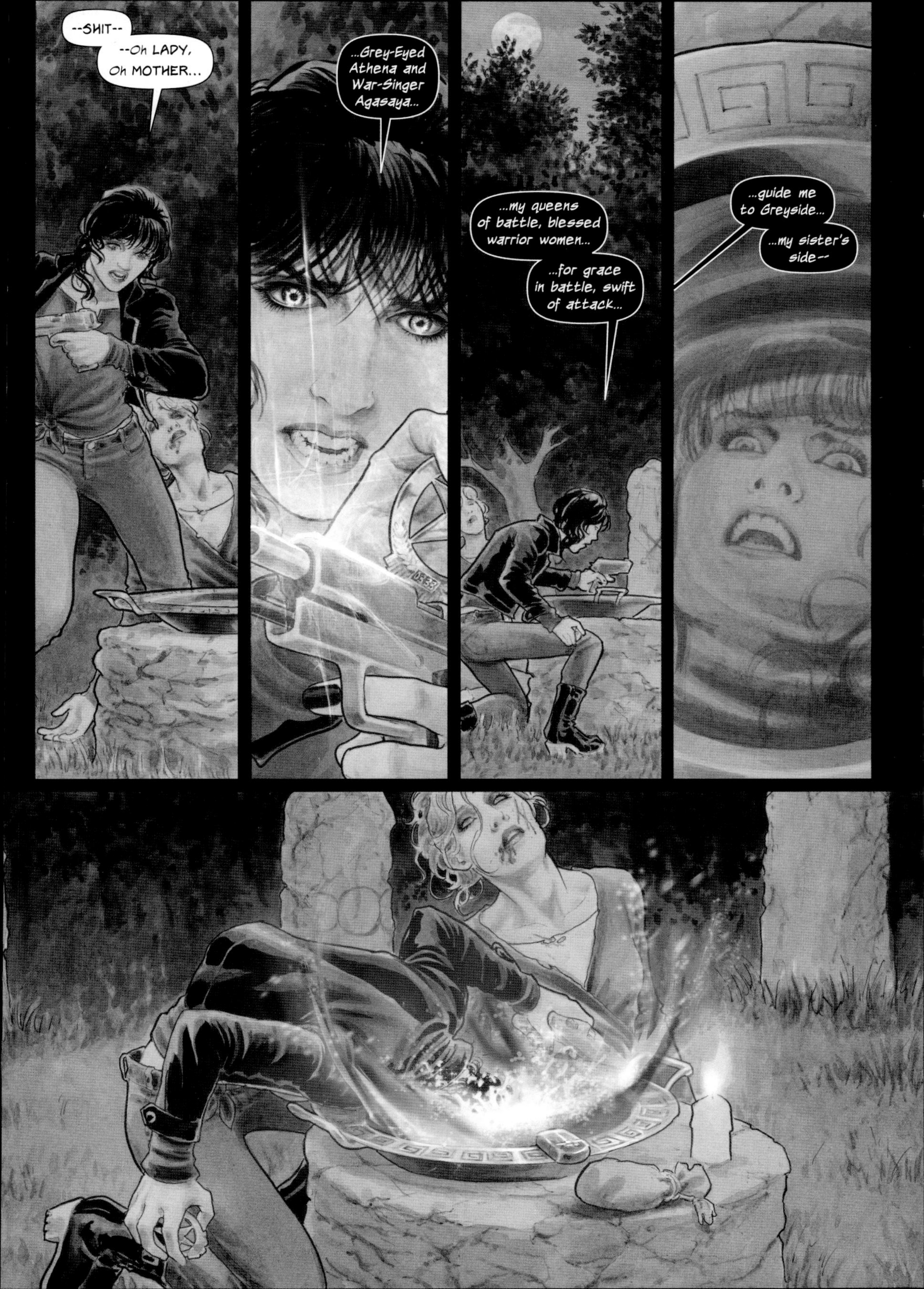
--SHIT--
--Oh LADY, Oh MOTHER...
...Grey-Eyed Athena and War-Singer Agasaya...
...my queens of battle, blessed warrior women...
...for grace in battle, swift of attack...
...guide me to Greyside...
...my sister's side--

This is what happens when you peer into the dark places.
What happens when you sneak into the hidden spaces.
The only question left, the one you must consider...
...which of your entrails would you like first for dinner?
WAIT.
WAIT.
Wait?
Whyfor would I wait?
SHE'S NOT TALKING TO YOU.

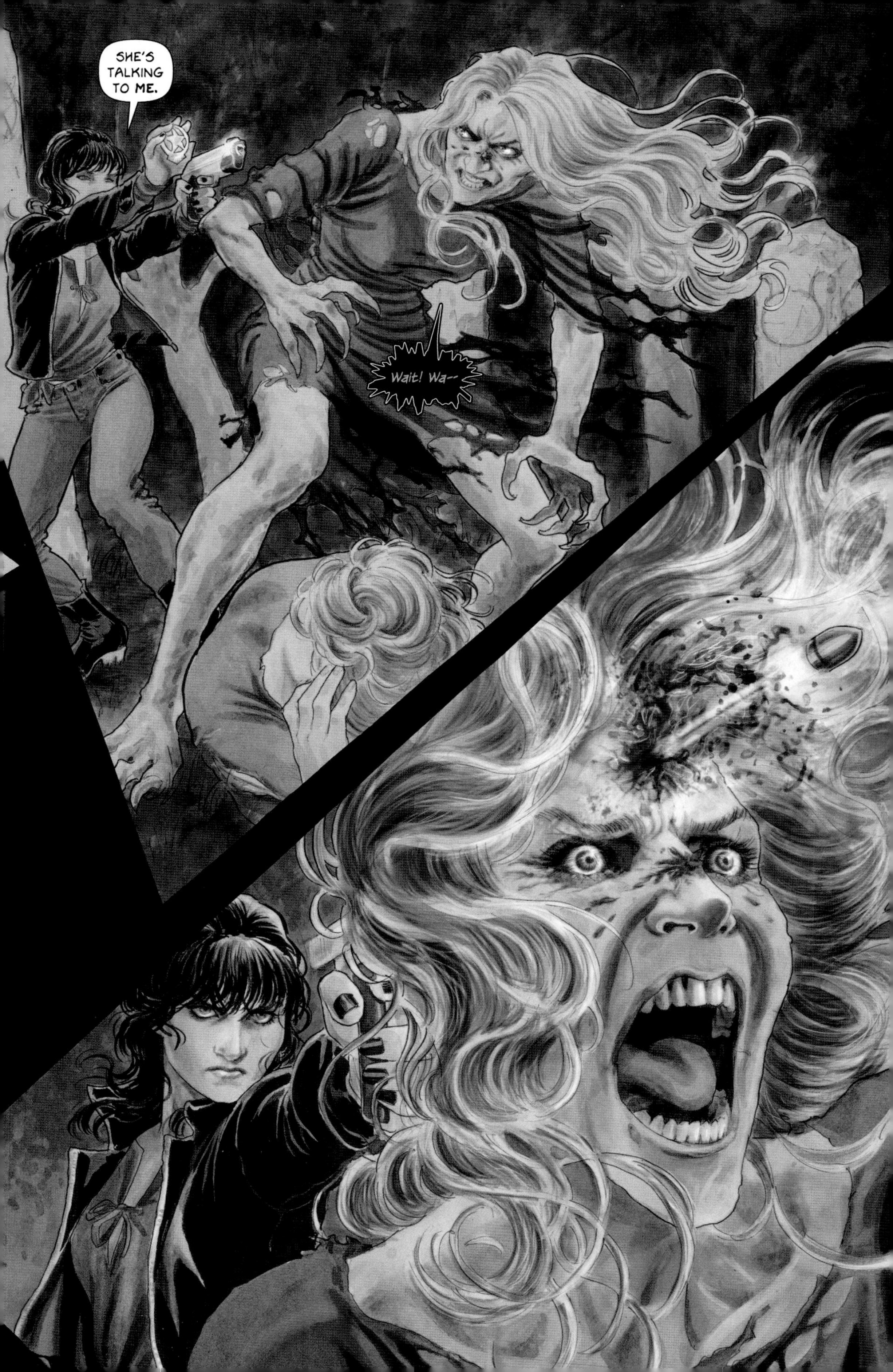
SHE'S TALKING TO ME.
Wait! Wa--

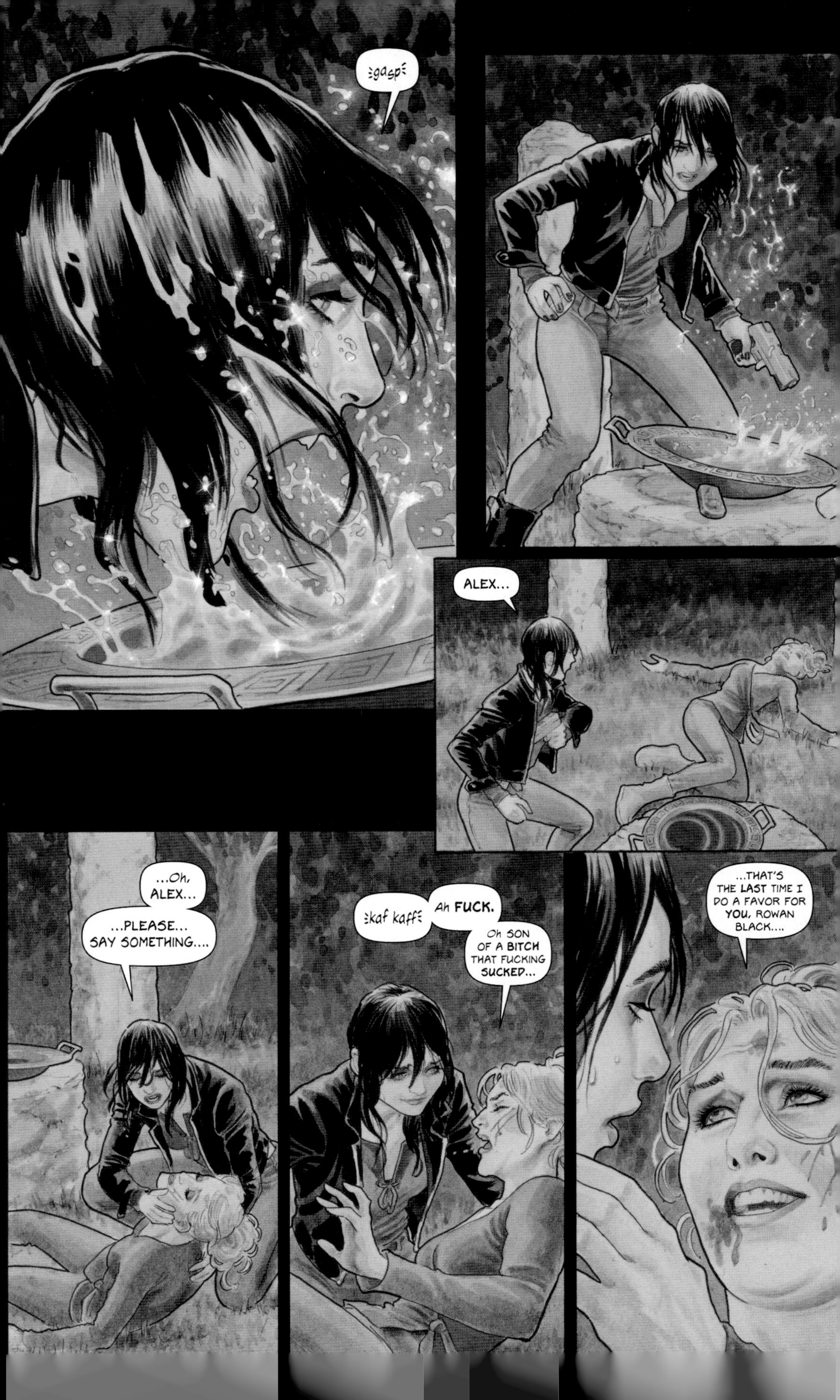
gasp
ALEX...
...Oh, ALEX...
...PLEASE... SAY SOMETHING....
kaf kaff
Ah FUCK.
Oh SON OF A BITCH THAT FUCKING SUCKED...
...THAT'S THE LAST TIME I DO A FAVOR FOR YOU, ROWAN BLACK....

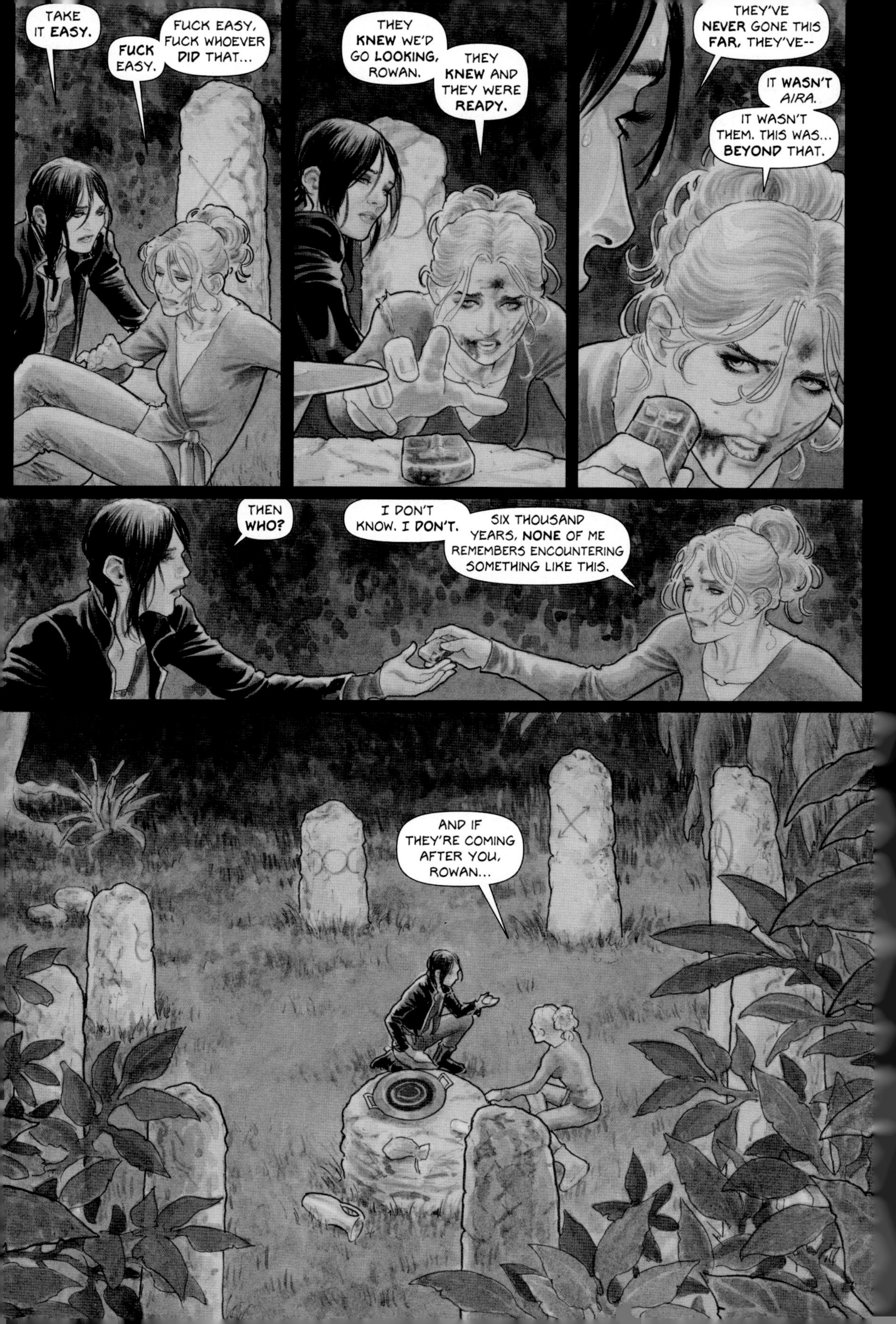
TAKE IT **EASY.**
FUCK EASY.
FUCK EASY, FUCK WHOEVER **DID** THAT...
THEY **KNEW** WE'D GO **LOOKING,** ROWAN.
THEY **KNEW** AND THEY WERE **READY.**
THEY'VE **NEVER** GONE THIS **FAR,** THEY'VE--
IT **WASN'T** *AIRA.*
IT WASN'T THEM. THIS WAS... **BEYOND** THAT.
THEN **WHO?**
I DON'T KNOW. I **DON'T.**
SIX THOUSAND YEARS, **NONE** OF ME REMEMBERS ENCOUNTERING SOMETHING LIKE THIS.
AND IF THEY'RE COMING AFTER YOU, ROWAN...

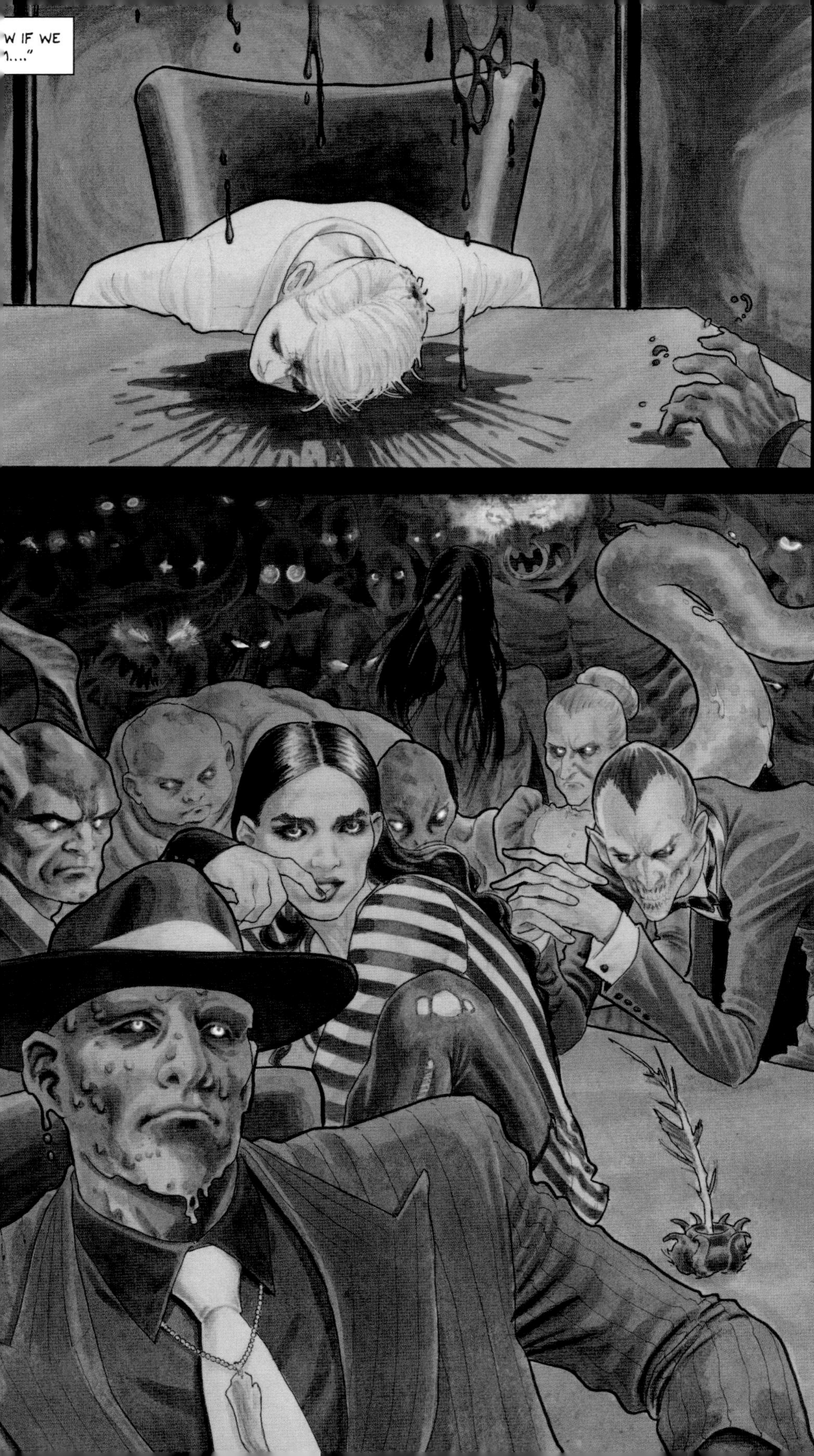
W IF WE

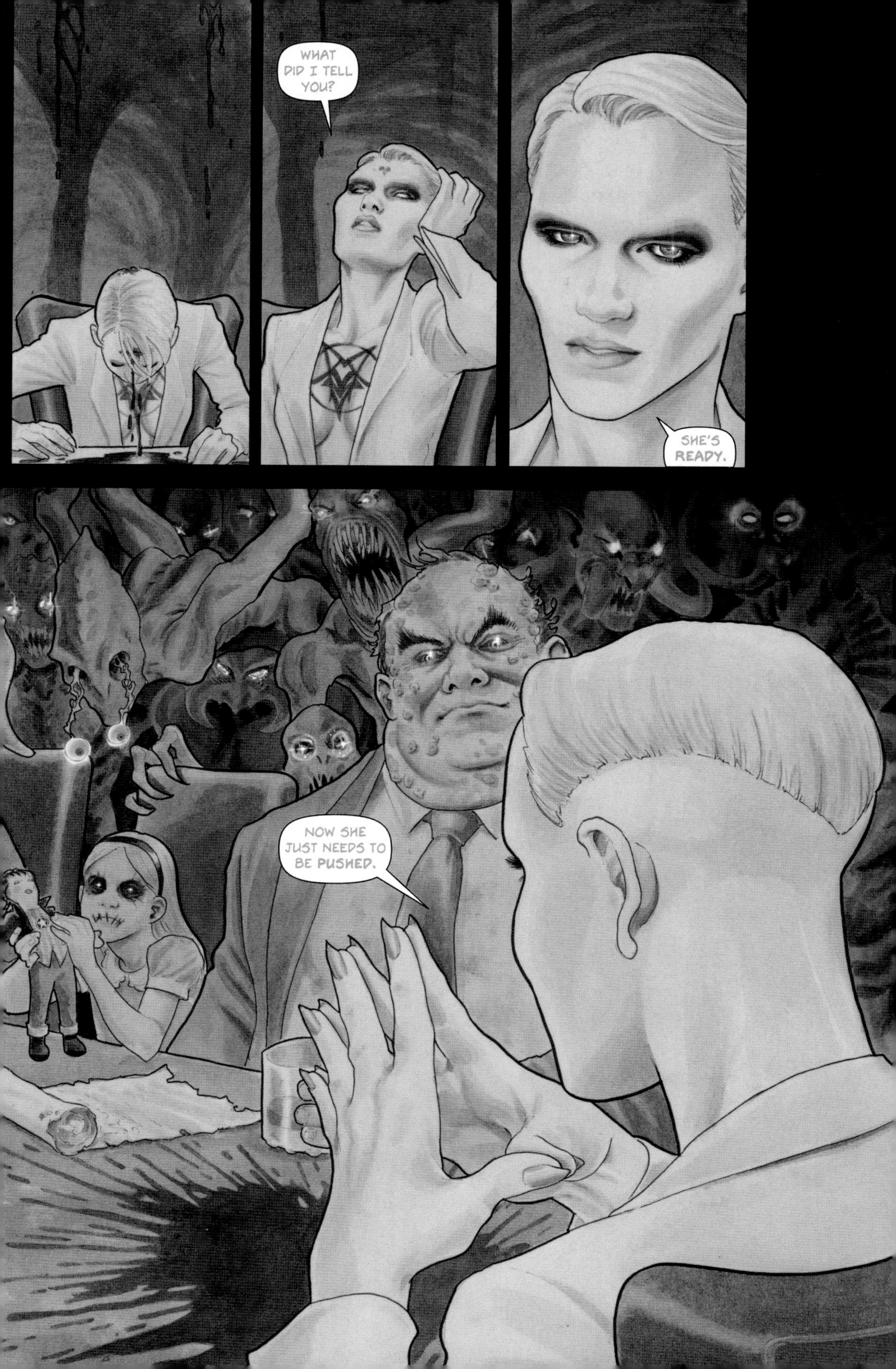
WHAT DID I TELL YOU?
SHE'S READY.
NOW SHE JUST NEEDS TO BE PUSHED.

VARIANT COVER GALLERY

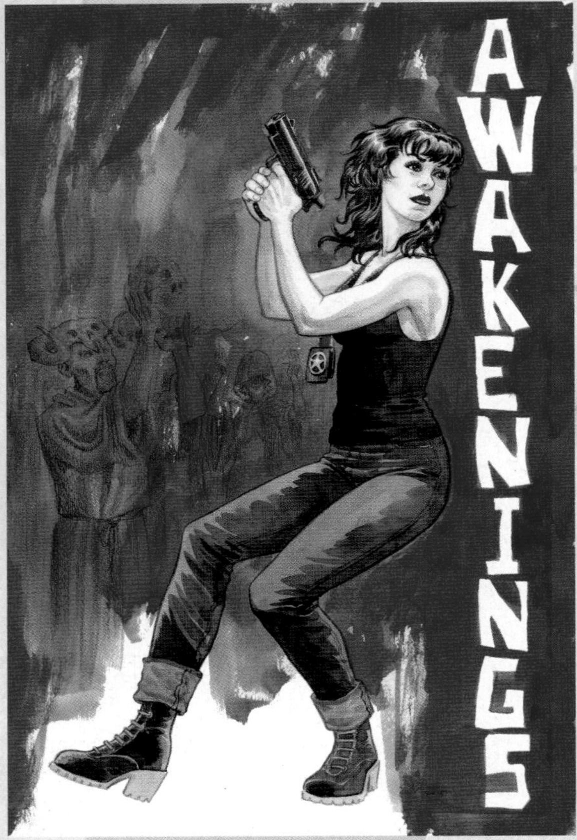
AWAKENINGS

Issue 001 "B" Cover by
JILL THOMPSON

Issue 001 "Magazine" Cover by
RICK BURCHETT

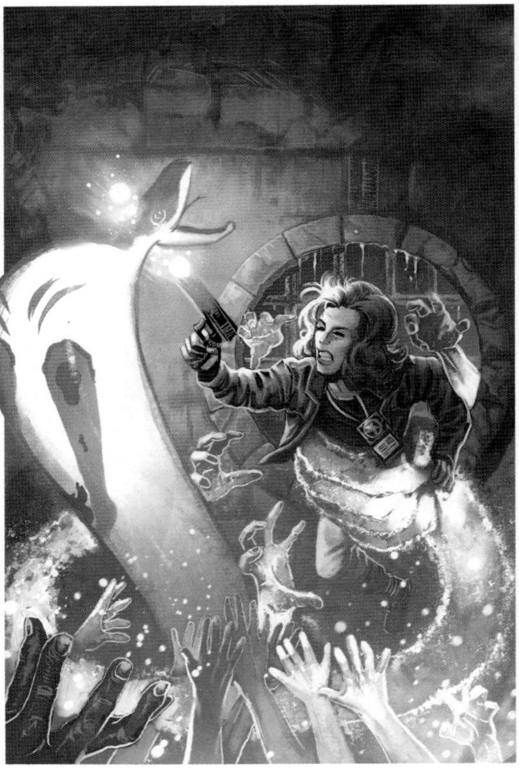

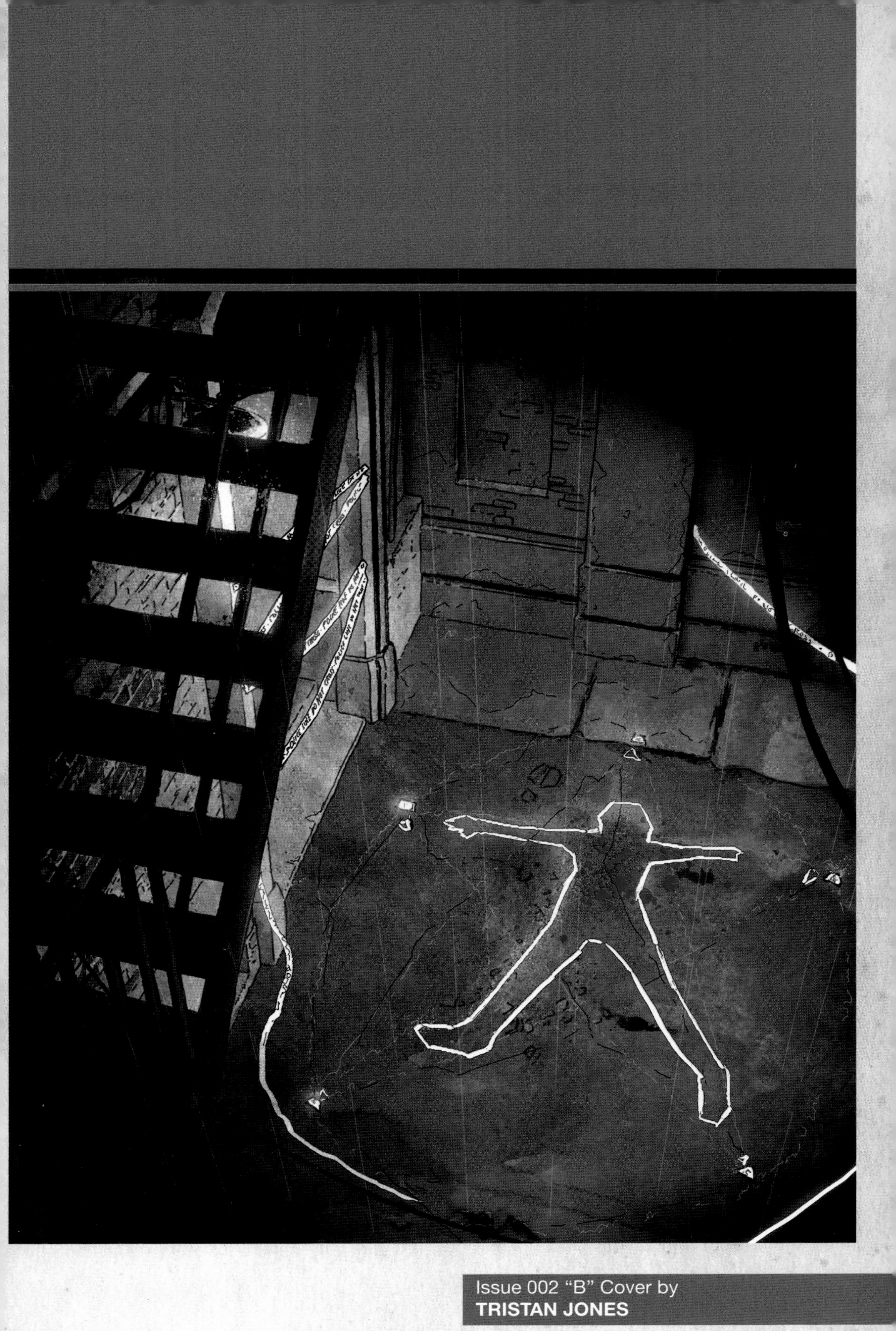

Issue 002 "B" Cover by
TRISTAN JONES

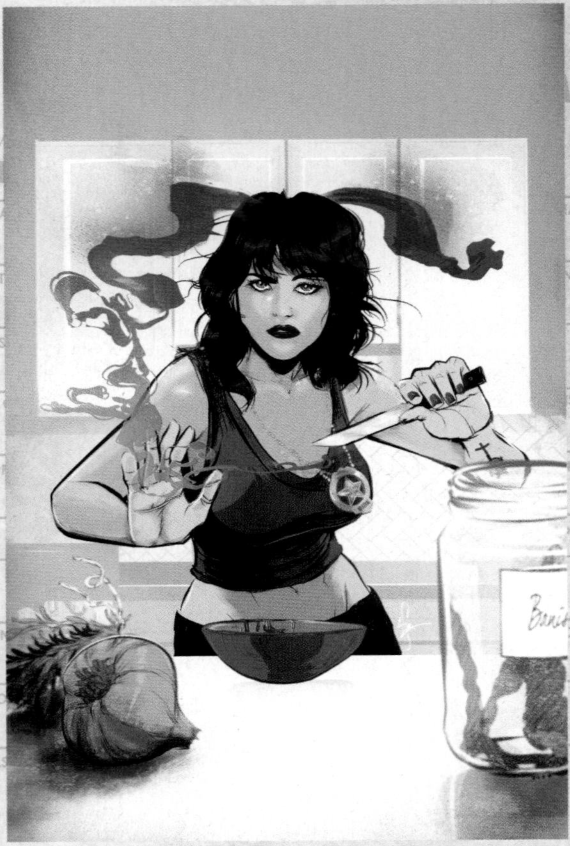

ICIDE REPORT

FORM

PO

CITY OF PORTS

AST NA | AME | RACE | SEX | AGE | RESIDENCE OF PERSON KILLED | OFFENSE

REPORT | NSHIP | RACE | SEX | AGE | ADDRESS OF PERSON KILLED | PHONE

OFFENS | AFTER INVESTIGATION CHANGED TO

PLACE | SION | PLATOON | BEAT | OFFICERS MAKING REPORT | I.D. NO. | NAME

DAY OF | RTED | REPORT RECEIVED BY | RECEIVED — TIME — TYPED

TION OF DEAD PERSON

AGE | IDENTIFYING SCARS, MARKS, ETC. | CLOTHING

CORON | OF ARRIVAL | A.M. | P.M. | NAME OF PROSECUTOR ATTENDING—TIME OF ARRIVAL

PRONO | PERSON WITH WHOM ACCUSED LIVED OR ASSOCIATED

DETAILS | TIGATION) | USE BOTH SIDES OF THIS SHEET.

Issue 003 "B" Cover by
AFUA RICHARDSON

Issue 004 "B" Cover by
MING DOYLE

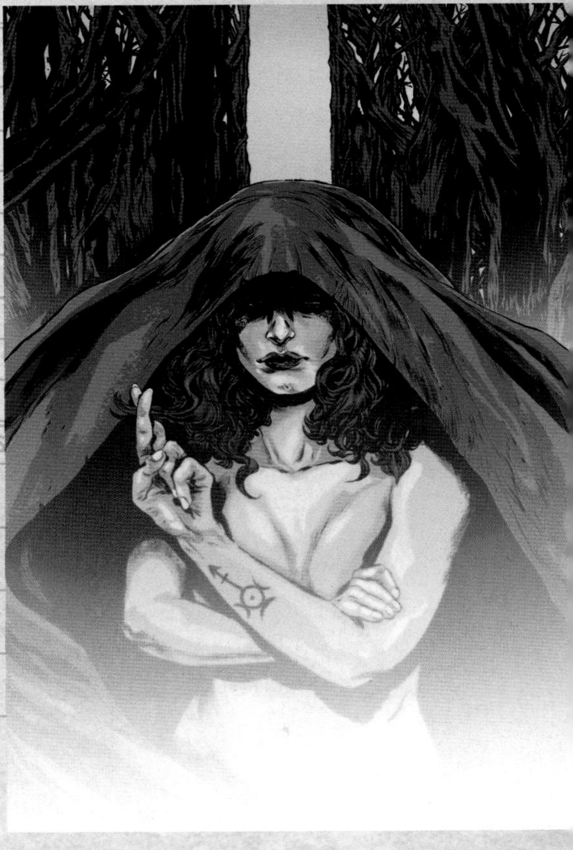

WITNESS TAKEN INTO CUSTODY | ADDRESS

KNOWN, SUPSECTED OR POSSIBLE MOTIVES

DESCRIPTION OF SUS

NAME IF KNOWN | ALIAS | ADDRESS

BEARD | NATIVITY | OCCUPATION | DRESS AND OTHER MARKS

NAME IF KNOWN | ALIAS | ADDRESS

BEARD | NATIVITY | OCCUPATION | DRESS AND OTHER MARKS

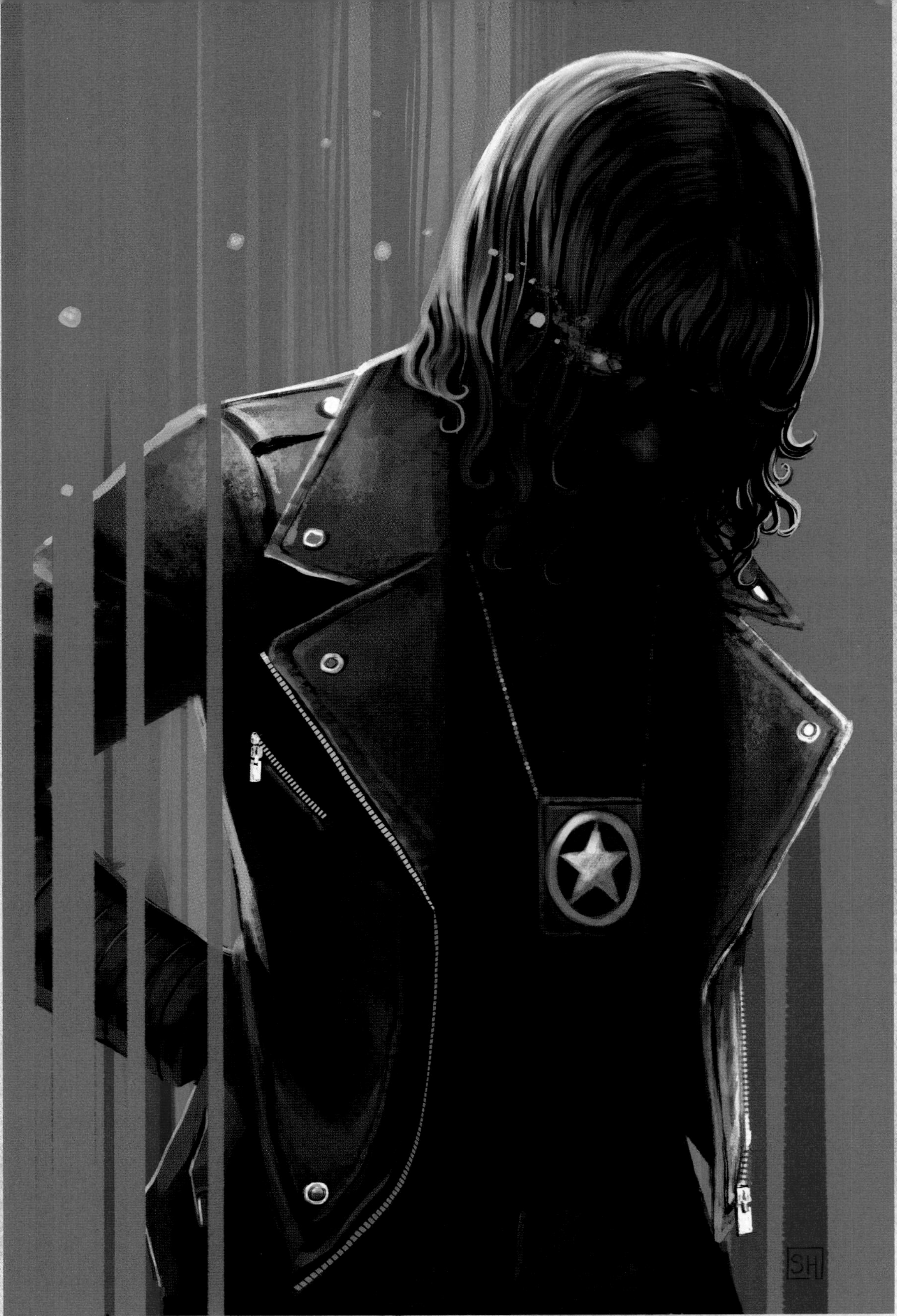
SH

Issue 005 “B” Cover by
STEPHANIE HANS

About the Creators

GREG RUCKA is a **New York Times** bestselling and Eisner Award-winning author of hundreds of comic books and two dozen novels. He is the co-creator of **Lazarus** with Michael Lark, published by Image Comics, as well as the comic **Stumptown**, with Justin Greenwood, from Oni Press. His next novel, **In The Eyes**, is due out in late 2016. He lives in Portland, Oregon, with his two children, and his wife, writer Jennifer Van Meter (**Hopeless Savages**, **Prima**). He believes in the magick of words.

NICOLA SCOTT is an Australian comic book artist working in the American industry since 2001. After working for Dark Horse, Image, and IDW, she quickly became a fan-favourite working exclusively for DC Entertainment on monthly titles **Birds Of Prey**, **Secret Six**, **Wonder Woman**, **Teen Titans**, **Superman**, and **New York Times** Bestseller **Earth 2**. She lives in Sydney with her husband, writer Andrew Constant, swears too much and will eat your bacon.

JODI WYNNE is an American letterer with a background in architecture and graphic design. She began work in comics as a character model, 3-D model maker, and cover colorist at Marvel with Michael Lark on titles such as **Daredevil**, **The Amazing Spiderman**, and **Dark Tower**. Current projects include **Lazarus** and **Slaves for Gods**. She lives in Texas with her husband, Aaron, and their two boys, Jackson and Sonny.

CHIARA ARENA is an illustrator and digital colourist. She lives in Sydney and she started her career in 2012 working as a digital colourist for Italian (Rizzoli Lizard and Panini comics), American (Scholastic), and French (Ankama) publications. She can be found online at **http://cargocollective.com/chiararena** and on Facebook at **https://m.facebook.com/chiara.arena3**

JEANINE SCHAEFER has been editing comics for over ten years. Titles include Marvel Comics' **X-Men**, **Wolverine**, and **She-Hulk**, DC Comics' **Robin**, **Citizen Jack**, and the upcoming **Prima** from Image Comics, and **Jonesy** at BOOM. She founded **Girl Comics**, an anthology celebrating the history of women at Marvel, and edited the Eisner-nominated Marvel YA **Mystic**. She lives in Los Angeles with her husband and adorable tornado/daughter, and sporadically runs a tumblr celebrating the special relationship between nerds and cats.

ERIC TRAUTMANN is a writer, graphic designer and occasional editor based in the Pacific Northwest. He is the book designer on **Black Magick** and **Lazarus**. He co-authored the DC/Vertigo original graphic novel **Shooters** (with Brandon Jerwa, illustrated by Steve Lieber), and has written for DC Comics and Dynamite Entertainment (including long runs on **Red Sonja**, **Vampirella**, and **Flash Gordon**). He can be found online at **www.erictrautmann.us** and at his wife's amazing comic store, **Olympic Cards & Comics** in Lacey, Wa.